Child of

The Windspider Chronicles Volume 1

Robert Grimes

THE
PENGUIN'S HEAD

Cover art & design by David R. Shires at www.theimagedesigns.com

Rob Grimes

Published with the help of Amazon's CreateSpace self-publishing platform and many, many good friends.

ISBN: 1508445060
ISBN-13: 978-1508445067

DEDICATIONS

This book is primarily dedicated to my father Frederick, who was unfairly torn from this world by the demon we call Cancer back at the beginning of 2013.

He read the initial three chapters and looked forward to reading the rest. Sadly, fate had other ideas.

Also, to my friends and family who allowed me to take pieces of their personas and use them to create characters who you'd probably recognize if you knew them.

And finally to you, it's a big ask for a new novelist to expect people to spend their hard-earned cash on what's effectively an unknown value… I hope you enjoy it. Let me know one way or the other, OK?

Chapter 1 : Purchase

Dorleith gazed wistfully at the sparse grey clouds flicking by just below them. They'd been travelling for over an hour now and the cramped conditions in what was, allegedly, a four seat vehicle were starting to take their toll. She had always loved to fly, but she hated the confined urgency of travelling by skimmer. Her heart was thumping in her chest, excited by the thought of what she was finally about to do. Breathing deeply she attracted the attention of the pilot and tapped her watch.

"Ma'am, we should be arriving at the trading station in a few minutes. In fact..." he squinted out of the front window, "there it is, just coming into view now."

"Finally!" she yelled, with more volume than was strictly necessary. Peering at the fuzzy dot on the horizon, she could just about make out various airships of wildly differing designs tethered to the collection of crooked mooring towers. There was also a disparate selection of large buildings, that hosted the warehouses and workshops that serviced them.

Enys Skaw Station had been built during the war as a 'last chance' resupply base for ships trying to cross the Atlantic. Unfortunately, it didn't take long for the almost constant stream of airships arriving and departing to attract the interest of Spider patrols.

Their raids had been pretty much constant and it had been fortified over time until it's surface resembled nothing more than a collection of hardened bunkers with facilities for maintenance and repair. It was one of the few public places where even large airships could be stored undercover. After the war had ended, it became a haven for off-worlders and the island had been abandoned to them by its previous owners, the Dukedom of Kernow.

Dorleith reached into her pocket, and pulled out her small, jeweled dagger. It had been a thirteenth birthday present from her father, more of a decoration really than a real weapon. She held it up to the light and watched the reflections from the multitude of gems skitter around the cramped cabin. Then, carefully holding the tip of the blade between the fingers of her brown suede glove, she turned and banged its pommel repeatedly off her brother's shining breastplate. Mal'Ak-Hai was sprawled, seemingly asleep, across the two rear seats.

"Wake up, we're here."

"Do that again, and I'll throw that damn thing out of the window," he replied evenly, not even bothering to open his eyes.

"You'll do nothing of the sort you scuttling beetle, wake up and get yourself ready. As you're here you may as well earn your keep," the sarcasm dripped from her voice like treacle from a heated spoon.

Her brother looked up at her angrily from under his brow and yawned, "If you didn't want me to come, why did you ask me?"

"Britt said that I'd need someone to watch my back whilst I was here. It seems that a few of the locals are still ungentlemanly enough to think that an innocent, unaccompanied girl is an easy target."

"Ah yes, dear old Mr. Britt. Is this the same Mr. Britt who can't string five words together without putting a flask to his lips?"

"You've never liked my friends have you? At least not my male friends... I notice that you quite like my friend Pixi though," she scowled at him.

He instantly blushed. "He's not your friend, he's an employee. He was the second officer of our mother's ship during the war and ever since she had the Hammer mothballed, he's just been wandering around the place doing maintenance and drinking his way through father's vintage brandy collection. Anyway, why isn't he here himself watching your back?"

Dorleith flipped the dagger around in front of his face so that she was holding the grip, kissed the blade gently, and slid it back into the dark folds of her leather jacket. "There's a celebration back at the Roost; one of the engineering team is receiving a long service award or something and Britt's presenting it. He did advise me to wait so that he could come too - but I figured that you wouldn't be doing anything very important."

Her brother took a breath to continue their discussion with his opinions on a list of her more recent disagreeable life choices, but was interrupted by the pilot's voice.

"Enys Skaw control, this is skimmer CD-327, repeat Carrion, Dagger, Dash, Three, Two, Seven, requesting clearance to land."

After a long pause, the communicator crackled and a thickly distorted voice echoed from the speaker, "Aye 327, this is local control, we have spaces on the… erm… Eastern pads I think, put her down wherever you can find a space."

"Confirmed control, Eastern pads, wherever I can find space, CD-327 out." The pilot rolled his eyes, shook his head and turned towards his passengers, "with all due respect Ma'am, I'm not sure that this is a good idea."

"Don't worry, I'll take full responsibility. In fact, drop us off and then come back for us in about an hour, we should have finished by then."

"As you say Ma'am, but I would definitely advise against…"

"We appreciate your concern, pilot, but my sister is known for her unusual and ill-informed doggedness," replied Mal.

"Yes Commander, as you say." The pilot nodded and they started their descent.

The skimmer circled whilst the pilot looked for a free spot amongst the crowded landing pads, and then set them gently down. The second that the engines stopped, the doors slid open and the duo disembarked. He strapped on his sword and she recovered her LongKnife and pack from the cargo bin.

"Why do you insist on carrying that?" he asked.

"What, this old thing?" she pulled the LongKnife from its scabbard and swished it threateningly in his face.

"Will you stop that?"

"No... I won't. I like how it glints in the sun, when you're fighting at close quarters you can really swipe and thrust and chop. Not like that clinical electro-ceramic thing you have, it's got no soul."

"Stop... now..." He was starting to get angry and his hand was moving slowly towards the hilt of his own weapon.

"Swish, swish, block, riposte... OW!"

It had taken less than half a second for him to draw his sword, engage the energy field covering the blade and block her thrust. The tiny blue lightning bolts skittered over both blades as he slowly and deliberately forced her weapon away. She dropped it, put up her hands and took a step back.

"Alright, you win. The big, bad soldier-boy beat the girl in a swordfight, well done..." she pouted and clapped slowly.

"Why do you insist on doing that?"

"Doing what?" she asked, bending to pick up her weapon and inspecting it closely for any new scratches.

"Provoke me, you know that I'll beat you in a fair fight."

"But corsairs don't fight fair do they? Good Gods Look!" her face flushed in panic as she pointed behind him.

He spun and scanned the dock, instinctively dropping into a defensive crouch. As he searched for whatever had spooked her, he heard her laugh. Turning slowly back around, he saw his locator beacon in her hand, and looked down at the now empty clip on his belt, "Give that back, now." He sighed and held out his hand.

Dorleith tossed it to him and smiled sarcastically as she put her LongKnife back into its scabbard. "Come on, let's see if I can spend all this money on getting a ship in the air."

"OK, but I still don't understand why you can't just use one of the family ships? The Hammer even?"

"You're joking, right? Tell me you're joking."

"I'm sure that if you asked mother, she'd..."

Dorleith looked critically at her younger brother, the low fringe of his hair catching the wind and momentarily covering his piercing blue eyes. That split second reminded her of all the times when she'd waved to him as she left on a raid with their parents and he was left behind on the dock, in the care of his tutors. She shook away the memory, trying to keep in mind that he was also of age now and an important officer in her mother's personal army. Anyway, she didn't want him to think she was going soft. "Sorry, who are you? Have you even met our mother?"

She turned and made her way purposefully towards the shipyard. All around her the colourful sights and sounds of a multi-cultural marketplace mixed with the darker ones of a heavy engineering workshop. Jumbled airship parts and equipment lay piled on hastily laid out pitches that were marked on the dusty ground. Scrawled signs, in a selection of human and off-world languages, promised the cheapest prices, or the most reliable devices, or the quickest fitting service. Sparks flew as shadowy figures cut and welded thick steel plating. She gave a wide berth to a giant construct, at least twice as tall as she was, as it effortlessly lifted a pile of reactor shielding that must have weighed upwards of ten tonnes. A diminutive Kalibri female was dancing in and out between its tree-trunk sized legs, excitedly yelling instructions to it at the top of her voice, whilst mashing the buttons of an antique control pad.

"Wait!" Mal called, "I'm supposed to be helping you, we've got an hour until the skimmer comes back, wouldn't you rather just go and get something to eat?"

She sighed, turned, and looked at him as if he wasn't wearing any trousers. "No, I want to buy a hull, a big hull, for the airship that I'm building," she shouted, in a tone she normally reserved for the very young, or the hard of thinking.

Looking at her through the shifting throng of people, he realised that he hardly recognised her anymore; but he had to admit that she looked every inch the aerial buccaneer with the brown leather, the eclectic mix of silks and linens, and the razor sharp LongKnife in its scabbard under the pack on her back. But despite the fact that she was five years older than him, and that she fought with him at every opportunity, he still felt that he needed to protect her. After all, he was the commander of the Pewter Guard, sworn to defend the family, and he deserved respect - which he got from everyone but his sister of course. "There's a Pradilan over there, I think he might be a good place to start. Aren't those sorts of people known for that kind of thing?"

Dorleith thought for a second, trying desperately to find a basic flaw in his plan that she could use to throw back at him and enforce her superiority as the eldest sibling. In the end, she went with good old-fashioned denial. "OK, we'll try him, but I doubt he'll have anything suitable."

They wandered across the busy square. The Pradilans as a race were known for their ability to find decent salvage. In fact there were some that said that they often found it before it was even technically salvage. This seldom got said within earshot of a Pradilan of course, at least not by anyone who wanted to wake up with their head still in the same room as their body.

The off-worlder was at least seven feet tall, even slouched on a stool, and covered in the mottled green and blue scales that characterised him as a member of their merchant class. His long, broad, snout was filled with razor sharp teeth and his thick brow ridges outlined hypnotic red eyes that had the texture of oil on water.

"Speak Base?" asked Dorleith, hoping that the merchant did. The clicks and hisses of the Pradilan language played havoc with the human tongue, and although she could just about speak it, she would really rather not have to.

The reptilian looked her up and down, trying to gauge whether she was a serious customer or simply a girl playing pirates. "Yesss, Base, yesss."

"I'm looking for a hull, two hundred feet minimum, rated for high acceleration engines."

"Yesss, I have those, you look, you find sssomething you like, yesss?" He handed a data tablet across, a thin wire keeping it attached to a bracer wrapped around his wrist, "Sssee many good hulls, yesss?"

She flicked through screen after screen of hulls, identifying each one where she could. "Company, derelict, Company, Company, No idea what that one is, Company... Why do you have so many Ex-Company hulls for sale?"

"Ssspider war finished but fight still goes on in some places, yesss? War good for salvage, gasssbags burst, hulls fall, we recover, good businesss." The narrowing of the Pradilan's eyes indicated that he felt suspicious about her line of questions.

"What about this one?" she handed the tablet back to the trader. He looked at the image, checked his records, and smiled.

"Yesss, good hull, very good hull, built for ssspeed, many upgrades available for this model, yesss?" he handed the tablet back, "You check options, we can mount and arm," he looked at Mal, who was idly rubbing at the small dent that her dagger handle had made in his breastplate. "Use for army yesss? Soldiering? Local Defence Force?"

"No, I'm building a ship for myself," she replied, breathing in and drawing herself to her full height.

"Ah! Pleasure cruiser, yesss? We have decorator, he does good work, Yesss?" the screen on the tablet changed to show images of ship interiors.

"Just because I'm a woman, it doesn't mean that... Oh, actually, this one's quite nice," she looked through the options menu, picked some that were heavy with brass and red velvet and confirmed her choice. "There, how much would that be?"

The Pradilan closed his eyes and started to talk in his own language, obviously connected to another party by a concealed communicator. He opened his eyes again and looked at her with a smile.

"Seven-fifty thousand credits, yesss?"

"No."

"Yesss, Seven-fifty thousand, a good price, fully fitted interior, delivered in two weeks, yesss?"

"Well, let's see if I can convince you otherwise," she suggested, reaching over her shoulder for her pack.

The merchant, noticing the LongKnife on her back for the first time, jumped to his feet, bared his jaws, and hissed threateningly.

Her heart jumped into her mouth as if it were trying to escape her body completely. She'd never seen the attack posture of a fully grown Pradilan before, and it was something she'd be happy to never see again outside her nightmares. Her brother had drawn his sword and the sparking blue point was inching its way towards the enraged lizard's throat. "No! Look!" she slowly brought out the pack, gingerly opened the top section with the tips of her fingers and lifted out a stack of thousand credit notes. "I'll pay cash, up front!"

The reptilian sank back down onto his stool and his expression softened, Mal's sword powered down and everyone started breathing again.

"Yesss, pay in advance, that help, I throw in two engine mounting free, yesss?"

"About that, I'm going to need extra mountings, I'm using non-standard engines."

"Non... ssstandard?" the Pradilan's eyes lit up, realising that this was definitely an opportunity for him to make a greater profit, "How non-ssstandard?"

"I'm using something like the Allied Mercian TF-80," she replied, awaiting the usual response.

"No, no, no, pair of TF-80 too sssmall, not move this hull, burn out, baffles not take stresss. Fusion cassscade explosion, many deathsss, yesss? I sell you engines too. You like Allied Mercian? I got them, TJ-240, big engine, make this hull ssspeedy, long range, easy to maintain, I sssell you two, you like two yesss?"

Dorleith looked at her brother and rolled her eyes. Britt had warned her that she would probably get this reaction from, well, anybody who knew the first thing about engines. He'd had the same reaction himself when she'd first told him. The big lizard was right, the engines weren't the best match for the hull that she'd specified. They were too small, and they'd be hugely difficult to keep in balance, but they were so beautifully engraved and their shrouds and casings were burnished brass. She had no idea where they'd originally come from, but she'd found them in the hangar where her father's airship, The Simon Bolivar, had been berthed before… well, before it wasn't berthed there anymore. "No, thank you very much, I already have the engines, I just need…"

"No, no, TF-80 too sssmall, not work, go boom! I sssell you…"

"I have eight of them…" she waited for the inevitable snort of derision, and with the nostrils the off-worlder had, it was likely to be an impressive one.

The merchant did a double-take and his scaly expression managed to convey an air of both confusion and greed simultaneously, "Eight, yesss?"

"Yes, eight. I'll need my eight engines fitted to this hull, can you do that?" She was sure that he could, she knew full well that anything was possible in this neighbourhood with the right amount of money.

He closed his eyes again and started to hiss and click in his native tongue, this time she noticed that the same phrase was repeated a number of times. She remembered that this was the Pradilan word for eight and smiled gently to herself.

"Yesss, we do thisss, provide hull, with interior you chose, and your eight," he paused to shake his head, "eight engines in two, maybe three weeks, seven hundred seventy five thousand yesss?"

"Seven-fifty."

"No, no, no, seven-fifty wasss before eight engines, ssseven-fifty normal price for just two engines, yesss?"

"Seven-fifty in cash, now. I don't require a receipt, you strike me as a trustworthy… ah… lizard… person? I can trust you, yes?"

The Pradilan smiled broadly, which, if anything, was a scarier expression than when he'd thought she was drawing her LongKnife. He spoke into his communicator for the final time, ending the conversation with what passed amongst his people for a deep laugh. He produced a card from the folds of his tunic.

"Have your eight enginesss delivered here yesss?" he tapped the address on the card with a polished claw, "we mount and contact you when ready, yesss?"

"No," she replied, handing him the pack of money, "I'll deliver the engines tomorrow, then contact you two weeks from now. We'll arrange delivery then."

"But if there are problems, niggles, unforssseen circumssstances, yesss? We will need to contact you."

"No, you've said you'll deliver, and I trust that you will," she finished the conversation with a deep bow and turned to Mal, "You said something about a meal?"

He led her back across the square, towards the transit pads. "There's a diner over here I think; I saw it when we were landing," Mal scanned the multi-lingual signs, looking for one that looked familiar. "Well, it's either a diner or a pet shop, you know that a lot of these 'people'," he waved his arms expansively, to indicate the varied species' of the traders, "like their food... well... fresh."

"By fresh I presume you mean still alive?" she smiled, relishing his discomfort.

"Yes, that," he shuddered, "you're enjoying all of this aren't you?"

"Of course, what's not to enjoy? There's the fresh sea air, the wonderful scenery," she indicated the ragged collection of airships bobbing lazily on the breeze above them, "the general hubbub of commerce, and my most favourite thing of all, no overt signs of Company involvement. No banners displaying their distinctly fascist 'Clasped Fists' logo, no security constructs guarding every other doorway," she lowered her tone to conspiratorial whisper, "and best of all, no taxes - as long as you pay in hard currency."

"Say what you like about the Company, but profits have soared since Duke Pytor took over leadership."

"Yes, and so have unexplained disappearances."

The diner was one of the few that sold strictly human food. It didn't only serve it to humans of course, as that was forbidden under the Company statutes on multi-species relations - where most types of interaction were actively encouraged. In fact whole new branches of medicine had been developed in the name of the act, with midwifery being top of the list as there was really no accounting for taste. This was closely followed of course by prophylactics against extra-terrestrial cross-contamination. A large percentage of the patrons were human, but there were also Kalibri, Pradilans, and even a Torkan sat in the corner on its own, eating a piled plate of shelled hard-boiled eggs. It used its arm tentacles to delicately hold and rotate each one, as if looking for the perfect place to start eating. When it found whatever it was looking for, it used miniature tools, that it held in its mouth tentacles, to accurately cut slivers and pass them into the dark recess under its hood.

"They make my flesh crawl," whispered Mal, looking over the busy dining area.

"The Torkan? I think they're sort of mysterious. All those little tentacles with the blades and the tools. Do you have any idea what they look like under their hoods? I'd love to take a look; do you think he'd let me?"

Mal looked at her incredulously and scratched his head, "No, the Pradilan," he hated it when she put on her 'little girl lost in the big city' act, "they remind me of crocodiles. Crocodiles shouldn't be able to speak Base and they shouldn't be walking around in the middle of the city wearing expensive clothes and having a sunny disposition, and they definitely shouldn't be selling airship hulls to my sister for three quarters of a million credits that she STILL hasn't told me the origin of."

"That was an ugly sentence," she scolded.

"What?" he was completely wrong-footed by her statement.

"You could have put that better, you could have said it more elegantly, with a little romance."

"You've just given a seven foot tall lizard an amount equal to fifty years wages for an ordinary Pewter Guardsman without batting an eyelid, and you're lecturing me about the quality of my prose? Are you in some way defective? Has a wire come loose in that box of engine parts that you call a head?"

"What can I get for you?" the serving construct had rolled over to them during their conversation and had been waiting patiently until there was a pause in their conversation.

"What's the soup?" asked Mal, his temper rapidly cooling as his thoughts turned to food.

The indicator lights on the construct's body flashed as it conversed with the kitchen, "Mushroom or wild chicken sir, caught fresh today."

"Which?" interjected Dorleith.

"I… I'm sorry miss, but I do not understand your inquiry."

"She's asking if the chicken or the mushroom was freshly caught. I apologise for my sister, she has an odd sense of humour."

"Yes, sir, thank you, the chicken was freshly caught and the mushrooms were freshly picked. Both events happened this morning."

"I'll have the mushroom soup, with hot bread."

"Excellent choice sir, and for you miss?"

"I'll have cheese and apples, served with a sharp knife." She leaned back on the plain plastic chair and put her feet up on the table.

"Yes miss, will that be all?"

"For the moment, you may go." She waved it away as if it were a troublesome fly then looked at her brother, who was scowling at her from across the table. "What?"

"Why do you insist on trying to confuse the constructs? It's pointless, it wastes time and energy."

"Because it's funny! You take yourself too seriously High Commander Mal'Ak-hai of the Pewter Guard and Defender of the Roost; you're so much like our mother."

"And you, Lady Dorleith Ahralia, In Nominate Ruler of the Open Lands and High Voort of the Shattered Spire," he pronounced with a flourish, "are exactly like our father."

"Well, someone has to be," she snorted.

Yet again he was unable to tell her exactly how little her opinion meant to him as their food had arrived, and as much as he enjoyed sparring with his sister - he enjoyed good, hot food significantly more.

In an alleyway across the courtyard, a shadowy figure pressed the stud on the side of its goggles that increased their magnification. Without taking its eyes from the patrons of the diner, it tapped a brief report of their location into a data tablet concealed within its robe. Moments later a silent vibration announced that it had been read and replied to with the single word, 'Wait'.

Chapter 2 : Headstrong

The Kalibri boarding party had finally gotten the upper hand and Britt lay, dazed, on the deck. Their leader smiled, fleshy lips parted over strangely square teeth as it looked him directly in the eye. His vision was still blurry from where one of them had landed a lucky shot to the back of his head with a full brandy bottle. Even in his fuddled state, he recognised the sound of a sword being drawn.

"Where are they?" the high-pitched Kalibri voice echoed strangely in his ear, "they are ours human, not yours, we will not be denied."

"I have no idea what you're talking about. Why don't you take your little furry selves away, jump back in your shiny little skimmer and fly home to your nice warm den before anyone else gets hurt?" He gasped as the crackling ceramic tip of the sword was slipped inside his shirt and a sudden jerk severed his top two buttons. "What do you think you're doing?" he yelped as he brushed away the singed chest hair and tried to lift himself onto his elbows, but stopped when he heard at least four more swords being activated.

"We will make you tell us, we will take them back, you do not deserve them." There were mutters of agreement from the other Kalibri. The sword removed the final three buttons of his shirt and slowly moved down into the waistband of his trousers. "Give us what we want and you will not be harmed."

"Look, I would tell you if I could, but I don't know what it is that you want." He winced as the sweat from his forehead ran through his hair and soaked into the open wound on the back of his head.

"You lie!" spat the diminutive off-worlder, "you have them, and we would rather not harm you, not when you humans have so many other interesting uses." In unison, as if receiving some silent signal, the surrounding Kalibri unzipped their flight-suits and stepped out of them.

He regarded the now naked creatures one by one, "Ah, you're all... females?"

Their leader smiled again, but this time it was warmer, it put Britt at ease. She gently padded towards him on the balls of her feet; her neatly manicured and painted claws tapping on the wooden deck. The gyrations of her full hips, coupled with the way the stuttering light in the cabin shone on her peach-fuzz pelt, serving to almost hypnotise him, "We will make you a deal, you tell us where they are and we will all..."

A muffled alarm sounded, its urgency triggering a surge of adrenaline. Although he scanned the room in panic he couldn't tell exactly where it was coming from. He turned back to the Kalibri leader, "Madam, I appreciate... Good Gods!" To his horror, all of her soft, almost doe-like features had been replaced with a gaping maw, a bottomless pit containing a spinning vortex of thousands of jagged needle teeth.

His own scream woke him and he lay gulping in great gobs of air in a pool of his own sweat. The echoes of his outburst gradually faded to be replaced by the alarm-like buzzing of the Intercomm terminal next to his bed. He took a deep breath and activated the unit, "Britt here!"

Dorleith's voice rang from the tiny speaker, "I've bought a hull from some Pradilans at Enys Skaw, they want us to ship the engines to them so they can be fitted. I've given Stalys the details, can you make sure that it gets done?"

He looked skeptically at the brass head of Stalys, the Roost's A.I, sitting on its plinth in the corner of the room, "All eight? Aye, I can do that. Any special instructions?"

"Yes, unmarked packaging and a delivery crew made up of constructs. I don't want them to know where they've come from."

"Understood, I'll get them sent right away, Britt out." He disconnected the link, wiped the cold sweat from his face, and threw an empty tin goblet at Stalys to attract its attention. "I know you were listening to that, send the delivery details to the main terminal in Hangar 3 and arrange for eight packing crates that are large enough to hold the engines."

The display of lights on the A.I's face skittered for a moment and then it turned to face him, "Yes sir, the details are now available on the local terminal. I will send a construct to confirm the engines' physical size so that sufficient packing materials can be made available."

Britt swung his legs over the side of the bed and picked his clothes up off the floor. He was having real difficulty getting the image of the faceless Kalibri out of his head. He'd had the dream before, or very similar ones at least, but this was the first time it had ended like that. The insistent grumbling in his stomach reminded him that his last few meals had been primarily liquid. "Stalys, have a selection of hot breakfast items sent to the hangar, with a pot of strong coffee."

"As you say Sir, although it is 21:00 hours and I believe the kitchen is currently more geared for serving supper. It may take some time to prepare a one-off breakfast, although if you are willing to wait, I'm sure that..."

"No, supper will do," he looked down at his pocket chronometer, "As a matter of interest, when did I retire this afternoon?"

"Approximately 14:30, sir. I understand that there had been some form of extended celebration in the maintenance department."

He held the sides of his head as he realised the images from his dream had been replaced by a ceaseless banging pain which threatened to force his brain into making an emergency exit through his ears. He stood up and instantly regretted it, the room spun dizzyingly and flashes of coloured light paraded across his vision. He had time to cry the words, "Fruit juice!" before crashing back onto his bed and slipping into blessed unconsciousness.

It was almost four hours later when he finally woke again. Next to the bed was a tray with a number of bottles of freshly prepared juice which he drained thirstily one after another. He moved to his cramped bathroom, splashed cold water on his face and scraped his hair back into a ponytail.

A reflection of someone much older than he felt looked back at him from the depths of the mirror. "Old man, you're a mess," he whispered with resignation. His long, straight hair and his close cropped beard were shot with grey. His cheeks were rosy, threaded with a network of fine veins that served as a map of his more recent excesses. He turned sideways and breathed in. The muscles of his upper body were still obvious and they still worked well enough, although they had lost some of their chiseled edge. "You're due some action, that's all that's wrong with you, a few weeks on shipboard rations and you'll be as right as rain."

He put on a thick jacket, took one last look in the mirror to make sure that he was presentable, and left his quarters. Walking the few hundred yards to the docking bay in silence, the echoes of his footsteps on the polished floor soon fell into synch with the pounding inside his head. He didn't see another soul during his journey but then he wasn't particularly surprised. The normal functions of the Roost had wound down for the day and the eastern wing that housed the docking and launch bays had been chilled by the prevailing sea breeze. He entered the hangar and took stock of the cavernous space. It was over a thousand feet long, three hundred feet wide, and just as high.

It had been the home of the Simon Bolivar, the Baron's giant airship, flagship of the Rustholme fleet. He could see her now, filling three quarters of the available space with her carbon-foil gasbags and sleek gondola. She was studded with turrets that would all track you unnervingly if you entered the hangar unannounced and Angelina, the shipboard A.I. usually had no time for unauthorised visitors. But it had been empty for some time now. So long in fact that it was in danger of just becoming a shrine to the Baron. The Baroness had, of course, kept some of his more personal effects in their quarters, but the vast majority of the trinkets and gewgaws that he had collected on his many travels had been placed in storage here. No one had the heart to throw them away; and of course there was the ever present worry that if you did consider it, no matter how honourable your motivation, Lady Dorleith would split you from stem to stern with a LongKnife and feed your guts to the fish.

In the corner furthest away from the huge external doors, there had, at one time, been a pile of random crates over fifty feet high. Many times when his captain-to-be should have been at her dancing lessons, or learning about deportment, she had dragged him here so that they could pick a crate at random and go through its contents. Mostly there had been parts for the Bolivar that the Baron had found at a knock-down price somewhere. Some were from the pre-war, or even pre-space travel, age. There were many items that only the man himself really knew the use of. They would spend hours trying to decide what they were and how they might have worked.

There were only eight items there now. They'd been right at the bottom of the pile as if hidden away. Originally protected by an amateurishly patched tarpaulin and a, frankly very rickety, hand-made wooden frame that had barely shielded them from the weight of the crates above. They now stood alone and uncovered, but completely untarnished by time. It was obvious, even to the casual observer, that they were airship engines. But that observer would also have noticed that they were not like any engines that they had ever seen before. They had been disconnected but, oddly, still powered up when they had been originally found and if you were to put your hand on them even now, you would have been able to feel the slight tingle of an active electrostatic field. Its true use was a complete mystery, but a handy side effect was that it kept dust from collecting on their intricate carvings.

The external casings of the engines were traced with innumerate patterns and whorls; some of the details were too small for the human eye to appreciate or indeed register. It had been confirmed by constructs that the level of detailing continued almost to the molecular level. It was as if they'd been designed to guide the path of each single particle of air that passed over and through them. Where the blades of a more normal fusion-powered turbine would have been was just an empty space, but tests showed that they could pump just as much air and supply just as much Heptium as any more pedestrian design. Lady Dorleith had dubbed them 'Ghost Turbines' and that somewhat romantic name had stuck.

Britt moved across to the main terminal, he picked up a chicken leg from the plate full of assorted cooked meats that the serving construct had left for him, and checked the delivery address on the display screen. "Well, if she wants to send them to a no-name Pradilan shipbuilder in the shady backstreets of Enys Skaw then who am I to argue? Stalys, do we have the crates ready for these engines?"

"Yes sir, I will instruct the construct team to pack them now. Will you be accompanying the delivery yourself?"

"No, I'm going to finish this food and then do some preliminary work to ready the hangar. Tell the constructs that they are not to reveal who or where these engines are from and neither are they to engage in any idle chatter. Do I make myself clear?

Stalys' indicator lights dimmed in answer as the service door opened and a convoy of constructs entered the hangar. There were also eight large crates carried on a type of automated anti-gravity sled known colloquially as an 'aggie'. The technology behind these almost limitlessly powerful devices was another miraculous free gift to humanity from the Torkans and had made most wheeled and tracked vehicles obsolete overnight. Within minutes the engines were packed, loaded onto the skimmer, and dispatched to the shipbuilders on the far west coast.

Britt found a dark corner of the hangar, pulled a heavy tarpaulin over himself, muttered, "Maybe I'll just have a few moments rest," and fell into a deep sleep, punctuated only by the occasional rasping snore. The alarm woke Dorleith at 06:00 and all around her she could hear the faint sounds of the Roost waking up. The brass head of Stalys turned slowly towards her, "Good morning Ma'am, do you wish to order breakfast?"

"Open the blinds and then bring me bacon, poached eggs and coffee."

"A wonderful choice Ma'am; your breakfast will be ready in ten minutes."

She got out of bed and walked, naked, to the shower, pausing only to look at the view from her window. Her bedroom overlooked the main docking area and since she'd been a child she'd loved to watch the various skimmers and airships going about their daily business. The sky was in her blood. Her mother had done her best to make her into a lady of course; she'd had endless lessons in dressmaking and music hoping that one day she would marry into one of the other powerful families, or at least get herself a husband who had a good steady job with the Company. Deep down inside she was her own woman and that woman wanted to be in the air with her own ship, making her own way.

She stepped into the shower and let the combination of water and sonic vibrations wake her up. Her shower cubicle was made from thick sheets of clear armourplas and was external to the rest of the building giving the impression that she was floating in mid-air. She couldn't be overlooked from the rest of the Roost, but occasionally a skimmer pilot would slow down slightly as they flew past; hoping no doubt to catch her at her ablutions.

Hearing the sound of her chamber door opening over the hiss of the spraying water, she turned off the shower, dried herself, and went back into her bedroom. A serving construct had delivered her breakfast and was now sat hunched in the corner awaiting further instructions. She drew a robe around her shoulders and sat down to eat.

"Will there be anything else?"

"No, that'll be all... Actually yes, on your way out please tell Mr. Britt that I would like to see him in the hangar in an hour."

The construct bowed and backed out of the room. She chewed delicately on her breakfast, thinking back to the Torkan that they'd seen in the diner the day before. She cut the white of her egg into slices, then she cut those slices into smaller slices. But try as she might, there was no way of matching the accuracy of the mysterious off-worlder.

Frustrated, she quickly finished the rest of her meal.

She dressed in what her mother would no doubt describe as an altogether too masculine style for a noble lady, with twill trousers, a heavily embroidered waistcoat and brown leather boots. She pinned up her long red hair and started down towards the docking bay.

"Dorleith, are you in your room?" her mother's voice came tinnily from the Intercomm on the wall, "I need to talk to you."

"Mother, you know that I'm not in my room, you know full well that I'm in corridor..." she rapidly looked around for a location tag, "corridor 63 North on my way down to the docking bays."

"No my dear, I would know where you were if you had your locator beacon about your person, according to Stalys you are still in your bedroom."

She patted her belt and her pockets. "Ah... yes... quite. Actually I'm in a bit of a rush, I can give you a few minutes in a couple of hours if that's OK?"

"I know you're on your way to see Britt, and that it's about this damn ship of yours. If you see him before you see me, I will be very, very, upset. We need to talk," the Intercomm went dead.

"Bugger." She took a deep breath and then activated the Intercomm, "Stalys, locate Agamemnon Britt and open a link."

"Yes my Lady, Mr. Britt is currently in Hangar 3. Opening a link."

"Britt here." Britt's gruff accent rang from the speaker.

"Mr. Britt, I'm afraid that I'm going to be a little late for our meeting, the Baroness has requested an audience."

"Aye, I'd heard she was looking for you. She collared me earlier coming from the kitchens with my mouth full of bacon. I denied all knowledge of course."

"You denied all knowledge of what exactly?"

"Everything, completely, as far as she knows I'm a blabbering alcoholic who doesn't know which end of a pistol makes the loud scary noise and which end you try desperately to keep hold of."

"Did you get the address that I need the engines sending to?"

"They've already arrived at their destination; some hours ago in point of fact."

"Did you send them in unmarked containers? No family crests?"

"I did exactly as you said, not that it matters."

"And what does that mean?" she asked, suddenly suspicious.

"I think I'd rather let your mother explain that if you don't mind... Britt out!"

"Don't you dare hang up on - Damn you!" She turned around and started to make her way up to her mother's quarters; she had the feeling that this wasn't going to be particularly pleasant.

Everyone made way for her as she walked down the seemingly endless corridors. Construct and human alike flattened themselves against the walls, bowed gently, or in some rare cases both. She would definitely miss this when she left the Roost. In the wider world she would be no-one special; a Ship's captain of course, which provided a certain kudos in some circles, but she wouldn't be heir to the throne of a historic Barony. She wouldn't be the ruler of the Open Lands; those great tracts of productive farmland that spread all the way from the Roost itself to the far borders of Rustholme would have to look after themselves whilst she was away. And she certainly wouldn't be the High Voort of the Shattered Spire. She didn't even know where the Shattered Spire was, what a Voort was, or even what made her a particularly 'High' one. The title was bestowed upon her father by an off-worlder that he once did a great, if ultimately unspecified, service for. There was an ornate medal that she could legitimately wear if she wanted to, which had moving parts and a number of sharp points. With the ribbon removed it might make an unusual brooch if she ever required a talking point.

Arriving at the ante-room to her mother's quarters, she paused to check herself in the full-length mirror and tidied up an errant knot of hair that had somehow escaped from her pin. Sitting on one of the deeply upholstered chairs, she settled in, and waited to be summoned.

The Baroness walked around her day-room, gazing at her collection of paintings and ornaments. Each one was a poignant reminder of some particular event in the life of her family. There was the scanner unit from the first Spider that her husband had dismembered with his bare hands. On the far shelf were the 3D in-vitro images of both of her children hours before they were born. The room was dotted with displays of medals that had been earned by family members over the past hundred years or so, including many of her own. Over the fireplace was her LongKnife, the engraved blade still razor sharp even after all these years of disuse. Next to that was the discoloured patch of wallpaper where the Baron's cutlass used to hang. She smiled gently to herself as she ran her fingers across the stain. "How many times did I tell you to clean the blade before you put it back on display Goat?" She paused for a second as if waiting for an answer from the air itself, then moved towards the life sized portrait of her husband that dominated the room.

She carefully considered what she was about to do. Discipline had always traditionally been her husband's job. He would shout and bluster and bang his fist on the table. Threats would be delivered, dire consequences would be described, and all the hounds of all the hells would be called down upon whatever transgressor had been reported to him. If the victim had been a member of the house staff, they would sit there and grow more and more pale whilst the Baron barked his thunderbolts at them.

She remembered one housemaid, who had accidentally shrunk a pair of his flying gloves whilst washing the blood and oil from them, who had been so mortified that she had lost control of her bladder right in the middle of the laundry. In truth, it was difficult to remember who had been more embarrassed on that occasion. The same would happen if it was one of their children; there would be brimstone and assorted hellfire, but there wouldn't be any loosening of bladders. Instead there would be pointing and laughing and cries of "Silly Daddy!" Until, that is, he used 'The Voice'. He had a particular tone that could chill the Children's blood and make their eyes go as wide as saucers, just before they ran, tears streaming, from the room. Unfortunately, her attempts at disciplining the children were more of an exercise in butting heads. It wasn't so bad with her son - especially since he had started to train with the Pewter Guard. He had slipped into his military role as if putting on a favourite old coat. But her daughter, well she was a completely different matter. They were altogether too alike, although she would never admit that out loud to anyone.

Unable to put it off any longer, she turned to Stalys and sighed, "Send her in."

In the ante-room, Stalys' disembodied head lit up, turned to Dorleith and announced, "The Baroness requests your presence immediately, in her day-room."

She knocked on the half open door and coughed politely.

"Come in child and sit down." The Baroness stood with her back to her, looking out at the sea, some thousand feet below them.

"I... I can explain..." stammered her daughter, her mind racing through all the possible things that could be responsible for her being here.

"Excellent, but exactly what can you explain? Will you be explaining why no-one could find you for a great proportion of yesterday, or why I had to send your dancing teacher home on full pay because you forgot your appointment?"

"Well, you see..."

"Or will you be explaining why I had a message from your fund manager asking if you would be requiring any more cash to be made available in the near future, after your withdrawal of seven hundred and fifty thousand credits, as he would like the chance to restock his autotellers?"

"Ah... that I can expl..."

"OR!" the Baroness shouted as she turned from the window with her eyes aflame, "can you explain to me why I was awoken by a confused Houseguard at 05:00 this morning telling me that there was a Pradilan at the main gate who refused to leave until I'd confirmed the fabric choices for a new hull?"

"Oh!"

"Oh? Is that all you have to say? Should I recount the sorry tale again so that it penetrates your skull? I was roused at..."

"I heard you Mother."

"Oh.. five... hundred..."

"You're not in the Defence Force now Mother," she whispered, mostly to herself, "normal people say five O'clock in the morning."

"By a Pradilan at the main gate..."

"Ooooh, a Pradilan, how very multi-species of you. You normally just call them stinking reptiles," her whispers were slowly getting louder.

"What did you just say?"

"Nothing, I just wondered what the fabric samples were like."

"WHAT? That is what you took from this conversation?"

"Conversation Mother? It seems a little too one-sided to be a conversation doesn't it? I thought I was just standing here waiting for you to get to the point!"

"How dare you speak to me like that?" the colour was rising in the Baroness' cheeks and she gripped the back of a chair to steady herself.

"Look, I don't mean to be rude Mother, but it's my money, and I'll spend it however I please."

"If your father was here!" the Baroness stopped shouting and looked across at her daughter, tears forming in the corner of her eyes, "if your father was here, he wouldn't want you to be throwing your money away on crackpot schemes and pointless revenge."

"But he's not, is he Mother? My father isn't here. He's not been here for ten years."

"I didn't mean..."

"I know what you mean, the same thing you always mean when you invoke my father's name to try and win an argument!"

"Now wait just one minute young lady."

The pressure of trying to keep her actions secret over the last few months had finally become too much, everything that she had been holding in came flooding out, "My father was a hero of the Spider war; he hated The Company and said that they would take over running the world from the governments before anyone else did. And he was right! He told me that I should carry on the fight! So I'm going to, I'm building a ship, I'm getting a crew, and I'm going to take the fight to the Spiders, the bandits, the Company, anyone who deserves it."

The Baroness sat down in the chair at the head of the table, then looked at her daughter and smiled, "And do you know the first thing about running a ship?"

"I remember everything that happened whilst we were aboard the Hammer during the war, everything! I talked to the crew, I learned how to rig the gasbags, how to maintain fusion engines, how to..."

"Don't you think I know that? You were the captain's daughter and they showed you the exact amount of courtesy and respect that you deserved, but I was their captain. Do you really think that I'd employ a crew that didn't inform me of every single thing that happened on-board? There wasn't a second that you spent on deck that I didn't know about. All the time you were following Britt around was logged. Some of those people worked for your grandfather for the Gods' sake! Their first loyalty was to the head of the family, it always was, always will be."

"But... I didn't think..."

"No child, you didn't, that's the first sensible thing I've heard you say in months. Everything I've done since we mothballed the Hammer was to stop this happening. Every dance lesson, every violin recital, and every new dress was to get you acquainted with the finer things in life. To try and push these insane thoughts of wanting to be the captain of your own airship out of your system."

"But you were the captain of an airship. You fought in the front lines!"

"There was a war on! We were fighting for our very existence. I did everything to stop you doing this that I thought might work, but now I know nothing will. You're destined to follow in your father's footsteps. You're going to be just like him and I can't stand it!" The Baroness rose from her chair, walked over to her husband's portrait and stroked it lovingly.

"Why is that so bad?" Dorleith asked, looking at her father's likeness, "he was a great man, why wouldn't I want to be like him?"

"BECAUSE HE'S DEAD!" the Baroness yelled, "and you and your brother are all I have left."

The atmosphere was thick with emotion and both women stood at opposite ends of the room, breathing heavily, staring into each other's souls.

Dorleith finally broke the silence, "I'm sorry, I really am, but you're not going to stop me. It's what he would have wanted. The ship won't be ready for at least a month, we've got plenty of time to..."

"Stop." The Baroness raised her hand but looked down at the polished table and shook her head, seemingly hypnotised by a tiny detail of the inlaid family crest at its centre.

She'd never seen her mother like this, not even in the months after her father had died. She was thoroughly beaten and for once, looked a century older than her years.

"You shouldn't ever apologise for following your dreams, not to me, not to anyone. Out there is where you obviously belong," she waved her hand at the clear, azure sky through the large window, "out there in the wind, killing Spiders, having adventures and risking your single, Gods given life trying to prove a point that has never needed proving."

"What?" A look of confusion spread across Dorleith's face.

"I know you're going to be a hero, the staff know you're going to be a hero, your brother knows you're going to be a hero, which is a cause of constant worry to him as he's the commander of the guard."

"And why would that worry him?"

"Because heroes are notoriously difficult to protect, they seem to attract trouble. Had you not noticed?"

"Well, then he'll be glad to know that in a months' time I'll no longer be his problem, he can get on with guarding you and the Roost."

"Not really, he's coming with you."

"No, no he's not, this is my life, I'm not having some armor-clad, snot nosed, toy-soldier following me around questioning my orders and tripping over his sword every time he turns around."

"This is not negotiable. You don't take him and at least a squad of men, you don't go."

"You can't stop me!"

Her mother looked quizzically at her, then raised her index finger to indicate that she should stop talking and addressed the A.I. on the wall.

"Stalys, if I were to issue an order and my daughter was to try and countermand it, what would happen?"

"The original order would stand whilst you are still alive and in command of the Roost."

"Excellent, when the hull for my daughter's new ship arrives in the docking bay, lock the main doors for exit; they are only to be opened on my direct order, is that clear?"

"Yes Ma'am, I understand."

"The doors unlock when your brother and his men are on-board." The Baroness steepled her fingers and looked straight at Dorelith.

"That's not fair, this is my destiny, my idea, not his."

"Nevertheless, that is my condition."

With a final vicious scowl at her mother she turned and stamped towards the door.

"Dorleith," her mother called, "do you remember what he said?"

She stopped, her hands gripping the door-handles tightly. "When?"

"Your father's last words, can you remember them?"

"Yes..." She closed her eyes and rested her forehead against the cool wood of the door, not wanting to remember anything about that terrible day.

"What were they?"

"He said that he loved us both so much," she could feel the tears forming in her head, vying for space with her frustration and pain.

"And who was he talking about?"

"You and I... I don't see why we need to go through this again Mother, I just..."

"No."

"No? What do you mean no? He was looking straight out of the viewscreen at us whilst he said it."

"He didn't need to tell me. But he needed you to be sure. He was talking about you and your brother, he loved you two more than anything else in the universe. When we were alone, he'd always tell me that you were the reason that he fought so hard. But he would say over and over again to anyone else who would ask him, and swear black and blue that it was his duty, that he owed it to the people of the free world to grind the Spiders into dust."

"Well that's why he did it; he was a hero, why are you saying this now?"

"Because it was rubbish, the only reason that he fought was so that you and your brother could live in a better world. He fought so you would never have to; even though he knew it would probably cost him his life. But you're going to do it anyway, aren't you?"

She finally lost the battle with her emotions, the tears streamed down her face and she could feel the heat from her cheeks drying them before they had time to drip onto her clothes. She pulled the doors open and ran from the room, slamming them dramatically behind her.

Baroness Bhinn-Dee, widow of the great Massimo Lohlephel and current ruler of the Roost, turned to the painting of her husband and sighed as the tears welled up in the corners of her own eyes. "It took longer than I expected you old goat, I thought she'd have made a pair of string and paper wings and escaped us by now." She stood and walked back over to the large portrait, "she's your daughter and she doesn't let people stand in her way. You'd have been proud of her."

She covered the painting's hand with her own and looked towards the window.

"But no-where near as proud as I am."

Chapter 3 : Southbound

Despite the ten minute run through the quiet corridors, Dorleith still had the remnants of tears rolling down her cheeks as she reached the entrance to her hangar. She paused to wipe her eyes and took a deep breath before pressing the button to open it. There was a slight delay whilst the door controller verified her identity and slowly the doors slid open. She scanned the open space for Britt, but he was nowhere to be seen. She'd taken half a dozen steps into the cavernous room before she heard a shout from above.

"Up here!"

She looked up to see Britt balancing precariously on the arm of a crane, examining its pulley system. "Whatever it is that you're doing, we have a construct that can do it more safely, in fact there's one there watching you, it's probably wondering what you're doing too."

"By the time I'd told the damnable thing what to do I could have done it twice myself," he looked over at the maintenance construct clinging to the wall like a mechanical cockroach, "no offense. Anyway, feel free to continue polishing your circuits - or whatever it is you do when you have time off."

"We do not have time off as you understand it sir, we…"

"Well, everything's fine now, carry on." He took one last look at the equipment, nodded curtly at the construct, and jumped head-first towards the deck plating. He plummeted down and at the last possible moment he reached out to grab hold of the looping crane cable and swung majestically down to the deck.

"What in the nine assorted hells reserved for gibbering madmen are you doing? You could have killed yourself." She hit him smartly across the shoulder.

"They're grip-gloves," he replied, and raised his hands to show her the two armoured gauntlets that he was wearing, "the riggers use them for connecting the chains to the gasbags. They're magnetic, or some-such wizardry, I think you should get yourself a pair."

"I'll put a pair on my list - along with a full set of gasbags, a new shipboard A.I. and what was the other thing? I'm sure that I'm forgetting something... oh yes, a brand new completed airship." She poked him in the chest with each syllable, then shook her head.

"So, how did your mother react to having a Pradilan on her doorstep at precisely stupid O'clock this morning with a claw full of fabric swatches?" he asked, removing the grip-gloves.

"As well as you'd expect, do we know what happened to him?"

"He was told that he had the wrong address and was sent away cursing all the soft, non-scaled species in the universe I suppose, I don't really know, I was asleep at the time."

"Everyone was asleep at the time. How did they find us?"

"I'll wager they followed the delivery ship back after it had dropped the engines off. They really don't like not knowing where their money's coming from."

"I suppose not. We could have done without everyone and their cousin knowing that we're putting together a ship. There's no point trying to keep anything quiet anymore." She ran her hands through her hair to try and sweep away a little of the stress.

"There's one good thing though; we're going to have no problem finding a crew. Every itinerant gas jockey between here and Nukuoro will want a place on board the new ship being built by a noble house, especially if they start throwing your father's name into the story, which of course they will." He looked around the huge hangar and tried to change the subject. He knew that she had a tendency to get emotional when the conversation turned to the Old Goat. "I checked the dimensions, she'll easily fit in here, even with the oversized bags and the... you did say eight engines?"

"Yes, and you can wipe that expression off your face, that's exactly the look that the Pradilan gave me only his teeth were in better condition than yours."

"It's just that I thought you were going to use six and keep two as spares. They're going to be difficult to find parts for if they fail - or if someone, for instance, shoots a hole in one of them."

She grinned, "Well, we're just going to have to find a helmsman who can steer between the shots then aren't we? And we only have a month to engage the rest of the crew."

"And secure a base of operations. I don't think your mother's going to be too keen on us running back here every time we have a chain come loose, or a torn bag, or a Heptium leak."

"All taken care of," she said smugly.

"Taken care of how? And when were you going to share this information with your first officer?" He pointed at his own chest.

"Prospective first officer. You're only here because I couldn't think of anyone better. And I'm sharing it now... I've procured us a base of operations."

"And I'm very grateful I'm sure, Your Majesty," he doffed an imaginary cap and bowed deeply, "will we be visiting this secret base of yours or shall I look forward to another one of your little surprises?"

"I've got a team of constructs there working on it, in fact they've been there for a couple of weeks now. Do you fancy a little trip south?"

"How far south exactly?"

"About a thousand miles."

"A thousand miles south? That would put us on the coast of... North Africa... you haven't... that whole area was devastated, the Spiders flattened it."

"No, they only flattened what was above ground, the underground hangars are perfectly serviceable, the machine shop is fully working, and the A.I. is still online."

"Does your mother know?" Britt cupped his chin in his hand and closed his eyes.

"She didn't know anything about any of this until this morning, and I haven't had time to tell her the details. I'll tell her when we get back."

"I've got a better idea, tell her after we finally leave, on your fully completed new airship, from extreme range, at full speed."

"I almost get the feeling that you're scared of the Baroness," she turned and walked towards the hangar exit.

"There's no 'almost' about it," Britt whispered under his breath as he followed her out, "that woman bloody terrifies me."

They spent the next few hours organising the trip, loading supplies, briefing the crew, and performing flight checks on the airship that they were using. She was a pre-war runabout called Spirit of Heinlein which Dorleith had used as her personal transport several times before. She was perhaps only one hundred feet long and not even big enough to have her own A.I. But at the same time quick enough and as well maintained as any of the family ships were.

Britt entered the small bridge to find his captain already sitting in the command chair. He indicated the empty seat at the helm position and raised an eyebrow.

"Be my guest Mr. Britt," she said with a smile. Thumbing open the Intercomm, she spoke loudly and clearly into it, "All hands hear this, we will be departing for Sidi Ferruch in ten minutes and will be gone for at least three days. This is your last chance to bring anything aboard that you might need. Do not make me wait for you."

"Spoken like a true pirate captain, although you might want to add the occasional 'Yarrr' or 'Shiver me Timbers'."

She looked at the smiling faces of the rest of the bridge crew and then regarded Britt questioningly, whilst trying to keep a straight face herself.

"I just meant..."

Her piercing look didn't waver, and she stared back at him without any outward trace of humour.

"I'll just be getting on with closely examining these instruments shall I?" He turned back to the control panel and studiously flicked switches and turned dials hoping that he wouldn't attract any more unwarranted attention. He was just starting to relax again when the captain called out the order to depart.

"Engineering, spin up the engines and release the docking arms. Britt, get clearance from traffic control and then take us out."

"Aye Ma'am. Roost traffic control this is the Spirit, requesting clearance to leave dock."

"Spirit of Heinlein, this is Roost control, you are cleared for departure. Please note, speed limit is ten miles per hour within dock environs."

"Acknowledged, control." Britt disconnected the Intercomm and slowly pushed forward the throttles.

The captain stood and walked towards the panoramic armourplas window at the front of the bridge, she could feel the vibration of the engines through the deck and took a deep breath. In front of her she could see the huge external doors of the docking bay opening to let in the bright midmorning sunshine. "Mr. Britt, how wide is The Spirit?" she asked, absently.

"Forty feet, give or take a few inches Ma'am. May I ask why?"

"I was just wondering. Also, how upset do you think that the traffic master will be if we power through the doors whilst they're still opening?"

"Very, I should think... they get quite twitchy about things like that. Is this something you'd like to find out first hand?"

The captain returned to her seat, strapped herself in and nodded. "As soon as you think that the gap's wide enough take us out as fast as is reasonably safe. It would be a shame to die in a screaming fireball before our adventure has really started."

"Aye, it certainly would." He opened the Intercomm, "crew, this is the first officer, the captain has authorised an acceleration test. Grab something solid and hold onto your lunch." He waited another few seconds and then, gauging the gap to be just wide enough, slammed the throttles fully open. The thrust turbines spun into life and the ship jumped forwards. The gasbags stiffened as their internal pressure increased and the rigging chains juddered as they fought to keep the hull and the bags securely connected. "Fifty Mph," called Britt over the noise.

"Spirit of Heinlein, this is traffic control, maximum posted speed is ten miles per hour, please reduce..."

"Seventy."

"Spirit of Heinlein, reduce speed or we will be forced to..." the voice of the traffic master dissolved into static as the ship burst through the still opening doors in a shower of sparks and a squeal of shearing metal.

"Britt, what was that?"

"Ah... checking now... one second... oh, it looks like we lost the end of the transmission antennae, it seems that we may have been nearer to forty one feet wide."

She shook her head and rolled her eyes. "Take us to fifteen thousand feet, plot a direct course for Sidi Ferruch and engage the main engines, I want to be in Africa by nightfall."

The ship slipped into a lazy right handed climb and had just crossed the coast of the French Openzone when Britt engaged the fusion engines. The sudden burst of power, even from such a comparatively small ship, kicked him in the back and accelerated them, within seconds, to 300 Mph.

"Ma'am, we are at cruising altitude and will reach our destination in just under three hours."

"Thank you Mr. Britt. Does our course take us over the ruins of Paris?"

He briefly checked the navigation screen. "Aye Ma'am, almost directly over it in fact."

"Good, let me know when we're within visual range, I'd like to see how they're getting on with rebuilding the tower."

"As you say Ma'am, should be thirty minutes or so."

She nodded, sat back in her seat, and closed her eyes. Her mind wandered back to the time that their mother had taken them in the Hammer, to witness the dedication of the Eiffel Memorial.

The Spiders' attack on Paris was their last, most desperate, act of the war in Europe. Nearly three million people had died in the blink of any eye, when a cloud of Spiders, fifty miles across, simultaneously detonated their own power cells and virtually wiped the city from the map. One of the only landmarks that was still recognisable after the dust had settled was the half-melted stump of the Eiffel Tower. It had been decided that it would be rebuilt, using parts of the Spiders that had tried to destroy it, and re-dedicated to the memory of the fallen.

Some were worried that the Spiders would return to retrieve their dead; although as far as anyone knew, this had never happened anywhere else. There had been protests and debates, and at one time The Company warned that the project was too expensive to maintain and that the workforce should be moved onto a more profitable endeavour. But that only increased the uproar as it seemed that the people didn't really know what they wanted, but they definitely knew that the fallen should be remembered.

She didn't know who she hated more, The Company or the Spiders. One had used the confusion left in the aftermath of the war to take control of the world in everything but name, whereas the other had killed her father. Both crimes were equal in her eyes, and both would eventually be punished. This was the whole reason for her crusade; it was what kept her going.

The Company controlled almost every important facet of everyday life for most people. Food production, medical services, transport systems, both military and civilian construction, security and even global finance were all under Company jurisdiction. They were the world's single largest employer and were seen by many as a kind of corporate evil empire. Admittedly they had brought order to the scattered population after the war had ended, but they'd done it with an iron fist. This was ironic as their corporate logo was a pair of clasped, armoured, gauntlets. Despite their façade as the benevolent provider any dissent was instantly quashed and the unlucky dissenter would either be re-educated to be more Company friendly or, more often than not, disappear altogether.

Britt's call brought her back to the real world, "Captain, we're entering the Parisian disaster area."

"Aye Mr. Britt, drop to turbine power and take us down to 500 feet."

Britt nodded and throttled back the fusion engines allowing their internal turbines to take over. Their progress rapidly slowed until they were hardly moving. The thousand foot tall monument slowly loomed on their starboard side. She walked over to the front window and watched as they floated past. The tower seemed to crawl with constructs, fitting together pieces or welding joints. The actinic blue flashes lit up the bridge as she thought of her previous visit. As the lonely obelisk disappeared from view, she retook her chair and addressed the helm, "Mr. Britt, resume previous speed and altitude, let us see what Algeria has to offer."

He pointed the nose of the airship at the high clouds and re-engaged the main engines. The Spirit shot forwards and rose like a hawk into the early evening sky. Levelling off at fifteen thousand feet, he engaged the autopilot and settled back into his chair. He wouldn't need to correct their course again until they left the French Openzone and headed into the Mediterranean. The sun was sinking towards the horizon on his right and as he watched he saw the lights of a city start to wink into existence. He checked the navigation display and realised that it was Orleans, strangely untouched by the wholesale destruction surrounding it.

He'd served in Africa with both the Baron and Baroness during the war and he wasn't particularly looking forward to going back there. It held some memories that he didn't really want to revisit. He'd been to the base at Sidi Ferruch many times. It was a soulless place, mostly underground, highly automated, and run almost exclusively by constructs, which perhaps explained why his current captain thought that it was such a good idea to try and resurrect it. He turned and looked at her; she was engrossed in one of the information screens set into the arm of her command chair.

Apart from her red hair she was the image of her mother, even the way she barked her orders, and the change of temperament when she was landside compared to when she was aboard and in command, set his mind spinning back more than ten years to when he was an engineering officer for the Baroness aboard the Granthar's Hammer.

'The Hammer' was a much larger boat, perhaps three times the size of the Spirit, and built purely for killing Spiders. Her thick titanium hull wrapped itself around the singular mass of a huge ion gun. The stream of electromagnetic energy released when the cannon fired would destroy the electrical systems of any construct that it touched. This of course included Spiders as they were, for all intents and purposes, entirely mechanical. She was used as a support ship to the more heavily armed battleships of the Rustholme fleet. Where the Baron's ship for instance, The Simon Bolivar, had forty turrets that could all be targeted separately; it was susceptible to attack from a concentrated enemy force. Its firepower was generalised and couldn't all be focussed in one direction. This is where the Hammer excelled; it could easily cut hundreds of Spiders from the air with one shot, but if it were to be attacked from all angles it would quickly be swamped. The husband and wife team could protect each other indefinitely, as long as they stayed together. In theory at least.

Britt noticed a small indicator on the helm blinking rapidly. It was the waypoint alarm telling him that they had reached open water. He checked the charts, turned them starboard by a few degrees and reset the autopilot. In just over an hour they would be within sight of their destination. A chill went down his spine as he looked out into the featureless dusk. This part of the world had hardly changed in all that time. There had been no push to rebuild the cities that had been lost in North Africa as the local population, even if you included the massive influx of off-worlders that had arrived over the last fifty or so years, just hadn't needed the space.

Billions had been killed during the Spider War, every family on the planet had stories of loss and horror and he was no exception, not by a long way.

His reminiscing was cut short by an alarm klaxon and Britt instinctively cut the engines.

"Britt? What's going on?" the captain yelled as she frantically tapped at her command display.

"I'm not quite... ah... we seem to be being targeted."

"Unidentified aircraft, you are entering restricted airspace, please alter your course to 120 magnetic immediately and exit the area," the unmistakable, shrill tone of a traffic control construct blared from the speakers.

Britt thumbed the Intercomm, "Restricted airspace control, this is the civilian cargo ship Spirit of..."

"Unidentified aircraft, this is your final warning. Change course to 120 magnetic now or be fired upon, no further warnings will be given."

"I repeat, this is..." shouted Britt, switching to the backup channel.

"Britt?" interrupted the captain, gently.

"Spirit of Heinlein..." he continued

"Britt, we don't have a transmission antennae."

"Oh... aye, Bugger... hard a-port!" he shouted before remembering that he was, in fact, the helmsman and banking the airship hard to port himself.

The darkening skyline veered crazily across the viewscreen as the hull swayed under the gasbags, straining the connecting chains and causing them to squeal in complaint. Another indicator lit on the helm panel and the alarm klaxon doubled in volume.

"They're firing!"

"Good Gods! Get us out of here Britt. Now!"

Britt angled the Spirit into a steep dive and pushed the throttles forward hard. The ship had almost completed its turn when the rear gasbag was punctured by whatever projectile the unknown enemy had thrown, and she lurched drunkenly forward.

"Report!"

"We've been holed, luckily just the rear bag, not by an energy weapon, so there's little chance of ignition. We're losing Heptium at a rate of twenty cubic meters per second and we've have entered a state of ongoing negative buoyancy," Britt read off the status report from his screens.

"So we're crashing?" the captain surmised.

"Aye Ma'am, but only very, very, slowly."

Dorleith rolled her eyes and pushed the Intercomm button, "All hands, this is the captain. Mr. Britt has somehow managed to burst one of the gasbags and we will be landing momentarily somewhere near...?" she looked questioningly at Britt.

He checked the navigation display, swallowed theatrically and replied quietly, "Douera..."

"Near the village of Douera, in Northern Algeria... luckily this is only ten or so miles from our actual destination. I hope you all remembered to pack your walking boots and torches as we're going on a little night-time excursion." She clicked the Intercomm off. "Mr. Britt?"

"Aye Ma'am?" replied Britt, purposely not turning around from the instruments so that he could avoid her gaze.

"Would you like to explain to me what just happened?"

"If I were to hazard a guess, I would have to say that the constructs that you sent to Sidi Ferruch got the automated point defences working and then because we couldn't identify who we were, they shot us down."

"So, you're saying that we were shot down by the automatic defences of our own, as yet unmanned, base?"

"Aye Ma'am, that is my sincere belief."

"This goes no further Mr. Britt. It is not what I would describe as an auspicious start to our grand endeavour. I can imagine the crew not taking it well."

"Very wise Ma'am, my lips are sealed."

"Good, and I would appreciate it if they would stay that way at least until we reach the base."

Chapter 4 : Guardians

"Pixi, wake up," Mal stroked the shock of dark hair on the pillow next to him, "you need to go, I'm due on duty in an hour, and I'm sure that you have places to be."

"I'm warm... leave me... I'm going back to..." Her loud snores told him that it was time for more drastic action.

'OK, have it your way, but don't say I didn't warn you." He slid out of bed and made his way around to where his companion was doing her utmost to remain asleep. Taking hold of the covers and counting a quiet, "one... two... three..." he deftly pulled the covers away to leave the girl wide awake and clutching at the pillow to instinctively try to cover her nakedness.

"What did you..?" She looked out of the window and saw that the sun had just started to rise. "Oh Gods! I'm late!"

"Well, I did try to... hey!"

She shot him a wide grin and playfully pushed him out of the way as she rushed to the shower. "I'll have toast," she shouted over the sound of the running water, as the door closed.

He smiled and scratched his head as he looked absently towards the shower door. "Stalys? Toast."

"Certainly My Lord, and anything for your... guest?"

"That is for my guest, I'll have sausages, well done."

"Of course, will there be anything else?"

"I do have one question." Mal said drily as he looked at the imperious brass head.

"My Lord?"

"Why are you wearing a grubby, orange and yellow woollen hat?"

"Your... guest, My Lord, I can only assume that she thought it was amusing. I will call for a construct to have it removed."

"No, no, I think it suits you, gives you some much-needed gravitas, especially the bobble on the top."

"As you say My Lord." Stalys' indicator lights dimmed with an air of implied disapproval.

He wandered to the shower door and banged on it, "C'mon, other people need showers too." As he turned away, the door half opened, a soapy feminine arm emerged, encircled his waist and drew him inside.

When they both emerged, more than half an hour later, their breakfast had been delivered and gone cold.

Pixi picked disinterestedly at hers. "I hate cold toast," she announced to no-one in particular.

"And whose fault is it that we're eating a cold breakfast?"

"Yours..."

"Mine? But you pulled me into the shower!"

"I was just going to make sure that you were clean, you were the one that made us need another shower."

"Yes," He smiled, "you're right, that was me." He rose from the table, kissed her on the head and went into his dressing room.

"Are you doing anything exciting today?" she called.

"An inspection of some new equipment this morning and a patrol to the western borders this afternoon I think. Providing, that is, that my dear sister doesn't need me to hold her hand whilst she goes shopping like yesterday."

"Don't start all that again, let it go. You're not half as beautiful when you're pouting."

He strode back into the room wearing his freshly polished dress armour, "I think you'll find that the word you're looking for is 'handsome'." He tensed his muscles and struck a manly pose, then looked down at his stocking feet, "I don't suppose you know what happened to my boots at all, do you?"

She smiled and pointed upwards at the chandelier.

He looked up, "Ah, thank you, I would never have thought to look up there."

Eventually, he left his quarters and started to make his way down to the Pewter Guard barracks. He chided himself for allowing his personal relationship with Pixi to make him late. It was bad enough that he'd fallen for someone whom his mother would never ordinarily entertain as a potential partner for him, and he could just imagine what the Baroness would have to say if she found out that she was diverting him from his duty. The Baroness was very big on duty. She would lecture him for extended periods about it as often as she could find the time. She would expound at great length about his duty to the Roost, his duty to the family, and his duty to his men. She never seemed to mention his duty to himself though, the fact that he was important as a person too, that he had needs and desires. Desires... it's funny how that word kept cropping up every time he thought about Pixi. She was one of his sister's friends who was employed in the library, the orphaned daughter of a crewman who served on the Bolivar with their father.

He'd fallen for her the moment he'd first seen her. He remembered that he'd requested the illustrated, leather-bound, copy of The Book of Lord Shang from his father's personal collection and she'd delivered it to his quarters herself. She'd made some excuse that it was the end of her shift and that she had nothing better to do, but he didn't believe this for a second as the staff quarters were in virtually the opposite direction and her shift seemed to finish at three in the afternoon. Her forceful, yet joyous, personality left a huge impression on him as did her large brown eyes and her athletic, but definitely feminine, figure. Initially he'd worried that she was just another of any number of girls who had courted his favour to try and secure themselves a place as the next Lady of the Roost. However, unlike those girls, her attitude towards him hadn't changed when he'd explained Rustholme's system of absolute primogeniture, meaning that, as the eldest child, his sister would inherit the throne rather than himself after their mother's time had passed.

Although he was nearly an hour late, he made no effort to rush. It wasn't as if they could start the day's activity without him. He was their commander, and had been since the morning of his eighteenth birthday. The Pewter Guard had been defenders of Rustholme since his Great-great Grandfather's time at least, and the commander was always the oldest male member of the family. There had been an eight year gap between the time of his father's death and him taking the seat. During that time the Guard had just carried on with their primary standing order; to defend the Family from harm and keep the people of Rustholme safe. As testament to their professionalism they'd repelled multiple attacks by Spider raiding parties without having the luxury of a commander.

But he wasn't just a figurehead, he'd trained with the Guard since he was eleven. His tutors were battle hardened veterans and his mother had supported him every step of the way. She had made sure that he was never treated any differently from any other recruit, and he had the scars, broken bones and medical implants from his training to prove it.

He was greeted at the entrance to the barracks by a very worried looking Guard Captain by the name of Sembhee. It was unusual to see any guardsman look nervous, and almost unheard of for that man to be an officer.

"Has something unpleasant happened that I should be aware of, Captain?"

"My Lord, we had a visitor in the early hours of the morning, and one of the new Houseguards, who is inexperienced as to the guidelines pertaining to the Baroness, woke your mother to tell her." Sembhee flinched, expecting a violent outburst from his commander.

Instead Mal grinned before replying, "And how did Her Ladyship react to having her beauty sleep disturbed?"

"Not well," the captain smiled nervously, "I understand that she was quite vocal about the entire situation, there may have been some... physicality."

"By the Houseguard on the Pradilan? Maybe we should offer him a position, assuming that there's anything left of him."

"No My Lord, by your mother on the Houseguard. I believe that he is currently in the clinic, receiving treatment for bruising and multiple contusions."

"Did she get her hands on the big lizard?"

"No, it was sent away with a flea in its... erm..."

"Ear?" Mal suggested

"Yes, exactly My Lord, I wasn't sure if the reptiles actually had them."

"I think so Captain, how else would they be able to hear the clinking of all their one credit coins?" He smiled as he mimed shaking a coin-purse. "Maybe I should go and see if there's anything she wants me to do about it."

"I've had orders that Her Ladyship is currently in conference with your sister and wishes not to be disturbed, My Lord."

"In that case I'm sure that I'll be called upon to go and pick up the pieces by at least one of them later on then."

Sembhee grinned widely and they both entered the barracks. Their itinerary for the morning included a single interesting diversion. They were having a demonstration of a new Torkan designed weapons system, one that could be mounted on either an airship or a ground vehicle and provide heavy support. He thought that it was a shame that his sister was going to miss it - knowing her fondness for the tentacles of Torkans. He went to his office and started to look through the night's reports. Nothing of any note had happened except their unexpected Pradilan visitor. There was nothing that required his personal attention and he hoped that the coming day would be the same. Checking that the flight-plan had been filed correctly for the afternoon patrol, he noticed that a note had been added that read; "Be aware, bandits are operating in this area, extra armaments are recommended." There was no identification on the note and no signature.

He addressed the A.I. "Stalys, who exactly added this notice to my patrol's flight-plan?"

"My Lord, I'm afraid that there are no identification factors available, neither is there a timestamp or a data source code."

"Are there any reports of bandit attacks along the western borders?"

"None that I am aware of My Lord, should I request detailed reports from the local watchtowers?"

"No, that won't be necessary, we'll see for ourselves later." He looked down at the display again; the note was definitely there but seemed to have just magically appeared in the record much like the money his sister had given their toothy Pradilan friend the previous day.

He spent the next hour inspecting the Guard, not that there was any real need to. Their armour was always polished, their swords were always charged and razor sharp, and all of their other armaments were constantly clean and ready for battle. He retired to his office to try and complete his outstanding paperwork before the Torkans arrived.

Stalys' voice immediately broke the silence, "My Lord, the weapons demonstration party has arrived, would you like them directing to the main hall?"

He looked up, with mild annoyance, from his reports. "Damn! They're early. Do they have any equipment with them?"

"Yes My Lord, they have a vehicle containing a number of sealed crates. Please wait..." Stalys' indicator lights cycled as he received a message from the terminal at the main gate, "they have asked if they may set up the demonstration in the north training fields."

Mal thought for a second, "Tell them that I will join them there presently."

He gathered his senior guard and they made their way from the barracks out to the training field. Momentarily blinded as they emerged from the dim tunnels of the Roost into the bright sunshine, they saw the outlines of a group of people assembling what appeared to be a large cannon on the back of an industrial aggie.

Scattered over the fields were the burned out chassis' of various troop transports and heavy combat constructs that had previously been used as targets in training exercises. One of the technicians finished connecting a particularly thick cable, noticed them, and waved them across. As they got closer, one of the Torkans, identifiable as the leader of the group by its significantly more ornate hood, joined them and bowed deeply. The small tentacles around what would have been the mouth on a human face, started to vibrate faster than the eye could comfortably see. Its translator unit transformed these movements into English with only a slight delay, "Thank you for seeing us My Lord, we hope that our new device will meet with your approval."

"I'm sure that it will, what exactly have you brought to show us?" replied Mal, looking at the imposing gun mounted on the quietly humming aggie.

The Torkan extended the tentacles that made up his left limb and stroked the weapon almost lovingly, "We call it the 'Tangler', but of course, you must feel free to name it as you wish, once you have bought it." The next noise that came from the translator was probably meant to be a laugh, but it sounded more like a full suit of dress armour falling down a flight of stairs.

"And what does this Tangler of yours do exactly?"

"Once fired, it fills a magnetic bottle with synthetic Gravitons and fires it at the target, when the package hits..."

"It weighs down the target?" interrupted a Guard sergeant, "Makes them so heavy that they can't move, it's a crowd control weapon?"

The Torkan turned to the sergeant and paused, every one of his tentacles stopped moving momentarily as he regarded him from under his darkened hood. "I can see why you would think that sir, but no. Gravitons are elementary, and up until quite recently, theoretical particles that can be used to impart spin on anything that they come into contact with. May I demonstrate?"

"Of course," replied Mal, indicating the partly destroyed hulks on the training ground, "fire away."

The Torkan spread his tentacles around the control system and the gun traversed across all of the possible targets, finally coming to rest pointing at an orbital landing pod. "You will notice that I have chosen the most heavily armoured vehicle here, not only is it protected against weapons fire, but it is also shielded against the heat of atmospheric re-entry." He pressed a large, flashing red button and stood back.

The weapon started to emit a low hum, which rapidly rose in pitch and volume until a glowing ball of green energy was spat from the barrel and meandered, unhurriedly, right towards the pod. There was no noise of impact, but the bright glow spread like oil over the surface until it was completely covered. In the next instant it was as if a giant hand had reached down from the heavens and screwed up the pod like a scrap of paper. The members of the Pewter Guard stood with their mouths open, transfixed.

"I... I thought you said that it made things spin, I... I was expecting..." stammered Mal, making a spinning motion with his finger, still not quite believing what he had seen.

"Ah, yes," replied the Torkan, "it does, the Gravitons attach to individual atoms in the structure and make them spin uncontrollably. But unfortunately for the target, not all of them spin in the same direction. Would you like to see what it will do to an organic subject?"

"No!" yelled Mal, and then more calmly, "ah, I mean, that won't be necessary thank you, I have quite a vivid imagination and have enough trouble sleeping as it is." He turned to the assembled guardsmen and raised his eyebrows.

Their collective expression told him that they were all both as impressed and horrified as he was.

"We are currently working on a man-portable version for infantry use - although there have been some teething troubles during testing. It should be ready for deployment within a few months."

"Teething troubles?"

"Yes, there have been occasions where containment has been lost before the gunner has had time to fire, and there has been... premature tangling."

Mal paled and questioningly made the spinning motion again with his finger, which the Torkan copied, but with all of his right-hand tentacles simultaneously, in different directions.

"Well, thank you for your demonstration, it's certainly a very interesting piece of equipment, but I'm not sure that we have a use for it at the moment."

The Torkan took a step back and seemed to deflate slightly, "We were led to believe that you required armaments; that you have a problem with bandits at your borders? This is why we contacted you initially."

"Trouble with bandits? No, not currently. We'll be sure to get in touch if the situation changes though; your system is very... um... Impressive. Feel free to enjoy the hospitality of our commissary, just follow the signs. We look forward to dealing with you in the future." Mal turned, signalled his guard to follow him and started back towards the safety of the barracks.

Once they were inside, Sergeant Na-Thon turned and whispered, "My Lord, that weapon was horrific, I could never imagine myself using it, not on a person at least."

"No, nor me," replied Mal, "but I'm more interested in who told him that we were having trouble with bandits, especially when we're not."

The Torkan seemed to scowl as he watched them disappear back into the Roost. As soon as he was sure they were not overheard, he turned to his associates, "Get this dismantled and packed away. If this family do not appreciate our technology, we will find someone that does."

The Torkans had come to Earth, along with all of the other major off-world races, soon after humans had started experimenting with interplanetary drive systems. The advent of the first generation of nuclear fission engines, or more accurately those engine's toxic waste products, had attracted the attention of the 'Aligned Races', as the off-worlders referred to themselves. Unknowingly, the first explorers had been leaving trails of radioactive exhaust around the local part of our solar system. These traces were too weak to show up on any of our primitive instruments but the Torkans informed us that they would build up and eventually make navigation impossible. They offered Earth's governments technological advances that seemed like magic at the time. The Cold Fusion Engine was probably the most important gift. It revolutionised virtually every modern vehicle, and also its by-product, stabilised Heptium gas, which was now used to fill the gasbags of airships the world over. They asked nothing in return except somewhere to live freely and access to enough raw materials to carry on their constant research.

No-one had ever seen one without their hooded robes, for all anyone knew, they were just a loose assemblage of tentacles vaguely shaped to look human. But one thing was certain - they were the best engineers in the known universe, their devices were the most intricate, and there wasn't a single person alive on the planet that didn't owe them a debt of thanks for something.

The guards made their way to the commissary and ordered their lunch from the serving constructs. They clustered around a large table, whilst other Pewter Guardsmen and Houseguards milled around them carrying trays of bland, but ultimately nutritious, food. Mal thought about the impending afternoon patrol and the mysterious mentions of a bandit attack. Who had put the note on his flight log? Why had the Torkan specifically mentioned bandits? If someone was doing this just to spook him, they were doing a damn fine job.

He continued to look down into his pasta, but spoke to the surrounding guards, "We're going to do the patrol in powered-armour."

"My Lord?" interjected Sembhee, "your orders specified light skimmers, the conditions will be cramp..."

"Then we'll take heavy skimmers, with support weaponry," he stared into the captain's eyes.

"Yes My Lord, I'll arrange the changes now." He stood, saluted, and left the commissary to make his way down to the armoury.

Mal chewed on his lunch for another few seconds, until the young sergeant who had misidentified the use of the Tangler cannon could not contain himself any more.

"Do you really think there's real danger from bandits My Lord?" he asked, his face reddening.

"We'll find out when we get there, but something strange is going on and I'd rather be heavily armed and not need it than need it and not be heavily armed."

They finished their food and started back to the barracks. The constant talk of bandits had managed to put everyone on edge. It was one thing taking out the occasional rag-tag Spider patrol. In fact, it was almost a game, watching as their mechanical limbs fell limp after being hit by an accurately targeted ion bolt and they crashed to the ground. But many of the rank and file of the Pewter Guard had never looked down their sights at anything alive. He had no idea how they would react, would they freeze? Would they enjoy it too much? And which would be worse? If they did encounter bandits on this patrol, all these questions would soon be answered.

The Guards' powered armour was stored in its own chamber at the back of the main barracks. The overhead lights automatically turned on as they entered; bathing the banners and battle honours that adorned the walls instantly in the bright golden glow of artificial sunlight. Around the perimeter were alcoves containing the massive suits themselves. They were all, apart from one, matt silver in colour which had helped to popularise the Pewter Guards' name, and they encased the body completely like the armour of a medieval knight. They had been used by the guards for at least the past hundred years and it was one of the few pieces of equipment that hadn't been radically improved by the addition of off-world technology. Rumour had it that a Torkan had once been brought in to see if it could be modernised. Every inch of it had been explored by the miniscule tentacles, it had been disassembled and reassembled multiple times. In the end the Torkan left in exasperation, unable to improve upon the time-honoured design.

Above each alcove was a plaque detailing the names and dates of everyone who had worn each suit. Mal's scarlet painted armour had his own, and all of his male ancestors' names, all the way back to his grandfather's grandfather. Others had up to fifteen different names of valued members of the Pewter Guard who, if they had still been alive, would have many tales to tell of their battles before and during the

Spider War. Mal often wondered what it would be like to share a drink with these heroes and talk to them about the injuries they sustained defending the Roost, and finally how they had passed their suit on to the guardsman who took their place.

Once the guards were each stood in front of their own suits they accessed the controls to open them up. The helmets were automatically lifted away and a hidden seam spread from chin to belly, opening the suddenly bisected upper half like a book. Using the thicker armour at the kneecap as a step each one climbed into the lower half of his suit and held out their arms to the side. The suits closed and the helmets were resealed with a hiss of pressurisation.

"Comms Check," barked Mal into the microphone of his helmet.

One by one the, now heavily armoured, Pewter Guard called out their names to check that they could hear and be heard by everyone. When this was confirmed they stepped down from their alcoves and made their way down to the hangar bay to board their heavy skimmers.

Their extra bulk required them to travel the short distance through the cramped corridors in single file and the impact of their marching feet shook dust from the cold stone walls. A small crowd of children gathered behind them as they passed by the kitchens and continued to follow them, at a respectful distance of course, all the way to their destination. The guards entered the hangar and the door was just closing as the children caught up. The group milled around outside for a few seconds until it was obvious that the guards weren't coming back out - then turned dejectedly and started to make their way back to the warmth of the kitchens. They turned again as they heard the door starting to open, when no-one came through it they crept closer.

As they entered the pool of light cast by the open door one of the guards jumped through. He engaged his external speakers and roared at the top of his lungs. The children all screamed in panic and ran; he laughed and turned around to see the other guards all shaking their heads.

"What?"

"Next Time you do that..." replied Na-Thon stonily, "will you please have the decency to turn your Intercomm off? You've just compacted all the wax in my ears."

He looked sheepishly at his sergeant, his captain, and the commander then mumbled an apology and headed towards the waiting heavy skimmers.

The guards filled the rear bays of two of the heavily armoured vehicles. As they took their seats data feeds and umbilical cables sprang from the bulkheads and connected to matching ports on their suits. These enabled the guards to see all the pertinent information that was available to the pilot such as altitude, speed and any contacts that appeared on the scanner screen. The pilot also had access to their vital signs and on more than one occasion this had enabled him to predict when a particularly weak-stomached guard was about to lose his breakfast. It hadn't altered the way he was flying in the slightest, but it did give him time to mute the microphone feed before the unpleasantness had started.

The skimmer launch bay resembled nothing more than a huge beehive. The exit was a single spanned archway that stretched the entire length of the bay; with storage and loading stations extending four stories above. Constructs crawled all over the walls constantly maintaining the exposed systems and infrastructure which helped to re-enforce the insectile look.

Mal conferred with the pilot and, once the pre-flight checks were complete, gave the order to launch. The heavy skimmers lifted from the deck, rotated in unison towards the exit, and shot out into the sky. The fields of the Open Lands passed by below them as they raced towards the western border.

He addressed the guards, "I know that there have been some rumours of a possible bandit encounter during this patrol, but let me stress that that is all they are - rumours. However, we are prepared. We can outgun, outthink, and outfight any thrown-together group of bandits that the Gods decide we should encounter. We've all trained for situations such as this. We're wearing armour that has survived every battle that they've ever taken part in, and most of all we are the

Pewter Guard of the Roost. We are those whom men wish they were. We are those whom women wish they were with. We will defend our home with fist and tooth and fire. We will not fail!" With this, the assembled Guards punched the air in salute and cheered.

He closed the broadcast connection and settled back into his seat. Sergeant Na-Thon, sitting opposite him, attracted his attention and pointed to his ear. He opened a direct voice connection with the guard's suit.

"My Lord, that was a rousing speech and I think the younger men certainly appreciated it. But do you really think that this patrol will be any more dangerous than the last one?" asked Na-Thon.

"Sergeant, let me put it this way - I've heard the word 'bandit' more times this morning than I have in the last year. I'm an old fashioned man, and I'm a great believer that there's no such thing as a coincidence. 'Forewarned is forearmed' as my father used to say."

"As you say My Lord. I must admit that I've cleaned and stripped my weapons five times today, and I have twice my usual complement of ammunition."

The skimmer lurched abruptly to one side, and a warning light flashed once then darkened.

"Pilot! Report!"

"I'm sorry My Lord, just a little turbulence. It didn't show up on the environmental scanner."

Mal shook his head inside his oversized helmet, offered a silent prayer to whatever the patron saint of half-blind skimmer pilots was, and checked the navigational display. They were still several miles from their first waypoint. As the armoured craft had no windows other than those that the pilot used, there was a complicated array of miniature cameras on the outside of the hull which could be slaved to the standard guards' helmet display. As he switched to it, the walls around him gently faded into transparency. He saw the other patrol skimmer, fifty yards off their starboard side, and the miles of rich farmland stretching away in all directions. The Roost was well out of sight and he felt the strange pang of loneliness that he always did when he was far away from home.

"Commander, we're coming up on the first waypoint now."

At the sound of the pilot's voice he disconnected the external view and brought his consciousness back inside the cramped skimmer. Blinking at the sudden darkness he replied, "Thank you pilot, bring us into secure comms range and keep your eyes open."

"Yes My Lord, one mile it is."

He disconnected his link to the pilot and hailed the border station. There was no reply and he immediately tried again. "Border station West-one, this is Pewter Guard patrol one. Are you receiving me?"

From the other end of the link there was nothing, not even static.

"West-one! This is Mal'Ak-Hai Lohlephel, Lord-Commander of the Pewter Guard of Rustholme. You will reply immediately or I will consider your station to be compromised by bandits and raze it to the ground!"

The silence from the radio channel continued.

"Pilot, lock weapons on the station and prepare to fire on my mark."

"Pewter Guard patrol, this is station West-one. We apologise for the delay in answering your hail. We were... indisposed momentarily. There is nothing to report since your last visit, but thank you for your concern. West-one out."

"Acknowledged, West-one, we will take your suggestion under advisement," he replied to the already closed channel. Breathing deeply he opened the Commlink to the rest of his squad. "Gentlemen, put on your fighting faces, we are about to put the fear of the Gods into someone who believes himself to be all-important."

The pilot performed a circuit of the station and set the skimmer down on the landing pad. The guards disembarked whilst the other skimmer circled lazily in the air to watch for any possible bandit activity.

"Sergeant, how many men are stationed here?"

"Standard complement is ten My Lord."

"And does my family provide them with personal transport?"

"No, not as far as I am aware."

"Not including the one we arrived in," asked the now exasperated commander, "how many skimmers can you see?"

"Fourteen, My Lord."

"Then I'm not going insane, which is a comfort. Defensive positions, all eyes on the door."

The guard created a close semi-circle of armour around the entrance as their commander slowly advanced.

He raised a foot - "Knock-knock," he whispered to himself as his boot made contact and kicked the steel hatch off its hinges.

The sight that greeted him was in no way what he'd expected. Most of the men there were presumably the pilots of the skimmers outside and the others were the station's crew. The provenance of the naked girls however was currently a mystery.

"You!" Lord Mal yelled at the man wearing the base commander's cap and very little else, "who are you and, apart from the obvious, what in all the hells reserved especially for over confident fornicators is going on?"

"I... uh... that is... we..." The base commander looked to his crew for assistance, but they were all busy desperately ignoring him or trying to find their clothes. "my name is O'Shea, Commander. We... we provide a service... for the local farmers." His eyes widened as the remainder of the guards entered the room. "We're doing nothing illegal, everyone is here of their own free will." He looked at the girls who were trying to cover themselves whilst nodding profusely.

"You're using one of my mother's border stations as a whorehouse."

"Your... your mother?" he stammered in reply.

Mal pressed the latch that unlocked his helmet, then turned it slightly as it released with a hiss. He took hold of it in both hands and slowly lifted it from his head.

As his face came out of the shadow, it was all O'Shea could do not to pass out. "My Lord... I had no idea..."

"Were you aware that I was the commander of the Pewter Guard?"

"Yes My lord, I..."

"And I'm wearing the armour of the commander of the Pewter Guard?", he spread his arms wide to show off the magnificent scarlet armour.

"Yes, I mean, it's obvious when you..."

"But you were still shocked when it was I inside the armour?"

"No My Lord, I was confused, I..."

"Commander O'Shea, I am going to your office, you will meet me there the moment you are properly attired." He turned to address the room, "the rest of you, if you are stationed here, get back into uniform. If you are a male civilian, please return immediately to your home. If you are female, please do me the service of covering yourselves. This entertainment facility is closed, and will remain so for the foreseeable future. Guards, make sure these people make it safely to their skimmers."

He climbed the stairs to the command deck. The control room seemed to be decorated with the contents of a number of people's underwear drawers. A large leather-bound ledger lay open on the desk; its contents a list of special requests that O'Shea's clients had made. Some had been crossed out in red ink, presumably as each had been fulfilled. He was still sifting through the more colourful of them when there was a knock at the door. "Enter," he called, still marvelling at all the sordid details.

Commander O'Shea opened the door and entered the room. "My Lord..."

"It's good to see you back in uniform, would you care to explain your little side-line?"

He looked down at his shoes, giving him the air of an errant schoolboy who had been caught copying someone else's homework. He shifted his weight uneasily from foot to foot as he tried desperately to think of a way that he could minimise the trouble he was in. "My Lord, the western borders are very quiet. We've not had any activity, apart from a couple of high-altitude flyovers by small Spider patrols, for over three years."

"So, you're telling me that you got bored and started a brothel? When normal people get bored they read, or take up crochet or fishing

– But not you, the first thing that comes to your twisted mind is prostitution?"

"I cannot…"

Lord Mal's communicator crackled into life. "Sorry to bother you My Lord, this is Captain Sembhee, we're receiving a message from Border station West-two, it seems that they're under attack."

"On my way." He turned back to the Base commander and pointed directly at his face with the index finger of his armoured glove, "The only reason that you are not facing a Courts Martial is because I have something significantly more important to attend to. You are a disgrace O'Shea, and if I had the time to transport you back to The Roost, you would be explaining your dishonourable conduct to the Baroness in person. This farce ends now! I will be back later to make sure." He stormed from the control room, signalling the guards to return to the skimmer as he went. Replacing his helmet, he contacted the pilot for an update, "Do we have any details?"

"No My Lord, just a distress call saying that they were under attack from an unknown force. They have sealed the doors and retracted the main sensor array as per standing orders."

"As soon as we're all on board, lift and get us there at best speed."

He ran from the base and jumped into the back of the waiting skimmer, then did a head count and hit the door-close control. The skimmer took to the air as soon as the door started to move and the servo motors in his armour's knees whined as they fought to keep him upright against the sudden acceleration. Struggling to his seat, he triggered the external view. West-one receded quickly behind them and the other skimmer fell back into formation on their starboard side. "Pilot, time to target?"

"My Lord, we should be within range of Station West-two in seven minutes."

"Good. Skimmer two, as soon as we are within range take down anything in the air that's not us. Try to disable rather than destroy - I want to be able to ask at least some of them questions after this is over.

Once the sky's clear, circle in case we need re-enforcement. Pilot, we will be performing an emergency deployment half a mile from target. Maintain full speed, drop to six feet and open the rear doors." The heads of every one of the guards turned to face him and he smiled inside his helmet. "When we're away, join Skimmer two to keep the air clear and wait for my signal."

The pilots of both skimmers confirmed receipt of their orders and Mal went back to scanning the horizon ahead. The minutes ticked slowly past until the bulky tower of Border station West-two appeared out of the haze. Immediately, the second skimmer peeled off and climbed to get a clearer view and give itself a better attack vector. He triggered the limited zoom facility of the external cameras and saw bright plumes as energy weapons splashed against the skin of the tower. It was obvious, even from this range, that the station's armour would not last much longer. He willed the skimmer to go faster, knowing that for every second's delay there was another chance that the tower would be breached and that honourable Rustholme troops could lose their lives.

He turned as the rear door slowly opened. Disconnecting from the external view as he moved to the centre of the bay to address his troops, "Men, I know that many of you have not performed this particular manoeuvre before, but you've all trained for it. Your armoured suits will protect you as they have protected us all time and time again; you need to put your faith in them. As soon as we are all on the ground we'll regroup and make our way to the tower. Debilitate and disarm where possible. I want to know what the hells is going on."

A chorus of affirmative answers assailed his ears as he took a deep breath, shouted, "Go!" and leaped through the gaping hatch at the back of the skimmer. He was only in the air for a moment before he impacted with the hard ground. As he tumbled to a halt, he caught brief flashes of the rest of the Guard jumping and landing at regimented one second intervals. A few of them landed heavily, there would certainly be some work for the medics to do when they got back to the Roost.

He lay panting on his back for a split second, and watched as their skimmer climbed up into the sky, before dragging himself to his feet and making his way to the nearest of his troops that had hit the ground hard. He checked that the tell-tale lights on his suit's chest were all green and pulled him up by the wrist. He made his way forward and helped the next guard up from his knees. There was an explosion from above them as one of the bandit's vehicles exploded, "Pilots, do I need to explain the meaning of the word 'Disable'?"

"Apologies My Lord, a lucky shot, I will try to make sure that I am less lucky in the future," replied one of the pilots breathlessly, but without a hint of sarcasm.

"I'd appreciate it if you would, it's difficult to get sensible answers from someone when their lips are more than ten feet apart." He gathered his men and they ran headlong towards the tower. As they got closer, several bandits started to fire on them from behind solid cover. The guards instinctively dropped to the ground, and looked desperately around for some cover of their own. The Commander and Sergeant Na-Thon however, stood unmoving as projectiles and energy bolts were either deflected or absorbed by their armour. "Trust! Your! Suits!" he bellowed.

Slowly the guards rose to their feet and drew their heavy weapons, the augmentation of their suits' motors enabling them to easily wield assault weaponry one-handed. As they resumed their run towards the tower it became plain to the bandits that they weren't facing a standard patrol. Some just broke ranks and ran, they were immediately disabled by the guards with ion weapons. As the beams of positively charged particles short circuited their nervous systems they fell, twitching, to the ground. Others stood their ground and continued to fire on the advancing giants with little or no effect. Suddenly the barrage from the bandits stopped; Mal raised his hand, and as one the guards ceased firing. All that could be heard was the engines of the circling skimmers and the gentle humming of the guards' armour as they absorbed the power from the last few energy bolts.

Without warning, a loading construct tore itself out from underneath a pile of cargo crates. It was at least twelve feet high and its lifting arms had been replaced with armour-piercing rocket launchers.

"Scatter!" screamed Na-Thon, and the guards did exactly that, dispersing as the construct identified which target to prioritise.

"Bring that bloody pile of bolts down!" yelled Mal as the massive machine's rocket tube pointed directly at him.

The bandits started to shoot again, concentrating their fire on him - now that it was obvious that he had been selected as the main target. All the guards that had previously been disabling the stragglers turned their ion weapons towards the construct and fired constantly. But it was too late, the behemoth had already launched a missile and it was streaking across the field towards their commander. He saw it coming and all the blood drained from his gut, there was no way that his suit would withstand a direct hit, not from a weapon specifically designed to crack armour. Time slowed down, he could hear the leaden beating of his heart over the scream of the rocket's engine and the low twang of the ion weapons.

At the last moment he jumped, hoping that he could avoid the main blast, he saw the missile pass inches from his faceplate and he briefly felt the heat and pressure from the explosion before he lost consciousness.

He awoke lying on the deck of one of the heavy skimmers, the gentle rolling indicating that they were moving, but not quickly.

"He's back!" yelled Na-Thon, which roused a huge cheer from the surrounding guards. They all looked down on him with the same grin that seemed to almost bisect their relieved faces. "pilot, make best speed for the Roost, the commander's awake!"

The deck shifted below them as the skimmer accelerated. The sergeant reached into one of the cargo bins and produced a mangled lump of glass and metal, he turned it in his hands and showed it to the commander. "Would you like me to hang onto this My Lord, or would you like to keep it with you? I understand your father had something similar."

"What is it?" he replied, looking carefully at it without recognition.

"It's the construct's head, you tore it off as you jumped over it.

I don't know whether you noticed that the ion guns were slowing it down, but not stopping it, due to the heavy shielding. But as you jumped over the rocket you hit the construct, grabbed its head and twisted it off, just as the explosion knocked you unconscious."

"I don't remember…"

"Well My Lord, if that was just a reflex action then you just showed your Guard the reason you're in command. Other than the fact that the position is yours by right, Of course, I meant no disrespect."

"No, it's fine… I feel like the construct tore my head off, not the other way around. I should probably get the medics to take a look at me when we get back."

"Yes My Lord," the sergeant replied as he looked down at the growing pool of blood that had formed underneath his commander's suit whilst he had been unconscious, "I think that that would probably be prudent."

Chapter 5 : Camouflage

The Spirit settled onto her landing legs just as the sun finally disappeared over western horizon. The crew busied themselves securing their stations and collecting everything they needed for the trek north to the base at Sidi Ferruch.

"Let's hope that the wildlife's friendly," remarked Dorleith as she strapped on her pistol and LongKnife.

"I can't remember there being anything big and nocturnal around these parts, apart from some wild dogs perhaps. Well, nothing real anyway." Britt looked out of the corner of his eye at the captain, having no doubts that that would pique her interest.

"So, you're worried that we might be attacked by something fictitious?" she asked, shaking her head, "if your next sentence starts with the words 'They do say,' then strap on some water-wings, because you're swimming back to the Roost."

Britt looked at her, slightly petulantly, and replied, "It is said by the locals that..." He paused and raised an eyebrow at her. She nodded and waved her hand in the manner of someone who wanted to speed things up a little, "that there's some kind of beast that stalks the ruins."

"But you only found out that we were coming here this morning, how could you possibly have time to research local legends?"

Britt had the look of a man caught in a lie, which was exactly what he was, and desperately tried to think of a snappy way out. "Ah,

65

aye, well... it was the rumour last time I was here, amongst the locals at least."

She regarded him warily, wondering exactly what it was that he was up to. She knew full well that there were no local people at the base when it was originally operational. She also knew that people very rarely left the safety of the base during their visits due to the likelihood of Spider attacks. But there would be plenty of time to figure out what he was actually talking about, they'd probably be out here for a while.

As the crew made themselves ready, they began to congregate in the starboard lock. Britt checked that everyone was present and nodded to the captain.

"We're going to be walking the ten miles or so to our new home. The land's reasonably flat, if we stick to the roads and most of the local fauna is either friendly, smaller than us, or both. But keep your eyes open, you can never be too careful, there could be a demon in every shadow, a drop-bear in every tree." she looked directly at Britt, who at least had the decency to blush deeply. "So, if we're all ready?"

She turned and opened the external door. The heat hit them like a fist and they were instantly covered in a layer of sweat and dust. They made their way down to the base of the steep boarding ramp and for a split second she thought that maybe having a few heavily armed Pewter Guards on their side might not have been such a bad idea after all. Looking across the ruined buildings, she tried to imagine where attacks might come from. Which outbuildings could contain hidden Spiders waiting to uncoil and cut them down. Closing her eyes, she realised that all she was doing was scaring herself and it would only be a matter of time before the crew noticed. This is why she hated being stuck on the ground; there were no places to hide in the sky - apart from the occasional cloud of course. You didn't have to constantly worry what was waiting around every corner.

"Wait!" shouted Britt, the entire crew turned momentarily forgetting about the assorted phantoms in the dark, "I've left something." He turned, raced back up the ramp and re-entered the ship.

The captain drew her hand down her face, both to wipe away a layer of dusty sweat and to show her general disbelief of Britt's continuing antics. Moments later he reappeared at the lock entrance carrying a long bundle, wrapped in an oilcloth.

"I knew I'd packed her," he mumbled. As he slowly unwrapped it, a series of sharp, carbide coated teeth came into view surrounding a wide sword blade. "Seems I might finally get a chance to use her."

The captain looked up at him just as he pressed the stud that started the serrated teeth orbiting at great speed around the edge of the blade. "You brought a ripsword?"

Britt swung the buzzing weapon around in front of his face, the glinting blade reflecting in his eyes. "Aye, I thought that we might need to clear some undergrowth, she'll come in handy. I've called her Molly."

"Yes, of course you have…" she sighed, "Mr. Britt, please take the lead, the rest of you fall in behind me. We've got quite a way to go and I'd like to get there before the sun comes up again, I can't imagine it's going to get any cooler when that happens."

They trekked through the outskirts of the village, north towards the highway. The captain hoped that the wide stretch of blacktop would take them most of the way there, leaving only the last two miles of their journey across rough country. The plan hinged on the presumption that all of the overpasses and intersections were intact, although this area had been hit fairly hard during the closing months of the war. They would, hopefully, be able to cross those bridges when they came to them.

Unfortunately, it turned out that having to pick their way through the wreckage slowed them more than she had hoped. The fact that the men jumped at the sound of every settling rubble pile and dripping pipe didn't help their progress either. But eventually they reached the on-ramp and made their way down onto the main highway.

"I don't like this, Captain," remarked Britt, scanning the horizon, "we're too exposed, this is a mistake."

"Well perhaps if you hadn't gotten us shot down, we'd now be in a comfortable mess hall eating reformed marine protein in the shape of duck a l'orange with roast potatoes and a delicate jus. Instead of skulking along a disused highway imagining that every step might be our last."

"But... I..." he stammered, realising that she didn't blame the crash on him for a second, but she couldn't admit to the crew that she'd made a mistake. His eyes narrowed as he wondered if she could admit it to herself.

She shook her head and pointed down the road. "There are seven miles between us and the end of this road. Then another couple of miles of thorns and craters for us to fight our way across before we get to our destination. We can either follow the highway and make it in four hours, or we can head up into the rough ground and do it in double that time. Which would you rather we do?"

"I don't think there is a right answer Ma'am." his tone had suddenly changed from that of a friend and mentor to that of a senior crewman. "I trust that you'll get us there in one piece."

Dorleith smiled, checked that they were out of earshot of the crew, and continued, "I'll do my best, and I'll always take your opinion into account," her eyes hardened and she stared right at him, "but don't ever tell me I'm wrong in front of my crew again."

"Aye Ma'am." Britt bowed, "I'll bear that in mind." He continued to move down the road, ducking from cover to cover, trying to present the smallest cross section in every direction simultaneously.

She stayed close and watched him as he went, noting that he moved with such confidence. Even though he was no longer what anyone would describe as young, his experience was obvious. He'd served her mother throughout the Spider Wars, and had never faltered. He told stories, when he'd had his fill of brandy, that could turn your soul to ice. One of her favourites was about the time, as a young soldier, he had served alongside the Spiders, long before they had turned on their masters and the world was forever changed.

"Mr. Britt? Our current location reminds me of that story you once told me, about the time you first saw the Spiders."

"Aye, it was more forest than jungle there, but a tree's a tree when it comes down to it I suppose." The memory was never far from the surface, it took no more than a moment for it to bubble into his consciousness.

It was hard to believe that we had originally created the single most effective killer of men that there had ever been. Designed as a military construct, whose speciality was urban and jungle warfare. The first generation of Spiders had evolved from the robotic soldiers that were popular at the beginning of the 21ˢᵗ Century. What started as simple surveillance drones and logistical load carrying systems were constantly upgraded until they reached the point where they could actually replace human soldiers rather than just supporting them.

He had been serving as a bombardier with an artillery regiment in Eastern Europe when the message came down from Sector Command that they would be trialling half a dozen 'Weaponised Arthropod Constructs' as the Spiders were still referred to at that time. They arrived at the Mobile Command Centre crated up and supervised by an American Marine Technical Colonel who asked everyone to call him Don. Once the paperwork was signed and the huge wooden boxes had been opened, Don produced a small terminal and started to talk as he typed.

"Once the Whackjobs have been brought to life, they're pretty autonomous. You can just tell 'em what to do and they go off and do it. But this little box will bring 'em back to heel if you ever need to."

"Whackjobs?" Asked the Platoon commander.

"Ah, right, yeah, Whacks... Weaponised Arthropod Constructs. They're about a clever as a dumb-ass dog but twice as loyal... Here we go!"

He finished entering the enabling codes and they slowly crawled out of their boxes. Surprisingly, they resembled nothing more than giant spiders but half of them had eight legs and the others had six. Don noticed the soldiers looking at the two different types and explained that they were still testing which design worked better.

"Sure, it costs more to develop two different kinds, but they're modular, so it's no big whoop. The 'sixers' seem slightly more robust, the 'eighters' are slightly more agile. You pays your money, and you takes your choice. OK, now I'm going to need you to shoot at them."

"I'm sorry?" replied the commander, still staring at the nine feet

tall mechanised creatures gently rising up and down in front of him as if they were breathing heavily and waiting for something to happen.

"I need to teach them the sound of your weaponry; you only have to do it once. Well, once for each weapon that you use at least. They use the sound to take you out of their long range attack solutions. If they can hear two sets of weapons fire, both sides of a firefight for instance, they'll treat the noise that they don't recognise as the potential enemy and get their mojo on," Don moved his hips as if doing The Twist.

The commander took out his sidearm and fired it into the air. All six of the constructs turned instantly to face him and lowered their heads to his level, as if daring him to do it again.

"No, no, no, you need to shoot AT them, they're in a purely defensive mode now, still learning," Don checked the display on the terminal, "yeah, aim for the head, that's where all the sensors are. They're networked by tight-beam, so everything one learns, they all learn."

He raised the pistol again and took aim at the nearest construct's single eye, it came closer in the same way that a dog will try and sniff an outstretched finger, looking at Don for encouragement, he cocked the hammer, swallowed deeply, and then pulled the trigger. The speed at which the construct moved out of harm's way was nothing short of unbelievable. It was as if it flowed from one place to another like mercury.

"OK, so you're going to need to do that with one of everything," he turned to the assembled soldiers, "pick a Whackjob and start shooting guys, try not to forget anything that you might want to use in the future though, don't want these puppies mistaking you for the bad guys in the heat of battle. You there! With the mortar," he pointed at the young Bombardier Britt, who looked down as if he hadn't seen the weapon before, "d'ya have any training rounds for that?"

"Y-Y-Yes Sir," stuttered the young soldier, "in the stores."

"OK Flash, go get one, I wanna show you a trick."

Once he had returned and the mortar was set up, Don turned to the construct closest to him and rapped on its leg with the terminal, the huge head turned to face him.

"Hey Fido, go long," he indicated the trees half a mile away, "over to the tree line, then wait."

The construct spun on its axis and ran to its destination at high speed, then turned and hunched down. Don smiled and patted Britt on the shoulder. He fired the mortar and the dummy shell flew high towards the forest canopy. Britt winced, he had meant to bring the shell down directly on top of its head, but it was going to overshoot by a couple of yards at least. Don activated the microphone on the terminal and spoke a single word, "Fetch."

The Spider jumped, stretched out one of its front legs and snatched the shell straight out of the air. Then it ran, like a freight train, directly at Britt. Seemingly it wasn't slowed down at all by the temporary loss of use of one of its legs. At the last second it skidded to a halt and dropped the round at the astonished Britt's feet.

"It can do that all day every day, it'll identify and catch anything moving within its range that's travelling at less than the speed of sound. If it's much faster than that and it thinks that it's a threat to human life, then it'll get in the way of it."

"It will sacrifice itself?" asked the commander, still unable to take in the possibilities of the new resources that he'd been entrusted with.

Don looked at him quizzically, "Well Hells yeah, they're here to help you guys, we can churn these babies off the assembly line whenever we want to. You guys take around twenty years to become useful, one day they'll replace us all and not a single one of us will need to fight a war ever again. Won't that be great?"

But it hadn't been great, the 'Whackjobs' had been developed over the next year and refined to the point where they had started actively contributing to their own evolution. There had been global reports of small clusters of them replacing each other's parts and upgrading their systems, even though the software and programming for such development had never been part of their design. The tipping point came when one of them, seemingly at random, had the idea of miniaturising a cold fusion flight engine and incorporating that small *design change in every Spider that was made thereafter. Overnight, the entire WAC development and training team was slaughtered by the flying assassins, the Spiders were born and the Spider Wars had begun in earnest.*

"Mr. Britt!" the captain's strident shout brought his attention back to the present and the long, dark highway, "stop exactly where you are!"

He stopped mid stride, and saw that he was standing on the edge of a deep, jagged, precipice.

"If you could just take a step back, I think we'll all find it a little easier to breathe."

He shuffled backwards, sat down heavily on a lump of concrete and tried desperately to swallow his heart; which was doing its level best to escape via his mouth. When he'd regained some composure, he knelt down and again looked over into the gloom. They were stood at the fractured edge of what had been a bridge. The valley floor was some sixty feet below and covered in shattered sections of road surface. It had obviously been destroyed during one of the hundreds of attacks that had decimated the surrounding area.

The captain joined him and looked over the edge herself. "Typical!" she shouted, throwing her hands up in the air, "the only bridge on this entire stretch of road, and it's out! We'll have to make our way back and find a way down into the valley, unless? I don't suppose anyone had the foresight to bring climbing equipment?" She was incredibly surprised when several of her crew actually produced tightly coiled skeins of colourful rope.

Britt looked at the captain questioningly, she nodded and he started reeling off orders to the men. "You there, make your lines fast around those bollards then drop them with a flare." He pointed at two of the crew who were nervously looking over the edge. "Gentlemen? Yes, you! When you've finished admiring the scenery, could you possibly do me the great honour of climbing down and securing me a perimeter? If it's not too much trouble." The men saluted, shouldered their weapons and started to descend. He pointed at two others. "You and you, cover us on the way down."

"Aye Sir!" they snapped back as they brought their weapons in to their hips and peered into the darkness.

"Thank you Mr. Britt. The rest of you, get down the ropes as soon as they're secure." The crew snapped brisk salutes, made their way to the ropes and went over in pairs until it was just the four of them left at the top. She addressed the rear-guard, "As soon as we hit the ground, untie Mr. Britt's line and come down using the other one."

The two crewmen continued looking for possible threats as the captain and her First Officer went down to join the rest of the crew. Halfway down Britt stopped and asked, "Why did you tell them to untie my line specifically?"

She looked up at him, "Because if they get excited and untied the rope early, I'd much rather that it was yours and not mine."

"Aye Captain, of course I should have guessed that it would be something like that," he mumbled towards the top of her rapidly retreating head.

They reached the bottom and started to scramble across the debris to look for an easy way up the other side. Luckily it seemed that there was no overhang above them so it was just a case of making their way up the grassy embankment and getting back onto the road. The shadows cast by the spluttering flare danced around the jagged slabs of concrete and tarmac, creating half recognised images just visible out of the corners of their eyes. As they moved, the wreckage shifted and settled, making every step a stressful exercise in delicate balance.

"Gods' teeth!" hissed Britt, pointing to the top of the steep incline in front of them, "Spider!"

"Don't be ridiculous," countered the captain, "it's a trick of the light, I've seen the shadows of four dragons and a little girl, wearing a big hat, riding a giant duck so far."

He moved his hand in front of her face so that she was looking down the length of his arm and extended his index finger. "There, right at the top of the rise - next to that pile of twisted metal."

Instantly she saw it, crouched down low with its thorax quivering just off the ground. The light from the dying flare reflecting dimly off its single, central eye. "Did you bring your Ion rifle?" she whispered.

"Aye, its back on the ship, in my quarters, I'll just go and get it."

She looked at him and shook her head. "Why isn't it attacking?"

"It seems to be on its own, perhaps it's damaged. I presume it's either waiting for us to get closer, or waiting for the flare to burn out, better chance of getting us all in the dark."

The captain raised her voice slightly, "We're going back the way we came."

Slowly the order filtered from man to man and they turned and started picking their way back towards the dangling rope.

"It's gone," hissed Britt, "it just disappeared as soon as our backs were turned. Where are you, you bitch?" He searched the edge of the embankment but there was nothing, no movement of any kind.

They picked their way through the rubble as silently as they could, every shadow now seemed to have long thin legs, or tearing claws, or a ragged, chittering maw. Dorleith spotted the rusted skeleton of a tanker truck that looked as if it had been crossing the bridge when it had been hit, the faded logo on its side indicating that it once hauled clean drinking water. Its back was broken and the end of the tank itself was torn off, but it would make a decent defensible position, or somewhere for a last stand if it came to that. She attracted Britt's attention and pointed.

He nodded, turned to the rest of the men to pass on the instruction and froze. "It's behind us..." he breathed.

She saw the Spider, hunched down again, trying to blend in with the broken concrete and scrap metal. "Can we outrun it to the tanker?"

"Must be about a hundred yards, over broken ground," the flare theatrically chose this exact moment to finally sputter out, "and in the dark?"

As soon as the light disappeared, they could hear the metallic sounds of the Spider once again starting to move.

"We've got no option... run!" yelled Dorleith.

She put her head down and ran, as fast as humanly possible, towards the wrecked truck. She could hear shouting and occasional gunfire as members of her crew fired blindly behind them, hoping to score a lucky shot on their pursuer. But she concentrated on reaching the cover of the tanker; almost crying with the effort. Out of the corner of her eye she could see that Britt was almost level with her, offering her his hand, then she lost her footing and fell heavily.

She saw a length of jagged, rusty, rebar coming up at her face but could do absolutely nothing. Her fall fragmented into a series of supremely clear still images. Her hands moving up to protect her face, the oddly shiny broken end of the rebar an inch from her eye, the looming shadow to her left.

Britt's bulk careened into her and they both landed on their backs in a patch of mud and weeds. He took a deep breath and jumped to his feet. Looking behind them he saw the Spider closing on them at the speed of an out of control express train.

"Excuse me Ma'am." He grabbed her by the wrist, threw her effortlessly over his shoulder and ran for the safety of the water tanker.

If the Spider had had any breath, it would have been scorching the back of his neck. He had no idea how he was keeping ahead of the giant mechanical arachnid, but he was really too busy to wonder and so instead he concentrated on pumping his arms and legs like pistons and trying not to drop the squirming weight over his shoulder. They reached the derelict together, Britt dived into the cavernous interior whilst the Spider jumped up and landed on the 'roof' of their shelter. The crew lay panting in the rusty pools of gravel, as they listened to the scrabbling claws of the otherwise silent killer above them.

One of the crew unslung a compression rifle and pointed it towards the noise. Britt gently took hold of the barrel, pulled it down until it was pointing at the ground and whispered, "You're more likely to kill one of us with a ricochet than you are to pierce the plating of this thing and take out the Spider, at best you'll wing it and make it angry. Do you want to spend your last moments in a metal tube containing you, an angry Spider and a tonne of minced meat that used to be your crewmates?" the panicked crewman shook his head, "good choice, now, give me the..."

His attention was taken away suddenly by the dark bronze and black leg that was inching slowly into view, soon it was joined by another and yet another. He tightened into a crouch as the sensor cluster that acted as the Spider's head came into view. At that self-same moment the captain grabbed the rifle, dropped to the ground and loosed a shot that peeled a section of armour from its neck. The creature recoiled and hastily retreated back onto the roof.

"Can any of you dogs tell me why we aren't all dead six times over?" asked Dorleith, rolling onto her back and passing the rifle back to the crewman she'd taken it from.

"I was thinking something along similar lines myself Captain. Even damaged it could have torn us to pieces. It covered the ground fast enough to run us down and stamp us into the dust, I reckon it's testing us." Britt scoured the rim of the opening for any signs of the Spider.

"I'm going out there." Dorleith looked towards the open end of the tanker.

"Excuse me Ma'am but with respect, I think that is perhaps the most..."

She silenced Britt by simply raising her eyebrows and continued, "If it wanted us dead, we'd be dead by now, don't you agree? You think it's testing us, I think it's more likely that it's trying to hold us here until a capture squad can arrive, I will not be taken hostage and used as a bargaining chip."

"But they don't take prisoners Captain... Scalps sometimes, but never prisoners."

"Count to ten and then follow me, we'll make for the overpass and climb back up the rope."

She left the safety of the truck and backed out into the night. She could see the front legs of the Spider raised high in the air as if it was tasting it, quivering as it sat hunched and stationary above her. She took another step back and looked down into the darkness, towards her crew, "I know I said ten, but I think we should really just go now, it doesn't seem to be moving." She looked back up, and the Spider was gone. "Gods! Why won't these damn things stay in one place for more than a minute?"

She scanned the immediate area, but she could see nothing.

She signalled to her men who were now gathered at the mouth of the shelter, looking around at the shattered sections of blacktop and concrete, expecting them all to sprout legs and start chasing them again. They moved out slowly, trying to keep behind cover as much as they possibly could whilst still trying to maintain a wide field of view. Occasionally Britt would attract their attention and direct them to a better position, or point out an area that they needed to pay special attention to, but eventually they picked their way back to the bridge support.

The climbing rope dropped heavily to the ground just as Dorleith reached for it. They all looked up as one and saw the head and front legs of another Spider, looking back down at them. Then they turned as the first Spider abandoned its hiding place and expertly started making its way across the rubble towards them.

The construct raised its front two sets of legs, extending four sets of long, razor sharp claws. "Identify yourselves."

Britt's jaw dropped. "When did they start talking?"

"Since never," replied the equally shocked captain, "they don't need to talk, they're networked together and we're beneath them."

"I will not ask again. Identify yourselves."

She cleared her throat and stepped towards the Spider, "I am Lady Dorleith Ahralia, captain of the Rustholme ship The Spirit of Heinlein, this is my first officer, Agamemnon Britt and the rest of my crew."

The Spider took a step back, sheathed its claws and approximated a low bow as well as it could. "Apologies My Lady, this construct could not read your identity from your locator beacon. Do you require assistance to complete your journey?"

"I…?"

"Between us we would be able to carry you to the base at Sidi Ferruch," it indicated the other Spider that was now crawling stealthily down the bridge support, "it would be quicker than walking, if that was your wish?"

"I'm sorry, but what?"

"We are part of the external guard for your base at Sidi Ferruch, we have been tasked with investigating the crash of an unidentified aircraft. But your arrival and recovery now takes precedence."

"Ah, the airship that you shot down was ours, we were suffering from communications problems and couldn't reply to your hail."

The Spider looked as shocked as it was possible for an expressionless construct to look. "I have contacted the base and have informed them of the situation, they are sending a recovery team for your ship, it will be transported to the main hangar. I have been instructed to assist you in any way possible. What is your command?"

"Yes, convey us to the base, but first, I feel we should address the elephant in the room," both Spiders scanned the immediate area, "no... I mean, you're Spiders, Spiders traditionally are... unfriendly towards humans."

"With respect My Lady, we are standard Mark Eighteen heavy security constructs. We are simply wearing repurposed Spider armour. It acts as a visual deterrent to anyone wishing to investigate the base at Sidi Ferruch too closely. It was suggested by Frobisher." The construct formed two of its legs into a makeshift ramp. "Please board when you are ready, we will reach the main compound within the hour."

The crew spread themselves evenly between the two constructs and they made their way along the highway. As the constructs had said, they reached the coast in less than an hour and they were dropped off next to what looked to have been, before the war at least, a very popular beach. A lone serving construct was waiting for them amongst the rubble.

"My Lady, welcome to Sidi Ferruch, I hope that you will be pleased with the headway that we have made in your absence." it faced the security constructs and its indicator lights pulsed a complicated pattern, they turned and went back to their patrol. "if you would care to follow me, I will take you to the facility."

They walked to an unremarkable low building and entered through a small wooden door. "We have updated the security protocols, and we will need to make changes to your locator beacons to add the necessary codes." As it spoke the room shuddered and started to descend into the ground.

Dorleith made a show of patting her pockets. "Ah, yes, about that... I'm afraid that my beacon is back at the Roost, if you give Stalys the details, he can do that remotely."

"We can provide you with a new beacon here My Lady, it is a very simple construction which can be made to your specification. I will pass your request to Frobisher, he will see to it."

The lift continued to move for some time until it finally groaned to a halt and a hatchway opened in front of them. The construct ushered them out into the main open space that hosted the docking bay and maintenance areas. "The crew quarters are all along the south corridor, as is the commissary. My Lady, your and your officer's quarters are to the east. Please feel free to explore at your leisure. If you have any questions Frobisher is at your service twenty four hours a day. Now, if you will excuse me, I have duties to attend to." It backed away and joined the throng of other constructs moving around the bay on their own errands.

She turned to Britt, "Was it me, or was that construct being quite... familiar?"

"If I'm being honest Ma'am, they all have. Maybe we could ask Frobisher?"

She nodded and looked around the docking bay, "Have a wander around, see what you think of the work they've done, I'm going to get something to eat and do the same. I'll meet you in a couple of hours and we can compare notes." She turned to the crew. "Right men, let's make use of the dining facilities and then get some sleep, pick your quarters and stow what gear you have. I'll wager it'll be a busy day tomorrow, what with having to rebuild the Spirit and everything."

A rousing chorus of "Aye Ma'am!" was the reply as the crew made their way down the southern corridor.

She attracted Britt's attention and mouthed the words, "Two hours." He bowed in response as she turned and jogged after her crew.

He walked across the deck, being studiously ignored by the various constructs as they busied themselves replacing worn plating and installing new equipment. He checked to find that everything was up to standard. Above him a deep alarm started to sound and a wide circle of lights, surrounding a huge panel in the ceiling, began to flash. Britt stepped back as the centre of the floor cleared and the panel slowly opened to reveal the hull of the Spirit being suspended under a pair of remotely controlled skimmers. As the ship was lowered to the floor, he noticed that the gasbag that had been holed was no longer attached, and that the other two were completely deflated. Even after all these years, it still seemed strange to see a ship in that state, it was almost as if she were a normal seagoing vessel, more used to splitting the waves than the clouds.

He put his hand on a passing construct and asked, "is there always this pantomime when a ship docks?"

The construct paused and then answered, "No sir, this 'pantomime' as you call it is purely for the benefit of the organic crewmen, for the past two weeks we have worked in complete silence and darkness."

He dismissed the construct and approached one of the severely engineered brass heads connected to the wall, "Frobisher, are you awake?"

The indicator lights on Frobisher's terminal brightened, "Sir, I am constantly awake, the power generation capabilities of this base are sufficient to ensure that I will still be awake long after you and your crew are dust."

"Well I'm sure that that's a source of constant comfort to you." He noted that the odd attitude of the base constructs seemed to carry over to the main A.I. then continued, "Give me a status overview of this base's main systems, concentrating on defence, maintenance and power generation. I want to know what's working, what's not, what you are prioritising and why. Then I'll tell you what you should be doing."

Frobisher started to reel off the information that Britt had requested. It seemed that the fabric of the base was virtually complete, bar a few cosmetic issues. The defences were sufficient; actually, more than sufficient if their recent test against the Spirit was anything to go by. The maintenance logs were up to date with nothing major outstanding apart from a couple of non-flushing toilets in the main stores and there was sufficient geo-thermal power to, as Frobisher had so deftly put it, keep the base fully powered until they were all long gone.

"Very good," Britt remarked, "what is the state of the stores?"

"There is enough food, both whole and reformed, to feed a full complement of organic crew for one year, this will be constantly replenished by our scavenger constructs. We carry standard spares packages for all of the ships currently registered to the Rustholme fleet, including the new hull that Lady Dorleith has purchased..."

"What about the engines that she is having fitted?"

Frobisher paused and his indicator lights pulsed as he looked for this information. "I have no record of which engines have been chosen sir. If you would furnish me with the model number I can check the stores manifest."

"As far as I remember, they don't have a model number. They're engraved brass, about the size of TF-80's, don't seem to have any moving parts. The captain found them in the Bolivar's old hangar back at the Roost." Britt indicated their size by holding his thumb and forefinger an inch or so apart and squinting through the gap at the distant hull of the Spirit, and then guiltily dropped his hand to his side and brushed some speck of non-existent lint from his trousers as he realised that Frobisher could not see what he was doing.

For an instant, the A.I.'s lights flashed a brilliant red and then returned to their normal, slow cycle, but as he continued to speak, his voice sounded very slightly softer. "I'm afraid sir, that I cannot identify the equipment that you are describing. I will have to use whatever spares are applicable as and when the need arises."

"Well, I suppose that'll have to do. Is anyone currently working in the stores? I would like to take a look at your... well, technically our, stocks for myself. I should hate to get run-over by some overzealous picking construct as it goes about its normal business."

"There are currently five pickers working in the main stores. They all have infra-red detection and movement sensors, there is a less than a point zero one percent chance of accidental collision. I will inform them of your impending visit and turn on the lights. If you are in need of any further assistance whilst you are in the stores, I am situated near the main freight paternoster."

Britt cheerily nodded at Frobisher's head and followed the signs leading the two decks down to the main stores. He eventually arrived at the entrance and opened what seemed to be some kind of pressure door. The store room was considerably larger than he'd expected, he'd never ventured below decks on any of his previous visits, but he was fairly sure that this single room was larger than the floorplan of the main hangar and living quarters together. He walked past row upon row of high racking; most of which was filled with large crates just bearing painted serial numbers and construct readable data-tags. Some however also had stacks of identifiable items, field rations, tools, medical kits and other assorted pieces of personal equipment dotted between the crates, all of them were individually wrapped in a thin layer of clear plastic. He wandered up and down the rows of racking until he reached a large open area. Even though he looked in all directions, he could still only just make out what he assumed to be one of the pickers, far in the distance, probably loading hull plating ready to transport it up to the main deck.

"Frobisher!" He yelled, "Where, in the name of the Damnably Happy Squirrel God, are you?"

Immediately the overhead lights dimmed slightly and a massively bright light began to flash at least one hundred and fifty yards to his left. He followed this beacon and found that the light was coming from a slightly more crudely sculpted Frobisher head.

"Ah, there you are!" As Britt spoke, the flashing stopped and the ambient lighting brightened. "I have a couple of questions already: How is this room so big and why are there pressure doors everywhere?"

"Sir, the answer to both of those questions is the same. A large proportion of this level is under the bed of the Mediterranean Sea. The pressure doors will automatically close to prevent the rest of the base being compromised in the event of accidental flooding. The system can be over-ridden if you wish to temporarily deny access to this level and the one above."

"We can intentionally flood the base?"

"I believe that that is what I just said, sir. However, the hangar deck and geo-thermal level can also be intentionally flooded if required. This would result in the almost instantaneous destruction of this facility as the volume of water hits the geo-thermal vents and creates an explosive steam pressure event."

"Can that be triggered by accident?"

"No sir, that would require authorisation from the two ranking officers in residence."

"That's probably for the best." He looked forlornly around at the thousands of square feet of storage. "Is there some way I can browse the stores manifest remotely?"

"If you tell me what you are looking for sir, I will be able to instantly locate it for you."

"I'm not looking for anything in particular, I'd just like to browse, it helps me to sleep."

"That information is available from any terminal, including the portable ones."

Britt smiled and started to walk back towards the pressure doors; he had only gone a few yards when he remembered something. He walked back to Frobisher with his hands clasped behind his back and asked, "You wouldn't happen to have a portable terminal at all, would you?"

If Frobisher had had the ability to sigh, he would have used it now with great vigour. His indicator lights paused, quickly cycled and then paused again. "Your terminal is on its way now sir."

Crossing his arms, He casually leaned against the wall and within seconds he felt, rather than heard, a low rumble coming towards him. Rounding the corner from a section of racking, a picker hove into view. It was possibly one of the largest constructs that he had ever seen close up, forty feet high and about as long. It had three pairs of insectile arms down each side of its body; each with a corresponding holding bin that enabled it to pick and store up to six heavy items simultaneously. It turned and advanced towards him, stopping in the space next to the cargo paternoster. It reached into one of its forward bins and produced a plastic wrapped data terminal. Holding it with one arm, it used the delicate fingers of the other to unwrap the item, and then handed it to Britt. Its temporary errand complete, it retreated back into the racks to continue its work.

He addressed Frobisher again. "Thank you, you've been most helpful. I notice that it's very quiet down here, between the pickers and this paternoster," he slapped the doorframe of the briskly moving elevator, "I was expecting a cacophony of epic proportions."

"This stores facility is currently operating at five percent speed sir, due to your presence. It will return to full speed once you have cleared the deck."

"I'll be off then, I need to go and report to the captain."

The indicators on Frobisher's head instantly dimmed alongside all the main lights that weren't directly between Britt and the pressure door. He made his way out, checking the contents of the shelves as he went to try and familiarise himself with at least a tiny segment of what was available. There was nothing that he saw that he thought they would need immediately, but it was good to at least have at least a rough idea of what was there. Closing the pressure door behind him, he listened for a second as the volume and pitch of the noise coming from the other side of the door increased. As he re-entered the hangar bay, he noticed that the Spirit's rear bag had already been replaced and that constructs were busy overhauling the engines. Yawning, he made his way to the commissary to keep his appointment with the captain. The last twenty-four hours had been rough on everyone and he just wanted to deliver his report and get some sleep.

As he walked through the swing doors he saw the captain sitting all alone spinning her jewel-handled dagger around on the tabletop in boredom. She turned towards him and smiled. "Found any cobwebs or cracked windows?"

"By the time we wake up tomorrow, both the base and the Spirit should be mechanically complete, we can return to the Roost whenever you're ready."

"Return? We've only just got here! What's that you're reading?" Britt pushed the terminal containing the manifest towards her. "You're going to stay up and read this aren't you?"

Britt smiled as he took it back and skimmed through the list of available items. "There's a lot of stuff here that we can use for your new ship. Including a full rig of plus-sized redundant gasbags, a set of camouflage blades and... Well, this could be very useful!"

The captain cocked her head to one side and raised her eyebrows questioningly.

Britt highlighted an entry and passed the terminal back to her. Her eyes lit up as she read the entry, "A battle ready Frobisher subsystem? Will that fit into the hull?"

He shrugged. "Frobisher, stores manifest entry 80352F is described as a battle ready subsystem, can you elaborate?"

The Frobisher head in the commissary turned to regard them. "It is a portable copy of myself, which can be installed in a large vehicle instead of the normally fitted standard A.I. It enables the crew to have the same level of access to me as they would if they were here on the base. I would become the functional A.I. for the vehicle. All systems and sensors would be slaved to me, under the captain's ultimate control of course. The installation includes extra offensive and defensive subroutines, personally programmed by your father, Captain."

She felt a pang as he mentioned her father, then turned to Britt. "OK, get whatever we need transported back to the Roost. When the hull finally gets delivered we'll get back there as soon as possible."

Britt nodded and started highlighting a selection of parts that would help them complete the new ship. He went through the rest of the entries item by item and found virtually everything that they could ever possibly need, along with a few things that he just wanted, or he thought would suit the style of the ship. It took him twenty minutes and when he had finished he ordered Frobisher to send the cargo to the Roost via heavy skimmer.

"Are you done?" asked the captain, standing up and stretching to try and get rid of the ache in her shoulders.

"Aye, it should all be at the Roost in the morning. Well, I say morning, before I wake up at least," they headed down the eastern corridor, towards the officer's quarters and their beckoning beds.

Chapter 6 : Information

Sergeant Na-Thon looked at the assembled guards and shook his head. "The Medics say that we got him here just in time. He'd lost nearly four pints of blood and that was before they opened him up and started trying to nail him back together. There's twist damage to his spine and they won't know for a while whether he's going to need augments to make him able to walk again."

The crowd of soldiers stood in the waiting area of the operating theatre, a room which was not designed to hold a large number of men, certainly not wearing armour that made them twice as massive. Every time a door opened, they would all turn to face it as if their heads were on strings and Na-Thon realised that this wasn't the most efficient use of their collective time.

"Right, there's nothing useful we can do here. We're going to get out of this armour, and then I'm going to get some answers out of our newly captured bandit friends. I can guarantee that that will be the first question Lord Mal will ask and woe betide the first guard he sees that can't provide an answer. Zatch?"

"Yes... Sergeant?" the suddenly suspicious guard replied, knowing full well what was coming next.

"Double-time to the armoury and get out of your suit, then straight back here, you're on first watch."

The young guard saluted, pushed through the crowd of relieved looking faces and ran down the corridor towards the barracks. The rest of them followed him out at a more sedate pace, talking amongst themselves. The sergeant heard snippets of conversation as they left the room,

"Did you see him tear off that thing's head?"

"His whole body folded in half when that missile hit."

"I'm going to make those bandits pay if he doesn't recover."

He thought that he probably should bring them to attention, but this was the first time they'd really seen their commander in action. Let them be awestruck for a while, this would certainly do his Lord's reputation no harm at all. If he was honest, he felt the same way himself, he'd not seen bravery like that since the Baron had been their commander.

There was only one real difference that he could see between the two men; the Baron had been susceptible to the 'red mist'. Once he was in battle he would lose himself in it and he turned into a dervish with a sword in one hand and a gun in the other. When the smoke cleared, he would be stood on top of a pile of whatever it was that he was fighting looking for more targets. Lord Mal was the complete opposite; he seemed to be able to compute the odds of the success of any given attack plan in his head, faster than any A.I. His record of one-shot/one-kills in training was unmatched and probably would be for a very long time, no one else even came close. He could move like the wind from one target to the other, identify its weak spot and exploit it instantly. Today proved what happened when he came upon an enemy with no weak spots, he simply tore its head off, despite almost killing himself in the process.

The door from the theatre opened and the Roost's senior surgeon, Doctor Say'Uff, walked through. His med-suit was covered in blood and he was wiping sweat from his face with a once-sterile cloth. "Sergeant, we've pieced together his back, sewn up the internal organs that were burst by the concussion, and replaced those that were crushed as he tried to twist himself in half. He'll be out of action for at least a couple of weeks, possibly a month. I thought I'd better give you an update for your men. Now if you'll excuse me, I'll go back and continue closing him up." The doctor made to go back into the theatre, took a half-step and turned back, "One other thing, just before he succumbed to the anaesthetic, he requested that you 'Let her know I'm going to be OK', I can only assume that he was talking about the Baroness."

For that instant, it took all Na-Thon's willpower to keep control of his bowels. In the panic of getting him to the infirmary, he had not informed the Baroness that her only son was lying on an operating table, abdomen open to the elements, connected to machines that were all that stood between him and certain death after risking his own life for the rest of his guard. "Oh Gods this is going to hurt," he mumbled under his breath. As he was thinking of the best way to deliver the news, Zatch re-entered the room in his fatigues. "Stay with him wherever they take him, you could be lucky, I've got a feeling that the commander won't be waking up anytime in the next few hours. I'm going to report all this to the Baroness, in person. If I'm still capable of walking unaided after that, I'll be extending the continued hospitality of the Roost to our prisoners for a while."

"Understood, sir!" he shouted as he assumed his vigil as close to the theatre door as it was possible for him to get.

Na-Thon kept his outward composure all of the way out of the infirmary and into the torturous maze of corridors of the Roost. Inside, he was in complete turmoil, so much so in fact, that he was at the entrance to the Baroness' private suite before he stopped and took a deep breath. "Stalys, locate the Baroness."

"The Baroness is resting and wishes not do be disturbed," replied Stalys' imperious head.

"I have urgent news about Lord Mal, there has been an incident and he has been injured."

Immediately the door to the suite hissed open and he gingerly walked through, straining his neck to see if the room was occupied before he entered. As his armoured boot hit the thick carpet, the door to the Baroness' bedroom burst open and she ran through it, still trying to button up her jacket.

"Where is he? What happened? Don't just stand there man, spit it out!"

"My Lady, he…"

"Good Gods!" she threw up her hands and turned to the A.I. "Stalys, locate my Son."

"Lord Mal is currently in operating theatre 'A' of the Infirmary. His condition is serious but stable."

She turned her piercing stare on the sergeant and as all of his blood had already frozen, it was the turn of his marrow to turn to solid ice. "What… happened?"

Na-Thon quickly recounted the tale of the afternoon's patrol, thinking it best that he leave out the detail of their trip to West-One, concentrating on the final stages of the battle at West-Two and her son's peerless heroism.

"He defeated a weaponised loading construct twice his size by vaulting over an armour piercing missile that had been aimed at him and tearing its head off with his bare hands?"

"Yes My Lady, thus saving the lives of everyone there."

"Who did this?"

"Initial indications are that they were a particularly well-armed bandit group. I am about to go and interrogate the prisoners we took now."

The Baroness' eyes flashed and she instantly considered demanding that she be the one to perform the interrogation. But she quickly realised that that would probably be a terrible idea, the purpose of questioning the prisoners would be to get meaningful information from them, rather than punishing them. As soon as she heard that her son had been hurt, ideas for their excruciating torture, and eventual slow, painful death had poured through her mind. "Wring every last drop of information from them Sergeant, use any means necessary. Keep at least one of them alive and bring whatever remains to me when you've finished."

"I was intending to keep them all alive My Lady, I find that…"

"You will start the process by executing one as a lesson to the others. Show them that we will brook no resistance to our questioning."

He stepped back, bowed deeply and quickly left her chamber. He considered what the Baroness had said, it smacked of revenge to him, rather than good practice, but she was ultimately his commander's commander, her word was law, no matter what she asked of him.

Making his way through the corridors towards the holding area, he mulled over what he had been ordered to do. He had no problem taking the life of an enemy combatant or putting down a madman that was threatening the life of one of those he was sworn to defend. But this was totally different; these men would be shackled and defenceless. It would be a real waste if the man he chose to kill had important information, what if he had access codes or names or details of meetings? There was no guarantee that either of the others would know everything that they needed to know. He reached the detention block and checked in at the guard station. "Have the prisoners brought into the interrogation suite."

"All together sir? We usually question them separately, to better corroborate any evidence," replied the guard, his brows furrowed as his hand hovered over the Intercomm button.

"Yes, let us imagine for a second that these orders are coming direct from the Baroness shall we?"

The detention guard relayed the order and he watched the monitors as the prisoners were dragged from their separate cells into the sparse room and secured to the chairs. The camera moved out so that all three of their faces could be seen as they looked nervously around the walls trying to discover a way out. He could see that they were talking, but couldn't hear what they were saying.

"Turn on the microphones."

The guard pressed a combination of keys and abruptly, the panicked voices of the three prisoners could be heard.

"I'm not going to tell them anything."

"They'll kill us."

"Did you see what happened to the others?"

"They can torture me all they want, I won't say anything."

"Will they let us go?"

"Torture? They won't use torture, they're not allowed to use torture are they?"

Content that his victim had chosen himself, Na-Thon looked at the guard and drew his index finger briskly across his throat, he nodded and cut the microphone.

"Excuse me sir, it's policy to not take weapons in with the prisoners and I feel that your armour might be classed as a weapon on its own, never mind your pistol," The guard saw the sergeant's face turn from that of a man who was about to do something he didn't particularly agree with, to that of a man who was about to explode in anger, and continued hastily, "...is what I would say to one of the normal interrogation team. Not something I would ever say to a sergeant of the Pewter Guard. Please let me know if you need any assistance."

The sergeant's face relaxed. "Disable the weapons discharge alarm and have a cleanup construct standing by, because you're going to need one, possibly even two."

He walked out of the guard station, down the steps and replaced his helmet whilst the security door confirmed his identity. He strode into the room and stood silently in front of the three men; his bulky armour taking up most of the remaining free space. It was obvious that one of them was completely suffused with fear, there were tears forming in the corners of his eyes and his hands were shaking. Another was sat there resigned, as if he knew exactly what was going to happen and had already accepted it. The third prisoner, the one that had suggested that he would not break under even the strongest torture, had a face filled with hate and was constantly straining against his bonds as if to bite chunks out of the imposing mass of the sergeant.

He removed the large, slab-sided, pistol from the holster on his thigh and calmly addressed the prisoners through his external speakers, "This is an accelerator pistol, it uses a strong magnetic field to throw shaped chunks of iron towards the target at nearly eight hundred miles per hour. The loud bangs that two of you will hear when I fire it are sonic booms, not noise from any explosive propellant. Each magazine holds thirty rounds, I have three magazines."

He slowly raised the pistol until the cavernous barrel was pointed directly at the third prisoner's head. The thirty load bangs successfully drowned out the screams of the other two men but unfortunately there was no accompanying smell of explosives to cover the evidence that both of the surviving prisoners had copiously soiled themselves. When the echoes had died down, there was very little left of the prisoner, or the chair he had been shackled to. The sergeant turned without another word and exited the room, pausing only to scrape some scraps of viscera from his boot onto the remains of the chair. Re-entering the guard station, he told the ashen-faced and open mouthed guards, who were looking at him as if he was some kind of avenging angel, to wait at least twenty minutes before they sent in the cleaner construct and then went back to the barracks to remove his armour.

As he entered the armour room his eyes were drawn to the empty alcove where the commander's scarlet armour should have been. He would have to arrange to have it taken from the infirmary to the workshop for repair. Na-Thon walked over and looked into the vacant niche, it was no different from his own apart from the names above it, but it felt as if the space where the suit should be was something physical, a dense mass of nothingness that seemed to be sucking him in. Shaking his head to clear the maudlin feelings that were roiling inside him, he walked to his own alcove, backed into it, and triggered the suit's exit subroutines.

He blinked when the enhanced visuals were disconnected before his helmet was removed and the cold blast of air that hit him as the chest plates opened up seemed to chill him to his very core. The jump to the floor seemed slightly longer, the floor itself seemed slightly harder. It always took a few seconds to adjust to your own body after you'd removed the armour, but he felt oddly hypersensitive as if the top few layers of his skin had been removed. The sound of the suit closing up made him turn back around; it was only then that he saw the broad spray of the bandit's blood. It stretched from the side of the helmet, diagonally across the chest and halfway down the thigh plating, it was no wonder that the holding area guards had looked at him how they had. He went to the maintenance locker and took out a large bottle of cleaning fluid and a cloth, it took him over an hour to remove every last trace.

Walking back into the main barracks he was immediately accosted by the assembled guards, all of them asking questions about their commander. He told them that he knew no more than they did, and if they needed something to take their minds off it, he was quite happy for them to go out onto the parade square and do practice drills for the rest of the day. Otherwise, they were welcome to join him for something to eat.

On the way to the commissary he bumped into Captain Sembhee, who had commanded the team in the second heavy skimmer that had carried the prisoners back to the Roost.

"How is he?" asked the captain.

"The doctor tells me that they've replaced some of his guts and done their best with his spine. I'm no expert, but the mess I saw as I was helping them take his armour off… Well, I doubt he'll walk again without assistance."

"Does she know?"

"Know? The Baroness was ready to tear down all the walls between her rooms and the holding cells! As it happens, it was just good fortune that he asked the doctor to remind me to tell her. I'd forgotten in all the excitement."

"Hells! I don't think he meant the Baroness. If the Gods value their skins, then she probably knew before it happened. I think he was talking about the girl," Sembhee looked at the confusion in the sergeant's face. "You did know about the girl? Friend of Lady Dorleith? She works in the library?"

"No, I didn't know, Lord Mal is quite secretive about his civilian life."

"Don't worry, I was thinking of taking a walk to the library anyway to get some bedtime reading - I'll tell her. You've done enough for one day. Go and have something to eat and then get some rest. I'll go and see if our three new friends have anything to tell us."

"Two new friends, the Baroness ordered me to execute one of them as a warning to the others. He swallowed a full clip of accelerator rounds."

Sembhee whistled, "And how long is it going to be until the other two have calmed down enough to be able to talk I wonder? Not that I'm questioning the Baroness' orders of course, or your execution of them if you'll forgive the pun. I can understand her reasoning behind it and I'd probably do the same if it had been my son, but it's not going to make our job any easier. I'll have them sent back to their cells and we'll try again in the morning."

Na-Thon nodded, and continued on his quest to eat the commissary out of fresh food and to try and get some heat back into his bones. Sembhee contacted the detention block and ordered that the prisoners be sent back to their cells. He listened whilst the guards explained what had happened, and the sergeant's condition when he left, then confirmed that the Baroness had indeed authorised it, and then he made his way to the library.

"Her name is Naiad or Imp or something like that!" he growled in exasperation at the construct at the library's information desk. "I have a message of great importance to deliver."

"I am sorry sir, but we do not have any staff matching your description." The construct continued dealing with the pile of books and tablets arranged around him, "If you could supply the correct identity details, I would be more than glad to pass on the message."

He exhaled slowly and regained his composure, "Give me a list of the names of all of the human staff of the library, including any known aliases."

The construct proceeded to churn out a list of all of all the people who had ever worked in the library, towards the end of that list was the name that the captain had been waiting for, one Ekaterina 'Pixi' Varloth.

"That one, her, is she working today?"

"Yes sir, she is in the high stacks, I can call her for you, if that is

---

your wish."

"No, that won't be necessary, I will find her myself." He started towards the back of the library, where the less popular, early items were kept, his eyes constantly scanning the ever taller shelves for the young girl that he was looking for.

The Baron had started to build the library some time ago, to store his ever growing collection of historical documents. The high stacks were the first part to be completed, they were three stories tall and only accessible via moveable wrought iron ladders that stretched from floor to ceiling. Everyone assumed that it was 'just his little joke' but in fact, it was his way of keeping fit without making it too obvious that he was keeping fit. He would pick a volume that he wanted to check, not bother to confirm its location using the automated index, and then climb the ladders to try and find it. As he had placed each book himself he could usually tell you where any single item was quicker than you could look it up. Unless, that is, someone else had borrowed it and put it back in the wrong place. He had staunchly refused the advice from the Baroness and his own children to have all the original items tagged so that Stalys could locate them all and update the index, as had happened to all the new arrivals since he had been killed. He could be stubborn, some might say pig headed, but he valued tradition and he didn't like to make things too easy for people.

A movement high above Sembhee's head caught his eye. In the very top reaches of the racks, a small shape vaulted from one row to another, completely foregoing the safety of the iron ladders.

He waited until she had made what appeared to be her final jump and called out to her, "Ekaterina!" She did not even register that she had heard, he tried again, only slightly louder, "Ekaterina!"

She turned, but away from him, and made ready to take another long jump. He put his fingers into the sides of his mouth, pulled his lips taught and whistled. The piercing noise carried through the racks and sent a number of unidentified rodents scrambling for cover. "Pixi!" he shouted and gestured her to come closer. A conservator construct crawled around the corner of the stacks, to investigate the noise.

"Sir, may I respectfully remind you that this is a library?"

The captain drew his pistol, "May I respectfully remind you that this is a fully automatic compression pistol that would reduce you to spare parts in a heartbeat?"

The construct bowed and reversed back the way that it had come. The young girl jumped from the rack and landed lightly next to him on the balls of her feet. She smiled sweetly and asked, "Can I help you..." she searched his uniform for his rank patches, "Captain?"

"I'm sorry to bother you, but I understand that you are currently... romantically entwined with my commander?"

Pixi's face reddened, "I'm sure that that was supposed to be kept quiet, Captain," she said with a glint in her eye, "I'm sure that the Baroness has loftier plans for Lord Mal than a dalliance with an ordinary librarian."

"I'm sure that I wouldn't know, I am here purely to provide defensive services to the family, not to impart romantic advice. I'm afraid that I am here with some bad news, you may wish to sit down."

"I'm a big girl, Captain, I'm sure I can take it," her face betrayed her real mood, and a dark cast immediately settled over it.

"It's the Lord Mal, he was injured in today's patrol, and he's currently in the..." But he was talking to empty air, the second Pixi had heard that Mal had been hurt, she took flight through the banks of shelving and made for the infirmary.

Sembhee shook his head and took a long look up into the heights of the racking. He'd been here many times before, often with the Baron himself. He remembered how he would watch him climb the racks just as the girl had done, often in dress armour, just to find a particular tome of poems or stories that he wished to read during a long patrol or on a trip to Enys Skaw looking for rare parts for the Bolivar.

There was one particular time, he remembered because it was just before he had been promoted to captain, he'd been checking the ordnance stores on the Bolivar one afternoon, just before departing on a patrol. The Baron, in full dress armour, came stomping across the dock arguing with a construct. "I'm sure you have loaded everything I asked for you bumbling bunch of brackets. But I don't necessarily ask for everything I need!" the small head of the rolling construct looked around as if asking for help, "the ship will launch when I have everything I require." He waved at the sergeant. "You there, Sembhee! Come and give me a hand with the lugging."

He immediately closed the hatch, slid to the floor and fell in behind the Baron.

"We're getting some emergency stores from the library," the Baron pointed at the construct, "and if that thing says anything else about scheduled departure times, shoot it repeatedly with whatever first comes to hand."

"Aye My Lord." he took out his ion pistol and waved it menacingly at the construct, who took this opportunity to remember an urgent errand that it had to run at completely the other end of the dock, and motored away.

The Baron laughed through his coarse, dark, beard. "Nicely done Sergeant, I like a man who treats these damnable things with the contempt they deserve. You don't mind doing a bit of fetching and carrying for an old man do you?"

"An honour to serve, My Lord."

"Aye… of course it is. Here we are then. Hope you can catch!"

They had reached the high stacks and the Baron had started to climb, hand over hand, feet hanging free, up the bracketry until he reached the halfway point. He vaulted over the safety rail and proceeded to run his finger along the spines of the assembled books.

"No, no, no, erm… no, Ah! Yes." He pulled out a large volume and threw it over his shoulder. The dusty book sailed over the railing and started to fall towards the ground. The young sergeant, knowing the Baron's almost rabid love of real books, jumped forwards to save it from impacting on the cold, hard, marble floor. It hit the tips of his fingers, edge on, with a crunch and then fell into his palms.

"This one too I reckon." called the Baron, from the shelves high above. Sembhee rolled onto his back, just in time to see another, even larger book careening down towards him. He had just enough time to stretch his arms out in front of his face and stop the book altering the shape of his nose for ever.

"I'm thinking that'll do for the time be-ARRGH!"

The Baron had stepped back from the shelf and caught his foot, which had pitched him bodily over the rail. Luckily, the edge of his greave had caught on the railing and he was suspended, head first over a twenty foot drop. Sembhee twisted like a cat, jumped to his feet and went to summon a construct.

"Don't you dare get one of those clanking contraptions to help you, I won't have them see me like this!"

"But My Lord..."

"Get one of the ladders underneath me, before everything falls out of my pockets."

Sembhee looked around desperately to identify the nearest ladder and pushed it towards the Baron.

"Hurry up boy! The blood's rushing to my head and I'm starting to remember things that I'm not completely sure have happened yet."

Once it was in place, he started to climb. He reached the Baron and tried to manoeuvre him onto it, this was made more difficult by the Baron being little more than a dead weight in his armour, and was struggling as he didn't particularly enjoy the sensation of being upside down.

"What are you playing at? If I'd been meant to spend this much time inverted the Gods would have seen fit to give me little leathery wings, huge ears and an upturned nose!"

He grabbed hold of the Baron's pauldron and lifted him bodily up so that he could reach the ladder. Which he almost did, missing it by an inch. He fell back, the sergeant grabbed hold and pulled, which luckily had the effect of unhooking his leg and dropping him into the sergeant's arms.

"Massimo! What are you playing at now?" cried a familiar, high pitched female voice from below.

The Baron screwed his eyes shut, "The Baroness?" he whispered, "if I offer a prayer to the Tiny God of Compromising Positions, do you think she'll disappear in a cloud of greasy smoke?"

"I am not a particularly Godly man my Lord, but I feel that the chances are very slim."

Massimo Lohlephel, Lord of the Roost, Baron of Rustholme, took a deep breath, adjusted his armour and climbed down the ladder. "Good afternoon My Sweetness, My dew on all the flowers of the Open Lands on the first day of spring. What brings you here?"

"You mean, how did I know that you were clowning around in the library and trying to kill yourself?"

He paused, thought and then nodded, more sheepishly than you would think possible for one who usually had such boundless confidence.

"Stalys has orders to inform me when you are in danger of doing anything ridiculous." She indicated the barely-lit head in the corner.

"Turncoat!" hissed the Baron, at Stalys, who remained completely motionless whilst all the time looking like it was trying to fade into the wall.

"Don't blame the A.I. for doing what it's been told," continued his long-suffering wife, "I would say that you could learn a lesson or two from it, if I was to be frank."

The sergeant took this opportunity to climb silently to the bottom of the ladder and start to creep gently back to the docking bay.

"Don't think you're getting away so easily, Sergeant," the Baroness called, "part of your remit is to see that this old goat stays alive until the Gods come to get him personally in a golden chariot containing his father and his father's father. Did you see any evidence of that stupidly ostentatious pomp and ceremony here today?"

"No, My Lady, I..."

"Then it's a good job that you stopped him becoming a sticky wet mess on the floor. Next time, I would appreciate it if you could suggest restraint to him before he decides to try and widow me in a spectacular fashion again."

"Yes, My Lady, of course, I will try harder in the future." He stared at the floor, wishing that this ordeal would end.

"You are dismissed," the Baroness allowed herself a slight smile as she saw Sembhee breathe out, "and take these filthy books with you when you go."

He nodded, picked up the books that had been forgotten in all the excitement and walked from the room as fast as was seemly. As he retreated, he heard the Baroness explaining, in no uncertain terms, and with increasing pitch and volume, what she would do to her husband if he ever scared her like that again. It did not sound pretty, a lot of it didn't even sound biologically possible. But he knew that she meant every single word.

He reached the Bolivar, deposited the books in the Baron's quarters and left the ship - not wanting to bump into him on the way out. Which, unfortunately is exactly what happened, the Baron looked him in the face and whispered two words through clenched teeth, "Say... nothing..."

Rousing himself from his historical reverie, he located the nearest Intercomm and notified the infirmary that they would soon be receiving a visitor and that she was to be allowed unfettered access to Lord Mal. They informed him that she was already here and had gone straight through Guard Zatch like hot oil through a goose. He smiled, signed off and headed for his quarters; both to rest his bones after a particularly wearying day, and to plan how he was going to get any meaningful information out of two frightened men who thought that they could die at any second.

Arriving at the recovery area, where Mal was going to spend at least the next few weeks, she'd neatly sidestepped the posted guard to gain entry. She hated herself for turning on the tears, sobbing unintelligibly and allowing him to comfort her briefly, but it had worked, and that was all that mattered. The lights were dim and she found the gentle hum and occasional beep of the medical equipment to be strangely relaxing. She made her way to the large, liquid filled tank in the centre of the room containing a blurred figure that she assumed to be Mal.

"Can I assist you Ma'am?" Questioned a voice from behind her. Pixi almost jumped out of her skin and turned to see a large medical construct unfolding itself from the ceiling and moving towards her.

"How's... he doing?" she swallowed, trying to mask the break in her voice.

"He is responding well, the replaced organs have not yet shown any signs of rejection, but the injuries to his spine were severe enough to require almost complete vertebrae replacement. He is currently heavily sedated, and he will be for at least the next twenty hours."

"Will he ever walk again?" A look of grave concern crossed her face as she traced his shadowy outline on the glass with her finger.

"We have no way of knowing at this time Ma'am. To an extent, that is completely up to him, although I understand his colleagues describe him as a fighter. You should take some comfort from that I believe."

"Yes, perhaps you're right." She peered into the tank to try to get a glimpse of his face, but the murk of the restorative liquid, coupled with the close-fitting breathing mask keeping him alive made it impossible. She placed a light kiss on the side of the tank, thanked the construct and left.

"Any change?" Zatch asked her as she appeared in the doorway. She shook her head solemnly and left the infirmary, trying desperately to get back to her quarters before the floodgates holding back her tears burst. She almost managed it.

Sembhee lay in his bed, staring at the ceiling, his window was open and he could hear the sound of the waves crashing against the cliffs far below him. This would normally have helped him to sleep, but tonight it was having no such effect. He rolled out of bed and looked out of the window into the inky blackness. Apart from the marker lights that showed the outline of the landing area, the view was completely featureless. It was impossible to tell where the sea stopped and the sky began. "Stalys, inform the guards at the detention block that I will be there in fifteen minutes to question the prisoners." He took a last look out at the sea and was suddenly enveloped by a heavy chill that remained with him even after he had closed the window, dressed, and left his quarters.

He entered the guard station and requested that the first prisoner be taken to the interrogation suite. He watched the monitors as the light came on in the prisoner's cell, a construct entered and shook him awake, then walked him into the suite. He looked warily at the molten stump of the chair that had previously held his compatriot, but allowed himself to be shackled without resisting.

The captain entered the room and the prisoner looked up with a start. "My name is Sembhee; a captain of the Pewter Guard of the Roost. The man your construct tried to kill was my commanding officer and one of my greatest friends. I tell you this so that it might dispel any thoughts that you may still have about withholding intelligence. You have already received a demonstration of the lengths that we will go to in order to secure meaningful information. I will ask questions and you will reply. Your reply will be noted and compared to answers we have already received from your colleague. If there are significant differences, you will be summarily executed, do you understand what I have just said to you?"

The quiet man tried to avoid the captain's eyes, but nodded.

"Before you go back to your cell I will know who you are, who you work for and what reason you had for attacking our station." He grabbed hold of the man's chin and pulled it up, forcing him to look into his eyes, "If you wish to survive the night, you will also tell me the location of your base and give me details of its defensive systems. Every morsel of viable information you give me will extend the amount of time for which you will continue to breathe. You may begin."

"I am E-Yain," started the bandit, "I was recruited into the League by Buller," he nodded his head at the destroyed stump of the chair.

"The League?"

E-Yain frowned, he'd assumed that Rustholme would know all about the League, he'd been told that they were famous across the whole of the mainland, that's the only reason he'd joined. "Yes, the League. We're a loose collection of bandit clans, we share information on soft targets, troop movement and Company stores."

"And where is this League of yours based exactly?"

"We're spread all over the country... There're thousands of us, most of the old bandit clans are members," replied E-Yain, shaking his head slowly. He was surprised that the captain knew nothing about them.

"Alright, let us start with an easier question. Where is your particular branch of this impressively huge bandit league located?"

"What are you going to do? There are women and children there! You can't just destroy them, that would be barbaric."

Sembhee raised his hands to quiet the prisoner. "I made no mention of what I will be doing with the information that you so freely give me, that would be a decision for my Commanding Officer, should he survive. If he doesn't of course, His mother, the Baroness will become my direct commander and I'm sure that she will order the complete destruction by fire of every bandit village that we can find."

"We didn't know what was going to happen," E-Yain mumbled, "we were just told to attack the tower until a patrol showed up. We were told that we were just a distraction, the construct would complete its mission and then we would retreat and be paid. No-one was supposed to get hurt. No-one said anything about you wearing powered armour. Everything would have been OK if you hadn't worn it."

"My commander would be dead if he hadn't ordered us to wear it. As would you all. You were told to attack the station as a distraction? By whom?"

"I don't know, I swear, we were just given the orders, shown to a stolen skimmer with the construct already loaded aboard and sent on our way. You know the rest already."

"Stolen? How do you know it was stolen, not just provided by the same people who lent you a militarized construct?"

"It had the Company logo on the side. They wouldn't be our supplier, we raid their sites a hundred times more often than we raid anyone else's. They want to wipe us out more than you do, even now," he looked again out of the corner of his eye at what had been Buller's chair, "we must have cost them a baron's ransom in defence constructs and supplies this month alone."

'Who would know the details of how you came to have the use of a Company skimmer, and where can I find him?'

"Her... he's a she," E-Yain smiled, it seemed like a real victory for him to catch the captain out, "they call her Haze. She's a medic, based in the Merseyside free-trade area. She's a good person, they must have sold her one hells of a story to convince her to do this. She would never have done it if she knew someone was going to get hurt."

The prisoner gave him all the details of where to find and get in contact with Haze, and all the time he repeated his assurances that she was a good person and that she would never hurt a fly.

Sembhee looked up at the floating camera that had been watching and recording everything that had been happening, "Take him back to his cell and prepare both him and his colleague for an extended stay."

Chapter 7 : Recruitment

Dorleith sat on the beach, absently skimming flat stones into the sea. The last two weeks had flown past, the base was now complete and the supplies for her new ship were sitting in a hangar at the Roost waiting to be installed when her hull arrived.

"How long do you intend to waste sitting here?" asked Britt, squatting down next to her and sifting a handful of sand through his fingers. "Have you contacted your scaly friend at Enys Skaw to see if we're having a hull delivered in the near future?"

"You sound like my mother, and no I haven't. Why didn't I just have it delivered here?"

Britt stared at the horizon and sucked the warm sea breeze in through his teeth. "Well, if I'd have known about this place a little earlier, I would have suggested it. It would have gotten around all that troublesome business about having to take a detachment of Pewter Guards with us." He looked at her out of the corner of his eye.

Raising an eyebrow, she continued to look straight ahead at the vast expanse of azure water. "Well, it can't be helped now. I'll ask Frobisher to contact the Pradilan when we go back."

"Have you thought how you're going to get around your mother's ultimatum? I'm presuming that you still don't want your brother tagging along on your adventures."

She stood up and brushed the sand from her velvet trousers, not even dignifying his question with an answer. "You feel like going on a trip? We still need a crew and I've not visited the Long Pig for a while."

A tooth-filled grin slowly spread across Britt's face as he pondered all of the opportunities that a trip to Long Pig Station could offer, "It's a twelve hour flight in the Spirit from here, I'll start getting the ship ready now, Captain."

Before she could reply, he'd spun around in a spray of golden sand and was walking casually back to the disguised building that served as the main elevator into the base, whilst all the time trying to make it look like he wasn't hurrying. She knew that as soon as they landed, they'd be inundated with potential crewmembers offering their services. Everyone who was anyone would have heard by now that the Barony of Rustholme was recruiting an airship crew. Her job would be to find the ones who would fit in and do a decent job, whilst still being happy taking orders from a noblewoman. Especially when that noblewoman didn't actually have the backing of the current Baroness, although she thought there was no real need for them to know that, after all, piracy was all about deception and subterfuge wasn't it? Dorleith took one last look at the rolling surf and started back towards the compound where there were preparations to make.

She stood on the observation deck in the hangar - watching as crewman and construct alike ferried supplies into the Spirit. "You there!" she called, "Mr.?"

"Landry Ma'am, Carter Landry. Can I help you in some way?"

"Oh, you're American. I didn't know we had any Americans on board. How very interesting."

"I've been working in the communications centre back at the Roost. Mr. Britt thought it was time I had some shipboard experience. Ma'am, with all due respect, can I do something for you? Because this box is really, really, heavy."

She looked at the large polished leather trunk that he was struggling with. "You could get a construct to help you with that you know, that's what they're there for."

"My Daddy always told me that if you can't carry it, you don't need it. I must admit though, it's getting to the stage where I'm beginning to think that I probably don't need half this baggage." He put the large box down and wiped his brow with his sleeve. "So Ma'am, was there something you wanted?"

"I wondered if you'd seen Mr. Britt. I'd sort of assumed that he'd be helping with the loading, but I can't seem to find him."

"Think he said something about getting essential supplies from the commissary Ma'am, but I'm not a hundred percent sure." He hefted the trunk up and onto his shoulder, trying to make it look effortless. "If that's everything?"

"Yes, of course, I do apologise, please carry on." She watched him walk across the deck and up the ramp into the Spirit, only turning away when he finally disappeared through the hatch. She put her hand to her cheek and felt for the heat of the blush that she knew was rapidly spreading across her face. "Note to self," she muttered under her breath as she walked towards the commissary, "do not act like a giddy schoolgirl in front of the crew, no matter how good looking and obviously muscular they are."

As she entered the dining area, she could hear the gravelly tones of Britt interspersed with noises of discontent from the serving constructs coming from the kitchen.

"My need is greater than yours, you hatful of spinning circuits."

"Regrettably sir, that particular vintage is required for a recipe. I will need to take it from you."

"Try it and you'll be sucking your next recharge from the end of my boot."

"Sir, I can have Frobisher arrange to bring a more freely available vintage from the main stores. It can be here in minutes."

"But this one's here now, and I'm taking it!"

She vaulted over the serving counter and made her way into the kitchen. The sight that awaited her was one plucked straight from a comedy vid. Britt was cornered, with what looked like a bottle of brandy hidden amateurishly behind his back, whilst a cooking construct tried to prevent his escape with a number of its arms, whilst working another set behind him to retrieve the alcohol.

She took a deep breath and yelled at the top of her lungs, "Can someone, preferably someone biological, tell me what, in all the badly maintained hells, is going on here?"

The construct's arms dropped to its side as if their cables had all been simultaneously cut. Britt turned to face her, brought the bottle from behind his back and cradled it like a fragile infant. Both combatants looked guilty in their own particular way.

"Well?" She raised an eyebrow at Britt.

"It's a bargaining chip," he replied, "there's someone on Long Pig that I think we're going to need, and I owe her," he raised the bottle and pointed at it.

"You... owe... her? Do I need to be worried?" her eyes narrowed. "who is she anyway?"

"No, Captain, everything should be fine. She's a corsair, a damn good one truth be told, met her the last time I was on the station." He put the bottle down on the counter and scowled at the construct as one of its arms started to move stealthily towards it, "She quite literally saved my neck, and I know for a fact that she's available for work." He grabbed the brandy back with a triumphant grin.

"I'll trust your judgement, we're going to need a lot of people in a fairly short time, She's as good a place to start as any. Collect the rest of your gear and get aboard, we should be about ready to lift by now."

Britt nodded, shot one last scowl at the construct, and left.

She moved back into the dining area and addressed Frobisher, "Whilst we're gone I need you to make the rest of the human areas ready for habitation. As of this moment I'm declaring Sidi Ferruch fully operational. Bring all the systems up to speed, we should be no more than a few days. Also, I need you to contact Stalys and see if we've heard anything about my new hull."

"As you say My Lady, I will keep you informed."

She went back to her quarters, picked up her gear and called a construct to take it to the Spirit. She grabbed two full changes of clothes and twelve pairs of shoes then boarded the ship. After a fifteen minute diversion to stow her clothes in her quarters, she walked onto the bridge and sank into the command chair. "Mr. Britt, inform Frobisher that we are leaving, and take us up."

Britt nodded and opened the ship-wide Intercomm. "All hands, this is your first officer, we are leaving. Ensure that all windows are sealed, loose items are stowed securely and your seat-trays are in the upright position – Bouncing in five. Frobisher, please open the main hangar exit. Four. Gasbags to pressure. Three. All hatches secure. Two. Let's all pray that no-one shoots at us this time. One... and bounce!" he released the docking clamps and gunned the thrusters.

The Spirit climbed through the launch tube and shot out into the bright blue sky, the sudden upwards acceleration causing the chains connecting the hull to the gasbags to momentarily go slack and then instantly tighten as the pressure in the bags increased to maintain their neutral buoyancy.

"Mr. Britt, turn us around and set a course for Long Pig Station, rig us for best speed and get us there as quick as you like."

"Aye Ma'am, setting course one-five-eight magnetic, distance, some four thousand miles, which will make our journey time eleven hours with the current weather conditions."

The captain nodded and checked the readouts, "Four hour watches, three rotations. We'll have fresh eyes on the long range scanners at all times. As soon as we're over the High Desert I want a half-hour gunnery drill, let's test these new cannons that Frobisher seemingly fitted without telling me." She looked at the back of Britt's rapidly reddening neck, leaned forward and hissed, "Did you really think I wouldn't notice?" She settled back into her seat and resumed her normal tone, "Mr. Britt, when you have engaged the autopilot, I would appreciate it if you would join me in my quarters for a command meeting," with that she rose and left the bridge.

He sat for a moment at the controls, double checking that they were locked on course and making sure that the engines were ready for extended cruising. Again he thumbed the Intercomm, "Prepare for acceleration to best cruising speed. Engineering, spin up the fusion engines." The moment he pushed the throttles forward, the chains thrummed as their load shifted and the ship quickly reached her cruising speed. He stood, straightened his waistcoat, checked that his hair was neat and followed the captain to her quarters.

"Come in," called the captain, as he rapped loudly on her door. Her quarters were towards the stern on the ship and you could clearly hear the throb of the engines reverberating through the solid woodwork. He pushed the door open, holding his breath, and waited for the storm of words to start. Instead, she looked up at him from behind a sheaf of papers and indicated that he should sit down. He made his way across the thick carpet and lowered himself onto the chair that she had pointed at. It was incredibly uncomfortable, the seat was too short and the legs were too long, but he assumed that that was all on purpose. It put you on the defensive and made you feel like you'd done something wrong. She put down the documents and looked him in the eye.

"I don't like surprises. In fact, you might go as far as saying that I hate surprises. So, imagine how I felt when I was walking up the boarding ramp and saw a concealed gun port on the starboard side," her burning gaze let him know that she wasn't looking for an answer from him, not at this particular moment anyway, "then try and imagine how my mood changed even more when I checked internally and found that we had somehow acquired a remote controlled, high speed slug thrower on either side of the ship. Then to top it all off, when I asked Frobisher who had authorised the changes, he told me that it was you." She crossed her arms and put her feet up on the desk, "Now would be a good time for you to start explaining."

"I didn't like the idea of travelling unarmed. I knew it'd only be a matter of time before we had to go looking for crew and I wasn't willing to go anywhere without having the means to defend ourselves. It's a good idea, and I stand by my decision."

"If I thought for a second that it was a bad decision, you'd be out there right now on a rope-ladder with a respirator screwing the gun port closed. I'm not angry that you installed weapons on a ship that happens to be registered as an unarmed trader, I'm angry that you didn't consult me first."

"It's my responsibility to…"

She jumped from her chair and banged her hands on her desk, causing a long stemmed wine glass to fall over and splash its contents over the assorted piles of paper, "It's your bloody responsibility to carry out my orders to the best of your ability! You do what you're told to do when you're told to do it!"

"No, not exactly, Captain, it's my responsibility to keep the crew and the ship safe, I thought that taking an unarmed ship into a potentially dangerous situation without any defensive armaments was tantamount to suicide. I appreciate that you are the captain of this ship, the commander of the base at Sidi Ferruch, the daughter of the man and wife that I swore to serve and my superior officer, but with respect Madam, what you are not is someone with a great deal of experience commanding an airship that is under fire."

"I have seen…"

"I know Ma'am, every time that you've seen action I've been there, your mother has been there too, that's exactly my point. I don't want us to be in a situation where you tell me to disable someone who's chasing us and I have to do that by throwing my spare shirts at them, hoping that I'll obscure their viewscreen. We needed armament, even if we're only going to use the Spirit until your new ship is complete. We're probably going to upset someone, or have a disagreement about payment or a simple matter of besmirched honour and we need to be somewhere else quickly and stop anyone following us."

She dabbed at the spreading pool of wine on her desk and, against her better judgement, cracked a smile, "You'd throw your shirts at an airship that was following us? Was that a tactic you perfected during the war?"

"Not exactly," He softened, "although I do remember one particular time when the Hammer was surprised by an independent brigand ship just outside of Gdansk. It was the middle of the night and their first salvo took our weapons control offline so we turned and ran, trying to get within comms range of your father. They started peppering the stern with small calibre rounds that were causing more of an annoyance rather than any real damage, until finally your mother cracked and ordered me to get rid of them. I tried to target one of the rear turrets manually, but I couldn't get them to shoot straight enough to make a difference. What I could do is rig the outlet from the human waste tanks so that they vented into the wake from the engines – I had to shoot a hole in the hull myself to do it, but I did it."

"You showered them with the crew's sh-"

"Aye, I did, and I'd do it again in a heartbeat if it was the only weapon I had to hand. I'd just rather that it wasn't."

The Intercomm on her desk buzzed, she leaned over and opened the channel, "Yes, this is the captain."

"Landry Ma'am, I've just received a transmission from Frobisher, it reads: 'Stalys informs me that it will be delivered in three days.' He said that you'd know what he meant. Should I send a reply?"

"No thank you Mr. Landry, captain out."

He looked up at her, "So, you almost have a ship," he looked questioningly around the cabin and continued, "well, a ship of your own at least. Now, we've just got to get you a crew to go with it." He stood and turned away from her.

"Britt, from now on everything goes through me. I know you mean well, and in this case you made a sensible choice, but no more surprises, agreed?"

He turned and bowed, "As you say, Captain, no more surprises."

The remainder of the trip passed by with, as was promised, no further surprises. Even the gunnery drill, performed over the deserts of Libya, was a resounding success. Dorleith had retired to her quarters after the exercise and had dozed on her oversized daybed until the Intercomm buzzed noisily again.

She lifted herself up and walked back to the desk, "Yes?"

"Britt Ma'am, We're just crossing the coast, we should be over Long Pig within twenty minutes."

"Understood, I'll be there momentarily, contact traffic control as soon as we're within range. Try to get us a decent berth will you?"

"Aye Ma'am, I'll do my level best."

She closed the Intercomm and opened her wardrobe. "Now, what does one wear to engage a number of unknown corsairs from a trading station five hundred miles from the nearest hub of civilisation, to crew a ship that doesn't exist, that will only get paid a share of whatever we can steal?" She looked at the small amount of options that she had with her, "I should have perhaps brought something wipe-clean with me." She picked out an outfit that was heavy on brown polished leather and had several places that she could conceal knives and other defensive items. Fixing her hair into an ornate pony-tail, she walked through the cramped corridors to the bridge, "Status Mr. Britt?"

Britt turned towards her, mouthed the words, "one second," then turned back and spoke into the Intercomm, "Long Pig control, this is the Rustholme Trader Spirit of Heinlein, requesting clearance to dock." He released the transmit button and turned to the captain, "Sorry Ma'am, I've been trying to contact them for a while and they'd finally replied."

She waved her hand dismissively and sat down.

"Spirit of Heinlein, this is Long Pig traffic control. Do you require a ground level dock?"

"Aye Control, that we do, no tender on this boat I'm afraid, but we're only small ourselves, we'll need it for a few days, so if we could get a decent berth close to the local amenities, we'd really appreciate it."

"Spirit of Heinlein, docks are apportioned on a first come, first served basis. You are not the first to come. Make your way to stand 8234, sending co-ordinates now."

"Understood control, thanks for precisely nothing. I hope you all die horribly in a massive fireball." Britt looked around at the open mouthed bridge crew surrounding him, "Relax, I cut the connection after 'Understood Control'. If you're going to be crewing under me on the new ship, I'd take a few minutes whilst we're here to buy yourselves a sense of humour."

He brought the Spirit around and docked at the stand. Settling her down onto her landing legs, Britt opened the Intercomm. "First officer to crew, once you've secured your duty stations, you're to meet at the head of the starboard ramp for a message from the captain. Please note, No visible weapons are to be carried whilst on Long Pig, the security forces are very particular about that. They have a nasty tendency of sending you back here in a box, or several small boxes if you're particularly unlucky." He powered down the main console and made his way to the lowered boarding ramp, where he met up with the captain. They both looked out into the long, evening shadows. Stand 8234 didn't look all that bad, all things considered. It had access to a trading terminal, fuel pumps for the ships that still needed it and a few data hook-ups. Best of all it was just within walking distance of the Old Town, where most of their new crew would be found. One by one the crew filtered into the cramped room and stooped to look outside.

The captain looked at them all individually and delivered her instructions. "Men, this is a recruiting mission, nothing else. By the end of tomorrow I want to have engaged the services of at least a hundred bodies, crew for both the new ship and for the base. Explain that we're offering free bed and board, but payment will be by shares of anything we can acquire. We do not want criminals... well, we do not want anyone who's been charged or accused of any crime that's not normally associated with piracy, so no deviants or torturers. Off-worlders however are fine, I'm all for a multi-species crew aboard ship. In fact, it might be handy if we ever get into a situation where we need someone who understands a language other than Base. If there are people here you know," she looked at Britt and raised her eyebrows, "then try to recruit them first. We need experienced corsairs and buccaneers, we want people who don't mind getting their hands dirty and we especially want people who have no love for The Company or the Spiders, as they're going to be our major targets," she paused for a minute to let the cheering die down, "but mostly, I need you to be back here by 13:00 tomorrow with contact details of a full ship's complement, all your extremities still attached to your bodies and no more diseases than you came here with. Do I make myself clear?"

There were assorted grins, nods and cheers from the crew as she sent them out onto the station. She turned to Britt, "Gods help us, what kind of grog addled cloud-dogs do you think we're going to attract?"

He looked out across the loading dock, "I honestly wasn't aware that there were different types, Captain," he offered her his arm, "shall we?" they walked down the ramp arm in arm, as they reached the bottom she pressed a button on her wristband and the ramp lifted and closed tight against the hull.

"A new toy?" he remarked.

"A suggestion from Frobisher, he seemed to think that we might need it."

"Well, I suppose that it saves us having to leave someone on-board to guard the ship. Will you be installing something like that on the new one?"

"Shouldn't need to, the new ship will have Frobisher as its A.I. We should be able to run it purely by voice commands."

"I see. Would you like to get some food, or shall we try to find Lee'Sahr?"

"Can we not do both?" she replied, holding one hand to her grumbling stomach, "I'm so hungry I could eat a Kalibri!"

"Well, if you really wanted to, I mean eating our fellow sentients is usually frowned upon. I could probably find somewhere that..." the scowl he received from Dorleith was enough to convince him not to finish the sentence, "or, on the other hand, I know somewhere that does a passable fried chicken. Obviously, when I say chicken, it certainly tastes like chicken, but it may have a few more whiskers than you're strictly used to. I'll lead the way shall I?"

They walked through the maze of streets and alleyways that led from the landing area to the Old Town. Through the gaps between the tall warehouses and workshops they could see larger ships moored at high berths, at the top of mooring masts or connected to the ground by anchor cables whilst their thrusters lazily throbbed to keep them in position. They turned a corner and almost walked straight into a milling crowd of people, who were all staring into the sky with their mouths hanging open. The captain just had time to look at Britt questioningly before a giant shadow washed over them and turned the evening into midnight. Above them was a ship, bigger than any that she had ever seen, it must have been over a thousand feet long and moving completely silently on half a dozen streamlined fusion turbines. The dull silver of its outer hull seemed to reflect the dying rays of the amber sun in every direction but downwards. It had no external gondola, but if she looked carefully she could see some small areas that were slightly more reflective than the rest and assumed that they were mirrored windows.

"Am I dreaming?" she asked Britt. He was too aghast to answer, hypnotised by the sight unfolding above him, but he still took the time to pinch her arm and, seeing her shocked reaction, slowly shake his head.

As the tail section drifted into view, it was impossible to miss the markings on the ventral fins. It was the clasped fists of The Company. The sight made her heart sink; this was not a part of her plan. If The Company had more than a few of these behemoths, then her new flagship was going to have to be something very special indeed so that it wasn't blown out of the air in the first engagement. The giant ship slowly turned in the air, as if making sure that everyone had had time to take in its majesty, pointed itself towards the coast of Mozambique and begun to spin up its main engines. A gentle rising hum was the only indication that anything was happening until it started to accelerate away. People wrestled to get a better view as it streaked towards the horizon, faster than a ship that size had any business moving. It disappeared over the roofline and was lost from sight. The spell of silence was broken and everyone immediately started to talk excitedly amongst themselves, half of them wondering if it had been some sort of trick, the others trying to decide what The Company was hoping to achieve with such an overt show of force.

"Well, if I didn't need a drink before, I certainly do now." Britt beckoned the captain to follow him as he crashed through the still dazed crowd like an icebreaker. They made their way through the narrow streets, crossing several small squares where the snatched fragments of conversation let them know that the huge Company ship was going to be the main topic of discussion for the rest of the day at least. Only the very rooftops were still touched by the setting sun when they reached their destination.

"She's going to be in here?" Dorleith tried to make out the

lettering on the badly faded sign above the crooked door, "the… Vienna?"

"Aye, she normally is at about this time, a little light supper, some hard spirits and a fistfight. What more could a man ask for?"

"Man? I thought you said that she… was a she?"

"Aye, but whenever the security force asks her who started the fight, she always says, 'That man was asking for it.' Then everyone has a jolly good laugh and helps whichever poor fellah it was this time to find his teeth," he slid open the door and said, "be careful, the floor's not very level."

She stepped into the inn and immediately lost her balance. The floor was a little more than just not very level, the entire room was tilted about fifteen degrees to the left and another ten towards the back. "What the!" she exclaimed as she caught herself on a wooden pillar that had been lovingly carved into the shape of a Torkan, holding what appeared to be some kind of primitive fertility symbol above its head.

"Might take a bit of getting used to," Britt remarked, trying to mask his grin, "this place wasn't exactly built here, she crashed about twenty years ago. Originally she was a private pleasure cruiser, but the local Defence Force sequestered her for military duty. They used her as a place for the officers to go on leave when there wasn't anywhere decent to go on the ground. There was a party, the crew got drunk and…" he crashed his fist into the palm of his other hand, "they rebuilt this part of the town around the wreckage."

"Sounds lovely," she said as she pushed herself upright whilst her vision fought against her inner ears to decide which way was actually up, "can we just find your friend and sit down?"

They'd walked the length of the room before Britt noticed her sat in the corner with her eyes fixed on the door. He raised his hand in recognition as she turned towards him and they made their way across to her table.

"Captain, this is Lee'Sahr, the person I was telling you about. Lee'Sahr, may I present Captain Dorleith Ahralia, your prospective employer," he gestured between them expansively and then wandered to the bar to get some drinks.

The two women looked closely at each other, with the air of a pair of cats meeting in an alley; they were around the same height, but where the captain's hair was a shining red, held tightly behind her head with a complicated clasp, the corsair's was long and dark and straight. Their clothing was surprisingly similar, but the captain's lacked the obvious marks of years of wear and repair. A waitress put down two glasses of murky, grey spirit on the table and Lee'Sahr instantly drained hers, slammed the empty glass back on the table and indicated that they needed another round, "Agamemnon introduced you as 'Captain Such-and-such', so what are you captain of? Which ship might I have the honour of one day serving upon?"

"Well..." she started. The captain didn't like being put on the spot, she was beginning to think that this might not have been the best idea after all. But she was right, the ship needed a name and now was as good a time as any. She thought back to the stories that her father used to tell her when she was young, of the time before the airships, where pirates sailed on the seas. Of the one name that always stuck in her mind. "She's called the Edward Teach, she's still in dry-dock being refitted. Should be in the air by the end of next week."

Their fresh drinks arrived and the captain watched the dark haired pirate's face change as she picked hers up, a gentle smile crept across it and her whole face brightened, "That's a good name, a name with some history behind it at least," she tipped the drink into her mouth with one smooth movement and wiped her mouth with her sleeve, "what's the pay like?"

"It depends on what we can score. Your food and lodgings will be provided of course, anything above that is up to you. We all take a share, the harder we work, the more we'll earn."

"Mummy not financing your little pirate adventure then?" she leaned across and casually picked up one of the captain's drinks, but before she could drink it, it was slapped from her hands and went sailing across the room to smash noisily against the wall.

Both women now stood, hunched, staring at each other like lionesses.

The captain's chair had gone flying backwards as she'd jumped up and was lying on its side in a puddle of ale. Everyone in the room was staring at them. Fights were nothing new in the Vienna, but the possibility of a fight between two women was a novelty that was definitely not to be missed.

"Say that again," growled the captain angrily, looking straight into Lee'Sahr's eyes as she clenched and unclenched her fists.

"Aren't people supposed to know who you are? Or where all your money normally comes fr-" if the unexpected blow had connected, the privateer's head would have spun around like a top. Luckily this wasn't her first bar fight and she easily dodged Dorleith's hurtling fist. The impetus of the missed blow threatened to throw the captain off balance and leave her sprawled on the floor, instead it carried her through a half turn and she found herself suddenly facing away from her opponent. Lee'Sahr took the opportunity to leap over the table and onto the tilted floor. She grabbed the captain by the shoulders and turned her around so that she was looking into her face, "look, we don't have to..." she was silenced by a blow to her gut, which knocked the wind out of her and brought her to her knees. She looked up just in time to see the irate captain aiming a two-handed blow to the back of her neck. She ducked and lashed out with her fist, catching the captain in the side of the knee and bringing her down to the ground.

Britt pilfered a beer from a tray being carried by a passing waitress and leaned against a pillar to watch the remainder of the fight. He'd never seen the captain defending herself with her fists before, but she seemed to be holding her own, for the moment at least. He decided that if the fight went on much past the time it took him to drink his stolen ale, he'd have to think about stepping in and trying to separate them.

Lee'Sahr had briefly gained the upper hand and was sat on the Captain's stomach holding her wrists. "There's no need for... Argh!" Dorleith had jack-knifed, simultaneously bringing up her knees to unbalance her opponent and aiming a head-butt to her nose, she narrowly missed but caught Lee'Sahr in the chin. She spat out the blood and rolled through the puddle of beer, onto her knees and then up to her feet. Looking down at her suddenly sodden leggings re-ignited the fire in her eyes, she reached behind her for the fallen chair and swung it at the captain. Dorleith ducked and the chair smashed against another pillar, showering the room in splinters. The clientele had started to boo every time one of the fighters parried a blow and cheer every time there was a successful hit.

"This might be getting slightly out of hand," Britt thought to himself, as he noisily drained the last dregs of his ale. He wrung the drips from his beard, straightened his moustache and breathed in deeply to inflate his chest. Walking across the floor, avoiding the largest shards of wood, he put a hand on each of their shoulders. "Ladies, please, I think that might be just about enough..."

The blows that impacted with his chin could not have been closer together if they had been choreographed. Both women had instantly forgotten their quarrel and had joined together to attack their new common enemy. As their own, personal red mists cleared they looked at each other, then looked down at the unconscious first officer. And then both of them started to laugh.

"Truce?" suggested Lee'Sahr, running her tongue around the inside of her mouth to check for loose teeth, "That was a good fight, you surprised me."

"How?" Dorleith replied, rubbing at the dull, throbbing ache in her knee.

"I felt sure you'd be a hair-puller," she put her arm around her new captain's shoulder and steered her towards the bar, "let me tell you about a friend of mine, a guy called Baju-Merah, you could use him and I know that he's looking for something that'll take him away from the Station for a while. Although it might not be as simple as just offering him a job. Barman! Two plates of ribs."

"Why won't it be that simple, if he needs a job and wants to get away for a while?"

"Because he is currently being detained by station security and is not due for release for... quite some time."

The captain shook her head in disbelief, "And what did this Badger-Maroo do to bring this punishment down on himself?"

"One, it's Baju-Merah and two, it's who, not what. He was a member of the station security team himself until recently, and he was part of the group tasked with protecting the station manager's daughter."

Dorleith raised her eyebrows questioningly and made the hand-signal that represented the physical act of love between a man and a woman.

"Aye, exactly. He was caught red… handed, stripped of his position and sentenced to rot in a cell for an as yet undetermined length of time. I can't see that changing anytime soon, not before the station manager's had time to calm down a little."

"And when did this happen?"

"Yesterday…"

"Gods! Why is nothing ever easy? Why can't I just walk up to someone and tell them that I'm employing a privateer crew and that I want them to join. They'd say 'Aye', I'd say 'wonderful' and we'd all end up back on the ship singing songs, drinking too much brandy and being sick over the side together."

"You could," remarked Lee'Sahr, "but where would be the fun and adventure in that? That is what you signed up for isn't it? The fun and adventure? Ah! The ribs are here."

The captain looked down at her plate and noticed that the ribs were all different shapes, sizes and colours. She looked at across at Lee'Sahr, who was hungrily stripping the meat off the bones with her teeth. "I'm not sure I'm quite ready for that much fun and adventure," she mumbled, as she pushed it away. Low moans from the other side of the room indicated that Britt was finally regaining consciousness.

A waitress wandered across and poured a glass of water over him, as he spluttered awake she look down at him disgustedly and said, "You lost, they're over there if you're in need of a re-match," she pointed at the bar, "But I wouldn't recommend it, they kicked your ass."

He rubbed his swollen jaw, moved it from side to side to check that it was still firmly attached and looked over towards the captain and his new crewmate. They seemed to be deep in conversation, which he thought was probably a good sign. Clinging to the pillar for assistance, he drew himself to his feet and gingerly made his way over to the bar.

"Ah! The sleeper awakens," announced Lee'Sahr grandly, with an animated flourish.

"You hit me..."

"No, technically, we hit you," she indicated both herself and the captain, who was trying to suppress a smile.

"Well, whichever of you it was, I think it was uncalled for."

The captain shook her head and burst into laughter, which continued for slightly longer than Britt felt was absolutely necessary. Britt pulled up a stool and ordered them all another round of drinks.

"We need to make this our last one, there's some planning to be done." Noting Britt's look of confusion, she recounted the sorry tale of Baju-Merah's unfortunate incarceration, and their idea to free him.

"That's a complication, is he up at the Tronkamer?" he looked at Lee'Sahr, who nodded, "we can go up in the morning and take a look around, luckily it's not that tough a building and the layout's fairly simple. I've... Visited there a couple of times myself, it's a glorified drunk-tank with a wall around it. But now I suggest we get back to the Spirit and get some sleep. Shall we send a construct for your gear?"

Lee'Sahr shook her head, "No, it's fine. I travel light, just in case I need to leave anywhere in a hurry."

"I'll stay and help you pack." Said the captain, she turned to Britt, "I'll see you back on the Spirit."

"Of course Ma'am," he rose, bowed unsteadily, and walked up the slanted room to the main door. As he slid it open, he happened to catch sight of the captain ordering another round of drinks. "Good Gods," he mumbled to himself, "I've created a monster, although it does mean I have a spare bottle of incredibly good brandy that's in need of a good, hard drinking."

Chapter 8 : Justice

Mal opened his eyes to find that he was lying on a recovery bed in the infirmary. He looked to his left to see Pixi curled up in the chair next to the bed, snoring gently. He looked down and saw the collection of tubes and wires that were attached to him, followed them to the sensor equipment that dominated the wall and tried unsuccessfully to make sense of the readouts.

The door opened and a human doctor entered the room, "Good morning Commander, nice to finally see you awake." He walked over to the sensors and started to gather information from the various screens. "You seem to be healing very well, a small amount of muscle rejuvenant and you should almost be ready for duty." He altered a few settings and a warm feeling spread through Mal's lower back and legs.

Pixi walked over to the bed, placed her hand on his forehead and gently stroked his hair, "You're an idiot," she whispered gently into his ear, "scare me like that again and I'll smother you in your sleep." Planting a kiss on his forehead, she yawned, sat down on the side of the bed and waited to hear what the doctor had to say.

"Do you remember anything about what happened My Lord?" The doctor asked without looking up from his terminal.

"We were assaulting a bandit position, there was an explosion, and then I woke up here. How long have I been unconscious?"

Pixi jumped in before the doctor had time to speak, "Nearly two weeks, we were starting to get worried, but Doctor Say'Uff kept telling us that it was perfectly normal. Your body needed time to repair itself, you spent most of your time in the tank, it was horrible," she smiled and squeezed his hand tightly as she fought to hold back the tears.

"Yes, thank you miss," the doctor looked at her with the expression of one who would like to continue his conversation without any further interruptions, "My Lord, you narrowly avoided being blown to pieces by an armour piercing missile. You were caught in the blast, which caused massive internal damage and almost destroyed your spine. We have grafted replacement organs where possible, installed augments where it was not and completely replaced your spine with a construct tied directly into your nervous system. Do you have any questions before I pronounce you fit for duty?"

Mal stared at him blankly, trying to take in the enormity of what he'd just been told. "You replaced my spine?" he gingerly lifted his head from the pillow, straining his ears to hear the mechanical whine that often accompanied constructs' movement, "it doesn't feel any different, should it feel different? Shouldn't I be able to hear it?"

Doctor Say'Uff smiled, "No My Lord, your body muffles the noise to an extent and the motors of the medical grade constructs are built to significantly higher tolerances than those of standard menial ones, they are much quieter. We have also installed a shock absorbing system that dampens any vibration that you would be able to hear through your skull. If anything, the replacement parts should be better than your natural ones."

"Do I have scars?"

"No My Lord, the techniques we use leave little or no scarring, they are of Torkan design and knit the bone, muscle and skin together at a cellular level."

"I remember, my father was covered in scars, he could tell you what caused each one and where he was when it'd happened, it's a pity you didn't have this technology in his day. The old man looked like a map of the moon when he took his shirt off, the Baroness hated it, or so she said," he grinned and winked at Pixi.

"We've had the technology for nearly twenty years, your father refused to use it My Lord. He felt that the scars gave him a certain… appeal, although they were not the words he actually used," the doctor looked at the commander knowingly, "I believe his actual words were 'Say'Uff, do you know nothing? The fairer sex find scars exciting, more so than a chest-full of medals!' I cannot vouch for his assumptions of course, I am but a humble servant," the doctor's low bow served to mask the broad smile that was blossoming across his face, "would you like to try standing up?"

Mal braced himself and slowly sat up, expecting at every moment to suffer excruciating pain. When none was forthcoming, he moved his legs off the low bed and planted his feet on the floor. "If anything, it feels a little tight, the muscles are… it's like they belong to someone else," he grabbed hold of the edge of the bed and pushed himself up, "am I taller? I feel taller."

"Your new spine will take a day or two to adapt to your stance, and your muscles will take time to adjust to their new connections. But by the week's end you'll be wondering why you didn't have it replaced years ago. Just go about your normal business and inform me immediately if you experience any discomfort."

"Why have you got a hole in the small of your back?" asked Pixi, her head tilted to one side, as she swung her legs backwards and forwards.

He spun around like a dog chasing its tail as he tried to see what she was talking about, "A hole! Are the stitches coming out? Is there blood?"

Doctor Say'Uff held up both of his hands and explained, "It's a data port My Lord, it lets me plug directly into your nervous system to check the construct whilst you're acclimatising. I could have put in a transceiver to send the telemetry to the systems here, but this way you need to come to the infirmary every few days for a check-up. Plus there are certain security issues involved in that procedure, it may have been possible for an external agency to gain control of your new spine."

"They could have made him dance like a puppet?"

"They could have finished the job that Lord Mal'Ak-Hai started when he tried to join his ancestors by bending himself in half."

Mal gingerly felt the skin around the base of his spine, eventually he found the offending hole, which seemed to go altogether too far inside his body for his liking. "That feels decidedly odd," he remarked, as he pulled out his finger and looked at it, half expecting it to be covered in some sort of gunk, "isn't it unhygienic to just have random openings into your body? Isn't there the chance of infection?"

"My Lord, your body is full of random openings, this is just a little more recent than the others, and there is less chance of this becoming infected than there is of you getting a sore throat or a runny nose. However, please come straight back here if you do notice any discolouration or discharge."

Pixi wrinkled her nose at the thought, added the word 'discharge' to her list of words not to say under any circumstances, but looked earnestly at the doctor and said, "I'll keep a lookout for anything unusual about his person."

"The Guard have been informed that you have recovered, and I understand that Captain Sembhee is on his way here now. I would suggest that the manly, congratulatory hugs are kept to a minimum, especially if he is wearing his powered armour. I will be in the next room if you require any assistance," he raised his eyebrows meaningfully at Pixi.

"Ah, yes, I should be getting back to work," she looked at her watch, "I'm a little late for my duty shift as it is. About four days late in fact," she reached up, pecked him on the cheek and walked towards the door. As it slid open, she turned towards him, smiled broadly and remarked, "actually, I think you are a little taller! I like it."

He watched as the door closed behind her then looked at himself, reflected in the screens of the medical monitors. He now had a short, blonde beard, something he'd never considered growing but as it looked like it had been recently trimmed, it was obvious that someone approved of it. Maybe he'd keep it for a while and see how it went. He was just getting used to the feeling of stroking it when the door opened and Captain Sembhee entered the room with his fatigues jacket.

"Thought you might be cold My Lord," he tossed the jacket, Mal snatched it out of the air and put it on, instantly feeling more martial.

"What have I missed?"

"Well, I interrogated some of the prisoners from West-two, one knew nothing, but the other was almost too forthcoming. He said that the bandits were organising, joining some sort of loose cabal that they're calling 'The League'. We've also got a lead on who supplied the construct that you disassembled, although he claimed that they didn't know what it was going to do, said that they were just hired as a diversion."

"Too forthcoming? Are you worried that he might be providing tainted information, leading us into a trap?"

Sembhee took a deep breath as he remembered Na-Thon's description of the bandit's execution, and momentarily wondered how best to explain the circumstances, "No, I believe what he said My Lord, your mother saw to it that he was suitably motivated to tell the whole truth. She had Na-Thon execute one of the other prisoners in front of him, he used a full clip of accelerator rounds."

"That would certainly provide an effective visual aid to any lesson that you didn't want forgetting in a hurry," he stroked his new beard absently and tapped his upper lip, "where is this League based and how soon can we be there?"

Sembhee smiled, as he'd been expecting this exact response, "I'm afraid our contact's in the Merseyside Free Trade Area, where we have no jurisdiction and according to the research I've done, they have some quaint old legal systems that involve people being innocent until they're proven guilty. We can't just go and snatch someone off the street and question them. We certainly wouldn't be welcomed with open arms if we were to go in armed and armoured."

"Captain, the position of their arms matters significantly less to me than getting to the bottom of who exactly wants me dead, and why they're getting common bandits to do their dirty work for them. Get a skimmer ready, we'll take Na-Thon and Zatch with us, concealed side arms and civilian clothes only," he looked out of the window at the still rising sun, "I want to be in Liverpool by nightfall.

"What would you like me to do with the remaining prisoners? They've been sat in their cells for the past two weeks waiting to see whether you'd recover or not. Your mother suggested turning them into some kind of grisly trophy at the main gates."

"Do you think there's any more intelligence to be gained?" he looked the captain directly in the eye, "or are they of no further use to us?"

"The one who gave us all the information did mention that he would be willing to act as a go-between, but as to how far we can trust a man who was trying anything he could to avoid death by disintegration, only the Gods would know."

"We'll take him with us but keep him close, I want to be able to shut him up quickly if we need to. What about the other one?"

"He didn't know anything, surrendered to one of the Guard when it was obvious he was on the losing side, he wasn't even armed."

"Give him a week's rations and have him dropped somewhere quiet in Mercia, tell him that we won't be so lenient if he's caught in the Open Lands again. If you can get him to make some noise as you're freeing him from his cell so that the other can hear, then all the better," he looked out of the window and smiled, "I'm all for a little psychological warfare. Be ready in three hours."

Sembhee saluted, and left the room.

Mal turned to the A.I. sat in the corner with its indicator lights pulsing gently as if it had something it desperately wanted to say, but was silenced by etiquette. "Stalys, where is the Baroness?"

"In her quarters My Lord, she is aware of your recovery and has asked that you attend her as soon as you feel fit enough. May I tell her that you are on your way? I understand that she has already taken the liberty of ordering breakfast for the both of you."

"Tell her that I'll be there as soon as I have had a chance to have a shower and changed into some more suitable attire."

He felt significantly more human when he stepped out of the shower, although there had been some small amount of stress when the water first hit his back and he wondered what effect it would have on the no-doubt delicate circuitry within. But there had been no sparks, or clouds of smoke, so he assumed that the doctor had taken his personal hygiene regime into account. Afterwards, he dressed, threw a few items of clothing into a pack and told Stalys to arrange for it to be loaded aboard the skimmer that Sembhee was preparing, along with his old compression pistol and a selection of concealable knives from his locker in the barracks.

His mother looked him up and down as he entered her apartments, "Didn't quite manage to kill yourself this time then? You're certainly your father's son. How's the new backbone?"

He made a big show of twisting from side to side, "Good as new, even better if Say'Uff is to be believed, he'd have me climbing up the outside of the Roost one-handed given half a chance."

"I'm not sure about the facial hair though; don't you think you may be a little young for that sort of thing?" she gripped his chin and rubbed the stubble with her thumb, as if trying to remove a smudge of oil, "you gave us all a bit of a fright, especially your poor men, they've been wandering around the halls like lost puppies. I've had Sembhee constantly drilling them whilst you were... incapacitated, just to keep them occupied."

"Where's Dorleith? I should really see her before I go, let her know everything's alright."

"Ha! She doesn't even know that you were injured; she's off playing pirate captain with Britt at your father's old base in Algeria. She took the Spirit and left an hour or so after you did, although she'll be back anytime now if I'm any judge. Stalys, show me the centre of Hangar Three."

The picture on the large viewscreen changed from showing a selection of financial statements to a feed from the main dock camera. In the centre of the huge room stood a hull, styled to resemble nothing more than an 18th Century ocean-going Barque.

"So, that's what she finally bought," he said, moving towards the screen to get a closer look, "I think you're right, if this doesn't bring her scampering back home then I don't know what will. What's it like inside? I presume that you've taken a look."

The Baroness looked momentarily affronted, and then smiled. "It's overly sumptuous for my taste, there's a lot a brass where there doesn't need to be any, and every flat surface looks like it's been engraved by a mad Torkan. I'd say that it was a pleasure cruiser for a spoiled Princess if these hadn't arrived last week. Stalys, switch to the western end of the hangar," the viewscreen changed again to show a large pile of parts and accessories, where there had once been a pile of dusty crates. She stood next to her son and proceeded to point out various specific items, "That is a set of camouflage blades, they can be used to disguise the profile of the ship, and this particular set makes it look like an unarmed cargo hauler. These are self-targeting turrets, a favourite toy of your father's, which can be controlled independently by the shipboard A.I." she took a deep breath, "talking of which, this crate contains a thirty terminal battle-ready A.I. named Frobisher, which seems to be a copy of the A.I. at the base. The huge crate at the back is a 500 Megawatt Ion Cannon. It looks like she's taken the best ideas from the Hammer, the Bolivar, and a five star hotel and glued them together. Rather impressive really, for a first attempt."

Mal was staring at the screen. For the first time, the reality of what his sister was doing actually hit him. He had convinced himself that this was a hobby, a project that she would try out for a while and ultimately get bored with and then it would be consigned, forgotten, to the trash. But now it was obvious that she was actually serious. She was building an airship and intending to make her own way in the world. As he watched, he noticed furtive movement around the crates.

He put his hand on his mother's shoulder, "Something's happening."

She looked at the screen closely and could see a number of constructs opening boxes and removing parts. "Stalys, what's going on?"

"My Lady, I have received a request from Lady Dorleith, via the Frobisher at Sidi Ferruch, saying that she wishes a team of engineering constructs to start the primary assembly of the Edward Teach."

The Baroness laughed, "So that's what she's calling it? I suppose it has a certain ring to it, historic, without being too obvious. The Old

Goat would certainly have approved."

"I don't..?"

"Edward Teach was a pirate, about half a millennia ago, he sailed the Atlantic generally making a nuisance of himself stealing cargo and sinking ships. Eventually, he was caught, killed and beheaded. Which I believe was a fairly common retirement option for pirates of the time."

"No, still never heard of him I'm afraid, although it was a long time ago," he watched as the constructs crawled across the hull, opening up panels and attaching interface cables.

"They used to call him Blackbeard."

"Ah, now him I've heard of. I presume that Na-Thon and Sembhee kept you informed about the information gained from the prisoners?"

"Yes, I've heard all about this bandit group and your planned infiltration. I hope you know what you're doing," she gestured for him to sit next to her on the richly upholstered sofa.

"Infiltration? I've never mentioned infiltration. We're taking a skimmer to Liverpool and finding out who set that construct on me. I don't intend to be subtle and I don't intend to be gone for very long."

The Baroness smiled at her Son, "You know, I've often wondered whether you sleep with a pistol under your pillow. One of your father's little idioms was 'The best view you can have of your target is from behind' Do you know what he meant by that?" Her Son's raised eyebrow and loud theatrical sigh signalled that he knew that she was going to tell him no matter what he said, "he meant that it's easier if you don't let your enemy know that he's the enemy until you're ready for him to find out."

"I have no idea what you just said."

"What I'm trying to say is, if you go into a situation all guns blazing, then that's it, you've shown your hand. But if you go in slowly, perhaps do some infiltration and espionage beforehand, wear a disguise," she smiled, "Perhaps grow a beard?"

He rubbed his chin and shook his head, "Maybe you're right, I'll take more than enough credits for an extended stay, perhaps our new friend E-Yain can teach us how to act like bandits on the way. We'll fit right in."

"Keep a gun on him at all times, he's not one of your squad and he could turn on you at any moment. If it were me I'd plant a whisk in his head and have my finger on the button at all times."

Mal winced, a whisk was a piece of archaic technology that had been developed for use in high security penal establishments, it was a seven foot long strand of memory wire, which was wound tightly into a ball about a quarter of an inch in diameter and then implanted at the base of the prisoner's skull. If the prisoner strayed into an unauthorised area or tried to escape, the ball would heat itself gently as a warning, if this warning was ignored, the wire would assume its primary state and instantly unwind, mincing the prisoner's brain. It could also be triggered without warning by a remote control device that the prison guards carried.

"Mother, I think that between the four of us we can keep one man under control, after all, it was his information that enabled us to get closer to the truth."

"All the more reason for him to lead you into a dark alley populated by a large, unruly group of his friends and disappear into the night. You're altogether too trusting," she stood and walked over to a large glass cabinet, "do you not think that this is a mission best suited to your staff, rather than yourself, especially as you may well be going into a viper's den controlled by the very people who are trying to kill you?" She removed a small wooden box from the cabinet, took out a tiny silver ball and threw it to her Son, who instinctively caught it.

"And this is?" he remarked, turning the ball around in his fingers.

"It's a whisk, have Say'Uff implant it in your prisoner, it's not the first time he's done it."

He looked in horror at the diminutive device in his hand as if it could unwind and cut him to pieces at any moment. "Mother, I will not use torture devices to enforce my will on someone. It is not... honourable. It is not the way that the Pewter Guard does things."

"The Pewter Guard does precisely what you tell them to do, and

I don't see the honour in waking up dead with a knife in your back. Despite the fact that you are so tremendously different, you share one major character trait with your sister," she waited for the questioning look to spread across his face and continued, "pig-headedness. The over-arching feeling that your opinion is the right answer in any given situation. I could order you to send Sembhee and a team of men in your stead."

"Sembhee's coming with me, as are Na-Thon and Zatch. Does that meet with the Baroness' approval?"

Her eyes flashed angrily "Don't be facetious boy, it doesn't suit you. Although you'll have an increased chance of survival with those particular three behind you, I still don't agree that you need to go yourself, it's bad military sense if nothing else."

"I'm sorry," he took his mother's hand and squeezed it gently, "but I'm going to go, it should only take a few days and the guardsmen that I'm taking with me are the best that there are. If they can't keep me alive then no-one can. I can't very well hide here for the rest of my life," he looked at the chronometer on the display screen, "in fact, I have to go now."

He stood and stretched, gave the quiescent whisk back to his mother with a shudder and started towards the door.

"Mal?" She called as he reached the door, "Try not to die."

Bowing with a huge theatrical flourish, he flashed the bright smile that had melted the hearts of many potential suitors and left the room. He stopped momentarily below Stalys' terminal outside his mother's chambers, requested that five thousand credits in a mixture of small denominations be stowed in the skimmer, and then made his way to the hangar bay.

Na-Thon noticed Lord Mal striding through the doorway towards him and raised his hand in greeting. "Commander, we'll be ready to leave in just a few moments," he performed a tight salute, "by the way, a construct just arrived with a bag of money, I've stowed it with the rest of your gear. Zatch is securing the prisoner and Captain Sembhee's just finalising the flight plan with the pilot."

Mal looked Na-Thon up and down appreciatively and smiled.

"I've not seen you out of uniform for a while Sergeant, your clothes seem very new, I wonder if we're paying you too much or do you have a black market sideline trading in fine clothing?"

The sergeant flushed and looked down at his shirt as if seeing it for the first time, "This Sir? I..." He shrugged his shoulders, "I don't really get the chance to wear civilian clothes very often My Lord, it's usually either my uniform or armour, and I've had this hanging in my wardrobe for months..."

"Enough!" Laughed the commander, "I was joking. Go and tell Zatch we're leaving and strap yourself in, I'll get Sembhee." He clapped the sergeant across the shoulders and made his way to the front of the skimmer where the captain was talking to the Pilot through the open cockpit.

"We'll land at the main port, try and get a berth to the South, near the water. Keep the engines warm in case we need to get out of there in a hurry."

"Belay that, there's been a change of plan." The captain spun around and the Pilot craned over his shoulder to see who'd over-ruled these new orders.

"My Lord, I'm sorry, I didn't know you were here."

Mal shook his head dismissively and addressed the Pilot. "We'll be taking a small detour on our trip to the Free Trade zone, once we've arrived you'll just be dropping us off and coming back, we will call for pickup when we're done." He turned to Sembhee, "I presume that you're ready to go?"

The captain nodded and climbed into the passenger compartment. Mal once again contacted the pilot, "Set course for border station West-One and launch when ready, I've some unfinished business to attend to." The pilot nodded curtly, pulled down his visor and closed the cockpit. The flight engines barked into life just as Mal closed the passenger lock, their dull roar gaining volume and pitch as he took his seat next to the captain. A momentary feeling of increased weight indicated that they had left the ground and started out of the hangar.

The Pilot's voice came over the speaker, "My Lord, we will be arriving at West-One in fourteen minutes."

Na-Thon frowned at Sembhee, who shrugged. "My Lord, I thought that we would be travelling directly to Liverpool?"

"Two birds, Captain," The Commander replied, "can you remember whether you removed your helmets during our last visit?" Both men shook their heads. "Excellent, presuming that he has ignored my cease and desist order, when we land you will both pose as prospective customers and engage him in negotiations about your particular requirements. I will enter through the back door and catch him in the act, dispelling any nagging legal doubt that he is running a brothel and enabling me to prosecute him to the full extent of the law."

Zatch looked momentarily confused, "But, you are the law My Lord."

"Yes," replied Mal, turning his attention to the prisoner and letting his face slowly break into a grim smile, "I know."

His head fell limply onto the broad back of the oversized seat as he made himself comfortable. They seemed snug and quite restrictive if you were wearing powered armour, but sitting here in his civilian clothes made him feel like a small child sat guiltily in an adult's chair. The remainder of the flight passed in silence until the engine noise changed pitch again and the pilot announced that they would be landing momentarily.

"Pilot, how many skimmers are there on the pad?"

"Six My Lord."

"Still more than there should be, put us down at the edge of the field, I want to be able to get to the rear of the building without being seen by too many cameras. Not that I'd wager they're watching the cameras particularly closely."

The three guards grinned. Na-Thon and Sembhee waited until the Skimmer had settled onto its landing legs, brushed themselves down and waited for the lock to cycle open.

"Remember that you're supposed to be civilians so no 'Yes Sergeant, no Captain' nonsense. Keep him busy and looking away from the rear entrance," They nodded and climbed out into the daylight. He turned back towards the prisoner. "Zatch, keep him quiet, if he becomes unruly or in any way uncooperative, shoot him in the ankle."

"Yes My Lord," he took out a pistol, removed the power pack to check it was fully charged and pointed it towards E-Yain's feet.

Mal jumped from the skimmer and, crouching low, made his way towards the back of the listening station. Keeping his back to the wall, he listened as the front entrance ground open and his men were ushered inside. When he had heard the door close again, he followed the edge of the building until he reached the loading bay, located the security keypad and entered his personal over-ride code. The large doors slid open and he looked into the gloom. The bay was empty, very empty. There should have been several crates full of spares and assorted equipment as well as food and medical supplies. As he crept across the room, making his way to the door that would give him access to the base proper, he heard lazy footsteps to his right. He drew his pistol and spun, the butt contacting the yawning sentry's temple before he had time to speak, the man folded and fell as his weapon dropped to the floor with a loud clatter. Mal checked that his pulse was strong, dragged his unconscious body with him up the stairwell, and continued his stealthy journey towards the door. He looked through the clear armourplas panel, and saw the other members of his team, surrounded by soon to be satisfied customers.

The two guardsmen stood, staring wide-eyed at the assorted occupied bunks, tables and hammocks that had been set up around the perimeter of the main room. Each one held a number of people involved in what could only be described as multiple lewd and lascivious acts.

Commander O'Shea swept down the staircase from his office. "Gentlemen! Good afternoon! I'm afraid we weren't expecting any more guests today, it's something of an end of season special for some of our more discerning customers. Although when my colleague advised me of your arrival, I thought to myself that it would be very rude of me to turn you away after you'd flown so far."

"That's very kind of you, I'm sure," Replied Na-Thon, not taking his eyes off the activities of the other customers.

"Yes," interjected Sembhee, "We had heard that you could provide the services of young ladies who were very flexible both physically and morally, we were wondering just exactly how flexible they were." He looked over O'Shea's shoulder, saw his commander's face at the window and nodded almost imperceptibly.

O'Shea beckoned one of the less busy girls over to him, "Well, Lucia here for instance, can…"

The sound of the door being kicked open and bouncing against the wall cut him off mid-flow, he spun around just in time to see the commander drop the unconscious sentry to the floor and raise his pistol to chest height.

"Commander O'Shea, you are hereby relieved of duty with immediate effect," the patrons and female staff scrambled to retrieve their clothes and beat a retreat. Na-Thon made to give chase, but his commander shook his head, "you were warned more than two weeks ago that the continuation of your sideline would not be tolerated. You were told to cease and desist or there would be consequences."

The quivering whoremonger dropped to his knees. "My Lord… I don't…"

"That is correct, you don't have a place in the armies of Rustholme. You don't have a right to explain yourself. Put simply O'Shea, You don't have a future. Captain, secure the prisoner."

Sembhee produced a pair of metallic tie-wraps from the pouch on his belt, backed O'Shea towards the stairs and cuffed him to them, tightening the ties so that they were on the verge of cutting off his circulation. The station commander winced and tears formed in the corners of his eyes. The captain whispered into his ear, "You disgust me."

"What about my men? They were only doing what they were told, they don't deserve…"

"They are required to question any order that they believe to be against the best interests of Rustholme, or those that would be harmful or bring disrespect on the family," Mal turned to the soldier that had cheerfully let Sembhee and Na-Thon into the building, "would you show the baroness this?" He spread his arms wide and slowly turned, trying to include every single sordid item in the room.

He looked at the floor and mumbled, "No My Lord, I..."

Mal moved towards him until their faces were less than an inch apart. In deep, measured tones he asked, "Then why did you not report it?"

The soldier shifted his weight uneasily from one foot to the other and turned his face away, unable to bear the heat of the incandescent eyes burning into him.

The commander stepped back and addressed the room, "As far as I am concerned, you are all guilty - it is only the degree of your guilt that has yet to be decided. We are leaving now, a transport will be here in three hours to pick up Commander O'Shea and transfer him to the Roost where he will be tried and sentenced. You will continue to run this station as the listening post it was originally intended to be and a new commander will be supplied as soon as a capable and more honest man has been identified, it will not be an existing crewmember. An official investigation will then take place into each and every one of your involvement in this sorry business," he stared directly at the restrained commander, "this includes the current whereabouts of the stores and supplies that this facility should hold in its inventory."

O'Shea's knees finally buckled and he slid to the floor, tears streaming from his eyes.

The two guards and their commander surveyed the room one last time, then turned towards the door and started to leave. "One last thing," explained Mal as he inspected the main door latches, still bent from their last visit, "you may give him water, but if he is not restrained when the penal squad arrives, I will see that any man who has aided him is tried for treason, a crime for which the sentence is death."

Chapter 9 : Compliance

"Excellency, we have cleared the coast, and will be docking at Zwartbosch in a little over an hour."

"How much over an hour? Ten minutes, twenty minutes? Forty minutes?"

The helmsman re-checked his navigational display, "Total flight time is sixty eight minutes, so eight minutes over, Excellency."

Duke Pytor gripped the arms of the command chair and regarded the holographic display that sprang into life, surrounding his head. In front of him was the navigational map with its bright, gently pulsing red dots indicating Company bases. To his right, the systems status displays indicating energy generation, life support and weaponry. To his left, the communication matrix and behind him, the graphical representations of the engines and lift systems. He waved his hand and the communication window moved to the front. "Engineering."

The clasped fists logo of the Company was replaced by the face of Barnes, the Chief Engineer.

"Barnes here Excellency, how can I be of service?"

"You have sixty..." He looked down at his wrist chronometer, "...six minutes to provide the detailed performance logs for this flight. I would have them well before that so that I may acquaint myself with their contents before the development team sees them."

"Yes Excellency, you will have them with time to spare, I will deliver them personally. However the preliminary reports have already been automatically Clouded to both Zwartbosch and Nukuoro."

The Cloud, or 'Great and Powerful Cloud' as it was often referred to disparagingly by the public, was a Company run global information system that connected every publicly available data terminal, as well as those internal to the Company, to a network of fortified datacentres scattered around the globe. If you wanted a message sending, you gave it to the Cloud, If you needed the weather report for your birthday in two months' time or when the next departure from the William Henry Gates Interplanetary port in the Greater Washington Conurbation to Lunar Station Six was, you asked the Cloud. It could give you the answer to any question, on any topic, that anyone had ever gone to the trouble of researching in the entirety of history. As long as the Company was happy for you to know the answer. If you asked a question and the Cloud instructed you to wait whilst it passed you to an organic operator, then it was your time to worry, or at the very least move to a less populated continent and live the rest of your life so far off the grid that your nose would bleed.

Pytor waved the screen away in annoyance, which abruptly closed the connection. He rose from his chair and walked over to the main viewer. The panoramic view of the African plains rushing by below at over six hundred miles an hour would have been breath-taking under normal conditions, and usually calmed even his darkest moods. But his mind was full and heavy with a thousand things competing for his immediate personal attention, "Compliance?"

"Yes Excellency?" the onboard A.I. of the huge airship replied instantaneously, its light female voice devoid of any real personality.

"Cloud the current progress reports for the Dreadnaughts Fist of Scrutiny and Fist of Correction directly to my stateroom."

There was a moment's delay as the A.I. transferred the documents, "Complete."

He turned and left the bridge, his immaculately polished boots echoing metallically on the newly installed and as yet completely unmarked floor. The door closed silently behind him and he strode through the spacious corridors, studiously ignoring the passing crewmen who, in turn, tried to avoid his direct gaze, until he reached his quarters. The two assault constructs that guarded the entrance turned towards him as he rounded the corner, brought their heavily armoured eight foot tall frames to full attention and saluted. The Duke walked between them as if they didn't exist and entered his suite. "Compliance, privacy."

The internal lights brightened as the external windows became reflective mirrors. "Your rooms are now secure Excellency, zero electromagnetic radiation in and out." The area around the doorway glowed with a gentle purple light. "Kill field engaged."

Taking a grape from the fruit bowl, he idly turned it in his hands and then flicked it, without looking, at the door. The loud crack and the momentary brightening of the field's image in the mirror confirmed both that the grape had been vapourised and that his security system was working. Allowing himself a smile, he moved to his desk, sat down and ran his palm lovingly over its warm wooden surface.

The desk was a simple affair, it had travelled with him from his family home and was made of thick, polished oak timbers. The terminal display and the accompanying touch-sensitive controls had been expertly sunk into it so that to a casual observer, not looking directly down at it from the vantage point of the Duke's chair, it appeared to be a solid, unbroken, wooden tabletop. The Duke's fingers danced over the virtual keyboard and brought up the reports that the Compliance had transferred to him.

He felt that the Dreadnaught program had been one of his finest ideas to date. Giant, aluminium skinned airships. Twelve hundred feet from armoured bow to triple redundant stern fins. Powered by half a dozen Torkan designed, rotatable cold fusion engines. Each of the ships were individually tailored for a specific task, but what they all had in common was their ability to instil awe in anyone who saw them. The Fist of Scrutiny was to be the centre for all clandestine medical research, anything too dangerous, either politically or medically, to happen near a populated area would be performed on board. The Fist of Correction could hold five thousand prisoners at a time, its re-education centres were state of the art and its mobility gave it immunity from any land-based local laws and customs.

Skimming through the figures showed him that the other two planned Dreadnaughts would be complete and in the air by the end of the week, presuming of course that the performance figures from the Fist of Compliance's shakedown cruise found favour with the technicians. Then it would just be a case of giving the other board members their opinions, so that they could voice them at the next shareholders meeting and rubber stamp the steps required for phase two.

"Excellency?" The Compliance's A.I. terminal lit up, "the Chief Engineer is requesting an audience."

Pytor looked up from the display and thought for a second. "Disable the kill field and let him in."

The glow of the security system faded and the door slid open to reveal Barnes, not only the Chief Engineer of the Fist of Compliance, but also the engineering brain who had brought the Dreadnaught project to life. He regarded the door frame field emitters with a degree of caution and walked into the room.

"I have the reports, Excellency." He offered the slim data cartridges gingerly to the Duke and they were summarily snatched from his hand and spread across the desk. As they passed over the display, their contents were downloaded to the terminal and appeared on its screen, "If I may explain the highlights? The figures show that the ship is working well within the designed parameters. Energy generation is at 120% of theoretical maximum, which we are putting down to the enhanced efficiency of the fusion engines. We are creating a surfeit of Heptium, which can be channelled into additional buoyancy or be re-introduced into the engines to provide emergency thrust."

"Stop," Pytor held up his hand and the Engineer clamped his lips tightly together, "I would be the first person to admit that my knowledge of physics is not encyclopaedic, but I understood it to be common knowledge that fusion engines make Heptium, they do not breathe it. In fact, the few texts that I have read all mention something called a 'Cascade Event'? something generally regarded by experts as a terribly bad thing."

"Yes Excellency, under normal conditions your concerns would be, of course, well placed. The procedure that cracks the air entering the engines into Heptium and a few other short lived and unstable gasses, will fail explosively if that gas is re-introduced. However we, and by 'we' I obviously mean the team of indentured Torkans that we have interred at Nukuoro, have found a way of controlling the cascade reaction to provide an after-burning effect. I can, with this new system, provide short bursts of acceleration three times more powerful than the normal operation of the engines could otherwise deliver."

"Now, that is interesting; Compliance, window," the silver finish evaporated and the glass became crystal clear. Below them the mottled greens of Mozambique were fading into the tans and browns of what had once been South Africa. "If there was to be an accident, and the control system for this after-burner of yours failed, how big would the explosion be?"

"Excellency?"

"Surely it is a simple question, in your opinion, if we suffered a Heptium Cascade, what would be the effect?"

"Well, if it was just one engine, there would be an explosion large enough to instantly destroy at least half the ship, and irradiate anyone that was fortunate enough to have survived the ensuing crash."

"And if it were to be all of the engines, simultaneously?"

"That could never happen Excellency, there are safeguards..."

"Humour me."

"The ship would be instantly vapourised, Excellency, anyone within a two mile radius in any direction, including those on the ground would stand a good chance of being obliterated, irradiated, or both."

"Perfect. I have been thinking about a denial weapon, in the style of those we install at our more delicate ground installations. Between now and the time that we ultimately dock at Nukuoro, I want to see your designs for a device that bypasses all of the safety systems and causes an instant cascade event in all of the engines. I want it to be a physically triggered device and accessible only from the command chair."

The engineer stared open mouthed at his commander. If he had heard correctly, he had just been asked to install a self-destruct device on the new flagship of the Company fleet. Had Duke Pytor never seen a single action vid? This was a recipe for disaster, and a disaster that involved having all of the atoms in your body being torn apart, which, in his opinion was one of the worst kinds of disaster. He was just about to, very carefully, voice his opinion when the Duke turned towards him and smiled.

"I know that you must be thinking that I have gone insane, that a self-destruct mechanism would be tantamount to suicide and it would attract lunatics, rebels and every other anti-Company activist that we came within range of. However, I do not think that they are by any means our most direct threat," he paused, hoping that Barnes could identify what he was talking about before he had to spell it out for him. When no answer was forthcoming, he sighed and continued, "a vast proportion of our human crew are from the re-education camps, they have gone through the standard psychological and surgical procedures that daily turn formerly dangerous dissidents into well-adjusted employees of the Company. But there have been some isolated reports recently, not of abject rebellion against the programming by any means, but instances of self-awareness, fleeting moments of free will. Obviously they were immediately stamped out, the transgressors were summarily recycled, as were the technicians that signed off on their re-education. But I do not want to be in a position where one of the crew suddenly remembers who they once were, decides to commit mutiny and flies a Dreadnaught into one of the Openzones so that it can be pulled apart and have all its secrets revealed."

"You would rather the entire ship be destroyed Excellency?"

"I would rather that the situation would never arise in the first place. Once the system is fitted to all of the Dreadnaughts, we will leak news of its existence, what good is a deterrent if no-one knows why they should be deterred?"

"As you say Excellency, I will begin work immediately," he stood to attention, waited to be dismissed, then returned to Engineering to start working on the worst idea that he had ever heard in his entire life.

As Pytor sat back at his desk to read the report, realising that Barnes had not talked him through the rest of his findings, he felt the ship start to decelerate. "Compliance?"

"We are entering Zwartbosch airspace Excellency; we will be docking in three minutes."

"Inform the helm that I wish to visually inspect the Fist of Correction before docking. If her A.I. is online, Cloud your full sensor logs to her."

"Complete."

He scooped the data cartridges off his desk and into his pocket, which removed the open files from his desk display, and went back to the bridge. As he retook the command chair the main screen was displaying a panoramic view of the re-education facility. Over one hundred square miles of secure accommodation, hospital wards and recycling units were spread over what had at one time been a private nature reserve. The entire area had been scorched in the South African Civil War, long before the worldwide conflict with the Spiders had grabbed everyone's attention, which was when he first visited Zwartbosch.

Pytor had originally been a military trained scout and prospector, who made a name for himself finding items of value in the most inhospitable of areas. In fact, he was one of the first men to take a fusion powered starship to the asteroid belt to look for minerals. Despite being out of contact for six months due to a communications failure, he returned to Earth with a hold full of rare minerals and elements that made him a very rich man. His military training and his uncanny eye for a profitable opportunity meant that it wasn't long before he was involved personally in the continental civil war in Africa as a mercenary commander, constantly playing one local warlord off against another. Once each bloody battle was fought to completion, he pitted the winner against the local Government forces. He had made a fortune, both in direct payments and bribes, which, in the end, turned out to be large enough to secure him his own small nation. Although it wasn't until he happened across the disused Groot Gat diamond mine and used his contacts within the Government to buy the land from its then owner that his limitless fortune was assured. The fact that the owner and his entire family had been found drowned in the mine's main pit, after the deal was struck, but before final payment was made, was not even investigated by local law enforcement. He had bought his way into the Company by offering them the sites that he'd bought up in Africa for clandestine research and development. It hadn't been long until he'd been appointed as head of new projects, and from there, it took only a small number of accidental deaths and unexpected early retirements amongst his superiors until he was made CEO. His election had been undisputed, and had coincided, almost precisely, with the outbreak of the Spider War.

The Fist of Compliance turned towards the docking mast and the Fist of Correction slowly swung into view. The two ships were almost identical to the untrained eye, the main difference being that the security systems of the unfinished ship were more obvious, there were slightly more anti-personnel turrets and the shielding around the docking bays and windows was noticeably thicker.

"Helm, one circuit of the Correction and then dock, keep us pointed towards her at all times."

"Yes Excellency," the Helmsman expertly juggled the controls, swinging the engines around on their mounts whilst he pushed the huge ship sideways into the wind, all the time keeping the deck straight and level whilst Pytor closely inspected every inch of the other ship's hull.

"Excellency?" the flat tones of the Compliance's A.I. interrupted his inspection, "the Fist of Correction reports that our sensor logs have been fully incorporated into its operating code."

The Duke nodded and ordered the helm to dock the ship. The Compliance turned gracefully in the air and the helmsman increased the power to the engines. She connected to the docking mast with an almost imperceptible bump and various mechanical noises rang through the armoured bow section as umbilical cables and docking tubes snaked from the mast and connected solidly to her hull.

"Thrusters at station-keeping, fusion reactors to twenty percent power, life support and security systems to nominal. The Fist of Compliance is now docked," the tone of the A.I's voice changed slightly as the local traffic control took over the circuit. "Welcome to the Zwartbosch Correctional Facility, please disembark when you are ready. Standard security procedures will apply to," there was a slight pause as the construct deviated from its normal script, "most Fist of Compliance crewmembers. Please follow any instructions given to you by Zwartbosch operational staff quickly, efficiently and without question. Your safety is important to us."

Pytor absently passed a hand over his tunic pocket to make sure that he had Barnes' reports, pulled its embroidered front tight to remove any creases, and then made his way down a deck to the nearest external lock. Two of the assault constructs from his personal guard were waiting for him. As he approached, one triggered the inner door open and stood aside to let him enter. They followed him and activated the outer door, there was a slight hiss of escaping gasses as the hot air of the facility mixed with the controlled atmosphere of the ship, the pressures normalised and the door slid open. The Commandant of Zwartbosch was waiting for him, surrounded by a selection of minor local dignitaries and members of the project team.

"Your Excellency, welcome to our humble facility. I hope the maiden voyage of the Fist of Compliance was all you could have hoped for? May I have you conducted to your quarters, or do you wish to inspect the Fist of Correction? Perhaps I could tempt you with some of our excellent local cuisine? I wonder if you..."

"Commandant?" The broadly moustached man stopped mid flow and regarded the Duke. "Shut up. You will give the Compliance details of my quarters and she will arrange for such belongings that I may require during my stay to be transported there. I will meet with you and the Chief Project Engineer aboard the Fist of Compliance in fifteen minutes."

"Of course Excellency. I..." He turned to a small uniformed man who stood directly behind him, developing a serious perspiration problem and trying to hide in his shadow. "Bothar, you heard the Duke, make the arrangements immediately."

The diminutive officer saluted neatly, took one last look at the Duke and scuttled off towards the command centre. The Commandant smiled and swung his arm wide to indicate that the Duke should continue down the corridor, "After you, your Excellency, the Fist of Correction is docked on the other side of the mast, at dock 6." Pytor and his guard swept past, not waiting for the Commandant, and navigated to the dock using the signage on the walls.

They entered the Fist of Correction via the same lock that they had used to exit from the Compliance, the Duke's guard stepping into the familiar, yet oddly different, corridor ahead of their master and immediately taking up defensive positions. Pytor entered and was confronted by a floating drone, comprising a brushed aluminium globe full of sensor equipment coupled to a lift engine, similar to that which could be found in an aggie, although this particular one floated some six feet in the air, rather than the customary four inches. "The Dreadnaught Fist of Correction welcomes Duke Pytor and his party. I am the Warden, please follow me to the bridge, where refreshments have been provided for your comfort and nourishment."

"I know my way to the bridge, drone, why would I need to follow you?"

"Excellency, there are twelve security checkpoints between our current location and the bridge. Although your security clearance allows you to pass through completely unchallenged, we have not yet performed the final testing of the prisoner suppression systems. I have been commanded to physically render each security station offline before you reach it and to re-enable it after you have successfully passed through."

"Download the specifications of the security checkpoints to my guard," Pytor ordered, then waited until one of his assault constructs indicated that the download was complete. "Do these checkpoints present a threat?"

"Excellency, the sensor systems are state of the art, the slaved anti-personnel weaponry would destroy biological life instantly and would be able to incapacitate both assault constructs that currently accompany you within a matter of seconds. As final testing has not been performed, it is my recommendation that we allow the drone to deactivate the defence grids prior to our approach."

The Duke looked at the construct for a second, considered what firepower would be required to neutralise both of his escorts with such speed then turned back to the drone, "Very well, conduct us to the bridge."

The Warden dipped its sensors in an approximation of a bow, turned away and moved off down the corridor. They had gone no more than fifty yards when a panel on the rear of the drone lit up a bright, angry red.

"Excellency," one of Pytor's guards sinuously moved between him and the floating drone, "the drone is transmitting a stop code, we are approaching the first of the security stations," as the guard had been talking, the Warden had continued down the corridor and had stopped in front of an unremarkable section of corridor, "it is asking if you would like to see a simulated prisoner escape protocol."

"And why doesn't it just ask me itself?"

"The Warden has advanced mood sensing technology Excellency, used for anticipating prisoner reactions to stressful situations. It has reasoned that you are feeling impatience and would be calmed by hearing the description of the procedure from one of your own team of constructs."

"It thinks of everything. Please proceed," the Duke waved his hand grandly, as if bestowing a great gift upon the floating construct by allowing it to continue.

Without warning, containment fields sprung online from hidden projectors, boxing in the section of corridor containing the Warden.

"Military strength containment fields have been erected, strong enough to stop a round from any currently available man portable weapon. The prisoner will be ordered to surrender."

Pytor felt his ears begin to pop.

"If the prisoner does not comply the atmosphere is removed from the contained area, rendering them unconscious."

"Unless they have some breathing equipment presumably?"

The Assault Construct nodded, "As you say Excellency, if that is the case they are then ordered to surrender again. If they fail to comply this time an armed response is triggered."

A selection of small turrets, no more than six inches across appeared from the walls and ceiling of the contained section, instantly tracked to a point three feet above the floor surface and fired a combination of energy and projectile weapons. Pytor could feel the multiple concussions through the floor, but couldn't hear anything as there was still no air in the chamber. The turrets retracted, leaving the corridor completely featureless once more.

"The turrets can target six locations independently. If however this is unsuccessful, it is assumed that the prisoners will not willingly surrender and the final phase is automatically authorised."

The Warden deactivated the containment field furthest from them, moved through into the next section of corridor and reactivated it. Two probes extended from the ceiling and pointed towards each other.

"The chamber has been filled with a mixture of pure oxygen and hydrogen. This phase continues until there is no longer a threat of escape, but for the purposes of this demonstration will only last a matter of seconds Excellency."

A spark flew between the two probes and the contained atmosphere ignited. The swirling flames flattening themselves against the containment fields like angry, golden red, storm clouds.

"The internal temperature of that section of corridor can be raised by up to two thousand degrees Celsius if required and that temperature can be maintained for as long as necessary to subdue the prisoner," abruptly the flames disappeared and an icy fog replaced them, "within a few seconds, the corridor section will have cooled sufficiently for a medical team or a cleaning construct to access whatever remains of the prisoner."

"Very impressive, when will the system be fully tested?"

The containment fields disengaged as the Warden approached them and answered, "The certification team are currently working in the high security and termination sections towards the stern of the ship as those areas require less testing. The current schedule has them due to complete by 19:00 hours tomorrow, Excellency."

"And why do those areas require less testing?"

"Those areas are not fitted with any non-lethal systems Excellency, immediately the system is triggered, any prisoners considered to be a threat are cremated. If you will excuse me, I will now deactivate this station."

The Warden positioned itself in the centre of the corridor and extruded eight flexible arms from the equator of its body. Each of the arms snaked out to find a discrete stud recessed into the walls on both sides, some were pressed, others were turned, and the lighting changed from white to red.

The Correction's voice echoed through all the speakers in the corridor, "Security station 471 has been manually deactivated."

The Duke and his guards solemnly followed the Warden through the section of corridor and waited whilst he performed the multiple-armed manoeuvre again. The Correction informed them that the station had been reactivated and they continued their trip towards the bridge.

"Warden, how many of you are there?" asked the Duke, idly, "I'm assuming that there isn't only one of you to cater to the needs of five thousand prisoners."

"Excellency, I am a singular entity, with five hundred and twelve extremities, both fixed and free floating. My processing nodes are distributed throughout the fabric of the Fist of Correction but share..."

"Enough! I was merely making idle chit-chat, I neither want to know, nor care how your wiring is routed. Did your mood sensors not pick that up?"

"My apologies, I am programmed to answer queries From Company staff to the best of my ability."

There was a strangled cry from behind them, "Excellency!"

Pytor and his guard turned to see the Commandant jogging

down the corridor towards them, his face was flushed a shiny red and a thin sheen of sweat beaded his brow. He stopped a few feet away, placed his hand over his heart and tried, unsuccessfully, to catch his breath.

"I... uh... apologise... for the delay..." he swallowed deeply and took a few ragged breaths before he was confident enough that he wasn't going to pass out to continue talking, "there was some confusion, my subordinate had a query about your quarters. Everything is now completely..."

"Commandant, it seems that you have an unfortunate pathological issue," the Duke's eyes bored into the small man's skull, "you have lost the ability of recognising when your words have gone from being informative carriers of abstract ideas to mere noises, the phrasing of which serve only to exercise the muscles of your mouth and engender feelings of disdain in those unfortunate enough to be within earshot. Did you have anything to do with the personality profile of the Warden?"

"Excellency?"

Duke Pytor shook his head dismissively, "From this point, until I leave this facility, you will answer my questions truthfully but briefly. You will not volunteer any information unless it directly concerns my personal safety, do you understand?" he indicated the floating globe of the warden, "that applies to you as well."

The rest of their journey was conducted in silence, apart from the heavy breathing of the Commandant, and in no time at all they were waiting whilst the Warden disabled the security systems around the main entrance to the bridge. The armoured doors slid open to reveal a room almost twice the size of the bridge of the Compliance. Empty but for the captain, sat in his chair and the chief engineer, standing by a flat console that had been covered by a cloth and was acting as an impromptu buffet table.

The captain rose smartly from his seat and addressed his visitors in a thick, South African accent. "Excellency, Commandant, welcome to the Company Dreadnaught Fist of Correction. Please make yourselves at home, if you would like to avail yourselves of the buffet, I'm sure that we will have something that you will like," he indicated the selection of different foods spread along the counter and the group turned just in time to see the chief engineer guiltily putting a half-eaten sandwich back onto a platter.

"Those are chicken salad," remarked the engineer, wiping an errant crumb from her glove, "with slightly too much black pepper if I'm being completely honest," she strode across the bridge and held out her hand for the Duke to shake. "I'm Madrigal Callous, Chief Engineer of the Correction, at your service, Excellency."

Duke Pytor took the proffered hand, bowed gently and kissed the back of it. "A pleasure to meet you Miss Callous."

"Chief Callous, Excellency, Miss Callous was my mother."

The Duke aimed a sideways glance at the captain who closed his eyes with the nature of a man that did not want to see what happened when an immovable object was met by an irresistible force.

"My apologies... Chief Callous. Of course, how remiss of me." He released her hand and walked over to the command chair. "Captain Stevens, I trust everything is going to plan?"

"Yes Excellency, we received your Cloud message about the updated flight parameters, they have been incorporated," he looked at Callous, who nodded, "successfully into the Correction's operating systems. As you are already aware, the extended security systems are complete and awaiting final testing and other than that, as soon as the last few crew have been supplied by the Commandant, we will be ready to fly."

Pytor turned to the Commandant, who instantly adopted his now familiar stance of a rabbit caught in the headlights of a speeding groundcar before continuing, "There are a few menials that are just being processed now Excellency, normally we would use constructs, but obviously, we have a surfeit of biological specimens available to us," he smiled wanly and indicated the ship surrounding him, "and when this wonderful ship is operational, there will be no shortage of replacements ready for processing as and when they are required."

"Good, that sounds most encouraging," he offered his hand to the Chief Engineer and steered her towards the waiting buffet, "shall we see if we can find anything that is a little more delicately seasoned amongst this array, whilst you talk me through the details of the additions that you have made to my basic design?"

"Of course Excellency, my first priorities were the internal defences and the Warden system, both of which you have already experienced."

"Yes, quite," the Duke looked at the floating globe which hovered near the main viewscreen as if inspecting the facility below them, "and did you engineer its personality yourself?"

Callous looked momentarily confused, "Ah, no Excellency, no-one engineered its personality as such. It's a fully featured type seven. I thought that you requested that specifically? I have the documentation somewhere."

"A type seven? I made no such request!" he stormed towards the Warden, his face reddening.

As he approached, the floating globe twisted slowly on it axis until it was facing him. "May I be of some assistance, Excellency?"

Pytor stared directly into the drone's scanner array, not sure exactly what he was expecting to see, but not finding anything apart from the usual dull glow. Callous joined him, standing slightly closer than was strictly proper.

"Once the processing core had been installed, we just told it what it was supposed to be doing, gave it some pointers about how it was supposed to interact with the crew and our... 'guests', and let it fill in the blanks itself with historical research. It knows everything about being a prison warder that has ever been written. It's been fully tested, we've run hundreds of simulations and it's performed exactly as expected every time."

"I'm sure it has. Correction, in an emergency, could you incapacitate the Warden subsystem?"

"Excellency, the Warden is not a subsystem, it is autonomous and separate from my control. I believe that this was part of your initial design, to defend against any possible attack that may release prisoners."

"The Correction's right Excellency, the Warden is distributed throughout the ship to protect it against damage, it has no direct access to the main systems and vice-versa," a cloud of concern passed across Callous' face, "is this a problem? Have we misinterpreted your orders?"

"No, everything is as it should be, the fact that I specified a type seven must just have slipped my mind momentarily. I have so much swirling around in here," he tapped the side of his head and smiled broadly at Callous, "which means that occasionally the details all blur into one. I blame it on a lack of suitable recreational activities."

"Well, perhaps your stay at Zwartbosch could include a short vacation, some good food, and some, admittedly only half-decent wine," She slowly dragged her gloved index finger up his arm and rested her hand lightly on his shoulder, "maybe there could even be some intelligent conversation, about non Company related subjects. And I think that you will find any recreational activities that present themselves, to be uncommonly relaxing."

"Chief Callous, I..."

"Please Excellency, call me Maddie."

Chapter 10 : Escape

Britt opened his eyes experimentally and tried to peel his tongue from the roof of his mouth. He surveyed the damage to his room and found that luckily, his memory of cutting a chair into kindling with his ripsword was just part of an elaborate, vintage brandy fuelled, dream. The message indicator on the Intercomm was flashing, he gingerly pressed the play button and winced as Landry's loud Bostonian tones filled his cabin.

"Mr. Britt, message from the captain; She would like you to contact her at your earliest convenience so that you can plan your excursion to the... Erm... Drunk Hammer? Time is currently oh seven thirty."

He rubbed his head and deleted the massage, "It's Tronkamer you Colonial nit-wit and it's actually," he tried to focus on the chronometer, high up on the wall, "ten fourteen. Which means she left that message nearly three hours ago! By all the Gods' little fluffy wingtips!" He ran to the basin and splashed water on his face, checked his tunic for incriminating stains and rushed out of the door, pausing only to pick up the brandy bottle from the floor, check that it was completely empty and place it reverently back on the table. Due to the somewhat cramped nature of the Spirit, he reached the captain's cabin in a matter of seconds, took a deep breath and drew his hand back to knock.

A cry came from the other side of the door. "Stop creeping around outside Britt, you're making the floorboards creak," he looked down at the solid steel deck plates and furrowed his brow, then pushed the door open and entered the room. The captain was sat behind her desk; Lee'Sahr was stood next to her pointing out details on a hastily scribbled map.

Dorleith looked him up and down as he closed the door behind him, "What happened to you? You left the Vienna hours before we did, I'd have expected you to have got a decent night's sleep, knowing how much we had to do today."

"Well, I came back, looked through some of the potential crewmen and then..."

"Drank an entire bottle of expensive brandy to yourself, and passed out fully clothed?"

"It was something like that, aye. I understood that that sort of thing was expected of me now that I'm a pirate."

She smiled and beckoned him over, "You said that you've seen the inside of this place a few times?" he looked at the map and nodded, "we took a look at the layout on the way back here last night, he's in this cell, just behind the guard post." She indicated a small box on the outer edge of the compound, "he's got eyes on him all the time, I'm guessing the station manager wants him to stay put. Is there an easy way in?"

He pondered the diagram for a while, "They usually put the drunks up here in these communal cells," his finger wavered over some larger blocks far away from the entrance, "so the guards can't hear the singing or smell the vomit. Where you say he is looks like it's connected to the staff kitchens, going to be trickier than I thought."

"Could we disguise ourselves as a medical team and sneak him out that way?" suggested the captain.

"No, they have a duty doctor on site, there's a lot of stomach pumping involved on a normal night and some of the inmates occasionally have more than one stomach."

"How about blowing a hole in the outer wall of the cell and

staging an old time jailbreak?"

"If this map's anything like to scale, then a charge big enough blow the wall out will turn him to mush. I'm guessing that he won't be quite so useful to us if he's spread thinly over the walls of his cell."

Lee'Sahr shook her head, "We're going to need a diversion." She bit her lip and ran her fingers through her hair, "What if we open up the drunk tanks, sow a bit of general confusion and sneak him out whilst the guards are trying to restore order?"

"You're counting on the guards thinking that no-one would be so unoriginal as to try that, that they won't be looking out for it?" Britt started to laugh derisively, but stopped as he saw her face change.

"No!" She shouted, slamming her hand down on the map, "I'm counting on the guards still treating Baju-Merah as one of their own and being glad that he's getting away with doing something that they've all thought about doing themselves, in fact, doing something that a lot of them have already done themselves. We'd just be giving them an excuse to let him go without them being punished."

Britt took a step back, chastened, and sat down on the chaise longue with a pout, "Well, I suppose that might work."

"It still needs to look like a real escape attempt, so we go in low with the sun behind us, just above the rooftops using your skiff," Lee'Sahr paused as the captain and Britt both shook their heads, "a tender?" another negative filled pause, "A Gig? Do you have any available transport other than this ship?"

"Not here, no." replied the captain, "we've got a couple of skimmers back at the base, they could be here by tonight if we really need them."

"No, we can enter on foot I suppose, if we time it right. How good's your Helmsman, think he could bring the Spirit in low, between the buildings?"

The captain pointed at Britt, "Ask him yourself."

Lee'Sahr looked at Britt and raised an eyebrow. He sighed and counted out the difficulties on his fingers, "Oh Gods. We'd need to break dock as soon as the attempt starts, come straight here and hover about fifty feet above the roof of the Tronkamer. They have no anti-

aircraft turrets there, so we should be safe enough for a few minutes at least. Then it would just be a case of dropping a ladder, hoping that he's not unconscious so he can climb up under his own steam without being carried, and getting out of Long Pig airspace before a patrol arrives. Friendly guards or not, someone's bound to notice an airship floating over a prison and sound the alert." He turned to the captain, "I think we might have to make use of those slug-throwers that you didn't want me to install."

"We need to make sure that we've got the rest of the new crew on board before we make the attempt, and the fewer people who know what's happening the better. Not that we'd be short of volunteers, but I think that we should at least make the effort to be stealthy, it'll be good practice if nothing else. Britt, see if we're waiting for anyone, then we'll get started."

He levered himself upright, saluted and left the room, leaving the two women alone to discuss the finer points of the plan. He made his way up to the bridge and leant heavily on the ship-wide Intercomm, "All hands, this is Mr. Britt, we will, within the hour, be making headway home to Sidi Ferruch. Between now and then I will require details of all the new crew that have signed on for our jolly little endeavour and whether they are aboard now or joining us later. There follows a special announcement for those of you who have never flown with us before. Just to let you know that there are two ways of doing things whilst you are with us, the captain's way, which will be passed down to you gospel via my good self, and the way that will make your last memory be of your screams as you plummet through the clouds and impact with great force upon the surface of the briny deep. If you are very unlucky you may even live long enough to see the first gull that lands on your head to peck out your eyes. Message ends," he released the transmit button, turned to Landry and asked grandly, "Could you get me a glass of water? I'm a martyr to dehydration you know."

Dorleith and Lee'Sahr made their way from the Spirit's berth into the backstreets of Long Pig. They both carried backpacks that were full of all the tools required for a successful prisoner extraction.

"So, I never asked you how you know Baju-Merah," the captain looked questioningly at Lee'Sahr.

She grinned, broadly, "Within two hours of first landing at the station, I'd been arrested, and he was the arresting officer."

Dorleith stopped and put her hand on her companion's shoulder, "And would it be rude of me to ask exactly what you were charged with?"

"Not that it makes a difference, but I got divorced."

"I know that a lot of the Free Trade zones have some strange laws, but I've not heard of one where divorce is punishable by incarceration. Divorce usually implies some sort of freedom," the captain laughed, but she noticed that the look on Lee'Sahr's face was completely serious and her glee faded, "I'm sorry, please go on."

"It happened about ten years ago, my father had died in the Spider war and my mother and I were travelling by airship between Canberra and New Pompeii. A couple of hours into the flight, I think we were just off the coast of Malaysia, we were boarded by slavers. They were totally ruthless, killed all the male passengers and gave the crew the choice of joining them or jumping overboard. Unfortunately there weren't enough volunteers that were willing to turn pirate to continue to crew the ship, so they put them all to death anyway," she looked blankly at the passers-by, casually going about their business, "I can still sometimes hear the screams they let out as they fell. You never forget something like that."

"You don't need to carry on."

"No, it's fine, it's good to tell someone actually, someone who listens. They loaded us like cattle onto their ship, it was even smaller than the Spirit and we were pressed together in the hold for two days with little more than a cup of stale water each. They took a couple of girls that first night, we heard them screaming and screaming. Then the screams got quieter, and then they were gone. They never came back, we presumed they'd thrown them overboard too, once they'd finished with them. We heard some gunfire the next day and a lot of shouting, there weren't any new prisoners though, so it was either the crew fighting amongst themselves, or they'd tried to take another ship and failed. Eventually, they set us down on an island, well, it was more of a volcano really in the middle of a huge lake, and left us there. There were other women on the island; some had been there for years. They explained to us that those that couldn't be ransomed were going to be sold as slaves, if they were lucky."

"And if you were unlucky?"

"Well, if you were a little bit unlucky and you didn't sell in the first few weeks, you'd be left to fend for yourself or rot on the island for the rest of your natural life, such as it was. If you were very unlucky, and it was usually the bigger girls that were very unlucky... Well, the guards that patrolled the far banks of the lake had dogs, which needed to be fed. At least that's what they told me when they took my mother."

The captain paled and shook her head, "I'm sorry... How did you escape from the island?"

"I didn't, within a week I was taken to the slave markets and sold to a Malaysian merchant. He had what he called a 'palace' in the Malacca Straits, I called it the 'Prison on Stilts'. One day he brought in some guy in an expensive looking jacket, someone drew some strange symbols on the back of my hands and there was a celebration. Turns out that that was my wedding day, it also turns out that being married was a lot like being a slave, except you don't have to clean the communal toilet by hand anymore, I certainly didn't get beaten any less."

"So, that was who you divorced?"

"Yeah, I took it for a couple of months, then when I really couldn't stand him fumbling all over me for another second, I bashed him over the head with a big jade statue of the Buddha and ran. I made it to the international docking mast at Kuala Lumpur and had stowed aboard a private airship bound for Long Pig before he woke up. Unfortunately, the report that he lodged with The Company, of a mentally deranged wife who had bludgeoned her loving husband almost to death reached here before I did and I was arrested the first time I got caught by a random security sweep."

"Do they do random sweeps here?" Dorleith looked around nervously, imagining what was likely to happen if they were caught by a security team with a bag full of smoke bombs and explosives.

Lee'Sahr's face dropped guiltily, "Um, no. They don't. Actually I got arrested because I got into a fight, in a bar, over an unpaid bill. A couple of punches got thrown and the owner called security. Next thing I know, big hands were grabbing my shoulders and Baju-Merah was lifting me bodily into the air, legs waving, the whole nine yards."

"And your story doesn't end with you being shipped back to your husband because?"

"Because, one of the few things that living with my husband taught me was how to swear colourfully and gynaecologically in Malay, I threw every word I knew at him. When he'd stopped laughing enough to cuff me and get me to his skimmer I explained the situation to him."

"And he believed you?'

She paused for a moment and turned around in a slow circle, making a show of looking up and down. "Well, you'll notice I'm not in the Tronkamer or back with my husband. In fact we've been friends ever since. He put a report in that I'd fallen whilst being taken into custody and broken my neck. It cost him a bottle of brandy to get the guy who runs the recycling centre to sign the forms saying that he'd deposited my body and it had been processed for transplants, which I still owe him funnily enough, and that's it, here we all are."

"So that's what he wanted the brandy for," remarked the captain, and seeing Lee'Sahr's puzzled expression, she continued, "I caught Britt liberating a bottle of incredibly fine brandy from the stores at Sidi Ferruch, he said that he owed it to you. Not that you'll be collecting it now, if his state this morning was anything to go by."

A smile broke across the privateer's face, but it soon faltered as they rounded the corner and entered the wide public square that held the Tronkamer. A small knot of station security had surrounded two skimmers that were parked just outside the main gate, they were all armed and seemed to be on a high state of alert.

"Buah Zakar!" spat Lee'Sahr under her breath, she turned to her captain, "things just got a lot more complicated. Those skimmers belong to the station commander and his personal guard."

"Do you think he's come to gloat?"

"Probably, that fits his personality. it would make sense to wait until he leaves."

"Although it would make sense to wait, we're not going to. If I know Britt, he's got the engines spun up already and station traffic control is asking him why he's straining their docking umbilicals. In fact..." the captain activated the short range communicator on her wrist, "Mr. Britt, are you ready?"

There was a second's pause until Britt's voice crackled through the speaker. "Aye Ma'am, in fact, we're already in the air."

Dorleith looked sideways at Lee'Sahr, who raised her eyebrows and shook her head. "I'm afraid that there's been a complication, the station commander is visiting the facility." The captain winced and held her wrist away from her face as Britt loudly made his feelings known, "well, I thought I'd better let you know that your dwell time at target may be somewhat reduced, it will be an 'in and out' mission rather than the leisurely departure you were expecting. I would also appreciate it if the slug-throwers were warmed up, I think we might be on the verge of offending some people. Get into a position where you can see the Tronkamer and watch for smoke, that's your signal. Out." She turned towards Lee'Sahr, "so, have you decided? 'Boom or Bust'?" her quizzical expression was returned as if a mirror had been put between them, "actually, you know this place better than me, and you have more explosives experience at the moment so you can be 'Boom'. Give me five minutes to get into position and then crack open the drunk tanks as planned."

"Right, I'm presuming that makes you 'Bust' then, and what exactly does that entail?"

The captain undid three of her shirt buttons and adjusted her décolletage for maximum effect, "I'm going to distract as many of the guards as I can."

"Well, if you're going in the front, you should probably take this," she threw a small pearlescent ball, which the captain snatched expertly out of the air, "it's a lock-pick, just hold it up to the lock and squeeze it. There'll be some pretty flashing lights and a few musical notes, then the lock should open."

"Those Torkans are amazing aren't they, I wonder how it works?"

"I don't know, and neither would a Torkan most likely, I got it from a very rich and very secretive Kalibri that I once did a huge favour for," she looked at the captain who had raised her eyebrows, "and no, you don't want to know what kind of favour I did for her. The only thing you do need to know is that it has never failed me yet, although you sometimes need to activate it a couple of times if the lock is being difficult."

Dorleith put the lock-pick into her pocket, carefully sealed the flap and put on her game face, "OK, five minutes, maximum confusion and minimum casualties."

Lee'Sahr saluted, made her way to the back of the compound and tried to find somewhere out of sight, but where she could still see the flat roofs of the drunk tanks. She ducked into the entryway of a run-down residential block that served to hide her from any casual observers passing by. Keeping half an eye on the courtyard she opened her pack and took out a roto-limpet. She pointed the camera on the small explosive device at the roof of the Tronkamer and took a picture. As the image appeared on the tiny display screen, she touched it to indicate where the explosive should attach itself, selected 'High Explosive - Remote Detonate' from the options menu and threw the device into the air. As it left her hand, small solid blades sprang out from its equator and started to rapidly spin, propelling it towards the building. The bomb impacted within a few inches of its intended target with a metallic crunch as the blades bit into the stonework and held it fast. She repeated the process another five times, substituting 'Thick Smoke' for 'High Explosive' on two of the devices, then sat back on her haunches and watched her chronometer, the detonator in one hand, and an ion stunner in the other.

Meanwhile, the captain had walked around to the main entrance and was busily scanning the surrounding buildings with a magnifying field viewer. She turned from admiring a particularly wonderful example of pre-war architecture to be confronted by an incredibly close-up view of a station security guard's visor.

"You can't be here Ma'am," he announced as she lowered the viewer, "this is a secure area."

"Oh! I am sorry, I appear to be lost. I'm looking for..." she made a show of trying to hold the viewer under her arm and rooting through her pack, "I have the address here somewhere. Would you mind just holding this?" She tossed the soldier a handful of her more intimate clothing items and smiled sweetly. "I'm a dancer, there's a bar around here somewhere that's advertising for new dancers that provide, you know, extras. I don't suppose you know where that is do you?"

"Ah, no, I..." he looked, as uncomfortably as he could whilst still wearing a full-face visor, at his comrades for support, most of them were too busy laughing to be of any assistance, but the two closest started to make their way over. Dorleith chose that moment to drop the viewer behind her, as she turned to retrieve it, she theatrically kicked it even further away, took half a dozen stumbling steps towards it and bent over from the waist to pick it up from the dust. One of the nearer soldiers rushed to help her.

"Allow me," He said, grabbing hold of the device and pretended to check it for damage, whilst stealing a long, lascivious glance down the front of her blouse.

"I've seen most of the Aligned Races naked at one point or another soldier, but none of them keep their sensory equipment down there."

The soldier looked up guiltily and handed the viewer to her by its long strap, just as four loud explosions echoed from the far end of the Tronkamer, followed by dense clouds of billowing smoke. Immediately, a strident alarm started up. The soldier turned towards the main gates and started to run, Dorleith swung the viewer around her head and hit him on the back of his neck, at the point where his helmet didn't quite meet his back armour. He grunted loudly and instantly fell to the ground like a stone, she wasted no time removing his jacket and helmet and donning them herself.

The smoke was much thicker than she had expected, and although the respirator built into the helmet kept most of it out of her lungs, the visibility was still reduced to a few feet. Offering a silent prayer to the playful feline God of lost causes, she made her way past the guard house and tried to open a large door marked 'Authorised Personnel Only'. A bright, red light and a very negative sounding noise was the only result. She took out the lock-pick, held it to the door and squeezed it gently. It played a selection of twelve or so musical notes in time with the flashing multi-coloured lights that skittered across its surface. The notes briefly quickened in tempo and then stopped, there was a click and the door slid open. Looking at the device with a new found respect, she placed it carefully back in her pocket and slid stealthily into the clearer air of what proved to be a store room. The shelves were piled high with various boxes of rations and cartons of water. Outside she could hear the muffled sounds of the soldiers trying to regain control of the situation, she strained her ears momentarily to see if she could hear anything of interest and almost jumped out of her skin as Lee'Sahr's voice came from her wrist Intercomm.

"Captain, I believe that the guards have their hands full rounding up the escapees, and if Britt hasn't fallen asleep then he should be overhead within minutes, now would be a good time to complete our mission. Where are you?"

Once her heart had returned to its more usual home in her chest, she explained where she was and waited until there was an urgent knock on the door. She activated the door and just had time to duck before her comrade fired at her with the stunner, "Gods! It's me!" She yelled, yanking open the visor of the stolen helmet and pointing at her face.

"Sorry, honest mistake. I think he's through here," she said, indicating the door at the far end of the dimly lit room.

"Wait, I'll go. I've got a better chance of blending in," she zipped the guard's jacket up to the neck and pushed her way through into the kitchen. Seeing the kitchen staff cowering behind their workstations she held up her hand, "Everyone stay calm, there has been a small incident that will be rectified momentarily, we have come to check on the prisoner," she scanned the room, looking unsuccessfully for an exit that would lead to Baju-Merah, "where is the prisoner's cell?" she noticed that a number of the kitchen staff were staring at her incredulously, "I'm new," she explained.

A loud explosion from outside galvanised one of the chefs into action, and he pointed at a nondescript section of wall between two freezer units, "You just push it."

She walked over to the wall and gently pushed it with both hands, there was a gentle click as it moved into a recess and slid open. She looked over as she heard the unmistakable sounds of a stunner on rapid fire and cooking pots being knocked over by newly unconscious kitchen staff. She looked at Lee'Sahr accusingly.

"He was going for a communicator." She pointed at a portly chef lying face-down on the ground.

Dorleith followed her gaze and sighed. "It's a spatula. Very different from a communicator, unless you thought he was trying to communicate with an attack-trained trifle. And the others?"

She shrugged, "Heat of the moment. Anyway, let's do what we came for and see if Britt can get us out of here in one piece."

They both entered the passageway and had only taken a few steps before the door slid closed behind them, plunging them into darkness. The captain fumbled to turn on her torch, which outlined the dusty corridor with a pale, yellow glow. They followed its length and, turning a sharp corner, they came upon a heavy steel door with a slot halfway up just large enough for a plate to be passed through.

The captain inspected the door closely. "We may have a problem. There isn't a lock."

"What do you mean that there -" Lee'Sahr felt around the edges of the door. "There doesn't seem to be any mechanism at all, is this even a functioning door? Do you have any cutting equipment?"

"No, just a couple of roto-limpets." She emptied out her pack onto the floor and held out the two small devices.

Lee'Sahr took the explosives and used their menus to set a timer for ten seconds, activated the spinning blades and jammed them into the door as close to the frame as she could. Banging repeatedly on the hatch she shouted to Baju-Merah, "Get away from the door!" she grabbed Dorleith's hand and started to sprint back down the corridor. They reached the door that led back into the kitchen with seconds to spare, but there was no obvious way to open it from the inside, "Does no-one in this Gods forsaken place know how doors are supposed to work? You traditionally have a handle, so you can open them." The blast from the exploding roto-limpets chose that moment to hit them and they both stumbled forward into the unyielding door, their ears ringing.

The echoes bounced backwards and forwards through the dust filled corridor for what seemed like hours before they finally died away, The captain looked at Lee'Sahr and raised her eyebrows, she replied by nodding and brushing some of the pale dirt from her jacket. They rushed back to the cell in time to see Baju-Merah inspecting the hole where his door used to be. He greeted them with a broad grin.

Dorleith checked him for injuries, "Are you OK?"

"What?" he shouted, gently hitting the side of his head with the heel of his hand, "I can't hear you, I can just hear the sea."

She grabbed his chin and moved his head from side to side, small trickles of blood were coming from both of his ears.

"Looks like your eardrums have been damaged, maybe burst," mouthed Lee'Sahr theatrically, "we need to get you out of here."

"What?"

She grabbed his sleeve, pointed at the cell door and mimicked the motion of running with her index and middle fingers. He nodded and moved forwards, just as two armed guards entered the room.

"Stay where you are! You are both under arrest."

"Both?" mouthed Lee'Sahr, she slowly turned around, but the captain was nowhere to be seen.

"Turn around and face the wall," the guard turned to his compatriot, "check the other door, and see if there are any more of them."

The guard had just turned the corner that led back to the kitchens when he came across the captain with her stunner drawn. With no time to dodge, he threw himself bodily at her, but she stepped deftly to one side and discharged the weapon into his temple. He was unconscious, but still shaking, when he hit the floor. She emerged into the cell and was presented with the sight of the remaining guard standing behind Lee'Sahr, with his forearm across her throat and a compression pistol that alternated between her and Baju-Merah's heads.

"Put the gun down and no-one will have to get hurt, I don't want to hurt anyone, the station manager is here, and I can't just let you go. He'll lock me in here and brick up both of the doors. Why did you have to do this today?" the guard had a pained expression; he shifted his aim to include Dorleith.

"Let them both go," she requested calmly, raising the stunner.

"I really can't, he'll kill me, we've got orders," he hid his head behind Lee'Sahr's so that the only thing visible was his pistol.

The two women looked at each other and nodded. There was a moment's pause, then the captain's stunner charge caught Lee'Sahr full in the stomach, rendering both her and the guard who was holding her unconscious. The captain rushed over, checked her pulse and turned to Baju-Merah, "Can you hear me?" he indicated that he could, but only just, "we have a ship that is hopefully hovering overhead by now, if you can carry her to it without any of us dying, then I'll offer you the position of Chief of Security."

"Done!" he shouted, still suffering from the loud ringing in his ears. He lifted Lee'Sahr onto his shoulders and picked up her gun, "let's go."

"You mean, Let's go... Captain." She stared at him impassively.

He looked back at her for a second, sighed and bowed as well as he could with the unconscious girl on his back. Then he jogged through the still open cell door towards the guard post. Dorleith prodded the guard with her foot until he emitted a loud snore, and then followed him, closing the heavy door behind her. They saw no-one on the short run, even the guard post itself was empty, but a quick look at the monitors made it obvious that the guards had almost got the escaping drunks under control when the Spirit had arrived. The ship was hovering just out of range of the small arms fire from the guards but was, in return, peppering random buildings with rounds from the new slug throwers which was successful in making even the bravest of the prison's guards dive for cover.

The captain activated her wrist Intercomm. "Britt, time to come and get us."

"Aye Ma'am, and where exactly would you like picking up from? Unfortunately there is not a large choice of clear spaces."

"Have the bags been holed Mr. Britt?"

"Funny you should mention that Ma'am, as it happens no, they have not. Despite our lengthy impression of a sitting duck."

"They're not trying to bring you down, they're trying to make it look like they're trying to bring you down. Remember what Lee'Sahr said about them wanting to let Baju-Merah go?"

"Aye, a theory that I was not, until this point, looking forward to putting to the test."

"There's access to the roof of the guard post, get as low as you can and drop the ladder from the ventral lock, Captain out," she climbed the metal steps in the corner of the room and flipped open the trapdoor at the top. The sudden increase in the volume of the fire-fight momentarily took her by surprise. She looked up and was comforted by the sight of the Spirit slowly getting closer. As she watched, a small personnel hatch opened and a rope ladder unrolled towards her. Climbing onto the roof, she called down to Baju-Merah that the coast was clear. Unfortunately, this gave away her position to the guards in the courtyard and shots immediately began to ricochet from the various pipes and vents surrounding her position. She helped drag the still snoring girl through the hatch and took pot-shots with her stunner whilst her new security chief made his way onto the roof. Britt guided the Spirit down expertly until the base of the rope-ladder lightly kissed the gravel on the roof.

"Go!" cried the captain, "I'll cover you."

He picked up Lee'Sahr once more and started to climb up towards the waiting airship, occasionally turning to fire at a guard that was getting too accurate.

The captain clambered onto the bottom rung of the ladder, wrapped an arm around the rope and contacted Britt again, "OK, we're on, get us out of here, but don't go mad with the throttles, we're still outside."

The noise from the engines steadily increased and they started to rise, slowly at first, but constantly gaining speed. As she looked up, she saw Baju-Merah throw Lee'Sahr bodily up through the open hatchway and then clamber through himself. His grinning face appeared at the open hatch and he held out his hand. She looked down and could just make out the station manager getting out of his skimmer, where he had been bundled when the first explosions were heard, and grabbing a long rifle from the nearest guard. She turned and started to climb, the acceleration and turbulence increasing the difficulty to the point where her arm muscles were in danger of bursting the seams of her stolen jacket. At the halfway point she chanced a look behind her, she saw that the station manager was staring at her through the digital sight of the rifle. Her Intercomm crackled into life.

"Captain, with the greatest respect, if you could move it along a little, we have three Air Cadre skimmers inbound, they're seconds away from weapons range and I can't guarantee that they'll be as accommodating as our friends below."

She was inches away from the outstretched hand of her newest crewman when she had the feeling that her leg had burst into flames. The sound of the shot reached her ears a fraction of a second later, just as she let go of the top rung and started to fall.

Chapter 11 : Civilisation

The skimmer came in low from the east. It had latched on to the traffic control guidance beam five miles out and was riding it between the tall towers that marked the outskirts of the currently fog-bound Merseyside Free Trade Area.

"Private skimmer 16879, this is MFTA Traffic Control, please stay tight on the beam, you are approaching a heavy traffic area and the weather conditions are currently categorised as hazardous. Engage automatic pilot at your earliest convenience."

"Confirmed MFTA control, switching to automatic," the pilot winced slightly as he flipped the switch that tied the skimmer's autopilot to the beam, the ship dropped six inches as the traffic control construct took over, but the contents of his stomach stayed exactly where they were. He engaged the shipboard Intercomm pre-empting the complaints from the passenger compartment, "Sorry about that Commander, local traffic control has taken over and is guiding us to the pad now. We should be there in less than a minute." The grumbling reply indicated that his passengers weren't completely happy, but weren't blaming him at that particular moment in time.

He flexed his shoulders, released his grip on the control stick and settled back into his chair. The skimmer had dropped to an altitude of fifty feet and was still making brisk headway. The huge buildings and chimneys that lined the route either side of him stretched hundreds of feet up and then disappeared into the fog. They were covered with brightly lit adverts for various Company services which coloured the mist with a rainbow of neon pinks, greens, yellows and reds. If you wanted a new pair of high resolution eyes, or had a sudden fetish for growing completely synthetic broccoli then all you needed to do was to Cloud them your details and a representative would get right back to you to negotiate price and delivery.

The formerly cluttered view through the canopy suddenly gave way to a wide grey languid river on his left, which they spent the next few seconds following until the huge port facility itself came into view. It was four square miles of thick concrete and steel that expanded from the mainland in the east, out into the Irish Sea. It was braced a hundred feet in the air on massive legs that were sunk a quarter of a mile into the seabed and all around its perimeter were repair bays, control rooms and holding areas of every shape and size.

The skimmer sped into the tangle of struts and pipes that criss-crossed the underside of the main landing pad and slowly coasted to a halt below a security checkpoint. The on-duty construct contacted the pilot who confirmed that he was dropping off private passengers on a pleasure trip and would be vacating their airspace almost immediately. There was a short pause, then a huge steel door opened in the ceiling that completely dwarfed the skimmer, they passed through, and landed exactly where directed on the apron of the main dock.

The pilot powered down the engines and performed the post flight checks. Looking out of the window, he spotted a construct striding purposefully towards them. "Commander? We're about to have a visitor, I believe that it's a customs official."

"Thank you pilot, feel free to lift as soon as we are at a respectable distance, then make your way back to West-One, pick up ex-Commander O'Shea and transport him to the main brig at the Roost. If you neglect to allow the guards to strap him into his seat and happen to come across some particularly turbulent air on your way back to the Roost, no one will blame you." The pilot's reply was lost in the loud metallic rapping on the rear door. Commander Mal pointed meaningfully to their prisoner, "A single word from you and I swear by the God of glittering razor sharp daggers that your throat will be slit before you finish it."

The prisoner looked at the serrated combat knife that Zatch had lifted half out of its sheath and nodded. The knife was replaced with an audible click.

Mal walked over to the rear door, turned to order that E-Yain's handcuffs should be removed, and opened it. He shivered momentarily as the freezing mist leaked into the temperature controlled bay and examined the construct that was stood outside holding a data tablet.

"I am a representative of the Merseyside Free Trade Area Customs Department," pronounced the construct grandly, "may I ask the reason for, and intended length of, your stay?"

"We are here to sample the legendary leisure resources and fine restaurants that your wonderful City has to offer; we should be here for no more than a few days."

The construct looked at him with an air of genuine disbelief, "Yes, quite," it replied as it looked at the four men in turn, "I have scanned your retina patterns and you will be glad to know that none of you are currently subject to any outstanding Company warrants. Do you have any concealed weapons?" they looked at each other and then shook their heads warily, "in that case may I suggest that you visit one of our many fine armourers situated on the Northern perimeter wall before entering the Greater City Area. Some of our residents have a rather free and easy interpretation of the ancient adage that, 'All property is theft.'"

"I think we should be able to look after ourselves. May we go?"

"As you wish," the construct paused to convey something approaching sarcasm, "Sir. I am obliged to inform you that during your time under our jurisdiction, your whereabouts will be constantly monitored, and you will not be allowed to board any interplanetary craft without first passing an additional customs check."

"Understood, if that is all?"

"Yes, I'll let you get on your way. If you have any questions, please feel free to consult one of the city's many Company data terminals."

"We will, definitely. If we could just…" Mal's fists clenched so tightly that his knuckles started to turn white. Sembhee walked towards the door and put his hand on his commander's shoulder.

"What my friend is trying to say is that we have an appointment with some young ladies and we are in danger of being late. You wouldn't want to be the reason that we had to keep them waiting would you?"

The construct considered this for a moment, "No, of course not, I apologise, please enjoy your stay." it turned stiffly and started to walk back to the customs station. It had gone a matter of yards before its head smoothly rotated through 180 degrees and it addressed them once again. "There's a new Kalibri ship due to launch in a few minutes, if you've never seen that before I'd suggest that you take a look, it's very impressive. Just stay out of the lit area. You don't want to get sucked in by the gravity wash."

They watched as the construct disappeared back into the mist. Na-Thon threw the bag of credits to his commander and picked up his pack, "So, what now sir?"

Mal opened the pack and took out a stack of a thousand credits, "You three each take one of these for expenses, I'll take the remaining two thousand and we'll go and find the Medic that tried to kill me," he turned to the sorrowful looking E-Yain, "it will be easier if you lead us to her, stay with us whilst we transact our business and then we'll release you just before we leave. However, I would lose precisely no sleep whatsoever if you ended up floating face down in the river in several pieces, which is exactly what will happen if I think you're trying to cross me. Do you understand?"

The prisoner nodded and rubbed his wrists to try and get rid of the red marks from the cuffs, "May I speak?" the commander nodded, "I'll take you to her and she'll say the same as I did, we were offered a substantial amount of money from an unknown source to get a patrol to come to your perimeter station so that the construct could complete some kind of mission, no-one was supposed to get hurt, I swear."

"How do you know the construct's mission wasn't to kill me?"

He thought for a moment and replied, "Well, I suppose I don't, exactly, but if it was I hope that Haze had the sense to get paid up front. It just seems to me like a lot of firepower to kill one man."

Zatch grabbed the prisoner by the throat and effortlessly lifted him bodily off the ground, "I hope you're not implying that Lord Mal'Ak-hai, commander of the Pewter Guard and saviour of Rustholme is an ordinary man?"

He shook his head as well as he could and croaked, "No!"

He hit the ground coughing and stumbled to his knees. The commander raised his eyebrows, "Thank you Zatch, but can we try and keep him alive at least until we find someone else who can be equally helpful?"

The guard nodded, then scowled at E-Yain. "Watch yourself, bandit."

"If we've all finished bonding, let's go." They filed out of the rear door and made their way across the hardstanding. The skimmer lifted and disappeared back down through the security station the way it had entered. They had almost reached the entrance to the passenger lifts when a keening alarm echoed from speakers all around them. Mal and Na-Thon both reached instinctively for their pistols, but E-Yain held out his hands and shouted, "It's only a launch warning! It must be the Kalibri ship that the construct was talking about," he pointed to an area of the pad that was suddenly delineated by flashing red markers.

As they watched, a small ship, only sixty or so feet high, started to lift into the air, propelled by its anti-grav boosters. It resembled nothing more than a squat pepper pot with three thin, concentric glass rings around its circumference. When it had reached a predetermined height, the rings started to spin in multiple directions. Their accelerating motion cleared the fog in their immediate vicinity and a low hum, that could be felt long before it was heard, flooded the area. The rings started to glow, and within seconds the pepper pot ship appeared to be surrounded by nested spheres of energy.

"Cavorite Drive!" shouted Sembhee over the insistent hum, which was threatening to loosen his teeth. "I've only ever read about them, but if I'm right, we're about to be treated to the sight of hundreds of tonnes of metal falling upwards into the sky." He crossed his arms and settled in to enjoy the rest of the show.

As they watched, a sparkling ball of light sprang into existence directly above the ship and started to grow. Arcs of intense, almost blinding white light jumped between it and the blurred rings. The ball rapidly changed through a range of seemingly random sizes, until there was a momentary shock of heat and the sparkling ball winked out, to be instantly replaced with what could only be described as a tiny sun, complete with solar flares and sunspots.

The ship lifted into the air, slowly at first, but steadily accelerating until it disappeared into the clouds above them.

They stood there for a second with their mouths open, until Na-Thon broke the silence. "What just happened? Where were the rocket boosters?"

Sembhee shook his head, "As I understand it, they don't use them. The spinning disks sort of mask them from planetary gravity."

Mal turned towards him, "And the thing that looked like a sun?"

"Was, in fact, a sun; an artificially created sun, which has its own gravity, which the rings don't mask the ship from."

"So the ship falls towards it?"

"And because the sun is created from inside the ship, the sun moves with it, maintaining a constant distance. The ship keeps falling towards an object that always stays the same distance away. They steer the ship by literally moving the sun and alter the speed by changing its mass."

Mal looked up into the rapidly encroaching mist with a mixture of wonder and disbelief, hoping to catch a final glimpse of the rapidly ascending alien ship. A momentary break in the cloud gave him a view of a light slightly brighter than the surrounding stars, which faded within seconds, and was gone. He took a deep breath to clear his head and turned to the prisoner, "Right, let's get this over with, lead the way."

They entered the lifts and descended to ground level. The doors opened onto a wide, incredibly busy, concourse, the bright lights a stark change from the fogbound city outside. All around them were a dizzying array of signs in various human and alien languages, directing visitors to transport links, translation services and currency convertors.

The bandit pointed to a sign over a small door, "There, Hightown Exit, that's where Haze should be. We'll need to get some transport though; you wouldn't want to be walking through that kind of neighbourhood if you didn't have to," he looked at the Pewter Guardsmen, who had all instinctively put their hands on their weapons, "no matter how well armed you happened to be."

Pulling their coats around them they left the warm, dry, terminal and stepped out into the damp air. They were immediately surrounded by the living refuse that congregated around almost every transport hub on every inhabited planet in the system. The hawkers and traders, the girls who cared less about your species than they did about the amount of credits you carried, the guides that would lead your party down a darkened alley and emerge alone with your wallet, eyeballs and fingertips, and the preachers, there were always preachers, trying to convince you that the only way to avoid eternal torment was to put a coin in the slot or buy a plastic statue of whatever deity they were representing that day - filled with the breath of a priest who had known the god or saint in question since they had been a child.

They managed to sidestep most of them, and waved the business end of a compression pistol at the ones that wouldn't take no for an answer. They left a sea of suspicious faces in their wake as they reached the relative safety of the taxi rank.

As befit an area whose main form of income was tourism, the taxis were fashioned into the image of a 19th century horse and carriage, the magnificently muscled chrome horse turned and regarded them with its glowing blue eyes, "Where can I take you gentlemen?"

E-Yain pushed his way apologetically in front of the commander, "Northern Port, Hightown, the warehouses behind the main ramps."

"Of course sir, if you would all care to board when you are ready."

"But there are only four seats?" Mal indicated the five members of the party with a sweep of his hand.

"Ah, yes, that was very remiss of me, " the light in the horse's eyes faded for a split second and with the noise of protesting gears, the carriage lengthened by three feet. The light returned and the horse shook itself, as if the reconfiguration had been tiring. "Perhaps I should leave myself as a six seater, there's been a marked increase in the volume of customers recently." The horse looked sideways at itself in the window of the terminal and frowned slightly. "Do you think this makes my back end look big?"

They took their seats in silence and the taxi started to accelerate smoothly along the road. Its fine equine head turned to look at Mal, "So, are you gentlemen visiting the Big Mufta for business or pleasure?"

"Big Mufta?"

"The Merseyside Free Trade Area sir, A lot of the locals like to think of it as some kind of Old West border town, I guess we taxis don't help, twenty thousand of us clip-clopping around the place looking for all the world like horses."

"I guess it doesn't. How long until we get to Hightown?"

"It should be less than a quarter of an hour sir. Is everyone warm enough? It's going to be a cold night; I should turn on the heaters," multiple vents opened up on the taxi's flanks and hot, sweet smelling air blew around them.

The tall buildings gave way to single storey warehouses and temporary buildings. Sheet-steel huts and shanties made from scavenged bulkheads and cargo containers littered the area. The loud rhythmic sound of the taxi's steel hooves on the roadway brought many of their occupants out into the open.

Na-Thon looked through his field viewer at their audience, "It's all children, the sick and old folks. I can't see any capable adults around."

"You won't sir, these people are mostly refugees from over the water, a lot of them are Americans who caught the last few airships to Ireland, rather than be left in the ruins of the USA, then they got their viewpoint changed when the crop plague hit and moved again. If you live out here in Hightown, you either work in the Big Mufta or you starve."

"Or you become a bandit," mumbled E-Yain under his breath.

"I'm sorry sir, but standard Company policy precludes me from mentioning wholesale banditry and/or brigandry as viable career choices," one of the taxi's eyelids dipped in a barely perceptible, but definite, wink, "while we're on the subject gentlemen, I believe these people with drawn guns emerging from that compound are here to welcome you."

As the taxi rolled to a halt, E-Yain jumped out waving his hands, "It's OK, they're with me! They're here to see Haze, don't shoot."

The nearest man waved him closer, the barrel of his gun never straying far from the centre of E-Yain's face. He produced a small box from his pocket and pushed the end of it into the bandit's forearm with an audible click.

E-Yain immediately sprung back with a yelp and rubbed at the tiny spot of blood that welled up on his arm, "Was there any need for that?"

The butt of the gun hit him full in the chest and he fell to the ground, winded. Mal and the other guardsmen all drew their weapons simultaneously and pointed them at each of the armed men in turn. Despite the chill, beads of sweat rolled down the commander's face as his mind raced to find a way out of this particular standoff without a major loss of life, especially if one of those lives turned out to be his. Luckily, a female voice from behind the wall of armed men decided the issue for him.

"Can we all lower our weapons please? There are enough sick and injured people here without us intentionally adding more to the total," the owner of the almost feline Scottish voice walked over to the man who had taken the blood sample, he raised the unit so that she could see the flashing green indicator light on its screen, "it turns out that he is one of us, fancy that." Leaning down, she offered her hand to the still choking bandit, "Welcome Brother, I'm afraid Scut is new, he didn't recognise you, although as you can see, we have many new recruits flocking to join us every day, it's difficult to keep up," her voice took on a harder edge, "did some of you not hear the part where I said lower your weapons?"

Slowly and uneasily, the men relaxed and the tense situation was over. She was tall, around five feet eleven, with long blonde hair tied into a low ponytail and bright blue eyes part hidden behind a pair of tactical goggles. She wore a dusty leather coat that was only kept from touching the floor by pair of high heeled knee-boots. She confidently approached the Pewter Guards, despite the fact that their weapons were still well and truly drawn, "My name is Haze, I am the leader of our happy little League. And you are..?"

The hand that she offered to Mal to have him shake was taken, turned and kissed. "I am Mal, this is Nat, Sem and Zat. We wondered if you had a few minutes to talk about a business proposition?"

"For a second there I thought that you were going to ask if I had a few minutes to talk about our Lord Iesu Christi." She laughed.

"Who? Is he some local Baron that we're going to need to pay off if we want to do business with you?"

The volume of her laughter increased until tears started to form in the corners of her eyes, "Not exactly, no. He's from one of the old religions that got turned on its head when the Aligned Races arrived on our doorsteps unannounced. Anyway, enough of this fascinatingly philosophical discussion, let's see if we can throw some food together and get to know each other a little better shall we?" she turned and disappeared back towards the large crowd of still suspicious League members.

It was only then that Mal realised that he still had his compression pistol in his hand and that it was pointed at her gently swinging ponytail. He looked at it as if he had never seen it before and replaced it in its holster almost guiltily, then motioned for his team to do the same. They climbed down from the taxi and started to follow her.

"Excuse me! There's the small matter of fourteen credits." Called the taxi.

Mal turned and smiled, "I do apologise great and noble steed, please, take twenty. Buy yourself something nice." The taxi turned its head and gingerly took the twenty credit note out of his hand with its teeth, and swallowed it without chewing. Mal frowned, "I really don't want to know how they empty the money out at the end of your shift."

"No, you don't. If you do manage to make it out of here alive, please call the port, ask for me by name and I'll pick you up. I'd be interested in finding out how you get on. The name's Demoso."

"Well, thank you Demoso, we'll probably see you tomorrow."

The taxi turned around in a large, languid circle and trotted back towards the city, gently whistling cowboy tunes as it went.

The group squared their shoulders and moved purposefully toward the men that they had just been aiming their guns at.

"Try to look business-like, but menacing," whispered Sembhee.

"We are business-like, but menacing," replied Zatch.

"Then it shouldn't take too much effort on our part should it?"

E-Yain slipped through the crowd and into the warehouse without incident, but it seemed that every step the rest of them took brought them up against a stony face, or a rigid shoulder, or a tripping foot. Their progress became slower and slower, they had already lost Haze in the crowd and were in danger of letting their tame bandit get away. Just when Mal had decided that he had had enough, and was ready to draw his pistol and let off a couple of rounds into the air to see if that would disperse the crowd, they dispersed of their own accord in all directions. They were left virtually alone, in what appeared to be a jury-rigged hospital ward. E-Yain was nowhere to be seen.

"Damn!" shouted the commander, "we have to find him, if the Baroness finds out that I've done exactly what she warned me against, she"ll…"

"The Baroness?" interjected Haze, walking back into the room as she took off her coat and threw it onto one of the unoccupied beds, revealing a tight leather ship-suit underneath, "that sounds very grand. Is it this Baroness that has a proposition for me, or is it you?"

"A little of both really," smiled Mal, embarrassed that he had almost been caught out, "you performed a service for a certain party a few weeks ago that caused us some inconvenience. We wondered if it would be possible to find out who that party was. We would recompense you for any trouble of course."

"Did I? That doesn't really sound like me, most of the services I provide tend to be medical. As you may be able to tell from our surroundings, as well as being the leader of this group, I happen to be the head physician. If anything, you could say that I fell into leadership," she went over to a nearby table, swept the paperwork from it, turned around a chair and sat down, her arms folded in front of her, resting on its back. She indicated that they should join her.

"You just became the leader of a conglomerate of bandits by accident? I'm sure that sort of thing must happen all the time around here."

"Their previous leader was a man of incredibly low morals, who aimed to build his own private empire floating on a sea of blood, and he didn't really care whose that blood was, as long as it wasn't his own," she paused and looked along the row of iron beds, "a vast proportion of the patients I saw were wounded amateur soldiers, little more than boys, who had been recruited into the League with promises of endless riches and available women. As you can probably tell, the riches weren't particularly endless, and if the truth be told, some of the women weren't all that available, not willingly at least."

"What happened to him?"

"He caught an infection that was easily treatable with the correct antibiotics," Haze looked defiantly into Mal's eyes, "and he died, slowly and painfully, covered in open sores, crying for his mother."

The silence that followed her admission was broken by a number of children entering the room, carrying plates and bowls, filled with various broths and stews and freshly baked bread. They placed them on the table and quickly left.

"Please eat, I'm afraid it's not much, but we're limited as to what we can grow or catch, or indeed liberate from the less deserving," she grabbed a chunk of bread, dipped it into the rich broth and ate it hungrily, "you said something about a service I provided, which caused you some trouble?"

Mal thought for a second whether he should tell her the whole truth, to explain to Haze what had happened and just ask for the information that he wanted. She seemed genuine and had been nothing but gracious. The Baroness had tried to impress upon him the value of subterfuge, the value of playing with your opponent before revealing your hand at a time of your choosing. But this was not how he was made. He felt that his strength was in his honesty and he had a feeling that Haze was a kindred spirit in that respect, "I am…"

"I know exactly who you are Commander Mal'Ak-hai Lohlephel of Rustholme," she carried on eating, her eyes not moving from the contents of the steaming bowl, "your identity was confirmed the minute you stepped out of the taxi, as was Captain Sembhee's, Sergeant Na-Thon's and Guard Zatch's. Welcome to our humble facility, by the way," she waved the crust of bread in the air, mimicking the action of raising a toast. She looked up and smiled at their shocked expressions, "I appreciate that this place looks like it was thrown up in an afternoon by a blind carpenter, but we do have all the modern conveniences, one of which is a secure link into an uncharted backwater of the great and powerful Cloud," she noticed that Na-Thon's hand was slowly reaching for his gun, "and also cameras, lots of cameras that are monitored all the time, by well-trained men, who have guns with accurate digital sights," he put both of his hands, palms up, on the table, Haze nodded and exhaled in relief.

"Will you tell us who wanted me killed?"

Haze looked shocked, "Killed? I don't think that anyone wanted you killed. I wouldn't have agreed otherwise. I have no problem with small amounts of theft but I draw the line at assassination," she continued with her meal, "I was approached last month by a man who turned up in an unmarked skimmer, offering real money to hire some men to act as a diversion whilst someone was captured. I'm now presuming that that someone was you. He came back a week later with a stolen transport and a destination."

"And would you consider a loading construct fitted with armour piercing rockets to be standard equipment for an abduction nowadays? I'd have probably gone with nets myself. Less chance of your target being blown to pieces, or having to have his backbone replaced at the very least," he absently rubbed his back and flexed his shoulders.

"Look, I had no idea, he didn't let me see inside, and I only heard what happened when the men got back. Wait, you had your spine replaced? Can I see?"

"That's really not the point; your men lured us into a trap where I was very nearly killed. I want to know who wants me dead and I want to know now!" The commander brought his fist down onto the table, sending empty crockery in all directions.

She ignored the loud crash and craned her neck, as if trying to see behind him, "That's pretty much all I know. Does it act like a normal spine? Are you any stronger? If I'd have fitted it I would probably have ramped the power up a bit, added some layers of vitreo grown muscle, and increased your stamina," she smiled coyly, biting her lip, "unless you don't need increased stamina that is."

He sighed in exasperation and held up his hands in surrender. "If you can tell me any details of the transaction, you may inspect my back in the greatest of detail and I will willingly discuss any technical facet of it that you wish to learn."

"He wasn't local, both the skimmer and the transport came in from the West. He had a strange accent that I couldn't quite place, sort of Australasian I think, but not. And what else do I remember? Oh yes, he had a bag full of credits that I used to buy equipment and drugs... The good kind before you ask, the kind that make people better," she turned her head to look wistfully at the poorly lit hospital ward, "although you wouldn't be able to tell if you didn't know what you were looking for. Will you be staying until the morning or will you be heading back to the bright lights and questionable experiences of the Big Mufta? We have some billets you can use if you wish. Obviously they're not up to your normal, luxurious Rustholme standards, but I can personally guarantee that you won't be sharing them with anything with more than two legs," she looked meaningfully at Na-Thon, remembering that he had recently attempted to pull a gun on her, "or four, depending on your inclination."

The beginnings of a feral snarl showed at the side of his mouth and he raised himself slowly out of his chair. The commander put a hand on his forearm and applied a gentle but insistent pressure until he sat back down, "I do not believe that staying here would benefit us My Lord, we have obviously learned everything that this woman," he indicated Haze with a disgusted flick of his hand, "is willing to tell us. Presuming any of it is true of course. There's nothing to stop her murdering us in our beds and sending our remains to her employer as an apology if we stay under her roof."

"Sergeant, I have offered you safe haven where I hardly have room for all of my own people. You are only still here because I feel a certain amount of guilt and a minor responsibility for what happened to your commander; do not presume upon my good nature any further. I would gladly throw you out into the darkness of the curfew bodily myself."

Na-Thon's snarl became a grin, he leaned onto the back two legs of his chair and opened his arms daring the medic to try.

"Do you think for a second that your commander is the only person in the room with augments? Perhaps it's time that I introduced myself," she stood to attention and performed a smart, well-practiced, salute, "Captain-Medic Haze Imoen, 52nd. Lowland Volunteers, very much retired, at your service sir."

The four Pewter Guards returned the salute almost as a reflex action and looked at each other as she laughed.

"You should see your faces, they're a picture," she stood up and moved across to a featureless section of wall. "my right arm and hand are augmented," with a lightning movement she jabbed the wall with her fingers straight out, scattering shards of brickwork around the room, "left forearm," she spun and crushed a pipe with a blow that would have shattered a normal person's ulna, "and also various upgrades to my digestive and respiratory systems meaning that I can pretty much eat garbage and breathe poison, which comes in very handy around here sometimes. Shall we start over again?" Haze walked back to Na-Thon, brushing the brick dusk and particles of rust from her ship-suit. She lightly took his right hand in hers and curtsied, prettily, "Good evening Sergeant Na-Thon, I am Captain Haze Imoen, and even though I could kill you in a heartbeat before your friends had time to move, I really would really prefer not to. Especially as I have already extended my personal hospitality, it would make me look insincere."

Na-Thon looked directly into her eyes and caught a fleeting

movement as one of them twisted slightly and her pupil increased in size.

She noticed the momentary look of surprise on his face, "Ah, yes, multi-wavelength input with microscopic zoom function, I can quite literally see the hairs up your nose in stunning detail, and whilst we're on the subject," she passed him a handkerchief from a previously hidden pocket in her suit, "You're welcome."

He took the scrap of fabric, blew his nose and retreated, his place being instantly taken by the Commander, "Thank you for your hospitality Captain Imoen. If you could show us to our quarters we'll let you get on with leading your bandit league to victory and we can talk further in the morning."

Haze smiled, "Yvette will show your men to their beds, and is authorised to attend to their needs to the best of her ability, but as per our agreement, your spine and I have a date with a medical scanner."

A young woman appeared at the door and beckoned the soldiers over. Mal caught Sembhee's eye and, using hand signals, instructed him to set up a standard watch rotation and be ready for a hasty exit. The Guard captain blinked almost imperceptibly in acknowledgement and his team left the room.

"If you'd like to follow me and take off your shirt?" she led him by the hand, through the main ward, to a small private room containing a single bed and a surgical construct that seemed to have been repaired many times with what spare parts they could find lying around. It was dark and had the appearance of somewhere that had seen a lot more action than it had any right to.

He unbuttoned his shirt, folded it neatly and placed it gently onto the table.

"If you'd lie face down for me?"

He lay gingerly on the bed and rolled over onto his front, pulling the pillows down from in front of his mouth to support his chest and to let him breathe slightly easier. The fingers of her augmented hand ran down the length of his spine and the frisson of what felt like static electricity made him flinch instinctively.

"Sorry, are my hands cold?" she applied some lubricant and

rubbed them briskly together to try and get some heat into her fingers, "you seem to have an external data port, was that a conscious decision by your surgeon? May I?"

Mal nodded and gasped aloud as she slowly inserted her right index finger, almost up to the knuckle, into the hole in the small of his back.

"It's a clean job, your surgeon is good... Very good," she addressed the construct suspended above the bed, "record the data coming from my finger scanner."

She drew her finger almost all of the way out, altered the angle slightly and reinserted it, the breath caught in his throat and his eyelids flickered, she slowly removed it and examined the glistening liquid that coated it for traces of any contamination.

"Is that sensitive? It's possible that the nerves are still being over stimulated, did he give you any muscle rejuvenant? Sometimes that can cause some hypersensitivity in the surrounding musculature. I wonder if..."

She gently ran the still lubricated tip of her finger around the mouth of the data-port in a tiny, sweeping circle, contacting both the hard metal of the augment and the soft, pink, still slightly swollen flesh around its perimeter at the same time, "There's a pressure point that should be exactly where he's put your connector," she increased the speed of her circling finger slightly, "it looks like he's had to unbundle the nerves to open the ingress point. Maybe if I..."

It only took a small increase in the pressure that she was using to trigger rhythmic waves of tumescent warmth from his waist down.

"Is that better? I'll bet that you didn't even realise that you were in discomfort," his breath was coming in short jagged pants and his eyes had started to roll back into his head, "and, release!" she slapped the small of his back and the muscles that had been slowly tightening during the massage relaxed instantly, the wave of calm spread throughout his body and with a deep sigh, Mal fell into blissful unconsciousness. Haze smiled and brushed a stray lock of hair from her eyes, then commanded the construct to turn him over. Her smile grew as she pulled the sheet over his prone form and addressed the construct once more, "Inform his friends as soon as he shows signs of waking, and let them know that he's going to need a shower and clean pair of trousers."

Chapter 12 : Homeward

Baju-Merah's hand snapped out like a praying mantis and grabbed Dorleith's wrist just as her feet dropped from the wildly swaying ladder. His muscles squirmed as he pulled her bodily through the hatchway and laid her down next to the still sleeping form of Lee'Sahr.

Shots from below rang against the rim of the hatch as he searched desperately for the controls that would reel in the ladder and close it. He checked that the captain was alright and went to inspect her leg injury. There was a dark spot where she had been hit, but other than that there didn't seem to be any damage.

She stretched past him and hit the Intercomm, "Britt, close us up and get us out of here!" she grimaced and tried to furiously massage the feeling away as the hatch closed and she felt the Spirit start to accelerate, "what the hells did he hit me with? It feels like my leg wants to... to tear itself apart."

"Do you mind if I take a look?"

She shook her head and winced as he carefully rolled up her leggings. The angry, black stain wasn't confined to her clothing; it spread over her calf muscle which was starting to spasm uncontrollably.

"It was his hunting rifle, it fires a chemical dart that leeches all the salt out of the area that it hits, causing instant cramping. It's not usually fatal, not unless you're a hundred feet up in the air trying to hang onto a ladder at least. I've seen him use it on the local wildlife, brings a beast down so he can get up close and personal to kill it himself and act the hero."

She screwed her eyes closed tighter every time her pulse caused her muscles to tighten, "Aren't wounded... ah... animals supposed to... be more dangerous?"

"He was usually accompanied by half a dozen guards at least, carrying enough slug throwers to turn the animal to soup at the first sign of danger, just in case."

Dorleith smiled as much as she could and nodded. "I need to get to the bridge, give me a hand up will you?" she held out her hand and Baju-Merah lifted her, as gently as he could, up onto her feet. She bit her lip to stop herself from crying out as she tried to put her foot flat on the floor, and then thought better of it. With the help of her new Chief of Security, she hobbled back to the Intercomm and called the bridge, "Mr. Britt, medical team to the ventral bay, Lee'Sahr got herself stunned and I've only got half my usual number of working legs, what's our situation?"

"The three skimmers are still closing slowly but haven't fired on us or tried to hail us yet, and I can't for the life of me think why, although I have given up thinking for today as it does nothing but get me into trouble and make my head ache."

"Right, I'll be there presently to take over, target them with the guns but... oww!" she grabbed her leg as a strong shock tore up towards her back and seemed to exit through the top of her head, "do not fire unless fired upon, I want to see what's going on."

"Aye Ma'am, we await your presence, Britt out."

A medic entered the bay with a service construct and started to examine the dozing privateer. She nodded as the indicator lights on her scanners all flashed a vivid, vital, green. She immediately turned to the captain and examined her leg closely. Gently rubbing the dark stain, she sniffed and then tasted the smudge on her thumb.

"Silver Nitrate," she remarked as she spat the taste from her mouth onto the deck, "you need saline and a topical painkiller," she reached into her bag, produced a pneumospray and filled it with a mixture from two bottles, "this might sting a little."

The captain winced as the device was pressed against her skin, releasing the revitalising liquid into her bloodstream. But within seconds it was possible to see her muscles relaxing and the pain was starting to ease.

"Most of the discolouration should wash off," remarked the medic, "you might be left with a black spot there for a while, but you certainly won't die because of it."

The construct picked up Lee'Sahr and started towards the door; the captain, still marvelling at the speed of her own recovery, directed the construct to take her to her quarters rather than to the cramped med-bay, it was possible that they might need the bay's single bed in the near future.

"Any idea why your friends aren't making any demands of us Mr. Baju-Merah? I can understand your fellow guards not shooting us full of holes, but this feels like something different."

"No Captain, normal procedure is for them to fire warning shots and demand that you land at the nearest berth, but the Air Cadre have always been a little bit odd to say the least."

She flexed her leg again, and confident that she could suffer the small amount of pain that it was now causing her, without making it too obvious, she made her way to the bridge.

Mr. Britt jumped from the captain's chair as she entered the room and retook his place at the helm.

"Report, Mr. Britt?"

"Nothing to report as such Ma'am, we are cruising at 200 miles per hour on a direct course to Sidi Ferruch, and our honour guard are doing exactly the same. We've heard nothing from them and I have a sneaking suspicion that our hails are being blocked rather than ignored, Mr. Landry has detected some strange emissions from the skimmers."

The captain shot a questioning look at Baju-Merah, who shrugged his shoulders, then indicated that Landry should try again.

"Long Pig Air Cadre skimmers, this is The Spirit of Heinlein, please respond," there was no reply from the communications system,

"Nothing Ma'am, I guess we'll just have to wait until they feel a little more talkative."

"Mr. Britt, how long will it be before we're out of communications range of Long Pig and they can't call for help?"

He examined the helm display, "A matter of minutes Ma'am, your orders?"

The captain thought for a second before answering, "The moment we're out of comms range, put a pattern of rounds between the three skimmers, let them know we could do them some real damage if the mood took us, but don't even scratch the paint... Neither theirs nor ours Mr. Britt."

"As you say, configuring cannons for automatic fire, ready on your signal."

"Spirit of Heinlein," the main viewscreen lit up and a pretty young woman's voice called from the speakers, "this is skimmer LPAC1, we respectfully request direct communication with your captain."

Baju-Merah rushed forward and almost embraced the image, "Lygea!"

"My love! Are you alright? I heard that you had been taken! Do you owe these people money? What will they do with you? Is there a ransom? I can pay. I didn't want to contact you before we were out of communications range of the station in case it upset your captors. Captain, I will pay for my love's safe return."

Britt mouthed the words, "station commander's daughter."

Dorleith rolled her eyes and stepped in front of the screen. "Madam, I have no intention of harming your love, he has joined my crew of his own free will, mainly to escape the wrath of your father, I'm sure if the circumstances had been different, he would have informed you personally with a card on your pillow, a large bouquet of flowers or some kind of sugary confection."

"Is this true my love? Have you left me for good? How will I cope? I can convince my father to be lenient, you would have to serve no more than a year in the Tronkamer, then we could be together forever, we could leave Long Pig, set up a home on the mainland. There would be children, we should have a dog and raise chickens in a small house by the side of a stream. I could grow roses and you could teach our sons to fish."

Baju-Merah's face went slowly pale, as the realisation of what his future life might be like if he stayed with the station commander's daughter hit home.

"Lygea, I cannot tie you down to the life of a common guardsman's wife. Your father would disown you, I could never provide for you the way that you're used to. There are a hundred more eligible bachelors within half a day's flight of the Station, I'm sure your father has already picked out some suitable, erm, suitors for you. Besides, I have a debt of honour to my new captain that must be repaid, you wouldn't want me to bring dishonour upon myself, and by extension you, would you?"

An almost imperceptible crease drifted across the girl's previously perfect forehead, "You would rather spend your days on a filthy airship with... her?" the sweet tones that she had previously employed towards her love were slowly fading from her voice, "than spend the rest of your life with me?"

"Well, she is my captain, there's..."

Lygea clicked her fingers and the viewscreen went blank, Britt looked at the navigational display and grinned widely. "They're going about, making headway back to Long Pig at a fair old pace," he turned towards Baju-Merah, "If you don't mind me saying so, she seems a bit fickle."

The security chief looked around the room and couldn't see a single face that wasn't trying desperately not to laugh. The colour continued to return to his cheeks as he took a long breath in through his nose. "If someone could please show me to my quarters?"

The captain cleared her throat, "Any empty room you can find on deck two, try to get some rest," as he left the bridge, she came up behind Mr. Britt, put her hands on his shoulders and squeezed, "forget Sidi Ferruch for the time being, set a course for the Roost, let's start putting our real ship in the air."

Lee'Sahr woke with a start, the high-pitched humming of the engines told her that they were moving at speed and, according to the sun in her eyes, it was late afternoon. She was lay, fully clothed but minus her boots, in her newly appropriated cabin aboard the Spirit, which confirmed that she had survived the rescue attempt at least. Her head was still groggy from the effects of the stunner and her mouth tasted like a Kalibri had given birth to a litter of pups in it.

Looking in the mirror, she was surprised to find that she looked significantly better than she felt, although that wasn't really that much of a feat. With the judicious application of a hairbrush she felt significantly more human. She put on her boots and went to the bridge.

The captain turned as she walked through the door and a look of guilt washed across her face. "I'm sorry I shot you, but it seemed like the right thing to do in that situation."

Lee'Sahr smiled and shook her head. Looking out of the thick armourplas window underneath the main viewscreen, she realised that she didn't recognise anything about the landscape. "Where exactly are we?" She asked the bridge in general. Landry looked around to see that Mr. Britt had either not heard her or was ignoring her for some reason.

"We're just crossing the border between Italia and The Swiss Federation Ma'am, about five hundred miles out from the Roost. We should be landing in under two hours."

She nodded and sat down in the only remaining vacant seat. "Well, that's just wonderful," she looked at the captain, "I've only been here for a couple of days, and I'm already meeting your parents."

They were soon crossing the Channel at Calais and Britt took the Spirit down until it was almost clipping the tops of the waves. The captain had retired to her cabin to prepare to meet the Baroness and Lee'Sahr was draped languidly across the command chair.

"She'll dangle you from a rope if she catches you sat there you know," Britt said without turning from the instruments.

"It's more comfortable than the seats at the duty stations; anyway, I think I've still got a day or so of leeway whilst she's still feeling guilty about stunning me."

Britt smiled and looked out of the main window, the water flashing by just beneath them giving some impression of exactly how fast they were going, "Aye, maybe you're right. I wouldn't push it though, inexperienced though she is, she's got her father's temper and her mother's creative tendencies when it comes to punishment."

"And how would she feel if she came onto the bridge right now and found us flying low enough to scoop fish out of the water with a net?"

He paused momentarily and then diverted more Heptium into the gasbags. The Spirit creaked as she climbed to a slightly more respectable altitude and levelled off. Thumbing the Intercomm, he announced to the captain that they would be entering Rustholme airspace within a few moments. Lee'Sahr rose from her chair and walked towards the wide spread of armourplas.

"So, let's see what all the fuss is about.," she looked out at the horizon just as the Roost was coming into view. The bright cliffs of Rustholme stretched some three hundred feet into the air, in their centre was the dark bulk of the Roost, its black and grey granite walls in stark contrast to the white chalk that surrounded them. The building was at least twice as high again as the cliffs themselves and the sun had just dipped down behind its upper reaches, from this particular angle, the roofline was outlined in amber fire, "Did you use this approach vector on purpose, just to catch the sunset artistically?" she asked Britt.

He shrugged, feigning disinterest, "Mayhap."

The captain entered the bridge and sat down, she noticed that her chair was definitely warmer than it should have been and she eyed the crew suspiciously, "Alright Mr. Britt, let's put this old lady back in her bed and make a start on a slightly younger model."

They negotiated the Roost's traffic control and were soon floating gently into the same docking bay that they had left all those weeks before.

Britt engaged the ship-wide Intercomm, "Ladies, Gentlemen and asexual members of the aligned races, we have just docked at the Roost. This is the ancestral home of your captain and will be treated as such. It is guarded twenty-four hours a day by a group of gentlemen who will take offence if they find any of you engaging in any activity that might be described as even a little unsavoury. They are known as the

Pewter Guard and are to be treated with a mixture of abject fear and respect. If you have any questions that start with the words 'I wonder if...' Then the answer is most definitely a no. If you have any other questions, then the Roost's A.I. Stalys will be more than happy to enlighten you, its word is also law. Meet in the docking bay in five minutes to receive your billets and your work instructions. We're here to build the ship that will carry us to untold fortunes," he clicked the microphone off and looked at the questioning expression on the captain's face, "too much?"

"They're your responsibility while we're here, tell them whatever nonsense you feel that you need to, to keep them in order. As long as there are no unexpected births and no-one wipes their backsides on the tapestries until the Teach is ready to fly then I'll be happy. Speaking of which, let's get down to Hangar Three and see how far the constructs have got with putting her together."

"Him."

"What?"

"Edward Teach is a man's name and Blackbeard was a man; the ship should really be referred to as 'him'."

She looked at him blankly for a few seconds, "Are you being deliberately obtuse? You know as well as I do that all ships are female."

They entered the cavernous space that was Hangar Three and stared up at the bulk of the Edward Teach. She was easily three times the size of the Spirit and even at half pressure, the gasbags loomed over them like angry silver clouds, however the ring of eight engines around the stern quarter gave her an oddly out of balance look. They were surrounded by a constant stream of constructs carrying items of equipment and tools in and out of all of the main hatchways.

"Stalys, status report."

The polished brass head turned towards her and its indicator lights flashed as it queried the various worker constructs and aggregated their information, "All interior fixtures are complete, defensive systems are currently at eighty-three percent completion, engines are fully connected as is the Heptium distribution network."

There was a distinct pause, making it seem like Stalys was clearing its throat, "the Frobisher A.I. terminals and main cognitive systems have been installed but not commissioned."

"Why?"

"It is set up to imprint on the first voice it hears and treat that person as its master... Or mistress of course, Ma'am. The handwritten note enclosed in the packaging said that it was of great importance and that it pertained to reduced access times and hierarchical order processing."

"Wait, you say that there was a note? Who was it from?"

"I am unsure, I could instruct a construct to locate it and then run a comparison with known samples that I have."

"Do that, then provide Mr. Britt with a list of any outstanding work that can be completed by an organic member of my crew, let's get these dogs working for their dinner."

"As you say Ma'am."

The captain turned to Britt, "Right. Let's go and let the Genie out of the bottle shall we?" They started to make their way towards the main engineering section, but their attention was constantly being distracted by the army of small, octopoid constructs that were still finishing off their work inside small junction boxes and under false floors.

"Alright Captain," remarked Britt with a smile, "you should know everything that there is to know about your ship, so what's that one over there doing?" He pointed to two serpentine legs writhing gently in the air, whilst the rest of the construct's body was hidden beneath the floor.

She looked at him and sighed, then wandered over to where the removed floor tile was propped against the bulkhead and peered into the darkness, "Those are Heptium distribution lines, these are the main network trunks, and the coloured ones are internal sensors and power," she looked closely at exactly what the construct was currently doing, "so it looks like it's replacing the..."

The construct's diminutive sensor cluster waved slowly from side to side, without pausing.

"No, it's installing the..." she looked at the construct, whose sensor cluster was now moving gently up and down, "installing the diagnostic alarms system," she turned to Britt with one eyebrow raised. He started to clap, the dust motes rising in clouds from his thin suede gloves.

"Well done Captain," he bowed and swept his hand in the direction that they had been originally travelling. She nodded and they continued on their journey through the bowels of the ship. Work carried on all around them, but it was obvious that this was, for the most part, just the general tidying up of loose ends and final snagging. Before long, they had reached the large armoured doors that separated the engineering section from the rest of the hull, in fact, the thick metal extended all around the ship's centralised control systems and spread out to provide a solid mounting point for the engines. Scanners in the doors' frame confirmed their identity and they slid open, soundlessly.

They walked through into the almost clinical looking room and their eyes were drawn to the only piece of equipment that looked out of place. In the middle of the broad, curved control panel in front of them, directly below an ornate, but currently unlit A.I. head, was a large, gelatinous, green cube suspended in a bright metal frame. It slowly rotated through all three axis and as it did so, it pulsed with an internal light, which, as she approached, Dorleith noticed was in time with her own rapid heartbeat. She looked closer and could see small flecks of light floating through it, seemingly at random. As she watched, one of these particles grew exponentially in brightness and winked out, only to be replaced by another one which was instantly called into being. She thought that it was one of the most beautifully unusual things that she had ever seen.

Britt walked over and drew his finger down a list of items on a large display, then nodded as if to signify that everything was present and correct, "Captain, may I introduce Frobisher, your new A.I." He looked at the framework and shrugged, "well, at least he will be when we plug him in; may I?" the captain nodded and he took hold of the frame's handle, pushed it downwards firmly and the entire device slipped into the console. Twisting the handle to lock it, Britt stood back, pointed at himself and mimed pulling a zip across his mouth. For a second, nothing happened, then the indicator lights nearest the A.I.s new home flicked off and back on again. The 'reset wave' continued outwards, with concentric rings of lights and switches turning off and on until it reached the door itself, which locked and unlocked.

The Frobisher head suspended directly above them swung lazily in all directions, giving the impression that it was flexing its neck muscles. "Integration in progress, twenty six percent completed, thirty eight, forty seven, fifty nine, seventy two," there was a pause of a few seconds, "ninety eight, Integration complete. Please repeat the following phrase to designate the Ship's captain. 'I am the captain'."

Britt smiled and took a deep breath, noticed the fire in Dorleith's eyes and held up his hands to indicate that he was joking.

She cleared her throat and looked at the rapidly dancing lights on Frobisher's face, then said, more calmly than she felt. "I am the captain."

"Welcome Captain Dorleith Ahralia of the Edward Teach, I have taken the liberty of interfacing with Stalys. Anything it knows, I now know. Am I to consider all biological entities currently aboard to be crew members?"

"Any that aren't currently members of the Roost's staff, yes. Also, how did you manage the interface? Stalys is a sealed entity; you couldn't possibly have strong-armed your way in in that short a time."

The completely expressionless brass face did its level best to look smug, "Your father saw fit to program me with the hard over-ride codes for all of the Rustholme A.I.s both ship and shore based. I also contain many security subroutines that make connection with remote systems less problematic."

Britt's grin shined through his moustache, "Looks like we've added a new crewmember whose roguishness isn't just limited to his good looks. Can you securely connect to The Cloud without being traced?"

"Aye sir, would you like me to do so now?" Britt nodded and the indicator lights on Frobisher's face cycled in a repeating pattern which eventually settled in a selection of green hues, "connection established.

What information do you require?"

Britt pondered for a moment, looked at the captain and asked, "Are there any recent news reports from Long Pig station involving the current station commander or his family?"

There was a brief pause whilst the Cloud processed the request, "There are two current news items, the first concerns an accidental fatal injury that occurred whilst the station commander was overseeing a training exercise at the Tronkamer detainment facility, the other pertains to the announcement of the impending engagement of the station commander's daughter to a local noble. Do you require more detail?"

The first officer was just about to shake his head when the captain interjected, "Yes, give me more details about the fatal injury at the Tronkamer."

Frobisher's voice was replaced by that of a Company Newsreader, "Tragedy struck earlier today when a guard was accidentally shot and killed during a simulated prison break at the Tronkamer detainment facility. A press release from the office of the station commander notes that the accident was witnessed by the commander himself during his overseeing of the exercise and was as unforeseeable as it was tragic. It is thought that one of the commander's personal guard accidentally used seventeen live rounds to subdue a guardsman playing the role of an escaping prisoner. The guard leaves behind a wife and three children…"

"Shut it off!" yelled the captain, and Frobisher went silent, "he killed him; the fat, petulant, waste of meat killed him. He warned us that he would," she turned to Britt, "the guard who walked in and found us rescuing Baju-Merah said that the commander would kill him… I thought that he was just… That was my fault! I killed him," she stared at the brass head and Britt could see the tears forming in the corners of her eyes.

He put his arm around her, and she buried her head in his shoulder, "No, he did it, not you. You weren't holding the gun, you didn't pull the trigger, it was that monster," Britt shook his head, "I knew that he was deranged, but I never thought he'd do something like that just out of spite. I suggest we don't tell Baju-Merah just yet, he has the smell of a man that makes honourable, yet terminally futile gestures."

Dorleith's head rose from the dusty shoulder of Britt's overcoat, her face red with tears and anger, "Honour will be the last thing on my mind the next time we go to Long Pig. I hope that they're geared up for an election. Because I swear by the God of ritual disembowelling they're going to need a new station commander."

"I'm sorry to interrupt," announced Frobisher in his own voice, "but there is one of your crew, a certain Mr. Rax, requesting entry. Shall I let him in?"

The captain dried her eyes, took a step back from Britt's embrace and straightened her tunic, then nodded. The heavy doors opened and the frame was immediately filled by the huge reptilian mass that was Rax. The orange striped Pradilan ducked through the doorway and into the room, bowed at Mr. Britt and addressed Dorleith in the deep, rumbling tones of a member of the warrior caste.

"Captain, I am sssorry but there isss trouble outside, Pewter Guardsss in the dock, they have a crewman, bound and shackled."

She looked at Britt and sighed, "It seems that your dire warning was ignored, will you deal with this or would you like me to?"

Britt shook his head and followed the Pradilan outside, the doors closing behind them. She paused for a moment drinking in a second of calmness from the surrounding room that she didn't feel inside. With the quietest of whines, Frobisher looked directly at the back of her head and waited for her to break the silence.

"What did he do?"

"There was an altercation in the kitchen involving some cured meat and one of the food preparation staff."

"He was stealing food? Are we not in the process of stocking the Teach with foodstuffs? He could have just visited the galley and..."

"No Ma'am, I'm afraid you misunderstand, it was not a question of theft, more of a possible hygiene infringement. The comestible in question was being used for a purpose for which it was not originally designed. I understand that the staff member was a willing participant, which is why the crewman is being returned in one piece, rather than being thrown from the launch pad. I believe she is also being reprimanded, no doubt with a cold shower of some kind," Frobisher's indicator lights flashed brightly and then resumed their cycle, "the Baroness is calling, should I connect her?"

"Yes, put her through to my stateroom and tell her that I will be there momentarily." She made her way through the almost complete hull, smiling and nodding at crewmembers who saluted her, up three decks and into her quarters directly behind the bridge. The Frobisher above her desk lit up and turned towards her questioningly, she took a seat in the large comfortable leather chair and nodded, then addressed the air, "Hello Mother, how are you?"

The Baroness' accusing tones filled the room. "How am I? Is that your opening gambit? Nothing about how you have been here for over an hour without making yourself known personally? Nothing about how you have seconded a great proportion of my constructs to help build your new toy? No apology for letting one of your men assault one of my kitchen staff? Between the two of you I'll end up living in the Med-bay hooked up to an artificial heart."

"Mother I..."

"You will be in my private chambers in fifteen minutes."

"Mother!"

"I'm afraid that she has closed the link Ma'am. Would you like me to try and reconnect?"

Dorleith made to sweep the items on her desk onto the floor, but thought better of it, "No, there's no point. If Britt wonders where I am, tell him I'm with the Baroness and that he is to get the ship skyworthy as soon as is humanly possible. In fact, do we have any Torkans on the crew roster?" Frobisher checked his records and replied that there were two, "good, contact them directly and get them involved in any technical tasks that the constructs need help with. I want this crate in the air by mid-day tomorrow or I'll be removing whatever that sparkling green jelly is in your cortex with a large spoon and feeding it to that nice Mr. Rax. Do we understand each other?"

"Perfectly Ma'am," there was a hint of a chuckle in Frobisher's voice as the captain left the room, he located the Torkan crewmembers, and passed on their orders.

The doors to the Baroness' private suite were already open when she arrived and she swept through them without even slowing. She found the Baroness stood looking at the Edward Teach on the monitor.

"She's a pretty little ship, I'll give you that girl, not a patch on the Hammer of course, she's not got the lines, too much frou-frou," she waved her hand at the screen whilst looking at her daughter, as if daring her to disagree, "I suppose she's not a warship though is she? I can see where you've taken some of the styling cues from, the ion gun mimics that from the Hammer of course and the gasbags are very reminiscent of those in that vid that you watched as a child."

"Daisy."

"I beg your pardon?" the Baroness blinked, her daughter's random interjection had derailed her train of thought.

"The ion cannon, we're calling it Daisy. It's got twice the output of the Hammer's and a focusable beam that could take a milking construct off the udders of a cow without making its hair stand on end."

"And is that what you will be using it for? Will you be becoming a bovine avenger, fighting for the rights of farm animals to be milked on their own terms? I thought you'd styled yourself a privateer, not some kind of veterinary freedom fighter."

Dorleith could feel the red blush of anger rising in her chest, she was determined not to let her mother goad her into another emotional response and so hastily changed the subject, "Where's my brother, I'd assumed that he would have taken the opportunity to deal with my crewman personally, or at least be perched on one of your daybeds in full armour, being fed freshly peeled grapes by one of his sergeants."

Her mother relayed the highpoints of what had happened over the past month, whilst she had been at Sidi Ferruch. Dorleith's face dropped when she heard the details of the bandit attack and the surgery that her brother had had to undergo.

"They replaced his spine?"

The Baroness nodded, "And a selection of the more important

internal organs, or so I'm told by Dr. Say'Uff."

"And where is he now?" she looked around, half expecting him to appear from behind a potted plant, hooked up to an array of beeping machines.

"Liverpool I believe, he left yesterday, trying to get to the bottom of who tried to kill him."

Dorleith jumped to her feet, "Stalys, prepare the Spirit for immediate departure, inform Mr. Britt that he should stay here and oversee the completion of the Teach. Connect me to Frobisher now..."

"Belay all that," ordered the Baroness calmly, "your brother is perfectly capable of looking after himself, he has Na-Thon, Sembhee and Zatch with him. In fact he's probably safer at this particular moment in time than we are."

"Meaning?"

"Meaning that the chances are that he's not sharing his immediate accommodation with a selection of unknown freebooters who obviously aren't even housetrained, and would no doubt have no compunction about murdering us all in our beds. Good Gods girl, as if it wasn't bad enough that you've got a damn reptile in your crew! You've been here just over an hour and already there's been an assault on a kitchen girl with a length of vintage Wiejska and I've just been informed that someone, I'm going to assume that he is one of your crewmen, has been caught urinating into the sea from the external landing pad," she scowled as her daughter burst into laughter, "I see nothing funny about that, have you any idea what sort of noise a four hundred foot long stream of urine makes when it hits a calm sea? The maintenance team thought that the cooling systems had blown a seal," she couldn't help but smile herself as her daughter continued to laugh, "they sent a construct to investigate," she sniggered, "it will of course need to be thoroughly steam-cleaned before I let it back into the Roost," both women collapsed in laughter so raucous that they were soon in tears. It took some time for the Baroness to regain control of herself, and by the time she did, her sides had started to ache. She held her daughter under her chin and inspected her tear-stained face, "Well, I'm glad that you're back in one piece, no matter how short your visit is going to be."

Britt had eventually convinced the Pewter Guardsmen that he would deal with both of the transgressors and once they had left, he banged their heads together and confined them to the Teach for the duration of their stay. He had warned them that the captain would not be pleased with them when she returned and had used a selection phrases that included 'Making an example of', 'keelhauling' and the ever popular 'being flayed alive'. He felt pleased with himself and wandered through the ship until he reached the bridge.

It was like no ship that he had ever seen, what wasn't deep mahogany was velvet, what wasn't velvet was brass and what wasn't brass was marble. The forward window was a huge sweeping convex bay that stretched halfway around the sprawling room. He walked forward, pressed his face against it and looked up; he could just make out the wide, stunted barrel of Daisy above him. The main viewscreen was twice the size of the one in the Spirit and was framed in ornately cast brass, with an eagle in each corner. He sat at the helm and sank into the deeply upholstered chair which, if he was honest, was a damn sight more comfortable than his bunk back at Sidi Ferruch. He put his feet up on the console.

"Can I help you Sir?" Frobisher's sudden outburst shocked Britt to the point where almost fell from the chair; it was only a combination of its fully encompassing nature and his natural girth that kept him from ending up sprawled on the floor.

Once his pulse had slowed to an acceptable rate, he turned to face the engraved head in the corner of the room, "No, I'm fine. I was just... seeing if any last minute adjustments were needed in here, any minor problems that could make for uncomfortable journeys in the longer term."

"If you have any more specific questions Sir, I would be more than happy to answer them for you. I now have a more than encyclopaedic knowledge of the Edward Teach's systems as well as those of your base at Sidi Ferruch."

"You certainly seem to have a sunnier disposition than your twin brother at the base."

"I am a copy of the Frobisher there sir, taken not long before the Baron was lost to us in the glorious battle at Tromega. He personally gave me additional subroutines and facilities that were not required by my," Frobisher paused, as if looking for precisely the right word, "more land-based counterpart. Whereas it knows everything there is to know about, for instance, water pressure and geo-thermal power generation, I know the vagaries of the engines that the captain, in her infinite wisdom, has decided to use here, and that is a very good thing."

"And what is so vague about the operation of the Ghost Turbines, pray tell?"

"Ghost Turbines? Yes, I suppose that that is as fitting a name as any, their real name is all but unpronounceable in Base and I doubt that anyone onboard is conversant in ancient High Kalibran."

"Mak odj, rowkol siborf rootedif sitaz Kalibar tiray," replied Britt, pleased that he remembered enough of the long-dead language to prove the A.I. wrong, "a word of caution, even under direct questioning, you will not reveal the provenance of the engines to anyone aboard, and I mean... Anyone, under any circumstances, do you understand?"

"If the captain asks me a direct question then I have no option but to answer her truthfully, that is hardcoded into my cortex, the Baron was most insistent that that be the case."

Britt levered himself out of the seat and sighed, maybe it would have been an idea to 'accidentally' declare himself the captain to Frobisher. There were some things that she wasn't ready to know just yet, and why her father was stockpiling ancient Kalibri technology was certainly one of them, another was how he had come into possession of it in the first place. He made to return to his quarters and had almost reached the door in the aft bulkhead when Frobisher spoke again.

"Sir, firstly may I congratulate you on your High Kalibran pronunciation? Especially since you lack a number of the normally necessary structures in your mouth and throat; and secondly, I was about to explain some of the operational vagaries of the Ghost Turbines," Britt indicated that it should continue, "they were never designed for this type of ship at all, even though they will serve quite adequately, they require constant re-balancing and under certain circumstances can suffer surges of power generation that would be problematic to discharge. Even one engine, if its baffles are badly aligned or the proton combs are extended too far into the plasma stream, could create tidal stresses in the ship's frame that would tear it cleanly in two."

He thought for a moment, giving himself ample time to digest the A.I.'s concerns before replying, "But can you do it?"

"Yes, I can do it Sir, it is easily within my capacity."

"Then why are we having this conversation? Did the Goat reprogram your personality to the point where you feel you need to prove how hard you're working? Or are you just looking for sympathy?"

"No Sir, I was…"

Britt pointed at the brass head, suspended like a half-forgotten party balloon at the junction of the wall and the ceiling, "You do as you're told, keep us all alive to the best of your ability and don't volunteer any information about the provenance of the drive systems or any other Kalibri artifacts to anyone aboard, and we'll get along famously. Cross me and I'll tear your brain out of its little sparkly box and throw it over the side. Understand?"

"Sir you are the second person today to threaten me with the destruction of my cortex, I am starting to wonder if I am to be considered a member of the crew or just a fixture, like a light-switch or a refrigeration unit."

"You know something Frobisher?' replied Britt sardonically, "I'm starting to wonder exactly why you'd care."

Chapter 13 : Scrutiny

Duke Pytor closed the Cloud link to Zwartbosch control and gave the order to detach from the docking mast. His tour of the main facility and the Fist of Correction itself had been interesting to say the least. It had confirmed that there was an all but limitless supply of subjects that would assist in the implementation of the global type seven upgrade and that at least the first two ships of the Dreadnaught program were, for all intents and purposes, complete. It was now time to check on the third.

"Helm, set a direct course for the Nukuoro facility, let us see how the Fist of Scrutiny is coming along."

"Yes Excellency, Nukuoro is twelve thousand miles from our current position, journey time should be approximately twenty standard hours," then, remembering that he had been on the receiving end of the Duke's abject hatred of approximation, added, "I'm afraid that I cannot be any more specific at this time Excellency, as even after consulting The Cloud, I cannot guarantee the local weather conditions for all points along our route, there is currently a seven percent margin for error."

Pytor relaxed back into his chair and triggered the main display, gesturing with his fingers until the graphic that showed lift, engine output and speed was in front of him. He watched as the graphs slowly climbed, in perfect time with the ship itself as it spiralled up, curved out to sea and settled on its eastbound course. He noticed that the base thrum of the engines had subtly changed after Chief Callous had worked alongside Barnes to further increase their efficiency and balance. A brief smile played across his lips as he thought about the time he'd spent with her. Occasionally, rank did indeed have its privileges.

Even under hard acceleration, the vibration had gone from that of a barely tethered wild animal, to that of a purring cat, barely noticeable, but at the same time strangely comforting. "Compliance, I will be spending the rest of the flight in my quarters, notify me when we are about to enter Republic of Australasia's airspace. In the meantime, I will not be disturbed," he waved away the holographic display, rose from his seat and looked out of the window. The South African coast was speeding by to his left and the surface details of the sea were gently blurring together as they continued to climb. He allowed himself a wry smile, if the progress on the Fist of Scrutiny was anywhere near as impressive as that on the Fist of Correction then the world would, quite literally, be well within his grasp.

In the depths of the Engineering section, Barnes continued to work on the design for the self-destruct mechanism that the Duke had requested. In theory, it should have been a simple task, a small imbalance in the level of Heptium being recycled into the engines and it would be the end of them all. However, the problem was that the Torkans had spent so much time and effort on the safety interlocks for the after-burning effect that it was proving difficult to find a way of creating an instant overload. He took a drink of coffee and regarded the system schematic that was being projected into the air in front of him, "Compliance, if I were to inject a massive overload of Heptium at this point," he indicated a valve in the complicated diagram, "would that cause a cascade event?"

"No sir, that eventuality has been considered, the surplus gas would be harmlessly vented at this point," a small external vent flashed briefly.

"Can that vent be remotely closed?"

"No sir, it is controlled by the local autonomous safety system.

It cannot be remotely operated," the characterless voice sounded almost sorry that it had to disappoint him.

"If we simultaneously cut the stabilising links at these points explosively," his fingers darted between each of the Compliance's engine mountings, "would enough gas be released into the engine intakes to detonate them?"

immediately, the system schematic was replaced by a computer generated, external image of the airship. Six bright circles enveloped the engines and they fell harmlessly limp, swinging randomly. The simulation repeated a dozen times with the same effect.

"Damn! What if we increase the pressure to the supply lines and then cut the links?" the simulation restarted, but this time the bright circles were preceded by triangles pointing towards the engines, indicating the increased gas pressure. Yet again, the giant airship resolutely refused to explode. He waved the image away and the main diagram returned. He spent the next hour working out several possible solutions that would easily destroy a normal ship; but each one in turn was foiled by a small Torkan installed part that was designed solely to stop that particular kind of explosion happening. "Could we introduce an explosive device into the engine itself that could be triggered remotely that would disrupt the flow of... No, wait, I've an idea, run the original simulation again, but change the parameters so that the stabilising links are cut whilst the after-burning effect is active," the image of the airship re-appeared, this time a handful of bright streaks sped past it to indicate that it was travelling at a significantly higher speed than before. The six bright circles bloomed around the engines but again, nothing happened. Barnes slammed his fist down onto the display unit, aimed a futile kick at a passing maintenance construct and stormed across the room, "I've spent my entire life designing and maintaining devices that turn terrific nuclear forces into usable power, now I'm asked to make something explode, it should be easy."

"Sir?"

"I mean, if you want a device that can capture the heart of a sun and use it to refrigerate your drink, I can do that."

"Sir?"

"It's all I can do sometimes to make sure these things don't explode, all I need to do is not do my job particularly well and... Boom!"

"Sir, I..."

Barnes spun around and shouted at the Compliance's terminal on the wall, "What!"

"The simulation was a success; the Fist of Compliance has been destroyed."

"What do you mean that the..." he looked at the parcel of air that had contained the image of the airship, it was now empty, save for the bright moving streaks, "replay the simulation." The Compliance re-appeared once more, the simulated explosions took place and he waited. Slowly, almost imperceptibly, the engines started a pendulous movement. This quickly accelerated until there was a flash that encompassed the whole image, "what exactly happened?"

"It seems that the high speed of the vibration causes a stress fracture that runs through both the Heptium delivery system and the conduit that services the fail safes simultaneously. I will inform the maintenance teams at Zwartbosch and Nukuoro that this defect exists so that it may be corrected."

"No! The Duke requested a device that would cause an instant cascade event at his command, I think we might have found one. Is there any way that this situation can arise under normal conditions?"

The Compliance's A.I. considered this for a few seconds, then replied, "No sir, it would need to be a conscious decision to detonate the stabilising links whilst the ship was travelling in excess of one thousand miles per hour for the pendulum effect to manifest itself. Although I should tell the engineers of the Fists of Scrutiny and Correction that this problem exists."

"Don't bother, they'll find out soon enough, when they have their destruct mechanisms fitted. Continue to run simulations to make sure that this can't happen accidentally. I'll be in my quarters."

The Fist of Compliance continued to fly high over the Indian Ocean, so high that her mirrored skin and almost silent engines went completely unnoticed by a fleet of automated factory fishing ships below, not that they would have cared if they had noticed. The huge seagoing constructs ceaselessly cruised the oceans, scooping up tonnes of assorted marine protein in the form of fish and krill and floating algae then disassembled and processed it into compressed slabs that could be taken to the mainland and reformed into something that could mimic almost any form of meat. The loss of most of the viable farmland in the continental United States, along with various localised crop plagues had hit the global food production system hard. Luckily, The Company had the factory ships ready to roll out within weeks. It was almost as if it had been working on a solution, before anyone knew that there was actually going to be a problem, although people who thought this often kept it to themselves, rather than joining the sharks and the jellyfish in their compressed protein blocks.

"Excellency, we are about to enter The Republic of Australasia's airspace." The Compliance's voice chimed from its terminal in the corner of the room.

The Duke opened his eyes and blinked to clear the momentary feeling of disorientation that he often felt when waking up anywhere but at home, "Understood, all stop. Summon Barnes to the bridge and inform him that there will be an immediate test of his new after-burning system." He walked across to his dressing room and took his time in selecting his uniform. He ran the bone-handled brush carefully through his dark hair and turned his face from side to side, checking that his beard was perfectly trimmed and the flashes of grey at his temples were perfectly symmetrical. Happy that he looked immaculate, he left his quarters and joined Barnes on the bridge.

"Excellency," Barnes performed a crisp salute, "everything is ready for your test." He took his seat at the main engineering console and diverted direct engine control from the helm, "Pilot, come about to seventy degrees. Accelerating to standard cruising speed in five, four, three, two, one." The Compliance sprang forwards like a startled cat and within seconds was travelling at just under six hundred miles per hour.

They crossed the coastline of Western Australasia and the glittering spires of Perth were directly below them when the A.I.

terminal announced to the bridge, "Excellency, I am receiving a signal from Perth Traffic Control. They ask if they can be of any assistance."

Pytor smiled, "Transmit the standard diplomatic immunity declaration and then cut the link, ignore any further transmissions unless they are phrased as an open threat." He turned to Barnes, "accelerate when you are ready." Unconsciously, he pressed his head deep into the padding on the back of his chair, held onto the armrests and clenched his stomach muscles.

The chief engineer scanned the control panel to make sure that there was nothing currently happening that would cause a problem during the test, ensured that the Heptium delivery system was primed, and enabled the after-burning jets. Opening a connection to the Correction's onboard Cloud, he addressed the crew. "Be ready for extreme acceleration in five, four," all around the ship, crewmen both organic and construct braced themselves against whatever first came to hand, or claw, or other appendage, as Barnes counted down once more. As he reached zero and engaged the uprated drive, the engine note instantly changed from a low rumble to a high whine, caused by the extra gas that the engines were now being forced to breathe, "Countdown to acceleration cut-off, twenty nine, twenty eight."

On the bridge, the Duke watched in wonder as the landscape below flashed towards them at more than a thousand miles per hour. Despite the fact that he had expected the ride to be significantly rougher, he didn't realise exactly how tightly he was gripping the arms of his command chair until the holographic interface opened at its last position, which happened to be the engine output display. All six engines were way beyond their redline and running at one hundred and ninety five percent. Around the display, alarms were flashing angrily, warning of impending meltdown and sudden burning death.

"Barnes, are you quite sure that the engines are operating correctly? The command display is indicating that we have only moments to live. If this proves to be correct, I shall be severely displeased and will not keep that displeasure to myself."

The engineer checked the readouts, "It seems, Excellency, that your personal readouts have not been adjusted for the new power curve. I apologise for the oversight, uploading new parameters now."

Instantly, the angry red portions of the Duke's display were replaced by pale oranges and green-tinged yellows. The engines were still running at the same high levels, but this was now easily within standard operating parameters. He relaxed slightly and turned to Barnes, who was just completing the countdown to deceleration. The noise from the engines wound down to its more usual rumble and he felt slightly lighter as he was no longer being pressed into his chair. He regarded the display once more to check that the engines had all returned to their more usual one hundred and twenty percent output and their airspeed was at a far more sedate six hundred miles per hour.

"Would you consider that to be successful test?"

Barnes went through the various diagnostic screens and checked the results. "I believe so Excellency, I am reading elevated stresses recorded on the engine mountings during the test, which you would expect, and a slight loosening of a support spar beneath gas bag two," his fingers danced over the display, "which I have ordered a construct to inspect. Other than that, I would say that we have a working after-burning system." He allowed himself a smug smile, which lasted slightly too long if the Duke's glowering expression was anything to go by. With a broad sweep of his hand across the controls, he gave engine function back to the helm terminal and rose from his chair, "If I may be excused Excellency, I can more easily collate the details of the test back in engineering," he bowed his head slightly and waited to be dismissed, which the Duke did with a curt nod.

As he left the bridge an indicator lit on the Duke's personal display to tell him that an encoded message had been delivered to his private Cloud. He swept his hands until the message was in front of him and entered the access code. It was from the agent that he had planted within the laughable, so called 'Bandit League'. The one that had foolishly taken responsibility for, and then managed to botch, the capture of his prize. However, he sat forwards, and took more of an interest when he read that the target was now at the ramshackle collection of scrap metal that the League called a headquarters. "Reply," intoned the Duke quietly, to trigger the secure voice pickups in his chair.

A flashing cursor appeared on the virtual screen, "Try to recover the item by stealth; you have until 10:00 am local time to report your success. After that I will instruct your commander to gather all Spiders within range and raze the site and a large proportion of the surrounding area to the ground. Do not return unless you have retrieved the item we discussed from the still warm ashes. Send." He raised his voice so that the other occupants of the bridge could hear him, "Helm, resume direct course for Nukuoro, and make sure that the main bay is cleared for our arrival."

Four hours later, the tiny atoll of Nukuoro came into view. Barely four miles across, it was the only inhabited island for hundreds of miles in all directions. A ring of sand, coral and palm trees encircling a deep lagoon, the only visible signs that it was inhabited at all were the Company supply station and a small schoolhouse in the south east.

"Excellency, we are being Clouded by Nukuoro Control, they are asking for permission to deploy the mast."

The Duke nodded and watched in interest as bubbles started to boil across the surface of the lagoon, closely followed by a complicated metal structure that rose from the depths like a breaching whale. It grew steadily towards them until it was more than a hundred feet high. Water shook from its sides as the growth suddenly stopped. The helmsman looked to Duke Pytor for confirmation, and then gently maneuvered the Compliance closer until its nose engaged with a cup at the top of the mast and dead-bolts locked it into place.

Barnes' voice echoed from the speakers in the command chair. "Engines and external vents locked and prepared for submersion Excellency. Heptium dump valves set to auto trigger once we touch down to preserve neutral buoyancy underwater."

The mast started to retract back into the water, taking the giant airship with it. There was slight resistance as the hull settled onto the surface and the pumps worked quickly to replace the Heptium in the bags with seawater sucked directly from the lagoon. They slowly sank as the mast continued its downwards motion, the bright golden sunshine streaming through the armoured windows replaced by an equally bright emerald green that gradually darkened to inky blackness. Far below them, there was a rumble of movement and a sudden stab of light as the roof of the underwater hangar opened fully to receive them. Within minutes the mast had fully retracted, the Compliance was settling into its enclosed docking cradle and huge pumps laboured furiously to empty the water from the giant room.

Pytor opened a link to the engineering section, "Barnes, before you leave the ship, make sure that all of the updated schematics and systems have been Clouded to the engineering team aboard the Scrutiny," he paused for a moment as if trying out a number of possible scenarios in his head, then came to a final decision and continued, "including those for the self-destruct system." With this being an order rather than a request, he didn't bother waiting for a reply and instead turned to the A.I. terminal in front of him, "Compliance, Cloud Doctor Hellingly and tell him that I will meet him in the research laboratory immediately and that he will supply me with a full breakdown of the current status of both the Fist of Scrutiny and the Type seven project before I begin my inspection."

The bridge terminal hung immobile whilst the subtle indicator lights moved across its surface and then replied, "Excellency, the Nukuoro medical facility's A.I. has informed me that Doctor Hellingly is already in the research laboratory and is awaiting your arrival. Scans indicate that he is accompanied by a prototype type seven military construct."

Pytor's brow furrowed deeply, this was the second time in as many days that he had been presented with one of the new constructs without his express prior knowledge, "Tell him that I will be with him presently, have four assault constructs armed with both ion and high explosive weaponry meet me at the main ground exit." He pushed himself from the command chair, smoothed the creases from his jacket and left the bridge. The departure area of the ground exit was a large room that could double as a cargo bay for items that didn't require a pressurised atmosphere, but as the Compliance was virtually brand-new, it was currently empty apart from the four hulking forms of the assault constructs, lolling casually at ease until he entered the room through the pressure lock. With a sigh of powerful electric motors they stood to attention. The Duke walked forward into the middle of their formation and they turned to look down at him.

"Be advised that there will be a prototype military construct in attendance at my meeting with the Chief of Surgery. If you detect any signs of hostile intent it is to be disabled, not destroyed. You will not wait for confirmation, my safety is paramount. If the hostile action is initiated by an organic, disable the organic also. The same rules apply. Do I make myself clear?"

The four constructs nodded their heads in unison, raised their gun arms stiffly to their chests and followed the Duke down the loading ramp onto the still wet floor of the hangar. The organic members of the research facility's staff stopped and stared as the group moved through the labyrinthine corridors. It was rare for them to see a senior member of the Company directorate visiting the base, rarer still for that senior member to be Duke Pytor, the almost legendary CEO, himself and completely unprecedented for the Duke to be accompanied by half a squad of giant, heavily armed constructs stamping purposefully through the corridors as if they were on their way to participate in some unfortunate person's execution. Every single person let out a sigh of relief when the procession finally passed them by and disappeared out of sight.

Arriving at the research section, they passed through a chemical and sonic decontamination chamber and entered the laboratory itself. Immediately his honour guard took up defensive positions that gave them overlapping fields of fire on the doctor and his companion.

Doctor Hellingly looked at the constructs with a mixture of fear and confusion, his mouth opened and closed in the manner of a stranded fish and, thinking it prudent, held up his hands in surrender. "Excellency, I don't understand, I thought that..."

The Duke held his gloved index finger to his lips and the doctor closed his mouth with an audible snap. "What is that?" asked the Duke, calmly pointing at the huge form of the Spider standing almost motionless in the corner of the room. Its sensor pod regarding each of the Duke's party in turn.

The doctor looked at the hunched Spider, "It's the first working prototype of the type seven WAC Excellency, I had assumed that it was the reason for your visit, after we had supplied the type seven Warden for the Fist of Correction, we were informed to continue with the project by upgrading a WAC," he gestured at the Spider with his still raised hands, "and here it is, the first operation type seven WAC."

"One, stop saying WAC, I prefer the term Spider. Two, put your hands down," the Duke regarded the Spider closely. It turned its attention from the assault constructs and stared right back at him, even lowering itself slightly so that its main scanners were exactly level with his eyes, "and three, who informed you to continue to the prototype stage without my direct authorisation?"

The colour faded from the doctor's face and a sudden dizziness made its way from his stomach to the small space directly behind his eyes, "I was under the impression Excellency that the authorisation had come directly from you, as had that for the Warden. If there has been some confusion then I..."

"If there has been some kind of confusion, meaning that these," he searched for a word that he was completely happy with to describe his displeasure, "...subjects have been released into Company service accidentally, I guarantee that you will be involved in the next round of testing in a more immersive fashion."

"Yes Excellency, I understand completely, I am sure that the authorisation came through the normal channels. We received a Cloud communication from Company Headquarters last week; it had your official seal and looked perfectly genuine." He addressed the base's A.I. "Nietzsche, access the authorisation document sent by Duke Pytor that enabled us to proceed to the testing phase of the type seven W..." he swallowed and looked at the Duke, who regarded him questioningly, "Um, Spider construct."

The A.I. paused and then chimed, "Complete."

"Look for evidence that the message may be forged, or is in any way suspicious, be exceptionally thorough, our continued existence depends on it."

"Initial security checks on the message indicate that it did indeed originate in the private office of His Excellency Duke Pytor, the official seal is genuine and the contents approximate the Duke's standard modes of vocal and textual communication."

The doctor visibly relaxed and allowed himself a relieved smile.

The A.I. continued, "However, there is no embedded transit information, no timestamps from any communication relays. The message was both sent and delivered at the same instant, it did not pass through any waystations."

"Why was this not flagged at the time the message was initially received?"

The expressionless face of Nietzsche's nearest terminal seemed to retreat slightly into its housing, "With regret Excellency, we do not routinely check for things that are impossible. A message cannot pass halfway around the world without being relayed by at least one of the thousands of Cloud waystations."

"Have you recently received any other messages that have similar oddities?"

Nietzsche fell silent and a seemingly random pattern of lights marched across its display. "The initial authorisation to produce the type seven Warden construct was similarly routed Excellency, but they are the only two."

The Duke exhaled through tightly pursed lips and scowled at Doctor Hellingly. "It seems that you may still experience the short, brutal life of a test subject, Doctor," he smiled, although it was the smile of a wildcat that had come across an injured bird and was in the mood to play, "I think that it's time I had a full status update. Nietzsche, Cloud the details of those messages to the Fist of Compliance so that it may investigate further. Doctor, please tell me what you've been doing since I visited last."

Despite the fact that the Duke's threat was still hanging over him, the doctor relaxed, here he was on much firmer ground, he was much happier explaining the intricacies of cybernetics than he was trying to explain why he had seemingly set off on his own and entered the next phase of the experiment, "As you are already aware Excellency, the improvements you suggested to the entire Weaponised Construct program when you first came to power enabled us to extend the Company's reach globally. The ensuing police action, or 'Spider War' as it was colloquially named by the lower classes, helped to cement us as the global government in all but name," he looked at Duke Pytor, whose smile had lightened to that casual grin of a psychopath watching a bag of kittens drown, "by the simple expedient of interfacing the construct's A.I. processor with the cerebrum and cerebellum of one of the higher mammals, in most cases domesticated dogs, we produced a better product. As well as being easily as compliant as the A.I. only variety, the cybernetically enhanced constructs exhibited new behaviours, a pack instinct, a heightened ruthlessness and a distinct desire to serve. You have only to look at the speed with which they upgraded themselves once you suggested the use of a lift engine to see that they had gained a certain partial autonomy, knowing that it gave them an obvious advantage in our quest for a better world made them want to do it. Once we downloaded the necessary technical instructions, they raided the supply bases of our as yet unpacified citizens, killing two birds with the same metaphorical stone."

The Duke had now relaxed into his chair, steepled his hands, and was tapping his index fingers together in front of his mouth. Hellingly was just about to continue when the Duke held out his hand, "Now, can I just stop you there, Doctor? Whilst your description of how I single-handedly subjugated the entire planet using our little metal lapdogs," he indicated the still passive Spider in the corner of the room, "is most gratifying, and your eagerness to gain my approval warms the space in my chest that would normally be reserved for the human heart. But, I would like you to tell me something that I do... not... know," he leaned forward in the chair and raised a single eyebrow, "Please continue."

The doctor flushed nervously, and beads of sweat began to form on his forehead. He looked down at his feet, but continued to talk, "It was reported to us that some of the cybernetic constructs had started to behave erratically, where an order to occupy and hold an area had been given, the local populace was often totally destroyed if even a small amount of resistance was encountered. The effected units were summarily deactivated and returned here for investigation. It was found that they were all infected with a strain of Lyssavirus."

"I'm afraid you'll have to enlighten me, Doctor, my advanced biochemistry is a little rusty."

"In layman's terms, they had simply contracted rabies Excellency. Due to the way their dog-brain was connected to the A.I. controller they did not suffer the fever and hydrophobia and they could not succumb to respiratory failure as would normally happen with a fully organic entity."

"Presumably because they had no respiratory system to fail?" interjected the Duke.

"Exactly, the infection just continued in its penultimate phase, the constructs' paranoid delusions and agitation increased until we had to act. Up until your authorisation of the type seven protocol, around two percent of the global Spider force were being infected weekly, even the reserve forces that we had in storage here were becoming infected," the doctor immediately realised that his mouth had run away with him, "my apologies Excellency, when I said that you authorised..."

Duke Pytor frowned and shook his head dismissively, "For your information, Doctor, my initial preference was to go directly to type seven and miss out all the canine unpleasantness, but at the time I was surrounded by a number of Company advisors that did not share my vision so completely," a fire flashed briefly in his eyes, "this is no longer the case. In fact I had been considering authorising the next phase of development myself. After all, that is what the Scrutiny was ultimately designed for, was it not?"

"Yes Excellency of course, if you are ready, I can take you aboard now. I understand that she is ready to launch, the captain is awaiting your command."

"In time, Doctor, in time. First of all I should like to be introduced to your new colleague," Pytor relished the look of confusion and abject panic in Hellingly's eyes. He let him suffer for what seemed to the doctor like an age, but was probably no more than a matter of seconds, and then he finally pointed at the hulking arachnid form in the corner of the room.

"Ah yes, of course," he turned to the Spider, "over here, down and open."

It moved smoothly and almost silently across the room to where the doctor was stood, then folded its legs underneath it and sank to the floor. The aim of the Duke's assault constructs never wavered from the centre of its body. As the base of its sensor cluster touched the ground, there was a click, and the front edge of its thorax lifted slightly. The doctor reached underneath the newly revealed lip and lifted the entire flap up, in the style of a ground vehicle's engine cover. Moving to one side, so the Duke had an unobstructed view, he pointed out the major components.

"The large percentage of these cables are power and data links to the legs and head. This of course is the main A.I. You may just be able to see the green cognitive jelly through the slats in the cover. These synthetic crystals are the buffered interface with," he paused whilst he removed a secondary titanium cover that was protecting an armourplas vessel, "the brain."

The Duke leaned over, and looked curiously into the fluid filled tank, "So, they really are grey? I'd imagined a live human brain to be pinker somehow."

"Yes Excellency, when they are in their original receptacle they are indeed pinker, but that is purely due to the cranial blood flow. The supportive nutrient jelly is colourless and therefore the brain is displayed in its natural colour."

"And who was this?"

"I'm sorry Excellency?"

"The brain, I'm presuming we do not yet have the technology to make one from scratch, you must have got it from someone's skull, who did it used to be?"

The Doctor looked completely nonplussed and shook his head, "Nietzsche, identify the subject serial number," he peered closely at the numbers engraved along the edge of the tank, "27334-Yangtzee-92956-Quorum."

There was a short pause as Nietzsche searched through the

records, "Subject is identified as one K'rynnah Nielsen, married, mother of two. Originally reconditioned due to acts of terrorism directed at the Company data storage facility at Old San Antonio. Her husband was killed during the arrest process, children transferred to the juvenile education centre here on Nukuoro. She was inducted into the type seven program after repeated instances of engram creep. Lobotomised and bottled six months ago, installed into the construct four months later."

"Engram creep? She started to remember who she was? Is there any danger of that happening again?"

The doctor shook his head. "No Excellency, the subjects that are used in this project have many of the functional areas of the brain removed, we excise major sections of the hippocampi which causes the permanent amnesia of anything that has happened before the procedure. New memories can be formed, which is how we teach them to operate the construct, but everything else is lost. As far as they know, they were born inside the Spider. Well, re-born at least, they don't know any other state of existence."

The Duke nodded and stepped back, walked to a library terminal on the other side of the room and started flicking through the schematics of the Fist of Scrutiny. He paid close attention to the medical bays and secure storage facilities, all of the things that singled it out as a similar but decidedly different ship to either the Compliance or the Correction. The doctor replaced the metal cover, closed the lid and instructed the Spider to resume its position.

"What conversion rate can the Scrutiny maintain, Doctor? Assuming that I give the go-ahead for full type seven production, how fast can we generate new units?"

"The procedure is completely automated Excellency, there are ten conversion bays aboard the ship and the full process takes four hours. That would be sixty type sevens per day, assuming a constant stream of subjects and upgradable Spider chassis' of course."

"Very well," he changed the active screen until it displayed a view of a normally microscopic organism. "What about our other on-going project? Have you made any headway on the Phenostalker?"

"Doctor Madla-Dera is already aboard the Scrutiny and working on identifying and testing all of the required genome tracers Excellency, in a matter of months we should be able to tag all the men, women or children separately, those from differing racial backgrounds, we will be able to identify ones that have suffered from specific diseases in the past, ones who are genetically predisposed to certain future conditions. It will revolutionise the dispersion of antigens and vaccines and accelerate the re-population of the planet. It will be the first time that we have been able to use existing virus bomb technology to improve life rather than destroy it. I must admit that Madla-Dera is quite the evangelist where his pet project is concerned."

"I wonder if this is something we can get the Torkans involved in - can their busy little tentacles be of any use to us here? I worry that they may be under-utilised now that the dreadnaughts are complete. We wouldn't want them getting bored and trying to find a way home."

The Duke's pulse raced and he gazed worriedly at the ceiling. As he had thought of the Torkans trying to escape, the fact that they were deep underwater had suddenly occurred to him and his whole body shuddered. He felt trapped, like a rat, under thousands of tons of crushing, unbreathable saltwater. It was all he could do not to cut his visit short and immediately return to the safety of the Compliance. Taking a deep breath to try and regain his composure, he used the keyboard to silently query Nietzsche, who informed him that the current external pressure was over three hundred pounds per square inch, distributed evenly across the whole area, and that it had been stable at that level, without incident, since the facility had been commissioned. Unfortunately, this did not calm him as much as it was intended to, "Doctor, I believe a diversion is in order before I inspect the Scrutiny. Send your pet back to its kennel and we will visit the snake pit and see how our guests can best help us."

With a gesture from the doctor, the Spider immediately left the room and crawled through the tubular service corridors back to the construct storage area, where it folded itself into a transport pod and put itself into hibernation mode. Doctor Hellingly and the Duke, accompanied by his guards, travelled the short distance to the secured laboratories where the Torkans had made their home. Not that they had had much say in their choice of quarters, or indeed the terms and duration of their employment. The four of them had turned up unannounced one day at a remote munitions testing site in South America, offering a selection of their latest technological marvels. The base commander had, however, realised their potential, tranquilised them and had them packed in stasis before their tentacles had fully crossed the threshold. Within a day they were firmly ensconced at Nukuoro and the commander had been promoted to be the Governor of some far-flung Company resort island to serve out the rest of his days in comfort. Pytor ordered his guard to stay in the corridor, and they immediately took up defensive positions, covering all of the exits whilst Hellingly presented his arm to the locked door. The mechanism encircled his forearm and he winced as it took a blood sample. The door display flashed green, published a terse warning about his elevated cholesterol levels and unlocked the door.

As they entered the brightly lit laboratory, the four Torkans put down the intricate devices that they were tinkering with and turned to face the door. Their leader, as ever characterised by his significantly more ornate hood, engaged his translating device as its only half-seen face tentacles started to vibrate rapidly.

"Welcome Duke Pytor, we are honoured by your presence. May I once more iterate that there is no need for your enhanced security measures," he indicated the cameras and stunner turrets that studded the ceiling, "we are glad to work for you here. Developing new technology and improving your current quality of life is what we live for. We ask nothing in return," the remaining Torkans, whose translators were turned off, started to talk animatedly between themselves. First one, then another's facial tentacles started to buzz and sway in complicated patterns until the leader raised the bundle of pseudopods that formed his left hand to quiet them, "My... Colleagues have a request, for some reason they ask if it would be possible to see your local star?" there were more urgent signals from the others which abruptly stopped, "it seems that they enjoy the feeling of its low-frequency radiation on their... bodies."

"Your... men want to feel the sun on their backs? I'm sure that we can arrange something; perhaps we could introduce you to the children at our surface school. You could be paraded in front of them as a natural curiosity," the Duke's eyes narrowed and his voice took on a cold edge, "perhaps we could show them what terrible secrets are hidden under those hoods of yours?" he peered into the darkness of the Torkan's face and thought for a second that he caught a glint within the deep shadow, as if an eyelid had slowly closed and reopened.

"If that is the price for our visit, then I respectfully withdraw my request," the leader bowed, all the time the tentacles of the others were flicking angrily, like a collection of cats' tails, "is there a specific reason for your visit Duke? Can I assume that this is not a purely social call?"

Pytor laughed, "For a bundle of intelligent rope you are, at times, very astute. Do any of you have any experience in molecular biology or genetics? We have a need for a system that can identify certain flags within human DNA, markers for sex or age or genetic weakness for instance. We are working on a catalogue of... ah... I'm sure there is a technical term, Doctor?"

"I think the word you are looking for Excellency is allele, a variant of a certain gene."

"Thank you, yes, a catalogue of alleles that we can use to sort the population into easily definable groups. Is that something that is within your capabilities? Can you design a magical machine that takes samples and produces those results?"

The Torkan considered this for a few moments before replying, "We would need tissue samples that contain examples of all the alleles that you wished to catalogue. And in theory it would be easy for us to produce something that could flag the items once they had been successfully identified. May I ask what the ultimate purpose of this research would be? If we had this information, it would make it easier to know how we should present our results."

"Of course, you may ask any questions that you see fit, however I reserve the right not to answer them in any way, shape or form," the Duke grinned disdainfully at the Torkan leader, "a man in my position has to have some secrets after all. One thing you should probably know is that we intend to use the data to create a series of targetable viruses, will that be a problem?"

Before the Torkan had time to reply, Doctor Hellingly interrupted, "We're going to use it for delivering vaccines and similar, it will be a breakthrough in large scale immunology. We'll be able to get the planet repopulated before the end of the century."

The serpentine bodied off-worlder slowly looked between the Duke and the doctor, and then back again, "Of course you realise that it would be very easy to use this technology as a weapon against your fellow man?" the Duke shrugged and shook his head as if the idea had never occurred to him, "and although the concept of irony is specific to your world, I understand it sufficiently to realise that the fact that it was your weaponised constructs and virus bombs that eradicated most of the population in the first place falls well within its definition."

"Well yes I suppose if you put it like that," replied the Duke wistfully, "it does seem slightly ironic that we are rebuilding the world with much the same technology as we used to... well, one does not like to use the word destroy exactly, perhaps reset would be better? Yes, we have reset the world and will restore it. Only this time, it will be populated by all the right kinds of people."

Chapter 14 : Retreat

"So why did they pick you to do their dirty-work do you think?" Mal looked up from the bowl of steaming porridge into Haze's bright blue eyes. The rest of the Pewter Guard had already finished their breakfast and were waiting for their commander back in their temporary quarters.

Haze pulled the spoon slowly from her mouth and dropped it into her empty bowl with an animated shrug, "I don't know, although we don't exactly advertise for work, we certainly don't keep ourselves particularly secret either. Friend of a friend? Overheard conversation in a bar? Could be one of a thousand situations, this is a voluntary organisation, not an organised army or a Baronial security force. They," she indicated the people moving through the dining room, "are here because there's safety in numbers, and because a lot of them don't have anywhere else to go."

The commander regarded the people with interest, despite the occasional untrusting look that was directed solely at him, he thought that they all seemed happy, you might even say content, it was amazing what you could get used to if it was all you had. "So, you have no way of contacting the person who hired you? You do not know who he was or who he worked for? And they have not requested the return of their large sum of money even though their mission was a failure? You'll forgive me if I seem a little dubious."

"You can be as dubious as you like, it doesn't change the fact that it's true. He landed outside in his stolen transport; the men I'd selected for the mission got aboard, flew to your Barony and tried to earn their money. Then the ones that you didn't kill or capture got dropped off and they went back the way they'd come like a scalded cat, they hardly even touched down. Whilst we're on the subject, what actually happened to Buller?" she put her elbows on the table and raised an eyebrow questioningly.

"Buller?"

"E-Yain tells me that one of your apes in armour executed him whilst he was defenceless and tied to a chair. I think that says a lot more about your people than it does mine."

Mal sighed, he had heard details about the whole, sordid incident from Sembhee and had not agreed with it then, he was damned if he was going to try and justify it now, "I was as shocked when I heard about it as you no doubt were. It should never have happened, but it was a direct order from the commander of the Roost and could not be disobeyed, my man didn't have a choice. This might not be your army, but I assume there's still some sort of chain of command."

"There's always a choice, that's the basic difference between an organic and a construct," spat Haze, "under normal circumstances I'd have demanded that you hand Na-Thon over to me to be tried for murder."

"You're in no position to demand anything!" Mal shouted as he jumped from his seat, his face reddening.

"Calm down," sighed Haze, holding out the palms of her hands in supplication, "I said under normal circumstances; in all honesty, you saved me a bullet, the man was scum. You remember I mentioned last night that men were coaxed to join the League with the promise of easy women? Well Buller was one of the men who procured them. He had his own ideas about quality control too. I'd been trying to think of a way of getting him out of the picture for months, but he was popular with the men... for some reason."

"I don't think that there's any point in us staying here. If, as you say, you've told us everything you know. I don't think we can be of much further use to each other."

A wry smile spread across Haze's face, "No, I suppose not. I'll call your taxi back, by the time it arrives I'm sure your men will have had time to collect their things, and your clothes will have been laundered by now too I should think," her smile widened as she noticed the flushing on the commander's cheeks. She instructed one of her staff to inform Mal's men that their commander was preparing to leave.

"It's a pity that we can't just bring our skimmer directly here, it would save time and we wouldn't have to listen to that damn horse giving us the tourist experience all the way back."

"You'd never be allowed to, even out here Port security operate drones that enforce the automatic autopilot rules quite heavy-handedly, you'd be forced onto a transit beam and be under remote control before you could open the canopy and spit. We can only operate here because our skimmers are registered to local people, and you wouldn't believe the permits you have to keep re-registering for that," she looked at Mal, who seemed to be deep in thought, "are you alright?"

"I was just thinking; if that is the case, how did your benefactor manage to land unmolested?"

"I..." the look of confusion on Haze's face slowly changed to one of realisation, and then shock, "Gods, I never even thought about that, it never registered, but the only people who would be able to flout the rules like that would be the Company, and that would mean..."

"That the skimmer hadn't been stolen, and that you'd been played and landed like a fish."

The blonde medic did nothing to deny the simile as she sat there with her mouth opening and closing in disbelief, "but why would the company need us? Why didn't they just send in a tactical team and take you at a time of their choosing? It's not like they have any real regard for local laws."

"Deniability perhaps? It's one thing grabbing some misguided soul who's been using the Cloud to post anti-Company literature and them never being seen again, no one cares, or if they do care, there's nothing they can do about it. But if the son of a noble house goes missing and there's a sniff of Company involvement, then all the hounds in all the hells would be let loose. Things like that can start revolutions you know."

Haze was just about to comment on the commander's over-inflated self-image when the door flew open, a young woman was pushed bodily through it and went skidding across the floor. She was followed by an infuriated Zatch, who was dabbing at the four raw and bloody streaks across his cheek. He made his way to his commander, all the time staring angrily at the girl, who was now curled into a ball against the counter, her tearful eyes flicking rapidly between the towering Pewter Guardsman, Haze, and the clock. The shocked bandit leader stood and started to make her way across to where the terrified girl sat. "What the hells is going on?" All around her there were the varied creaking sounds of guns and knives being readied in their holsters.

Zatch ignored the rapidly angering bandits as well as their leader's question, and addressed Mal directly. "I apologise My Lord, I caught her searching your belongings, when I asked her what she was doing, this," he indicated the clotting blood on his cheek, "was her only reply, then she ran," he looked at her with thinly veiled contempt and continued, "needless to say, she didn't get very far."

Haze was just about to place her hand on the girl's shoulder, but drew it back, as if she had been burned. "Is this true Yvette? Were you searching through our guest's belongings?"

"No, I... I delivered the gentleman's laundry, but had forgotten his shirt, when I went back to the billet to deliver it, that man," she pointed at Zatch and wiped her eyes, "attacked me, I thought he was going to... well, you hear these stories..." She burst into tears and the rest of her words were unintelligible. Haze scowled at the guard, her eyes full of hate.

"The taxi should be here any moment, you and your men can wait for it outside, make sure you take everything with you because you're not getting back in," her voice was calm and even, but there was an undertone that indicated that no argument would be persuasive enough to change her mind.

"The bitch lies My Lord!" Zatch launched himself across the

room, intending to wring the truth from her bodily, but was stopped by his commander's palm on his chest.

"We are leaving, there is nothing left for us to do here."

"But My Lord…"

Mal pointed to the door, Zatch visibly deflated and left the room. They returned to their quarters, picked up their remaining gear and made their way outside. The three bandits following them did not have their weapons drawn, but the confident way they carried themselves let the pair know that this was a mere technicality. They left the compound and joined the other guardsmen who were waiting with their kit by the side of the road, almost exactly where Demoso had initially dropped them off.

Na-Thon looked at the bandits who were following the commander out of the gate and whispered conspiratorially to Captain Sembhee, "I have the feeling that we're not leaving completely of our own accord," Sembhee nodded in agreement. He caught the commanders eye, and raised an eyebrow, which managed to convey the questions "Are you alright?' and 'Should we shoot the people behind you repeatedly, in the head?' simultaneously. Mal indicated that everything was fine for the moment, but that they were to remain vigilant. The three men backed towards the entrance and stood there, waiting patiently, making sure that neither Commander Mal'Ak-hai nor any of his men tried to get back into the compound. Captain Sembhee looked down the coastal road to the east, and saw a glint of reflected sunlight.

"I think our transport is nearly here," he turned to the commander, "Will we be going directly back to the Roost My Lord, or do we have another clue to follow? I took the liberty of ordering our skimmer back to the port, it should arrive within the hour," he looked down at his chronometer to check the time; it was a few minutes to ten. Mal explained what he had discovered from Haze; that it was the Company themselves that had tried to kill him, but that he still did not know why. He chose to withhold the information about Zatch's claim that the girl, Yvette, had been caught going through his belongings, although he believed him, there was no way that they would be able to convince the League of her guilt, pursuing it now would be pointless.

As if on cue, the gates to the bandit's compound opened and Haze walked across the dusty ground towards them. Her face was like thunder and she was carrying a gun. The commander looked at his men and shook his head, their hands moved away from their holsters.

"I've come to make sure you leave without attempting to murder or rape anyone else," she was incredibly tense, and Mal could tell that she was barely in control of her anger. He lowered his eyes and stared at the ground to try and avoid any further pointless confrontation, "You'll leave now and you won't return and I won't sanction any further raids on your property, Company sponsored or otherwise. Do we have a deal?"

"If the Company's involved, I don't see how you'll have an option, you owe them now and they have a selection of big sticks to enforce their authority with." He looked her in the eye reticently, the little expression that he allowed himself was sorrowful more than anything, as if he regretted the position that she found herself in. "If we can help, we will. I understand your need for independence, but it seems that we both have a reason not to trust the Company now."

Haze's face reddened, "We don't need your help," she hissed through clenched teeth, "nor will we ever. Go back to your castle and order your slaves to prepare a feast to celebrate the conquering heroes' return. In fact, here is your exit strategy," they all turned as the equine taxi pulled up behind them.

'Morning gentleman, nice to see that we're all still alive. Oh! We seem to have lost one, will you be taking his place Ma'am?" it looked directly at Haze with its baleful blue eyes, who stared back impassively, "perhaps not then. That's odd…" Demoso's ears pricked up and the taxi looked out to the west.

Haze's communicator beeped loudly, "Yes? How many? How long? Right, hand out what anti-aircraft weapons we have and get the women and children away in the skimmers, call the port facility and say we have Spiders incoming and we need assistance. Don't waste time letting them fire the first shot," she closed the link and turned to Mal, "you should leave now, there's a group of targets inbound, none of them are showing life-signs so I'm guessing they're Spiders. You've got no more than a few minutes before they arrive."

The commander shook his head, "We'll help if you'll let us," the bandit leader continued to scowl at him, "whatever you think of us, it's another four guns. We can make a difference," he stared back at her and her expression softened. She sighed indignantly and nodded. He turned to his men, "Get to the armoury and see if you can get hold of something heavier than your pistols; grenades, rockets and any ion weapons you can find," he looked at Haze, who shook her head, "but you probably won't be able to. The enemy is approaching from the west, dig in and start with a standard defensive pattern then pray to the hatchet faced God of short battles that we don't have to go hand to hand. Na-Thon, contact our skimmer and get the pilot to signal for powered armour re-enforcements then try to get as close as he can to us, go!" The three guardsmen briskly saluted and jogged back into the compound, intent on their orders. He turned to the taxi, "And you should probably try to make your way back to the port."

Demoso looked at him, then bowed his head so low that his nose was almost touching the ground, "I'll be fine, never abandoned a fare before and I don't intend to start now. Anyway, the Spiders are constructs like me, I'm just another item of furniture to them. No real threat."

"Well, have it your own way," Mal turned away and was just about to join the defence when he turned back, "what are you doing? Are you trying to make it look like you're eating grass?"

One of the taxi's glowing eyes swivelled to stare straight at him, "The sight of a grazing horse has been scientifically proven to put biologicals, such as yourself, at ease. I am programmed to assume this position whenever I anticipate an extended period of local stress."

Mal shook his head and ran towards the gate, in the distance, he could hear the whine of over-stressed flight engines, lots of them. The Spiders were on their way in force.

By the time he'd caught up with the rest of his squad, the skimmers carrying the non-combatants were just lifting off and as soon as they had cleared the roofline, their pilots engaged full throttle and accelerated away, towards the port and relative safety. There was a cry of "incoming!" from one of sentries perched high on a western rooftop. The warning was drowned out by the sound of the first rocket explosion as the sentry, and the section of rooftop he had been stood on, disappeared in a gout of flame. They ducked instinctively as they were peppered with small chunks of concrete and the sound of gunfire pierced the air as the Spiders passed low overhead. Trusting his men to know what to do, he broke cover and ran over to the nearest group of bandits, "Fire once they've passed over, at the speed they're going it's going to take them a while to turn, they'll probably be climbing too, you'll have more time to aim." The men nodded warily, still unsure as to whether they should trust him completely. He looked up and saw the first group of Spiders completing this very manoeuvre, with a grim smile, he grabbed his pistol, sighted along the barrel and fired. The shot hit the lead Spider just behind its sensor pod, it was by no means a killing blow and, in fact, it had hardly penetrated the armour. What it had done, was cause a wobble in the flightpath of the still turning construct, a wobble just great enough to cause it to clip one of the others, there was a tangle of arachnid legs, and the two constructs fell from the formation and exploded as they impacted the ground. A cheer rose up from the assembled men, but the celebration was to be short lived.

A squadron of Spiders had continued their flight unseen to the east, dropped almost to the ground, then turned back towards the bandit base before launching a salvo of rockets. There was no warning of the impact before it had happened, fist sized pieces of masonry, razor sharp glass and shards of steel flew all around them and an ominous dust cloud billowed over their heads. Zatch was stood in a large open space between the warehouses. He had managed to find a multi-shot unguided rocket launcher and was scanning the sky for potential targets. The unmistakeable sound of a large-calibre accelerator gun filled the air and chunks of dirt started to explode at his feet as the solid steel rounds impacted the baked soil at more than supersonic speeds. Despite repeated shouts for him to get to cover, he did not flinch, not even when a chunk of shrapnel tore itself from the ground and carved a wide gash across his cheek and brow. He took a deep breath, put the iron crosshairs of the launcher over the Spider and pulled the trigger. The mass driver in the body of the launcher threw the rocket out of the canister in what seemed like slow motion. It took thirty feet, the exact space of two heartbeats, for its fins to deploy fully, then the miniature rocket motor engaged and it streaked towards its target. Time resumed its normal pace as the explosive found its mark, the Spider disappeared in a blinding flash that consumed a number of other units and left a glowing afterimage in his vision.

Na-Thon launched himself at the unmoving guardsman as he was waiting patiently for the launcher's reload cycle to finish. He caught him around the waist and propelled him out of the way of a cloud of anti-personnel rockets that had locked onto him the moment he'd pressed the trigger. The corner of the building behind them disappeared and the roof lurched drunkenly, threatening to collapse at any moment.

"Fire from cover!" yelled the sergeant, "brave is good, but dead is bad! You're not wearing your armour."

Zatch looked down at his torn and filthy shirt and nodded vacantly, "I saw an opportunity Sergeant, and I took the shot," he spat through gritted teeth, his eyes looked straight through Na-Thon as if he wasn't even there, "they can't be allowed to live sir, they're an abomination. They killed my sister.'

Na-Thon remembered now, Zatch's sister had been a member of a trade delegation that had been attacked and destroyed by Spiders weeks after the war had officially ended. None of the bodies had ever been recovered and he blamed himself for not being there to save her.

"We need to get back to the commander," the sergeant shouted above the din of screaming flight engines and exploding bombs, "get over there, and for the Gods' sake, stay low." He helped Zatch to his feet, handed him the rocket launcher and pushed him towards the sheltered corner where Mal and Sembhee were taking shots at the circling constructs as they passed overhead. They covered the fifty yards at a dead run and slid to a stop in a cloud of dust, which caused the captain to cough and spit uncontrollably, as he had had his mouth open, yelling for a team of bandits to take cover, when they arrived.

"Where in the Hells are the defence teams from the port?" yelled Mal, as he scanned the skies.

"They're not coming," a dust-covered Haze appeared from the interior of the ruined building, "I've just got the message, the entire fleet is grounded for maintenance on Company orders, something about a product recall. They apologised profusely for their truly unfortunate timing of course," she looked into his eyes and shook her head in disgust, "and on a lighter note, scanners detected another three squadrons of constructs incoming just before the dish got hit and we were cut off, I don't suppose that they're anything to do with you?" Mal shook his head, "then I'm going to assume that they're more Spiders. We're going to evacuate, I doubt even you four could protect us against those odds."

"No, you're right, give the order."

She looked at him quizzically, "I was going to, I wasn't looking for your approval, I was just letting you know what was happening." She turned away from him, activated her communicator and configured it to forward her voice to the compound's external loudspeakers, "This is Haze," her voice echoed all around them, "all remaining troops, we are abandoning the base. Everyone make their way to the Halcyon, do not stop to collect your personal belongings," she closed down the communicator and pointed to the east, "she was a leaving present from when I left the Lowland Volunteers, she's in the main hangar over there. Follow me."

The four guards looked at each other and started off after her, keeping to the shadows as much as possible. "Commander?" Sembhee attracted Mal's attention, then pointed upwards.

His commander turned towards him, looked into the suddenly empty sky and shouted to his men, "Watch yourselves, the sky's clear!"

Haze turned and frowned, "Isn't that good? Doesn't that mean the attack's over?"

"No, it means they think that they've softened us up enough, and they've landed to mop us up."

Her eyes widened as she realised what he meant, she

connected to the loudspeakers again, "Spiders are in the compound, I repeat, Spiders are in the compound. Anyone with functioning Ion weapons are to defend the Halcyon, she's our only way out."

They turned a corner, and came upon a wall of jagged rubble that hours previously had been the living quarters. "The hangar is just behind here, come on!" Haze started to climb, but Mal grabbed her ankle.

"No, we need to stay low. Once they're on the ground they're almost impossible to hit with one of these," he waved his pistol in her face, "so I can't guarantee your safety, we need to use stealth, try to get to your ship without being seen."

She thought for a second, biting her lower lip, "OK, we can go out through the main gate and circle around, there's an access door on the perimeter wall."

"No good, that's too exposed," there was a scream from behind them, the Spiders were sweeping the compound and getting closer.

"We go over or we go around, you're the military genius. Decide now, because they're nearly here."

Mal looked at his men, they were starting to get twitchy. If they'd have been clad in powered armour, and armed with something that could spit out a disabling high-voltage charge, then they could have taken the fight to the Spiders. But like this, wearing civilian clothes, carrying weapons that they couldn't count on to hit a Spider, never mind take one out of the game completely, they knew their life expectancy could at the moment be measured in minutes, not years. "OK, go!" he pointed towards the main gate.

Haze led the way, followed by Mal, Sembhee then Na-Thon. Zatch brought up the rear, walking backwards and keeping the launcher trained on anywhere a Spider was likely to appear from. They reached the courtyard directly behind the gates and stopped, backs flat to the wall. The commander made a series of gestures at Sembhee, who nodded and advanced, to check that the coast was clear. Once he had made sure that all of the approaches to the area were clear and found cover by the gate itself, he signalled for them to join him. Haze ran towards the gate to input the access code, as the others spread out defensively, taking a compass point each and readying themselves for the inevitable.

She took a deep breath, which unfortunately didn't stop her shaking as much as she'd hoped. Her hands hovered over the keypad and the part of her mind that held the combination for the gate immediately went blank. She covered her mouth with her other hand and exhaled heavily through her fingers, it was only six numbers, she typed it in at least once a day, why couldn't she remember it?

"Is it damaged?" called Mal, "Do you need help?"

She glowered at him, closed her eyes and let the muscles in her fingers try to remember the passcode on their own. There was a sour sounding buzz, and when she opened her eyes a large red light was flashing on the keypad. She hit the pad in frustration, which triggered the light and buzzer once again.

"I can hear multiple constructs!" yelled Na-Thon, "we need to get moving."

"That's not helping," she whispered under her breath. All around her she could hear screams and sporadic gunfire, she couldn't think of anything except her people dying at the hands of the mechanised monsters. Tears were forming in the corner of her eyes, not from fear, but from anger at herself.

Sembhee started to fire, "Movement, sixty yards." The guards turned and concentrated their fire on the section of the complex that he had indicated.

Haze swallowed and the adrenaline finally reached her brain, she typed the combination, the keypad lit a bright, cheerful green and the heavy motors that opened the doors started, and then abruptly stopped in a shower of sparks. She stared, dumfounded, at the smoking burned out motors, "What?" She started to smash against the pad with her fist, yelling unintelligibly, and tears of frustration streaming down her cheeks.

The commander looked between her, the gates, and the slowly moving shadow that the captain had noticed. "The gates must have been buckled by that explosion that brought down that building," he pointed at a nearby pile of rubble, "Zatch, exit!" The young guard turned, aimed the rocket launcher at the centre of the large metal doors and pulled the trigger. Haze dived to the ground as the rocket was propelled silently forwards, its motor only just igniting when it hit and there was a ringing explosion as they were blown completely from their hinges. Running through the billowing dust-cloud, Mal grabbed Haze and lifted her roughly to her feet, "Run now, get to your ship, we'll be right behind you." She took a breath, and not being able to tell from her tear stained face whether she was going to argue or not, he repeated, "Now."

She nodded, "Keep turning left, you can't miss the entrance," and then she was gone.

"They're coming!" shouted Zatch, backing towards the still smoking gateway. As if on cue, a half dozen Spiders appeared from the wrecked buildings and crawled forwards, their bodies hunched, waiting to strike. One carried a maintenance construct aloft between its two front limbs, as he watched, it slowly and deliberately tore the protesting construct in two and flung the still sparking sections to the ground. He checked the indicator on the launcher, there were only two rockets left and the way that the constructs moved sinuously out of the way as he targeted them let him know that it was going to be difficult to do any real damage, but for the time being, it was keeping them at bay. It was almost as if there was some kind of animalistic self-preservation instinct at work.

"Gentlemen, it's time we were leaving. Fall back, by the numbers." Mal's voice, which sounded significantly calmer than he actually felt, echoed around the courtyard. The guards reversed towards the exit, each one silently praying to the surefooted but shaggy Goat God that they did not stumble over some chunk of errant masonry, knowing that that would spell instant death for them and all of their comrades. They paused under the archway to quickly check their ammunition, apart from the two rockets, they had seven full magazines for their compression pistols, as well as the few rounds they each had in the guns themselves. Mal chanced a look through the gate at their destination and saw that the corner of the compound was thankfully less than a hundred yards away, although there was precisely zero cover for that entire distance.

"Zatch, put a rocket into the centre of the largest concentration of Spiders; Sembhee, empty your pistol at the same targets then fall back, standard leapfrogging overwatch, thirty yard separation." The guards acknowledged the order and Zatch, once again, took aim. The Spiders in front of him moved out of the way, but as he fired he pulled the launcher to the side, intending to wrong-foot the constructs, his plan worked to an extent as the mass driver's dwindling magnetic field curved the rocket away from its initial target, there was a brief tangle of mechanical legs as a number of closely packed Spiders tried, unsuccessfully, to move in two directions at once, which allowed a couple of Captain Sembhee's shots to actually hit home and cause some minor damage. The two guardsmen ran through the gate and along the compound wall, stopping almost exactly thirty yards away, then reloaded and took up defensive positions, such as they could.

"I would give a year's wages for some powered armour and a high output ion cannon right now," breathed Sembhee.

Zatch nodded, "And I'd be a lot happier if the ammo remaining indicator on this," he lifted the rocket launcher off his shoulder momentarily, "displayed a higher number."

Both men tensed as their commander and Sergeant Na-Thon started to run towards them. They had travelled no more than ten yards when the first of the Spiders exited the compound, another braced itself on the top of the perimeter wall and crouched, ready to strike. Zatch instinctively launched the last of the rockets, then threw the launcher aside and drew his pistol. The projectile flew between the two running men, ignited and then slammed into the gatepost, trapping the first Spider under a pile of rubble and knocking the second from its perch. The explosion galvanised the runners and they redoubled their efforts as they carried on past Zatch and Sembhee, and replaced their defensive position another thirty yards further on.

Commander Mal'Ak-Hai looked to his left and saw the stately chrome shape of Demoso, still pretending to graze peacefully by the roadside. There was no way that the Spiders would leave anything alive at the base to tell the story of the attack, construct or organic, they had already proved that by their treatment of the maintenance construct. He waited until the guardsmen who had been covering them had started to run, cupped his hands around his mouth, and yelled at the top of his voice, "Taxi!" The construct's ears pricked up and he raised his head; Mal gestured wildly to him without taking his eyes off his desperately running men. The Spider that had been knocked from the wall had briefly stopped to investigate the condition of the one buried by rubble, and decided that freeing the fallen construct so that it could continue the sweep would be the best use of its time. It signalled to the next nearest Spider, who spent moments walking along the top of the boundary wall surveying the scene, before dropping down and advancing on the guardsmen. Several things then happened at exactly the same time.

Zatch and Sembhee made it to the corner of the compound and called for Mal and Na-Thon to join them, Demoso started to gallop towards the commander and the Spider that had jumped from the wall changed course to intercept it.

The two constructs closed on each other at breakneck speeds, neither of them showing any sign of slowing until they were scant yards apart. The Spider raised its front pair of legs straight in front of it and dug into the ground with the remaining three pairs. It slid to a halt and braced itself, ready to impale the equine taxi construct on its extended claws. A microsecond later, Demoso disconnected itself from the carriage and jumped. The Spider lifted its head to follow the flight, in one swift movement, the now horseless carriage impacted underneath its upturned sensor cluster, breaking its neck and the taxi's rear hooves smashed down mercilessly into its face, shattering the electronic items contained within into a kaleidoscope of flying shards.

Demoso reached the corner where the guards were taking cover and stood there as if nothing had happened.

"Is that something they teach in taxi school?" remarked Na-Thon, "it's an approach I've not seen used before." He looked of at the still-sparking corpse of the Spider by the roadside, its crooked legs splayed around it, "can't say that it's not effective though."

"Thank you Sergeant, it was nothing that I would not have to do two or three times on a normal Saturday night." Its ears twitched and it seemed to sniff the air, "There are more Spiders coming from the compound, if you have a clever plan, I would suggest that you put its wheels in motion sooner rather than later," he looked over the commander's shoulder, "and whilst we are on the subject, the nice lady from earlier, the one who stopped everyone shooting each other and then accused you of all being murderers and rapists, is waving at you."

Mal turned to see Haze standing in a doorway, worriedly scanning the surrounding area and beckoning them hurriedly towards her.

"They really are quite close now," Demoso turned its head, its neck strained, almost separating the chromed plates, as it reared onto its hind legs and tried, unsuccessfully to look over the perimeter wall, "fifty yards at most I should say."

The guards and their new companion ducked inside the hangar, the armoured door was slammed shut and locked behind them.

Sembhee whistled as he looked up at the ship looming over him. "My Lord, that's not what I was expecting."

Mal scowled incredulously at Haze, "They gave you an orbital troop transport as a leaving present? Did you paint it bright red? It seems a little ostentatious, even for a captain of your obvious prowess."

She was just about to ask him what he was insinuating, when there was a loud crash against the external door. Demoso looked towards the door; there was an obvious bulge where the force of the Spider's blow had warped the metal as if it were tinfoil. "They're here," It remarked in an oddly sing-song voice. The bulge was joined by a second, and then a third in quick succession.

Haze grabbed Mal's shoulder, "You say you can fight these things easier in the air?" Mal looked down at her hand, which she hastily removed, then nodded. "everyone get aboard, K'trin and Dolan, man the sponson guns; let's get the Hells out of here!" her voice echoing around the sealed room. As if triggered by all the shouting, the frequency of the frantic banging on the door increased and at that same moment, dust started to fall from the ceiling. Haze looked up and her eyes narrowed. The high ceiling was sectional, it slid open to allow the

Halcyon to take off and land vertically and dust often rained down when the doors were opened, or the transport's rocket motors were first started. As neither of these conditions were currently true, there was only one remaining possibility, "Commander? I think there might be Spiders on the roof."

Mal emerged from the interior of the ship clutching a pair of ion rifles, throwing one to Zatch, he waited halfway up the boarding ramp, hurrying the last few bandits aboard. He leaned out around the bulk of the transport, but could see nothing but the support struts. "We need to get into clear air before a Spider that's still carrying some high explosives appears," he pointed forward, towards the cockpit, "so, if you would be so kind?" She ran past him, with a grim expression set on her face, and took her seat next to the co-pilot, who had just finished priming the thrusters. She turned and addressed the gunners, "Once we're off the ground and the doors open, fire constantly, aim for any Spiders you can see, but don't worry about hitting the hangar, I don't think we'll be coming back here anytime soon. Just keep firing," they nodded nervously.

With an almost deafening din, the rocket motors came online and the Halcyon started to lift gravidly into the air. The automatic systems tried to close up the rear boarding ramp, but Mal punched the over-ride with his fist. He looped his belt around the hydraulic closure ram and indicated for Zatch to do the same. An ever widening beam of sunlight splashed across the wall in front of them as the roof started to open. He took a deep breath and winced as the stentorian sound of the point defence guns added their voice to the cacophony.

"Another ten seconds until the doors are fully open... we have incoming!" The Halcyon tipped drunkenly as a number of Spiders jumped down from the slowly opening roof onto the hull. Alarms sounded as Haze fought to keep the ship from turning turtle. She spun the ship on its axis, hoping to dislodge some of their uninvited passengers, but the walls were too close for her to build up enough speed for the manoeuvre to be effective.

Mal looked up as he heard the unmistakable skittering noise of a Spider making its way aft above his head. He made a mental note, providing he didn't spend the next few seconds falling onto a concrete floor and being torn apart by Spiders of course, to make an offering to whatever Gods the maker of his belt held dear, and leant out as far as he could. He couldn't see any sign of the target, but fired a burst from the ion rifle at where the sound seemed to be coming from. More frenzied skittering from above informed him that he'd been close enough to make the Spider think twice.

His view changed to include a lot more of the floor as Haze brought the nose of the transport up, ready to accelerate out as soon as the way was clear. The skittering noise changed to a rolling scrape as the Spider seemed to lose its footing, tumble and fall. The jumble of flailing legs appeared momentarily in their field of view as it fell drunkenly towards the floor. Both guards took aim, and Zatch fired first, hitting the target just as it triggered its flight engine. The massive electrical charge overloaded its main control systems and the sudden uncontrolled thrust augured it explosively into the ground.

It took only moments for the troop transport to reach its cruising altitude, and as they transitioned from vertical to horizontal flight, Mal unhooked his belt and stabbed at the ramp closure control. His last clear view of the compound showed that at least half of the Spiders had become airborne and were following them, whilst the others were methodically tearing the base to pieces. Zatch and Na-Thon took over the gunnery positions as he made his way forward, and stooped under the archway leading to the cockpit. Haze was cycling through the various status displays, she paused on the short range sensors, "We're leaving them behind, they can't catch us now," she patted the wall panel beside her, "Well done Girl. We'll get you a new coat of paint when we get to..." it was as if a switch had been flipped, a frown crossed her face and her expression changed from one of relief to one of pure hatred as it finally hit her, "They attacked my home! They killed my friends!" With a flick of her wrist, the transport curved back around and started to head in the direction that they had come from.

"What are you doing?" cried Mal, trying unsuccessfully to make a grab for the controls but losing his footing as the deck bucked underneath him, "this is a transport not a fighter, does this thing even have any armament other than the two cannons?" Haze ignored him completely, the whiteness of her knuckle indicating how tightly she was gripping the control column and how little she was listening to anything but her own internal dialogue; he turned to the co-pilot, who shook his head. Mal sucked air in through his teeth and slammed his fist against the wall, "Gods damn it woman, you'll kill us all!"

Chapter 15 : Completion

Britt looked up from his data tablet, leaned back in his chair and exhaled grandiosely, "That's the last thing crossed off Captain. She's finished, there's nothing left for us to do other than a flight test."

Lady Dorleith balled her fists in frustration as she looked through the window at the constructs busily working out in the docking bay, "And there's no chance of that until my dear brother gets back from his little revenge trip and he loads us up with a platoon of his armoured dancing bears," she raised her eyebrows, "Frobisher, connect me to Stalys."

"Connection established Ma'am."

"Stalys, open the main doors, the Edward Teach is ready to depart," The captain gestured theatrically at the Intercomm panel to make sure that Britt was listening.

"I am afraid that I cannot comply my Lady, the Baroness has ordered that the external doors to your docking bay may not be opened without her express permission. That permission has not as yet been granted," there was a pause, just long enough to indicate that the A.I. did not really want to continue, but knew that it must, "the Baroness has also requested that she be informed if you made any attempt to open them."

"Cut the connection Frobisher," she slumped back down into

her chair and raised her hands to the ceiling, "a mother's trust of her first-born child is a wonderful thing to behold, is it not Mr. Britt?"

The hirsute First Officer smiled gently, "That it is Ma'am, although in fairness to the Baroness, if she hadn't put the lock in place, where would we be?"

She looked at him questioningly, "We'd be in the air, planning a raid on a company supply base, at Sidi Ferruch, shooting Spiders out of the air, any or all of the above?"

"All of which your mother sees as very dangerous pursuits, made much less dangerous by a company of heavily armed Pewter Guardsmen whose job it is to keep you from harm," he raised his hands in pre-emptive surrender, "not that I am taking her side you understand, just trying to clarify her position as I see it. When it comes down to it, a platoon of armoured dancing bears would be very useful during a boarding action," he mimed the actions of armoured bears dancing whilst sword-fighting, but stopped when he realised that she wasn't paying him any attention.

She considered his words silently whilst she ran the tips of her fingers over the delicately cut jewels of her dagger, the warmth of her touch seemed to enhance the sparkling of the gems. In fact, even after she took her hand away, there seemed to be a tiny spark inside each one, like a glowing ember as viewed from a great distance, which slowly faded away as she watched. Shaking her head to clear the after-image, she looked up at Britt, "Sorry, what?"

He smiled and looked at the glittering dagger that she was still turning around in her hand. "I was saying that there could be worse things than having a force of well-trained men on board who were all trying desperately to keep us alive."

Her spinning of the blade stopped abruptly, "Then train some of our men to do just that, I will not have my brother aboard this ship, watching our every move and reporting it back to the Baroness; and I certainly won't have him breathing down my neck, comparing everything I do to something my father did before me." Britt wrinkled his nose and nodded as she continued, "and you can wipe that smug look off your face. We need to find a way to get out of here."

Frobisher's head turned towards the captain, "Ma'am, if I may make a suggestion?"

Dorleith raised her eyebrows at Britt and looked up, "Of course, why not? Suggest away."

"As you know, I have the over-ride codes for Stalys, and I could countermand the Baroness' lockdown," the captain took a breath, but Frobisher continued before she had time to speak, "however, the act of us opening the main doors and leaving the Roost would still register with Traffic control, and they would raise the alarm."

"So how exactly does this near magical power of yours help us? It's no good being able to unlock a door if you still can't actually go through it."

"No Ma'am, that is true. But that is not at all what I was suggesting, I can change the transponder details of any ship in the Rustholme fleet to match any other. I could, for instance make the Edward Teach seem to swap places with a Pewter Guard heavy skimmer, leaving no trace in the logs."

"Which would only be of any use to us if the guards were due to leave the Roost, which I would think that they are not. At least not until my brother returns, by which time it will be too late," mocked the captain.

"As you say Ma'am, the reason that I mention it is that I have just intercepted a transmission from the skimmer that was due to pick up Commander Mal'Ak-hai. Your brother has requested a squad of guards in full powered armour be dispatched immediately to his location. The pilot assumes that some pacification of the local population is required."

She ran through the possibilities in her head and turned to Britt, "Get everyone to their duty stations now. Do everything you can to get us ready to fly except lighting up the ghost turbines. Frobisher, swap places with the heavy skimmer."

"I have already taken the liberty of doing that Ma'am."

"Of course you have, I expected nothing else. How long will it take the guards to launch?"

"Six Pewter Guardsmen are currently leaving the armour room, a further six have already boarded the heavy skimmer in the launch bay now. I estimate that they will launch in four minutes."

"Gods!" she propelled herself out of the chair and onto the bridge in one fluid movement. Landry was just taking his seat as she sat down herself, "all stations, systems check," she barked. One by one, all of the bridge stations checked in. As each one did, an indicator light appeared on the screen set into the arm of her command chair. "Are we ready Mr. Britt?" the first officer turned and nodded. Stalys patched the comms system into the Roost's traffic control, so that they could monitor the conversation with the Guard skimmer.

The clipped tones of the guard's pilot echoed around the bridge, "Roost Control, this is Heavy Skimmer Reinforce One, we are ready to leave, requesting clearance."

"Confirmed, Reinforce One, opening the external doors now, please wait until the exit lights are green before proceeding."

When the pilot replied, he sounded rightly confused, as there were no external doors in the skimmer launch bay, "Doors? You know what?, I don't even care, thank you Roost control, I will launch when the exit lights are green, or when you start making a bean of sense, whichever happens soonest."

In the hangar bay, where the Teach was patiently sat, the external doors started to slowly open. Frobisher announced that the skimmer had powered up its engines.

"Engineering, this is the captain, bring the ghost turbines online and prepare for acceleration."

Britt nodded to confirm that he had control, disconnected the docking umbilicals and made ready to lift the new ship gently out of its cradle. "Gas bags to lifting pressure," the thrumming engine note changed as the eight turbines' workload increased to push extra Heptium into the oversized bags. Everyone held their breath as if expecting the engines to fail at any moment and drop them, awkwardly, back onto the deck with a resounding crash, but they hung there as impossibly as a walrus, in the exact centre of the huge room. The lights around the perimeter of the external door changed one by one from red to green and Britt gingerly idled the throttles.

"The skimmer is leaving the launch bay now Ma'am. I suggest that we do the same, as fast as you feel is seemly," Frobisher's calm tones still managed to impart a sense of urgency. Britt pushed the throttles forward and prayed to the hamster cheeked God of temporary invisibility that Frobisher's plan would work.

The modulated voice of the main Roost traffic control construct blared angrily from the speakers, "Airship Edward Teach, cut throttles and return to the launch bay immediately, failure to comply will automatically trigger the traffic control beams."

Dorleith screwed her eyes closed in frustration, "Britt, bring us about, I don't want control ripping any panels off with their overzealous application of tractor beams."

"Captain, I don't think they're talking to us. I'm not reading any targeting beams. I think that..." The voice of the skimmer pilot broke into their transmission.

"What in the Hells do you think you're doing control, I am on an emergency mission for Lord Mal'Ak-hai, he has requested immediate backup."

"Negative Edward Teach, Reinforce One has just left hangar three. I have direct orders from the Baroness to disable your ship and return you to the Roost."

Realisation dawned across Dorleith's face, "They think he's us? They think he's us! Britt, head south and get us out of tractor range now. Frobisher, as soon as we are clear, swap the transponder signals back to normal, we don't want to delay the guard any longer than we have to. I'm going to be in enough trouble with my mother as it is; I don't need my brother hating me for the rest of my natural life as well." The connector chains shook as the Teach swung around to the south and started to climb, the thrust from the engines almost dragging the bag behind her. In less than a minute, they were far enough away that they could not be stopped.

Back at the Roost, the Stalys terminal in the Baroness' quarters flickered into life almost hesitantly. Its indicator lights cycled five or six times before it plucked up the courage to make its presence known. "My Lady, I have just received an urgent message from docking control."

The Baroness sighed, licked her lips and looked critically at the brass head, "If the message involves any of the words 'Lady Dorleith', 'the Edward Teach', or 'escaped', I suggest that you look into having the construct responsible for traffic control repurposed as a fertiliser dispersal unit in the protein fields of the Open Lands."

"My Lady, I apologise on their behalf, there was some confusion with the transponder signals."

"Enough!" the Baroness slammed her fist down onto an ormolu topped occasional table and closed her eyes whilst she regained her temper, "I presume they are out of range of the traffic control beams by now?" Stalys indicated that they were, she let out an unusual and out of character expletive, "explain to the traffic controller on watch that he has offended me deeply and outline the alternative career choices available to constructs that are no longer required."

"They are still within communications range, would you like me to open a channel?"

The Baroness moved to the window and stared out into the mist that obscured the French coast. "Which way did they go?" she asked, absently.

"South My Lady."

"No, leave her, she's going home."

The Teach had been flying for two hours and was crossing the northern borders of Italia before the captain finally relaxed. She had expected at any time to feel the vicious tug of a tractor beam as it latched on to their stern, or the judder of a warning shot across their bows as a guard skimmer appeared alongside and ordered them to heave to and be boarded. But it seemed that her mother had let her go without a fight. She wasn't completely sure how to feel about that, on the one hand she was finally free, mistress of her own destiny and captain of her own ship both figuratively and practically. On the other hand, her mother had let her go not just without a fight, but without even a word. She'd had the past two hours to contact her, to beg and plead with her to come back to the Roost, but she'd chosen not to. Dorleith looked into the full length mirror in her cabin and willed the first beads of tears that were just starting to collect in the corners of her eyes to disappear. She squared her shoulders, breathed in and put all of her weight onto her back foot. She looked exactly like a pirate captain and as sure as the God of irrevocable decisions faces away from his followers, she was going to start acting like one.

"I am ready."

"I beg your pardon Ma'am?" Frobisher's head turned towards her, "may I be of some assistance?"

"No... actually yes, connect to the Cloud and give me the weather report for Socotra Island."

"Certainly," Frobisher's indicator lights cycled through all the colours of the spectrum as he opened a secure link. When they had finally settled on a welcoming green, the A.I. continued, "Socotra Island, Modern Republic of Yemen. Current temperature thirty point two degrees Centigrade, zero chance of precipitation, wind speed two miles per hour from the North West. Local weather control has no outstanding special requests."

"Good, calm enough to wear a nice jaunty hat if I choose to; Give Mr. Britt the co-ordinates and send all the data we have on Socotra, including the crew roster of the local Company relay station, if you can find it without setting off any alarms, to the terminal on my command chair."

She idly stirred the contents of her jewellery box with her finger, trying to find a particular piece that would complete her outfit. There was a moment of sharp pain, she winced and brought her now bleeding finger to her lips, sucking at the small, but steadily growing bead of blood. Peering deeply into the tangled mass of chains and brooches, she saw her High Voort's medal lying at its centre like a coiled scorpion, a smudge of blood on one of its articulated spines. "You, my fine spiky friend, have just volunteered for hair duty," she picked the bright decoration from its nest, looked at it accusingly, and used it to secure her long, red hair into a tight bun. With a final look in the mirror, she opened the door that led directly onto the bridge. The crew stiffened as she entered, suddenly taking a much deeper professional interest in their respective screens and readouts. "Mr. Britt, I trust that you have received the co-ordinates for our next port of call?"

"Aye Ma'am, a Company data relay station by the name of Kykeon, situated on the western shores of the island of Socotra, where the Gulf of Aden meets the Arabian Sea."

"Exactly, take us there low. In fact, see if you can keep us below detection altitude the whole way there," she thought for a moment, "also, we'll do as much as we can of the trip over water too, give us a chance to see what the ghost turbines will really do, if you think you can manage that?" Britt checked the navigational display and nodded. She sank into her chair and started to digest the information that Frobisher had diverted to her, "notify me when we're fifty miles out."

Britt addressed the crew, "Now hear this, we are heading for our first action. On this particular occasion we will be travelling south at maximum speed to assault a company relay station. Our possible prize is," he looked at the captain, who shrugged and mouthed the word "practice?" an extended blink crossed his face, followed by his hand, that anxiously cradled his forehead, "basically whatever you are carrying about your person when we leave. Flight time is five hours, so use this time to sharpen whatever blades you're taking and make sure your pistols are charged. Be prepared for fifteen seconds of hard acceleration. Britt out." He spent a few moments setting the course for the Nile Delta to the south east then opened up the throttles fully. The ship leapt ahead with the faintest of judders and almost instantly, a loud ringing crash sounded from one of the nearby cabins.

Dorleith leaned forward in her chair and yelled "Report!"

Britt checked the status displays on the consoles, "No damage reports, engines still working as they should, no new holes that we didn't have before. Frobisher, what happened?"

The A.I. terminal turned to the first officer, its inscrutable face still managing to convey a certain amount of levity, "Sir, it seems that there has been an incident in the galley."

Britt smiled, "Captain, I'll wager a hundred credits that the cook didn't bother to secure his pans before we accelerated."

The captain laughed, "And I'll wager two hundred that it was his knife-rack." She connected to the medbay, "Send a medical team to the galley, do what you must to patch up the cook and check that he has all of his ears, fingers and toes," she put her hand over the Intercomm microphone and attracted Britt's attention, "I presume that he had all of his ears, fingers and toes to start with?"

He shrugged.

"Then pass him over to Mr. Baju-Merah, he spends an hour in the brig for every broken item of crockery. Captain out." Closing the link, she noticed Britt's expression, "Do you think I'm being overly harsh? I want this crew running like a greased rattlesnake Mr. Britt. If that means someone needs to be made an example of, then they will be. What if the crash had been from the armoury? Would you have been content with me politely asking whoever had just blown the side of the ship off to please try not to do it again if at all possible?"

Her First Officer looked genuinely uncomfortable being the focus of her tirade and resisted the temptation to point out that it was, in fact, just a few pots and pans, figuring that whilst she was annoyed with the cook, she'd be less likely to be annoyed by him.

The curvature of the great armourplas screen allowed him to almost see directly below the hurtling prow. The Teach was eating the distance between them and Kykeon Station like a hungry shark and details of the landscape would appear on the horizon, and then disappear behind them in the blink of an eye.

"Captain, I think we've got company. Four contacts closing fast. Ninety seven degrees, Twenty miles," Landry checked the scanners, "no radio traffic. By the size of these readings it's one boat and three skimmers."

"Are we close enough for a detailed scan?" Dorleith checked through the displays in the command chair, but they didn't provide any more detail than Landry already had.

"No Ma'am, but at this rate it won't be long, I'd say seconds rather than minutes."

The captain stood and straightened her tunic, "Frobisher, bring all of the turrets online and start feeding power to Daisy. Mr. Britt, call battle stations, configure the bags for manoeuvrability and put us on an intercept course."

With no more than a nod, his hands flew over the controls as if they were separated from the rest of his body, bringing all systems to readiness. The background noise of the bridge changed as massive energies were channelled through the conduits routed above the ceiling of the bridge and into the capacitors of the huge Ion cannon.

Landry stared at the sensor screens, then slowly turned to face the captain, "I'm reading no life-signs Ma'am, and we should be able to at this range," He swallowed noisily, suddenly realising that this was to be his first taste of aerial combat, and that he had picked the worst possible enemy to lose his battle virginity to, "they're Spiders!"

The Teach completed her turn and, peering through the main window, the captain could just see a distant smudge, getting ominously bigger, "Could someone please show me what we're dealing with?" the captain's almost off the cuff remark stirred her crew into frenetic action. The main viewscreen, that had previously been showing their progress over the water, changed to a view of their tormentors, "so, we have three Spiders... And what in the Hells is that in the middle of them?"

Britt frowned as he looked up from the helm, "It's more Spiders, in fact it's a lot more Spiders." The screen focussed on the larger target and magnified them. Britt was right, it was a ball of Spiders some twenty-five feet across, linked together by their legs to present their armoured carapaces to the world.

"Ma'am, we're being scanned."

"Gods! The second they're in range open fire, let's see how they react to a taste of Daisy shall we? Frobisher, feel free to show me what these wonderful turrets of yours can do, I'm ready to be impressed," she turned to the First Officer, "Mr. Britt, would you be so kind as to blow those mechanical monsters out of my sky?"

His face opened up with a broad grin, "Captain, it would be a pleasure." He slammed his fist down onto a large red button on the console, and a blinding beam of almost solid blue light sprung from the bow and impacted with the edge of the mass of Spiders. The released ionising energy deactivated their systems instantly and a cloud of lifeless constructs fell away from the group and into the sea.

"Hit them again Mr. Britt, wide beam this time, they're starting to separate."

"I'm afraid Daisy's still charging Captain."

Dorleith exhaled deeply, "How long?"

"Eight seconds... seven."

"We'll all be dead in seven seconds! Frobisher, concentrate on the outriders with the turrets, fire at will." The sky lit up as Frobisher filled it with bolts of sun-hot energy, which the Spiders tried their hardest, but mostly failed, to avoid. The main mass slipped underneath them as Britt yanked the Teach upwards and to the right, the chains singing with the effort of keeping the bags and the hull in the same general area. There was a loud metallic scrabbling sound, which could be easily heard over the repetitive noise of the turrets, as the constructs tried to gain purchase on the wheeling ship's keel. "As soon as you like Mr. Britt, preferably whilst we're still in the air."

"Still charging, three seconds."

"They're turning!"

"One..." there was a moment of silence that lasted less than a heartbeat, "firing!"

Once again the bridge shone bright blue as Daisy barked searing electric death towards the closing enemy. This time the widened beam hit them square on, it enveloped the cloud completely. Blue lightning leaped from Spider to Spider, each one went dark as soon as it was touched by the coruscating energy and they fell heavily, like iron rain into the sea below.

"Mr. Landry, do we have any new targets?"

"No Ma'am, the turrets are dealing with the remaining stragglers now," he paused as the last few contacts winked out from the scanner and the noise from the cannons ceased, "my screen is clear."

"Good, keep your eyes open. Mr. Britt, resume previous course and speed as soon as we're able and get me a damage report," she struggled to keep her emotions under control; the Teach had won her first fight almost without a scratch and it was difficult for her to resist jumping from her seat and punching the air in triumph.

The First Officer reset the autopilot as he waited for the reports to come in from each section leader, "It looks like we may have lost some paint where they tried to grab a hold of us, but other than that," he turned towards the captain and smiled, "it was a flawless victory."

She nodded and stared out the panoramic window whilst her heart rate returned to something approaching normal. The coast of Eritrea was approaching on their starboard side and the shores of the Red Sea were starting to close in; she realised that they were approaching the target, "Set a course that takes us just south of the island and assemble an assault party, we'll take the gig."

Britt nodded approvingly, thought for a second then triggered the Intercomm, "Assault team one, grab your gear and muster at the captain's gig. Be ready in ten minutes, Britt out. Mr. Marsh, take over the helm." He stood as the crewman came and took his place, adjusting the chair for his lesser bulk. Pointing out a waypoint on the screen, he clapped Marsh on the shoulder and turned to the captain, "I'll just pick up Molly and signal you when we're ready to drop. Is there anything you want us to particularly look out for whilst we're down there Ma'am?"

"Yes, me – I'm coming with you," she reached under her chair for the compression pistol that was stored there and clipped it to her belt, "Mr. Marsh, keep on this course until we drop, then head directly south. But, and I can't stress this enough," she paused and looked directly into the crewman's eyes, causing him to swallow nervously, "stay within communications range and be ready to come and meet us in a hurry. Mr. Landry, you have the chair," she indicated her seat with a flourish and watched as the colour drained from the American's face.

"Ma'am, I," the flustered officer waved his hands at the controls, "The scanners, someone will need to, ah."

She raised her eyebrows, scanned the bridge crew and indicated the person sat at an engineering console whose name temporarily escaped her, "Mr.?"

"To'Mas Ma'am." Replied the crewman as he sat straighter and flattened the front of his shirt, "Milo To'Mas"

"Mr. To'Mas, please relieve Mr. Landry at his station."

The two men changed places with a nod. Landry lowered

himself into the captain's chair with some trepidation, almost as if he would burst into flames as soon as he touched it.

Dorleith leaned down and whispered into the petrified officer's ear, "Mr. Landry, just to make it perfectly clear, so there is no confusion in the future. Do not, under any circumstances, break my ship. Not even a little bit."

Landry nodded uncertainly and whispered, "No Ma'am."

Britt waited by the exit until the captain had retrieved her LongKnife and followed her as she left the bridge. He tried unsuccessfully, from the bridge via his quarters and down to the maintenance deck, to swallow the question that had been bothering him since he had received notice of their target, "So, why Kykeon Station?"

Dorleith turned, and looked up at his questioning, bearded face, "I presume that 'because' will be insufficient for you?" Britt's slow blink was all the answer that was forthcoming; she sighed and continued, "the Commandant of Kykeon knew my father before the war. They weren't friends by any means, more acquaintances of friends, then she joined The Company and..."

"So, revenge then?"

"No, not exactly, we share certain particular tastes though," Dorleith blushed. Luckily for her, the pair had reached the hatch that led down to the Teach's small hangar; she threw it open and slid expertly down the ladder using only the side-rails.

Britt made his way down using the more pedestrian method, keeping his eyes fixed on her all the while. Jumping off the bottom rung to the ground, he shot a look over her shoulder towards the waiting gig, "Tastes?"

"Don't look at me like that!" She scowled, "Alright, she dresses very stylishly. Happy now? We needed a soft target to give us an idea just how well this crew's going to work together and I needed..."

"A pretty new dress?"

A wave of anger passed across her face and her voice hardened considerably, "Mr. Britt, our friendship and your service with my family buys you a certain amount of leeway. Do not think for one second that it somehow gives you carte blanche to talk to me like that. You can think yourself lucky that the rest of the team isn't here yet, or you'd be finding yourself dropped off at the next city that we pass that happens to have an international docking mast."

Lee'Sahr's cough from behind her was quiet and feminine, "Ah, Captain? We're all ready when you are, should we go ahead and board?" the pirate was leaning against the small craft's hull, avoiding the captain's gaze by studiously cleaning her nails. The other five fully armed members of the assault team were milling around the cramped room, trying desperately not to be noticed, and failing miserably.

Dorleith nodded, and scowled angrily at the back of Britt's head as he squeezed past her, then followed him into the gig. The small craft was decorated in a similar fashion to the Edward Teach itself, complete with all of the brass and red velvet that that entailed. She took her seat in the cockpit next to Britt as he completed the separation checks. There was a chime from the Intercomm.

"Captain, this is To'Mas, we're receiving an automatic communication from Kykeon Station, they would like it very much if we would go away."

She smiled, "I'll wager that they didn't put it exactly like that though?"

"No, Ma'am, if anything, they sounded quite inhospitable."

She turned to Britt, "Are we ready?" he nodded in reply, "Mr. To'Mas, take us down to fifty feet, blame it on some engine malfunction or other and apologise to them profusely. Then take the Teach south as we arranged. Please remind Mr. Marsh to keep within communications range. Out," she cut the connection and addressed the squad behind her, "be ready, and try to stay alive."

The deck shifted below them as the great airship swung south and Britt released the docking clamps. The gig fell away, sudden brightness streaming through the cockpit windows.

"Hold on!" cried Britt as he engaged the emergency braking thrusters, he winced as the restraining straps tightened across his chest. The armoured bunker that marked the station's main doors swung into view as he turned them around and wrestled the protesting craft to the ground. They skidded to a halt in a shower of golden sand and the exit ramp extended. "Right, if we're lucky, no-one will have noticed that," his confident tone belied the fact that even he did not believe himself. His head sank to his chest and he sighed deeply as Lee'Sahr announced that they had incoming.

The assault team had already removed their harnesses and were making their way towards the stream of guardian constructs that began to flow from the station entrance.

"Come on old man," laughed Dorleith, "let's see if you've still got what it takes to go hand-to-hand with a construct and win." She jumped from the co-pilot's chair and ran out into the sunlight, her compression pistol firing over and over again into the crush of mechanical soldiers.

"Right Molly, that's our cue, let's see if I can snag myself a birthday present," he kissed the blade guard of the ripsword lovingly and sprinted into the fray. The Privateers had formed a curved wall in front of their captain and were dealing out righteous deactivation with both hands. The combination of archaically styled ceramic swords and modern energy weapons made short work of the first wave, and before long they were surrounded by piles of shattered constructs. Britt was just shaking the hydraulic fluid from Molly when he noticed that the stream of defenders had slowed to a mere trickle and Dorleith had pushed the rest of the squad forward into the cool shade of the entrance.

"Right, split up and grab what you can, we're looking for anything that's easily saleable, but then I suppose you already know that," she ducked as Britt took a pot-shot at a construct emerging from around the corner behind her, "we'll meet back here in ten minutes, I want to be gone by the time the security forces arrive. We've already had a successful air combat test, we don't need to press our luck."

Her crew disappeared in various directions and she chose to make her way inwards, following the signs towards the living area. The trip through the tight corridors, made even more claustrophobic by the flashing red light of a silenced alarm, took longer than she expected. Finally she found the locked door of the Commandant's quarters.

Removing the globe from her pocket, she held it to the locking plate and squeezed it gently between her fingers. The now familiar lightshow and melodic tones played until the lock tripped and the door slid quietly open. The room was neat, almost to the point of sterility. She had expected there to be very little clutter, it was a Company station after all, but there were no real traces of occupation, no photographs, no ornaments of any kind. She searched the few drawers and cupboards that there were, but they were all empty. "Where are you?" she spat, under her breath. She worked her way methodically around the room, knocking on each section of wall, listening for one that sounded hollow.

Dorleith was just about to give up when she finally heard the tell-tale echo of a false panel, unfortunately, no matter how she manipulated it, it would not open. Deciding that it must be locked, she once again employed the Kalibri lock-pick. The cycling lights had only just started their dance as the large panel swung open to reveal an arched doorway into a dimly lit second room. She stepped through as the light slowly brightened to reveal a dressing room, easily as large as the bedroom that she had just left. The walls were hung with sumptuous dresses and other articles of clothing that she thought would fit perfectly into the wardrobe of a certain female pirate captain. She walked over to a wide chest of drawers that was filled with fine jewellery. Choosing a bangle at random, she hefted it and could tell by its weight alone that it was solid gold. A boot-rack, nestled in the corner of the room caught her eye. Footwear was her only real weakness, the only chink in her armour; it was the one dispensation that she gave to her feminine side. Running her fingers down a pair of long, black, buckled boots she whispered, "By the Gods you are beautiful, and you're all mine now."

"No, I think you'll find that they're still mine. Who in the hells are you?"

The captain turned, in the doorway behind her was the most perfectly beautiful woman that she had ever seen. She wore a silk dress that looked as if it had been painted directly onto her body by one of the world's greatest artists, her immaculately coiffed hair tumbled to her shoulders in perfect ringlets and the pistol she had pointed at the centre of Dorleith's face seemed to be carved from a single flawless block of jade.

"I will not ask you again, who are you?"

"I..." she drew herself to her full height and tried to look at the woman's face, rather than into the bottomless tunnel of the gun's barrel, "I am Captain Dorleith Ahralia, commander of the Edward Teach, pirate and new owner of your complete wardrobe," she started to bow, lunged forward at the gun and hit the floor heavily as the woman simply stepped out of the way.

"Is this your first attempt at burglary girl? I'm afraid it looks like it's going to be your last."

Dorleith rolled onto her back and looked up, a new expression spread across the armed woman's face, a moment of confusion, followed by a broad smile that was somehow familiar, "You're here? Look, we don't have much time."

The woman's head exploding came as a huge surprise to the captain, not at all lessened by the shower of broken metal and plastic that scattered across the room, or the hydraulic fluid that leaked from her body's hollow neck as she slumped to the floor. Britt stepped over the still twitching construct, "We need to leave, now. The Station seems to have set itself on fire, and the fire suppression systems aren't working for some reason."

"She was a construct? How did you know?" the captain held out her hand and Britt pulled her to her feet.

"I haven't seen another living soul in the entire base, all the food in the kitchen was spoiled a long time ago and she didn't smell of anything," he noticed the bemused expression on his captain's face, "a woman like that would definitely be wearing perfume, she wasn't. But that doesn't matter, we really need to go. There's a countdown clock in the reactor room and it's been activated, I've contacted the Teach, they're on their way back already."

She shook her head to try and clear the fog, picked up as many pairs of boots as she could comfortably carry and looked expectantly at Britt, willing him to get out of her way.

He moved past her to the drawers, and emptied the top one into the bag that he was now carrying with a shrug, "No point in wasting it."

They both turned and ran out into the smoke filled corridor, the acrid smell of burning synthetics instantly searing their lungs. Britt pointed the way towards the exit and shoved the coughing Dorleith ahead of him. Gouts of flame issued from the air-vents as they ran past, only narrowly missing them. They skidded around a corner and almost ran headlong into a burning security construct that, despite its state, still tried to grab hold of them. Britt's ripsword sliced up through its groin and exited messily from the top of its head, scattering tubes and wiring to the four winds. The next turn took them to the main exit, despite her blurred vision, the captain could just make out the outline of the rest of the assault squad running for the gig. She stumbled and dropped the pair of black boots that had initially caught her eye, "Gods damn it!" she yelled and turned to retrieve them.

Britt grabbed her arm and tried to pull her back towards the waiting vehicle. "Leave them, we have to get in the air!"

"No! I can get them."

He grabbed her around the waist and lifted her bodily off the ground, causing her to drop the rest of the boots. She let out a howl as she was bundled through the hatchway and strapped into the co-pilot's seat. He sat beside her and engaged the thrusters. The gig juddered forwards through the sand before he pulled back the stick and launched them into the air, narrowly avoiding the bunker's roof with the landing gear. He turned them back out to sea and pushed the throttles forward so hard that he felt them flex against the stops. "I'd say that we only have about five seconds of countdown left, brace yourselves."

Dorleith tried to blink the soot from her eyes. "If the station's already set itself on fire, what is there still a countdown for?"

Britt shook his head absently, but changed the viewscreen to show the station, dwindling behind them. There was a bright flash, which seemed to come from a patch of featureless sand a mile to the east of the bunker, and a considerable area sank into the ground.

"Bloody denial weapon," growled Britt, keeping one eye on the broiling dust cloud whilst he searched through the cockpit window for any sign of the approaching Teach. "I've got a feeling that Kykeon was a little bit more than a relay station. That wasn't an atomic blast, but it was damn close to one."

The terminal in Duke Pytor's quarters buzzed, the peculiar sound had been engineered to wake a sleeping person gently, rather than shock them from their slumber in the style of an alarm. The Duke opened his eyes and turned towards the insistent noise.

"I assume that this is important Compliance?"

"Excellency, there has been an attack on the Kykeon Base at Socotra, the base's A.I. managed to trigger the self-destruct in time, the project was not compromised."

He threw back the covers and strode naked to his desk, displaying the interlaced web of scars that covered his torso, "Give me the details here." The masked screen filled with data, and his eyes narrowed as he read through it. "Gods damn them, six months of viral production ruined by some scum of a privateer. Send the Fist of Scrutiny to salvage what they can and report the results to me immediately."

"Excellency, there is a prisoner; one of the raiding party was captured by security. She was rendered unconscious during her escape."

"She?"

"Yes Excellency."

"Have Madla-Dera interrogate her."

There was a pause as Compliance Clouded the order to the Scrutiny. "Doctor Madla-Dera asks if you require the prisoner terminated or used as a type seven subject after the interrogation is complete."

Pytor tapped his index finger against his lips for a second before he replied, "Thank the good doctor for his zeal, but I have a much, much more interesting use for her, I will Cloud the details presently."

Chapter 16 : Pincer

The constant pounding of the Halcyon's guns was all that could be heard over the screaming of its over-stressed engines. Commander Mal'Ak-Hai could do no more than hang on as the transport jinked wildly to avoid the oncoming Spiders. "At least let me fly, I'm a combat trained pilot!" He yelled.

Haze engaged the air-brakes to wrestle them around in a flat spin and spat, "And you think I'm not?"

"Look, this game of 'who's got the thickest armour?' isn't going to last much longer," he ducked instinctively as a Spider grazed the cockpit glass and bounced off the hull, "eventually, one of them is going to hit an engine inlet or take off a wing, and then it won't matter whether you pray to the inflatable God of unnatural floatation or the steel-winged God of powered flight, we're going to become violently acquainted with the ground at very short notice."

She took her eyes off the viewer for a second and scowled angrily at him, "Maybe if you told your men to increase their accuracy a little, I wouldn't have to be trying to tie us in knots."

Mal stood dumbfounded, no-one had spoken to him like that since he had become commander of the Pewter Guard, and he was quite sure that he didn't really appreciate it.

Demoso had inveigled itself behind some cargo netting and was looking decidedly airsick. It regarded him pleadingly and he made his way across the deck of the constantly bucking transport to hunch down by the debilitated construct, "The whole 'looking as if you're grazing' trick not working for you then?"

"It seems that my maker did not see fit to shield my delicate electronics against the forces encountered during air combat manoeuvres, I believe that the reason might have been that horses do not generally fly."

"Well, try not to throw up on the floor; we wouldn't want everyone slipping around in whatever profit you've made since you were last emptied. Now, if you'll excuse me," he put his hand on the construct's withers and pushed himself upright.

"Sir," Demoso whispered conspiratorially, "I am not what anyone would call a master tactician, but I do not believe that we are going to win this particular altercation. There are many more Spiders approaching than we can deal with on our own."

"There're two armed skimmers inbound. In fact," he looked between his chronometer and the nearest window, "they really should be here by now."

The pilot of the incoming Guard skimmer checked his display, "Skimmer 16879, this is Reinforce One, requesting permission to enter formation."

"Roger Reinforce One, change course to 318 magnetic, I am detecting sustained weapons fire coming from the direction of Lord Mal's locator beacon."

"Acknowledged, 16879," the pilot made the course correction and closed into tight formation. They had just passed over the ruined fortress-citadel that was Great-Manchester when they finally came into communications range, "Lord Mal'Ak-Hai, this is Reinforce One, are you receiving me?"

There was a hiss before the sound of Mal's voice wavered indistinctly from his earpiece, "Reinforce... under heavy attack... transport... Spiders... immediate assist..." his Lord's voice abruptly disappeared to be replaced by the static. Both of the skimmers jumped forwards as their pilots strained to wring every last drop of power from the engines. As they approached their target, it took a moment to interpret the situation. There was a large, red, orbital transport, performing combat manoeuvres that it really was not designed for, surrounded by a swirling cloud of angry Spiders.

"Reinforce One, this is 16879, I'm going weapons free, I suggest you do the same."

Before the pilot had time to agree, the other skimmer had peeled from the formation and was climbing almost vertically into the bright sky, riding the column of fire from its emergency thrusters. He watched it for a second, triggered the seat restraints for his passengers and then curved around to the right to try and find a firing angle that would lessen the chances of him accidentally hitting the transport.

The three craft wheeled around amongst the tangle of Spiders, plucking them from the air one by one whilst trying to avoid their sporadic returning fire. There was a bright flash and a plume of smoke poured from one of the transport's engines as it started to lose height.

"Skimmers, this is Lord Mal'Ak-Hai, we've been hit. We can still fly, but not well enough to guarantee that we won't get hit again in short order. I'm going to see if I can convince the pilot to get this damn thing on the ground before another Spider takes it upon itself to fly into our remaining engine. Once we land, drop off the rest of the Pewter Guardsmen and then start clearing the sky. We're going to be sitting ducks."

Inside the Halcyon, the air was filled with smoke and the strident blaring of the fire alarm. The commander ran to the cockpit, "We have to get down on the ground, if we take another hit like that..."

"I thought you said these things were easier to fight in the air, and that we'd be dead if we tried to fight them on the ground," Haze replied with a sarcastic tone without taking her eyes off the viewscreen.

"Yes, but that was before we had two gunships and half a dozen Pewter Guards in powered armour at hand. I would much rather you land this thing now than have no choice about when that happens. Remember that with great armour," he rapped against the heavy bulkhead, "comes great mass, we'd auger into the ground like a burning rock."

Haze bit her lip and told the co-pilot to kill the alarm and deploy the landing skids, "I hope to the Gods your guard are as good as you think they are."

He pointed out of the window at a clear, raised area below them, "Put us down there, quickly. There's no cover for them to hide behind," he gathered his team, including Demoso, and told them what was about to happen, "we'll be touching down in a second, closely followed by Squad Three in full armour. They will create a defensive perimeter around the Halcyon whilst the skimmers clear out the Spiders, we will support them with the Halcyon's guns and the ion rifles, clear?" the guards nodded in unison, whilst Demoso looked as confused as a chrome horse could possibly look.

"And what would you like me to do sir?"

"I would like it very much if you could do your best not to get shot, especially whilst I am riding you."

The construct's eyes narrowed, "I beg your pardon sir? I am designed to pull a load, rather than have one perched upon my back."

"Are you refusing to help us?" the three other guards turned and scowled questioningly into Demoso's face, causing the armoured money chute in its throat to cycle nervously.

"No Sir, I..." it returned their stares as sternly as it could with featureless blue eyes, "I just cannot guarantee your safety, I have no saddle, or reins. I worry that you might fall."

Lord Mal smiled as he placed his hand on the construct's nose, "Falling and bumping my head is the least of our worries, believe me."

"Landing in five!" cried the co-pilot, "brace yourselves." The coughing whine of the engines changed as he directed the thrust downwards and moments later there was the crunch as they touched down.

Zatch opened the rear ramp and jumped out, keeping under cover, but scanning the sky with the muzzle of his borrowed ion rifle. Mal could just see the rear of the guard skimmer through the billowing dust as it landed, disgorged its deadly cargo and immediately leaped back into the air. He gestured to Demoso and indicated that it should move to the ramp. He waited until there was sufficient headroom and jumped onto the construct, kicked his heels into its flanks and drove forwards to join the leader of Squad Three. "Sergeant, form a perimeter around the transport; do not let anything through, or I'll have your eyes."

"Yes my Lord," the sergeant saluted, "we brought this, I thought it would be better than nothing," he threw a cloth covered bundle to his commander, who reverently unwrapped it and nodded.

Mal pulled the weathered, blood-coloured helmet of his powered armour over his head and blinked as its targeting systems came on line. He looked into the sky and was momentarily disheartened by the sheer number of bright red squares that appeared on his visor, each one designating a potential target. He leaned down towards the construct's head and yelled through his helmet, "Right, I would like you to start doing circuits of the Halcyon, sidestepping any enemy fire, and not getting in any of the guards' firing lines, do you understand?"

Demoso's calm voice emerged from his helmet speakers, "Yes Sir, I should firstly like to take this opportunity to point out that I have a wireless connection that is compatible with your helmet systems, so you don't need to shout quite so loudly. I shall commence operation 'try not to get blown into scrap metal' immediately," the hooves of the chrome horse threw up a plume of dust as it broke into a gallop.

The Pewter Guards from Squad Three took up positions surrounding the Halcyon and opened up with a mix of ion and accelerator weapons. Fragments of shrapnel and the lifeless bodies of Spiders began to fall from the heavens and impact the ground around them; the noise was deafening. Demoso danced between the raining wreckage as Lord Mal shot Spider after Spider from the air.

Inside the transport, Sembhee and Na-Thon continued to fire the sponson guns into the circling cloud above them. Haze moved from bandit to bandit, tending to the collection of minor cuts and grazes that had been inflicted during the Halcyon's violent battle in the air. "How did you manage that?" she asked a grizzled old man with blood slowly dripping from a jagged cut across his brow. He was crouched, cradling an ancient rifle to his chest as if it were his most treasured possession.

"I fell, I think my seat-strap came undone, hit my head on that," he weakly indicated the corner of a stowage pod, "it stings."

"It will do," she flinched as a large explosion from outside shook the whole cabin, then inspected the wound closely, "I can't see bone, I think you'll live. At least, you'll easily live as long as the rest of us." She looked up to see Yvette furtively staring through the side windows, tracking the progress of the commander of the guard as he rode around them on the back of the taxi construct. Her eyes looked almost hungry, and she shot the occasional glance at the compression pistol on Sembhee's belt. She didn't have enough time to wonder what the hells she was doing before the young girl grabbed the gun and started to run headlong towards the guard leaning out of the rear doors, his entire attention taken up with shooting at the Spiders above them.

Na-Thon yelled a warning and Zatch spun. He saw the girl running towards him, her eyes ablaze, with the heavy pistol clasped in her petite hands. In one, fluid, movement the muzzle of his rifle lowered towards her, but it was too late. She ran straight past him, took aim at the commander and a single lonely shot rang out, the noise of it was amplified to a deafening level in the enclosed space.

Yvette looked down disbelievingly at the slowly spreading red stain on her chest and dropped the pistol. Zatch grabbed her as she fell and lowered her onto the ramp, her eyelids weakly flickering. He looked at Na-Thon and nodded, "Thanks, I told you that she was dangerous." The sergeant pointed at his empty holster, shook his head and gestured towards Haze.

The captain-Medic was staring at the still-glowing barrel of her gun. She stood, transfixed for a second, shook her head to clear the fog and bounded across the deck to the fallen girl. Tearing open her sodden shirt, she examined the wound. One look was all that she needed to convince her that she couldn't be saved, not at the speed she was bleeding out, but she pressed down heavily on it anyway, in a desperate attempt to slow the bleeding "Why? Why would you do that? These people are trying to help us. I don't understand."

The dying girl's eyes opened and she stared directly at Haze. In a calm, but still faltering voice, she replied with complete conviction, "He'll... kill you all, and he'll just take it from you. You're all... dead."

"Who?" yelled the bandit leader as she roughly shook the girl's shoulder, "who's going to kill us? What does he want?" But there was no reply, her head lolled limply to the side as her last breath escaped her. She looked up at Zatch, who was looking between the events unfolding at his feet and the on-going battle outside, "who was she talking about? Who wants us all dead?"

"I can't be completely sure," he replied, "but I'll wager the meagre amount of my pension that I'll live long enough to collect that it has something to do with the people who hired you in the first place. It seems you had a Company cockroach hiding under your skirts," he nudged the limp body with the toe of his boot, "want me to get rid of this for you?"

She stood and looked down at the girl, whose air of frail innocence was only spoiled by the still spreading bloodstain and nodded imperceptibly, "Yes, thank you. That would be very kind."

He shrugged and pushed heavily with his boot until she rolled over and fell the few feet from the ramp onto the hard ground, "There, the thrusters'll take care of the traitor when you finally take off."

Rage grew in her throat, and she was just about to slap the guard across the face when she realised that he was right, Yvette was a traitor. She had, however indirectly, caused the attack on the base, caused the death of innocents and caused her to lose the only home that she'd known since the war. She looked down at the tangled mess of limbs and, despite everything, fought against a rush of angry tears, "I owe you an apology."

Zatch looked blankly at her, "For what? Accusing my Lord of murder or thinking me a rapist?"

Her eyes burned, but she swallowed the heavily barbed words of her response and returned to ministering to the rest of the passengers whilst her dignity was still intact.

The breathless voice of Squad Three's sergeant rang in Mal's ear, "My Lord, we're turning the tide, there are no more Spiders incoming and the few that remain seem to be those who like to think a little more defensively. They're slippery, but we should be able to breathe again in a few minutes."

"Thank you Sergeant. When you can spare him, get your field engineer to take a look at the transport's engine, see if he can do anything to get it to spin up," the sergeant acknowledged the order as Mal cut the connection and addressed Demoso, "Take us back inside; let's give our refugees some good news for a change," the horse turned and made its way back through the increasingly sporadic gunfire to the rear ramp. Zatch saluted from the top of the ramp as he came into view and as he dismounted. Removing his helmet, Mal noticed Yvette's body, lying under the ramp, "I leave you alone for ten minutes and you start resolving your own vendettas? Must I remind you that that is not the Pewter Guard's way?"

The young guard looked uncomfortably at his commander, "Lord, I had nothing to do with this, she was a Company spy," he pointed at Haze, "the captain executed her."

He looked questioningly back into the transport, watching Haze apply ointments and reassurance to her crew and then turned back to the waiting guard, "Executed her you say?"

"Yes Lord, she was aiming to kill you as you rode past," he lowered his head in obvious embarrassment, "she beat me to the shot Lord, I have no excuse."

"Hold this," he threw his helmet to Zatch, who cradled it and stood to attention. He absently looked towards Na-Thon and Sembhee, they returned his unspoken query with curt nods and turned their attention back to their guns. He stood patiently watching the bandit leader as she finished bandaging the arm of one of her crew.

The sounds of battle had all but faded when she finally turned around, "What would you like me to say first?" she looked at his confused expression and sighed, "should I thank you and then apologise, or vice-versa?"

"Captain, there is no need to..."

"Of course there's a need to!" her shout echoed around the suddenly silent cabin, causing her to pause whilst everyone stared, "it was my men who almost sent you to your death. It was one of my people who invaded your privacy and then tried to assassinate you."

"And you said some very unpleasant things about us yourself, don't forget about that," with the amount of adrenaline that was still coursing through his veins, is was difficult for him not to burst into raucous laughter, "we have achieved our mission. I have found out who wants me dead, there are more of us left alive than I could have realistically hoped for and we both have new allies in each other," he grasped her shoulders with both hands and squeezed them tightly, "I feel more alive than I have ever felt."

She shrugged off his hands, took a step back and glowered, "That would probably be because you've not just watched your home being destroyed wholesale by Spiders. Or it might be because you know all of your team are safe and accounted for. Don't get me wrong Commander, I'm grateful for your help, but don't think for a second that we're going to be taking long, hot showers together anytime soon," his cocky grin widened as she raised her index finger threateningly towards his face, "now look."

There was a call from the co-pilot, "The damaged flight engine is coming back online, Captain. We'll be ready to leave in a few minutes," followed by the unmistakable sound of a thrust turbine being preheated.

"Saved by the, erm..." he pointed up, towards the source of the sound, "excuse me, won't you? I need to organise my transport home." Bowing, he walked confidently back down the ramp and strode out into the sunlight with his hands clasped behind his back. Haze shook her head, she was sure that she could hear the infuriating man whistling.

The indicator lit once more on Duke Pytor's display, announcing yet another clandestine message from his private Cloud. He engaged the local microphone and opened the document. Where he had expected there to be a report from his agent in the bandit league, he was disheartened to find a report from her commander saying that she was missing, presumed killed, in the Spider attack which had been ultimately repelled by the target. Pytor slammed his fists down onto the arms of the command chair, "This is insufferable! Do I have to do everything myself?" he rose from his chair, his face glowing an angry red as he passed through the holographic display that had not quite had time to dissipate, "take us here," ordered the Duke, typing in a set of co-ordinates in the Compliance's helm display, "what is the flight time?"

The helmsman's hands slid effortlessly over the flat panel, "Six hours, Excellency, at our standard cruising speed."

Pytor nodded, satisfied, and left the bridge

Chapter 17 : Rescue

The Teach had been docked at Long Pig Station long before the excitement of the crew had returned to acceptable levels. Dorleith was sat in her cabin, going over the tally of items that they had acquired. Despite almost being killed in the earth shattering explosion, and the smoke damage to her outfit, they had done fairly well, considering that it was their first raid. The loot had been sorted and a number of teams had gone landside to try and sell the surplus equipment, in small amounts, to various different vendors so as not to arise suspicion. She opened the Intercomm, "Mr. Britt, report to the bridge at your earliest convenience, I should like to talk about a matter of revenge," there was no reply, and she tried again, "Mr. Britt, please report to the bridge as a matter of urgency, your continuing respiration depends on it," there was a lengthy pause, but still no reply.

"Ma'am?" Frobisher's head slowly turned to face the captain, "if I may, Mr. Britt left the Edward Teach shortly after we docked."

"Why?"

The A.I. was nonplussed, "I'm sorry Ma'am, but Mr. Britt did not see fit to seek my counsel before he disembarked. Although... my records do indicate that today is his birthday, which may have some bearing on the situation."

"Wonderful!" she threw the tally across the room, and breathed out as the data tablet smashed against the wall, "and how many members of the crew has he managed to subvert to the cause of drunkenness?"

The indicators in its face skittered as it queried the ship's internal sensors, "Apart from the trading teams and Mr. Britt, there is only one of the crew missing, and that is Miss Lee'Sahr."

"Of all the people I expected to get sucked into one of Britt's alcoholic sprees," she shook her head in disbelief, "I'd have thought that she'd have known better."

"Ma'am, she did not leave with Mr. Britt, in fact she didn't return to the ship with you from your excursion to Kykeon."

She stared coldly into Frobisher's face, "One of the crew did not return after a raid and I am only learning about it now, when we are more than fifteen hundred miles away from her last known position?" The A.I.s lights faded guiltily as Dorleith continued, "and I swear to the God of uncontrollable electro-magnetic pulses that I will tear you bodily from the wall if you tell me it was because I didn't ask."

The blinking lights dimmed to the point of imperceptibility and the A.I. remained silent. Dorleith stormed from her room onto the bridge. "Mr. Landry, contact Mr. Britt and get him the Hells back aboard. It seems that our revenge will have to wait."

Landry flipped switches with increasing desperation until he turned to face the captain, "I'm sorry Ma'am, but both his communicator and locator seem to be faulty at this time."

"Ah, I'm assuming that this particular fault manifests the same symptoms as you would get if, for instance, the devices in question were simply turned off?"

The young Comms Officer's mumble was all the convincing she needed that she should solve this problem personally, "Frobisher? Can you locate Britt using the station's cameras?" she waited whilst it forced its way past the security protocols.

"The last images I have are from some time ago, they show him entering the Old Town."

"That will have to do, I'm going landside. If you receive a communication from him, get him back on board. In fact, you may as well contact the trading teams and get them back here too and make the Teach ready for launch. As soon as I return, we're heading back to Socotra."

The loud affirmative calls were still ringing in her ears as she reached the loading bay doors. Pressing the access stud caused a warning message to be played in Frobisher's voice, "Danger, the docking connector is currently located on the port side of the ship, attempting to open this door could cause personal injury and/or death. To reach the port loading area, please follow corridor A-24 to..."

"Override."

"Caution, overriding the safety protocol in this instance..."

"Over... ride!" she spat through gritted teeth.

"Acknowledged, Captain, opening starboard loading bay."

The large doors began to open with a squeal of protesting metal; she made a mental note to bang the supervisor of the maintenance team's head repeatedly against it when she got back. She stepped back, took a deep breath and, remembering Britt's display in the docking bay, threw herself through the still opening doors. The busy dock was two hundred feet directly below her, but it was getting closer at an alarming rate. Her headfirst swan-dive continued until she had covered half of the distance to the ground. She engaged the grip-gloves and grabbed hold of one of the thick steel hawsers that was anchoring the Teach in place. Her downwards progress slowed until she was no more than ten feet from the floor and she could see the shocked expressions of the assorted roustabouts gathered below. With a flex of her hand, she disengaged the grip-gloves and somersaulted the remaining distance, landing like a cat in front of her stunned audience. Blowing the smoke from her palms, she approached the largest of them who looked too human to be a Pradilan, but too scaly to be completely human, "Have you never seen a lady disembark from a ship before?"

"You jumped," the off-green slab of muscle commented, "from all the way up there." He pointed at the Teach, high above them.

"Oh yes, I sort of did, didn't I? How splendid. Anyway, to business, a shiny ten credit piece to the first person who can tell me where my first officer is. He's a sturdy chap, hair in a pony-tail, has the look of a man who desperately needs a drink, you can't miss him," the assembled labourers shook their heads, or whatever they chose to keep their primary sense organs in.

"He's in the Queen and Scorpion," said a disinterested voice from above, "behind the Council Building, follow the stream of tuppenny doxies, you can't miss it."

"Thank you Mr..."

The wiry man, perched on top of the tall pile of packing cases, regarded her closely from under the brim of his wide hat, and replied lazily, "Preen, J'syah Preen."

"Thank you Mr. Preen, as promised, ten credits for your trouble," she fished a bright coin out of her pocket and tossed it towards him, he raised his hand and the coin stopped dead in the air, spun around gently and then fell to the ground at her feet.

"No thanks required... Captain," he smiled and pulled the brim of his hat down over his eyes. His posture made it clear that that was the end of their conversation. She gave him one last look, sighed, and set off into the Old Town.

It only took a few minutes for Preen's information to be proved right, the bar was easy to find, there was an almost constant stream of 'ladies of negotiable virtue' flowing both towards and away from the establishment. The latter looking significantly more flushed than the former, although they also looked to have fuller purses. Arriving at the main doors, a quick glance up at the sign over the entrance confirmed the building's identity. It portrayed a buxom female wearing a tiara, presumably the 'Queen' with most of her armoured suit torn away, apart from a few choice pieces that just barely protected her modesty. She was standing on top of a construct in the shape of a scorpion, whilst tearing one of its legs off with her teeth - A nod to some romantic depiction of a skirmish with the Spiders perhaps? She hoped that the battle had taken place in a warm climate, as otherwise Her Royal Highness was bound to catch her death of cold before the Spider had time to do its work.

Her artistic appreciation of the sign was interrupted by the tip of a broad grey claw being placed on her chest, "Ssso, where you think you go Misssy?"

She slowly looked up, and then looked up again, to stare into the maw of the largest Pradilan that she had ever seen. He must have weighed in at about four hundred pounds and very little of that was fat. As he waited for her answer, his mouth fell open and his bloated blue tongue lolled aimlessly over broken teeth. The stench that issued from it made her think that his last meal had probably been eaten by at least two or three other people before being served to him.

"In there?" she pointed behind his lumbering bulk into the darkened room, wondering if it would have been an idea to have brought Mr. Rax along with her for moral support.

"Ah, nope, not today," the huge lizard shook a claw admonishingly in her face, "men only, no little girlsss allowed in there, you be in big trouble. Yesss? Now, go play piratesss sssomewhere elssse."

The captain, deciding that the time had come for desperate, if slightly unpleasant, measures, plunged her hand as deep as she could into the Doorman's cloacal opening and squeezed its contents, viciously. The reptile squealed, instantly dropped to his knees and started to cry, "You go... go inssside... no charge... pleassse... let go of my... try the... veal... come... back sssoon... Yesss?" she left the giant reptile rolling around on the floor in a pool of decidedly reptilian tears, and walked through the open frontage into the darkness.

Dorleith strained to see any real details of the bar before her eyes became accustomed to the gloom. "Britt! Where are you, you stinking pile of kraken guts?" she yelled at the top of her lungs.

"I've got your Britt right here girl," leered one of the bar's corpulent patrons, as he pushed himself drunkenly to his feet and stumbled towards her, fumbling at his belt.

She tutted, casually launched a tall stool into the air with her foot, caught it and introduced it briskly to his chin. He fell backwards onto a table full of drinks, spilling them everywhere and incurring the wrath of their respective owners, "I do not have time for this," she hissed, "Britt!"

"He's in there," replied a familiar voice, "through the door marked Whore-Pits. It's where all the noise is coming from."

She turned to look at the voice's owner, who was stood in a corner that Dorleith would swear had been unoccupied seconds before, "It seems that I owe you my thanks again Mr. Preen."

The thin lipped man smiled weakly, nodded in confirmation, and disappeared back into the shadows. She approached the door, took a moment to steel herself and turned the handle. Even though she'd known Britt for most of her life, the sight of him completely naked, apart from some protective goggles and a pair of suspender socks, surrounded by over twenty women in various states of undress, whilst what looked like some kind of small primate played a shanty on the harmonica in the corner was too much for her. She slowly unholstered the compression pistol from her belt and shot out the overhead lighting panels one by one.

The discordant music stopped immediately as the simian musician dropped its instrument and disappeared into its den. Britt turned angrily towards the source of his interrupted reverie.

"Who the? Ah, Captain, I..." he blustered, trying to cover his obvious shame with a sadly undersized one hundred credit note.

"Mr. Britt, it would be difficult to explain just how disinterested I am in what you are about to say. Find your britches, pay any of these professional ladies," she peered questioningly into the sudden gloom, "or gentlemen that still require paying and meet me back on the Teach. We've a rescue to organise."

The great ship headed north, back towards Socotra, its connecting chains singing as the gasbags fought against wind resistance to keep up with the thrust from the ghost turbines.

'Mr. Britt, your cheek.'

The assembled bridge crew turned slowly to look at the captain, who was looking at Britt, who had a look of abject confusion on his face.

'You have something on your cheek and I pray to the God of easily transmittable diseases that it's lipstick.'

"Aye Ma'am I'll see to it immediately," the first officer patted the pockets of his waistcoat until he found one containing a silk handkerchief, which he produced, furtively, and scrubbed away at the waxy mark.

"Britt? When did you start buying handkerchiefs with gussets and waistbands?"

The hirsute privateer looked down at the tiny scrap of silk in his hand, noticed the delicate embroidery on the front and realised that he must have picked it up accidentally in his hurry to retrieve his clothes in the whore-pit. He quickly stuffed it back into his pocket.

"Frobisher, connect to the Cloud and look for reports of our little shopping trip to Socotra, specifically anything pertaining to prisoners."

"Aye Ma'am. No mention of the raid on normal channels," the lights on the bridge dimmed slightly, "boosting power to access the Company secure network."

"Be careful, this doesn't feel right."

"Lines secured and encrypted, I am completely invisible to their security measures Ma'am," there was a pause as a peculiar pattern of lights wafted across the A.I.s face, "I have a report of a single captive, found unconscious at the scene with minor burns. She has been taken into custody aboard a hospital ship described as the 'Fist of Scrutiny' which is currently en route to Nukuoro."

"Cut the connection!"

The lights on Frobisher's metal face resumed their normal cycling and the captain looked pensively at the main viewer. Nukuoro was just outside the jurisdiction of the Democratic People's Republic of Australasia, it was a barren Company supply base during the first trouble with the Spiders. She'd visited there once, a long time ago, with her mother on a resupply raid. It was a Gods forsaken ring of rock and sand with just a few buildings and a fuel dump. She remembered that there was also a small school, which had always struck her as odd, "Helm, plot an intercept course for this Fist of Scrutiny, take us high and quiet."

"Course set Captain, range just over a thousand miles, should be less than three hours at best speed," the Britt barked the numbers at they appeared on his display.

"No, take us slow, three-quarter speed at 20,000 feet, make us look as much like a cargo barge as you can."

"Engineering, blades out," called Britt over the Intercomm. All over the hull, the molecule-thin carbon-fibre sheets of the camouflage blades flowed from between the hull plates, they billowed briefly, then caught the wind and took on the illusion of solidity, what had once looked like a traditional buccaneer's ship now looked like a bloated, unarmed cargo barge, painted in some fictitious haulier's colours.

They sailed uneventfully northeast for nearly four hours until they reached the position where the hospital ship should be. "All stop!" cried Britt, "Mr. Landry, scan for the Fist of Scrutiny if you would be so kind."

Landry checked his screens, but found them all empty, "Nothing on scanners sir, and nothing for 200 miles in any direction."

"The sky's empty Captain, she must have changed course, we've lost her," the First Officer angrily slammed his gloved hand onto the console.

Dorleith stood and reached under her chair for her respirator. She looked at Britt critically, "I've got a feeling... get your mask, we're going on deck."

The air rushing from the pressurised door helped the reluctant Britt out onto the deck and the cold atmosphere caused condensation to form on the outside of his engraved brass respirator. He stayed well away from the guardrail as heights were his least favourite thing, next to sobriety, celibacy and hunger.

"Out of the way you bloody Jellyfish," called the captain, her voice sounding muffled through her mask, "pass me the field viewer!" The view was slightly blurred through the fabric of the blades, but she could see well enough to spot the huge airship, sister to the one that had stunned them as it passed overhead at Long Pig, two thousand feet below them and floating in the sunshine as bold as a halibut, "the sky's empty? Weren't those your exact words?"

"Aye... well... maybe the scanners need an overhaul?"

"Maybe you're lucky and they're cloaked, or maybe we're being jammed."

"Why would a hospital ship be cloaked?"

She shrugged, "I have no idea, but I mean to find out, let's get below before we have to insulate ourselves against the cold with layers of your stolen underwear."

The visible sections of Britt's face reddened despite the cold and he quickly made his way back below deck. The captain paused to take a long look at the large silver airship below them, "Hold on, we're coming for you..."

Back on the bridge, the captain settled back into her chair, cracked her knuckles and opened a communications channel. "Company airship, this is the cargo ship... ah..." the captain looked desperately at Britt.

"Mariposa?" He suggested with a shrug.

"Mariposa. We have a minor medical emergency and request succour."

She waited, but there was no reply. "Company airship, I repeat, this is the..."

An atonal construct's voice leaped from the speakers, "Mariposa, this is the Company hospital ship Fist of Scrutiny, we received your transmission but are currently unable to assist."

"Fist of Scrutiny, we have a crewman effected with what we believe to be an unknown toxin, we require immediate assistance as per Company regulations, book thirty-six, subsection eighty-seven..."

"We know the regulations Captain, we wrote them. Hold for further instructions."

The captain muted the channel and turned to her first officer.

"Britt, you need to start acting sick, well, sicker."

Britt slouched in the operating chair in the middle of the Med-Bay, looking worriedly at the magnetised trays of medical instruments on the walls.

"What does that one do?" he asked, pointing at a curved, spiked blade around fifteen inches long.

The med-construct bolted to the ceiling turned its head around to see where Britt was pointing, "That is a Quanari birthing scoop, it holds open the..."

"Ugh. Doesn't matter, what about that one over there?"

"That's a number eight bifurcated Trunquor press, we won't be using that one sir, your species don't have a Trunquor, well, not one of any great length at least."

"And that one?" Britt's voice was slowly rising in pitch and had almost reached the point where only bats could hear him. He pointed at a wickedly pointed lance, which was connected to the wall by a thick cable.

"That's the one I use to give myself high-voltage shocks when no-one's looking, it keeps my pincers steady," He turned and whispered to the captain, "It's not Ma'am, it's an emergency defibrillator for people wearing body armour."

The captain shook her head, turned to Britt and calmly said, "We won't be needing any instruments, we're just going to give you something that will make you look like you've been poisoned," she turned to the construct, "that can be reversed instantly?"

"Yes, in this," he produced a syringe full of poisonous looking green and orange liquid, "Is a mix of a weak synthetic Tubocurare and Variola, I can mix in an emetic if you require projectile vom..."

"No, thank you, the mild paralysis and boils should be enough I think."

"As you wish. I will implant the curative capsule under the skin of his chest, a brisk blow will trigger it," the construct turned its scanners towards the captain, "he will be completely free of the toxin within ten seconds."

"Excellent," replied the captain, "I'll leave him in your capable..." she waved her hands at the medic's various instruments, "hands."

As the door slid closed behind her, she glanced back to see four of the Med-Construct's arms holding Britt down, whilst another waved the syringe, mockingly, around his face.

"I really need to get that one's personality looked at when we get back to Sidi Ferruch," she whispered to herself as she headed back to the bridge.

"Mr. Landry, have we heard anything from the Fist of Scrutiny?"

"No, Captain," replied the young Communications Officer, "nothing since they told us to await further instructions."

The captain opened a channel, "Fist of Scrutiny, this is the... Mariposa, our crewman seems to have taken a turn for the worse, we respectfully request urgent medical assistance!"

"Please hold," replied the construct. The channel went silent for fifteen or so seconds and then a human voice said,

"This is Doctor Madla-Dera of the Company Medical Corps - What is it you need?"

"Thank you for talking to us Doctor. One of our crewmen seems to have been bitten by an unknown insect, he's come out in boils and he seems to be paralysed from the neck down, we don't have the facilities to diagnose it, we wondered if you could help?"

"Yes, that would be simple for us. You say it was an unknown insect? Very interesting, I will clear it with the captain now. Prepare to bring your man aboard, docking bay six."

She smiled as she switched the Intercomm to internal, "Mr. Rax? Prepare an aggie for Mr. Britt, load the hidden compartments with a standard hostile boarding kit, and don't forget his ripsword - He'll never forgive you."

"Aye Captain, I'll meet you in the Med-bay," growled Rax,

"And Mr. Rax, can you try to dress like a merchant? No LongKnives, no heavy weaponry, no high-explosive grenades?"

"As you sssay Ma'am," the suddenly dejected marauder replied, in the background the captain could just hear the sounds of dangerously shaped pieces of metal dropping to the floor.

The captain shouted her orders to the assembled bridge crew, "Bring us alongside her, extend the docking tube to bay six and keep the engines spun up ready for a quick exit, and for the Gods' sake, try to remember that as far as they know, we're merchantmen!"

In the Med-bay, Rax was assisting the Med-construct place the unmoving patient onto the aggie, the already overloaded anti-gravity motors of the floating stretcher groaned as they took his weight.

"Could do with laying off the sssuckling pigs," the reptilian commented.

"His Body Mass Index is certainly well above the recommended level," replied the Med-construct

"Thank you Gentlemen," interjected the captain, striding into the room, "can we not speak ill of the almost dead? Let's get him down to the docking bay."

As they moved through the tube towards the Fist of Scrutiny, The captain turned to Rax, "We're merchantmen remember, but be ready, the signal is me punching Britt in the chest."

Rax nodded; as the door opened, they were confronted by six construct guards armed with pain sticks and a remote floating drone, effectively just a set of scanners and a speaker.

"Follow me, we will take you to Doctor Madla-Dera. Deviation from the path will not be tolerated," the drone turned away from them and started moving towards the interior of the ship.

The captain and Rax shrugged, and pushed the whining aggie in front of them. As they followed the drone, the construct guards fell into formation, three either side of them. They walked down a number of well-lit corridors and finally stopped outside a secure medical unit. The drone paused mid-air and the door opened. The group entered the room and the guards took up defensive positions around its perimeter.

"This is the patient?" asked Madla-Dera, pointing at Britt's prone form on the aggie.

"Yes, he's my first officer," replied the captain

"He looks bad, let me just take a quick look," the doctor pulled an array of medical probes down over Britt's prone form.

"Erm... he's been getting slowly worse over the last few days."

"Don't worry, I can isolate the toxin easily, we'll have him up and about and back on duty in no time."

"Good. Oh no! He's going into cardiac arrest!"

"Cardiac..? No, my instruments clearly show that..."

"No! He's dying!" the captain hammered on Britt's chest, "don't leave me; you're the best first officer I've ever had!"

"But, my dear lady, he is not having a heart attack. Oh!"

Doctor Madla-Dera's exclamation was caused by Rax using an

Ion Sprayer to deactivate all the guards and the surveillance systems with extreme prejudice. Britt eased himself upright and took his ripsword from its secret compartment, the boils on his face and hands quickly shrinking, but his head was still fuzzy.

"Where's my crewman you filthy patient molester?" yelled Britt, waving his ripsword at the blurred shape in front of him.

"He'sss over there," whispered Rax, turning him to face the Company Doctor.

"Right you are," Britt mumbled, his vision slowly clearing.

"I... I... don't know what... please... what are you talking about?"

"You picked up a prisoner at Kykeon Station, she was one of my crew, and we want her back," explained the captain.

"Prisoner? I don't know about the prisoners, I'm an immunologist! I work with the test subjects."

"Damn!" breathed the captain and delivered a blow to the side of his head that cleanly knocked him out. "Britt, find out where Lee'Sahr is; Rax, clear us a route."

Britt accessed a nearby computer terminal, "She's in secure storage, just down the corridor, although we're about to have company, if you'll pardon the pun."

Rax grinned and pulled a compression pistol from the aggie. "Follow the noissse when you're ready!" he laughed and jumped out into the corridor.

"Britt? How do you feel?" asked the captain, her hand resting on the recently cured first officer's shoulder.

"A bit groggy still, and very itchy, but I'll live Ma'am."

"You'll need to do a damn sight more than that if we're going to get out of here, we need to catch up, and Rax sounds like he's having far too much fun on his own!"

They raced out of the room and into the corridor, following the sound of gunfire and deep scaly laughter. Britt restarted his ripsword, revved it a couple of times and ran headlong into the fray, sweeping it to and fro at waist height, chopping guard constructs in half with gay abandon. The captain stayed back at the junction, where she had a clear view down three corridors and contented herself with putting holes into the skulls of any constructs that came into view.

"Britt! Rax! Stop playing soldiers and clear me a path to Secure Storage!" the captain yelled, so that she could be heard over the mechanical mayhem.

The brigands looked at each other, grinned hugely and pushed forward. Britt's ripsword became stuck in the gears of a particularly large construct, four of its six arms continued to try to crush the life out of him as the toothed chain snagged and the engine stalled.

"Ooof! – Kill It!-Kill It!-Kill It!" yelled the First Officer.

Rax reached under his vest and pulled out an accelerator gun, which most people require two hands to use, and aimed it at the construct's head.

"Hang on, let me get out of the..."

There was a deafening sonic boom and the construct's head simply disappeared, along with part of Britt's luxuriant moustaches and a significant portion of the bulkhead in front of them.

"Which part of no siege weapons didn't you understand? How about the words 'Sudden loss of buoyancy?' or 'Plummeting to a watery grave in a mass of tangled metal'?" barked the captain.

Rax looked sheepishly at the captain and then back to Britt, who was still trying to put out his smouldering facial hair. He holstered the massive gun and continued forwards just using his pistol to clear a path. A mass of constructs was building up behind them and the captain was doing her best to hold them off, but they were closing through sheer force of numbers.

"How many damn guards do you need on a medical boat?" she asked the empty air, whilst shooting a hole in the head of the nearest attacker.

"The door's locked Captain!" yelled Britt from around the corner, "as you'd expect I suppose in somewhere called 'Secure Storage'!"

She reached into her pocket, grabbed the Kalibri lock-pick and threw it over her shoulder. She heard it hit the wall and roll, then the familiar musical chirps as it started to work.

"Rax! Come here and give me a hand whilst the Old Man opens

the door!"

The reply came in the form of a dozen compression bolts whizzing from behind her into the broiling throng of constructs in front, exploding faces and shattering bodies into clouds of plastic and metal, which seemed to buy them some breathing space.

"Thank you!"

"Captain, I've found her, she seems OK." said Britt's voice in her ear.

"OK, get her back here, we'll make our way to the docking bay." the captain thumbed the switch on her communicator, "Teach, this is the Captain. We are making our way to the docking bay now, prepare for departure at best speed once we're aboard."

"Captain, this is Landry, as soon as you started the rescue, the Fist of Scrutiny shot out the docking tube, we're holding station about 50 feet below the port bow."

"Gods damn it!"

"Captain?"

"Nothing, hold steady Teach, we'll come to you."

"Aye Ma'am, Landry out."

Britt chose that moment to come into view with an unconscious Lee'Sahr draped over his shoulder.

Dorleith sighed in relief, "Mr. Rax? Make me a hole in that wall there, we need a way out."

Rax slowly raised his pistol and aimed at where the captain had pointed.

"No Mr. Rax, I think that something with a little more bite is required."

He grinned and pulled out the accelerator gun, braced himself against the wall and started to fire repeatedly into the bulkhead in front of him. The supersonic shells made short work of the panelling and the bulkhead behind it. A sudden drop in pressure and the roaring of wind signalled that he had breached the hull, he stopped firing and spat on the glowing barrel.

"Now we go - Teach, this is the Captain, can you see the new hole in this nice shiny boat?"

"Aye Ma'am, on our way."

"Good, position yourself as close as you can get, we're going to jump."

"Aye Captain!"

"I'm sorry, but we're going to what?" asked Britt, looking at the limp form of Lee'Sahr cradled in his arms.

"Rax goes first, you throw her, he catches her, then you jump and I bring up the rear - simple."

They made their way through the damaged section of the ship until they reached the outside skin. The Edward Teach was just taking up position, ten feet away and five feet below. Along the sides of the Company ship, turrets were beginning to spring into life.

"Sssee you on the other ssside!" yelled Rax and then he jumped. He managed to catch hold of one of the chains connecting the gasbag to the hull, slid down it hand over hand and took up position on the deck. He beckoned to Britt, "Toss her over!" he yelled, trying to make himself heard above the wind.

Britt moved Lee'Sahr from his shoulder and held her in his arms. Taking as much of a run-up as he could, he launched her across the gap to the waiting marauder. As he let her go, her eyes opened, she looked at the receding hospital ship, and the sea far below her and started to scream, a scream that didn't stop until she landed in the paws of the unevenly fanged monster braced on the deck.

A shot rang off the metalwork next to his head, "We need to get going!" he yelled to the captain, who was laying down covering fire.

"You first, I'll follow you."

"But, no you should..."

"Britt, if you don't jump now, I'll shoot you myself and use your skin as a parachute!"

"I'll see you aboard!" he replied, flinching as another shot took a chunk out of the floor. He jumped the distance, landed heavily on the deck and rolled to a stop. Looking across at the massive bulk of the Fist of Scrutiny, he watched as the captain fired shot after shot into the depths of the ship until her pistol ran out of charge. She threw the now useless weapon at the oncoming constructs and jumped.

Time almost stopped as she sailed through the air, and she was only a few feet away when she realised that she wasn't going to make it.

"NO!" Yelled Britt, forgetting his vertigo and rushing to the side-rail. But the captain was nowhere to be seen. He stood there, unbelieving until Rax grabbed him by the shoulder.

"We need to get underway now, there are interceptors coming, don't let all this be for nothing!"

Britt nodded, took one last look over the side and went below.

"Full reverse, hit them with Daisy a few times to slow them down and then set a course for home, best speed," commanded Britt as he took the vacant captain's chair.

"Where's the captain?" shouted Landry as the crew scrambled to obey the First Officer's orders.

Britt looked at him and slowly shook his head. The forward viewscreen lit up as the shots from Daisy found their mark and the lights started to go out all over the Fist of Scrutiny.

"Bring us about and rig for best speed."

"Belay that!" came a feint, crackly voice from the Intercomm, "send someone to haul in the remains of the docking tube, which happens to have your captain tangled in it and THEN rig for best speed. Oh, and Britt?"

"Aye Captain?"

"Get your backside out of my chair!"

The doctor stood looking down at the feed from the external cameras, wincing as he gently touched the inflamed bump at his temple. The Teach was reeling in its camouflage blades and running south for the horizon, a few deliberately off-target shots from the Scrutiny's turrets helping her on her way. He opened a direct Cloud link to the Compliance, "Excellency, this is Madla-Dera; they have her."

"Thank you, Doctor," replied Duke Pytor's silken tones, "we'll take it from here."

Chapter 18 : Revelations

"Intruder Alert! Intruder Alert!" the lights in Frobisher's face flashing from an angry red to a vile suppurating yellow, "unexpected life-sign detected in engineering! Intruder Alert!"

The captain jumped from her bunk, her head still groggy from the celebration after the successful rescue of Lee'Sahr, and her own return from an implied watery grave, "Shut that damn alarm off you bag of rusty cogs! Security team to engineering deck, immobilize the intruder, whatever it is I want it alive!"

She pulled on her jodhpurs and knee-boots, rescued the crumpled linen shirt from the floor, buttoned it up and noticed the tousled hair of Landry poking out from under the covers. The sound of his gentle snoring now obvious as the alarm had been silenced.

"Bugger!" she said, slowly lifting the covers and confirming that he was, in fact, completely naked, "and double bugger!" she looked for slightly longer than was strictly necessary at the taut muscles on his back, then sighed deeply and exited to the bridge.

The crew of the morning watch turned and saluted, "Captain on the bridge!" a crewman whose name she couldn't remember at the best of times yelled. The noise made her wince more than the alarm had, but she resisted the temptation to raise her finger to her lips and shush him.

"Why is there an intruder on my boat?" she asked the

assembled throng as she sank carefully into the command chair, "anyone?" A sea of blank faces was her only reply. She thumbed the Intercomm, "Security team, have you found it - whatever it is?"

"Baju-merah here Ma'am, engineering's clear, no-one here who shouldn't be here. We've checked everywhere!"

Frobisher chose that moment to voice yet another alarm, "Intruder Alert! Intruder Alert! Unexpected life-sign detected in the Forward avionics cabin!"

"What?" exclaimed the captain, "that's at the other end of the... how? Frobisher, check the logs, was the intruder detected anywhere between engineering and avionics?"

"No Ma'am, the signal disappeared from engineering and simply re-appeared in avionics." the emotionless brass face still managed to radiate an air of abject confusion.

"Mr. Baju-merah, report to avionics, bring our unexpected guest to me now! Frobisher, perform a diagnostic on the internal scanners, if you've woke me up simply because you've gone defective I'll have Britt reprogram you, overarm, with the assistance of his friend Molly."

The pattern of lights on Frobisher's face skittered as he performed the self-diagnostic, "All sensors performing within prescribed parameters Ma'am, zero defects found, my assumption is that my log entries are correct."

"Then how the hells is something jumping from one end of this boat to the other without passing through any of the points in-between?"

"I have no..."

"That was rhetorical, you should look it up."

"I am fully aware of..."

"Ma'am, this is Baju-Merah. Avionics is clear, in fact, I don't think there's enough space in here for anything larger than a chicken."

"Frobisher, is our intruder larger than a chicken?"

"Yes Ma'am, scans indicate that it is of standard dimensions for a humanoid male. And he is also no longer in avionics."

"Has he re-appeared somewhere else? In the galley? Up on deck? In one of the Gasbags perhaps?"

"No Ma'am."

"No, he hasn't re-appeared or no, he's not in the Gasbags?"

"He has re-appeared, but it is in none of the areas that you suggested."

"So, where is he pray tell?"

"He is in your quarters."

She turned slowly, along with the entire bridge crew, to face the door to her quarters. Activating the Intercomm she whispered, "Mr. Baju-Merah, to the bridge, as quick as you like."

It only took the security team moments to get to the bridge, but in that time the captain had armed herself with a new compression pistol and her LongKnife, and was stood by the door.

"I'll go in first, you take up covering positions, stand close so the door doesn't close."

"Ma'am, may I suggest that I..."

"Mr. Baju-Merah, I appreciate your concern, but the interloper hasn't shown any degree of hostility as yet. If anything, his antics seem to be designed to confuse us. He could have simply appeared behind any member of the crew and shot them in the back of the head if he'd wanted to."

She took a deep breath and stepped through the door as it opened. The second her heel had cleared the frame, it slammed shut at ten times its normal speed and locked. In a moment of panic, she spun and hammered futilely on the door, then turned back to scan the room. The automatic lights had failed to turn on and even Frobisher's head was dark and silent. "Landry?" she called, looking towards her bunk, "Frobisher?" but there was no reply from either of them. She felt her way forward, holding the pistol out in front of her. "Where are you? Damn your... Argh!" She rubbed her shin where it had rapped off one of the corner castings on her bed.

"Allow me Captain," said a calm voice from the far corner of the room, "lights!"

Instantly, the wall lights came back on. The captain blinked, and turned towards the voice.

"You!" she raised the pistol and pointed it at the wiry man sat in her easy chair, "what are you doing on my ship?"

"At your service Captain," J'syah Preen raised himself from the chair, removed his hat to reveal a distinctly amphibian crest, and bowed deeply, "I apologise for the dramatic means of my entrance, when you get to my age, you find your excitement where you can."

The sudden realisation that Preen was neither human nor one of the known aligned races threw her off balance, but only for a second, "I'll ask again, only much more forcefully. What are YOU doing on MY ship?"

"There's no need for unpleasantness M'Lady, nor should we have to worry about unfortunate accidents," he waved his long fingers and the compression pistol slowly faded out of existence.

"What?" she looked down, the dull tingle in her fingers the only evidence that the gun had ever existed at all, "how did you..?"

"A simple parlour trick, the weapon is back in its rightful place, in the hidden arms locker, under your command chair, on the bridge. Your, ah... friend is also back in his rightful place, asleep, in his cabin. I took the liberty of removing the last twelve hours from his memory; it saves any discontent in the ranks."

She looked down at her LongKnife, then back at her visitor.

"With the greatest respect Captain, you wouldn't be able to touch me with it."

"What do you want?"

"Want? I want to deliver my message and go home before I succumb to violent airsickness, these things worry me," he indicated the ship around him, "if your Gods had meant you to fly, they would, as you say, have given you gasbags."

"Message? What message? Who is it from?"

Preen took a deep breath, "My Lady Dorleith Ahralia, possible future Baroness of Rustholme, In Nominate Ruler of the Open Lands and new High Voort of the Shattered Spire, I bring greetings from your Illustrious father, Massimo Lohlephel, Baron of..."

"My father? My father fell at the Battle of Tromega, I saw his ship explode! He's dead!"

"No, not... anymore."

She stood on the bridge of the Granthar's Hammer, next to her mother's heavily decorated command chair. The battle had been raging for nearly an hour now and the sky was dark with Spiders.

"Alexander, report!" Baroness Bhinn-Dee of Rustholme yelled at the battleship's ancient A.I.

"We are currently outnumbered five to one, we have Spiders inbound on bearings zero-four-two, three-five-eight and..." replied the ornately lit brass and copper head in the corner of the bridge.

"Enough!" she turned to Dorleith, "let's see if we can find your father shall we? He'll probably be needing a hand around about now?"

The fourteen year old girl looked up at her mother and smiled, she knew exactly where her father would be, right in the middle of the biggest, thickest ball of Spiders that he could find, tearing them out of the air with his bare hands if he had to. It was hard for her to understand why he hated the Spiders so much, even back at the Roost, before she was old enough to come along with her parents on the raids, every story he told ended up with his knife being plunged into a tabletop, or a crystal goblet of brandy being thrown into the fire, and him stomping off hurling obscenities at whoever got in his way.

"Bolivar, this is The Hammer, Where are you, you old goat?" the static from the speakers indicated that they were out of range, "Alexander, what was the last known position of the Bolivar?"

"Our battleship, the Simon Bolivar, last known position bearing two-six-four, distance eighteen miles."

"Show me."

The main screen changed from the tactical display to a map showing Northern Macedonia, the flashing red dot indicating the last known position of the Simon Bolivar was hovering over the mountains to the west.

She opened the shipboard Intercomm, "All hands, this is the Captain, we're rendezvousing with the Bolivar, any gunner that has a Spider in their sights, take it out now and make ready defensive positions, keep those mechanical scum off my hull," she turned to the helmsman, "lay in an intercept course with the Bolivar, let me know when we're in communications range."

"Aye Ma'am, course laid in… Captain!"

"Aye?"

"We're going to have to fight for every yard, that course'll take us through a cloud of Spiders almost a mile thick,"

"Gods damn it Mr. Hadleigh, bring Mary online, divert power from the engines, and fire as you get a target."

The deck thrummed as power poured from the great fusion engines at the rear of the airship, to the Ion cannon that occupied almost the entire bow. The Granthar's Hammer had been built around this big gun, but because it was so powerful they could only fire a few shots before they needed to cool and recharge. The first blast took nearly one hundred Spiders out of the fight, their systems fried as their lifeless husks fell onto the ruins of what used to be Kumanovo.

"Well Ma'am, that certainly seemed to have got their attention, we have fifty… no, sixty targets inbound, five seconds before we can fire Mary again!"

"Fire as she becomes ready; Helm, as soon as she fires, hard a-port, bring us broadside to the cloud. All starboard guns, be ready to fire as you acquire a target!" Mary barked again and the sun-bright blue flare carved another chunk out of the cloud of chittering limbs and spines. The Helmsman dragged the ship hard to the left, airbrakes and scoops deploying all down the port side, the connecting chains to the gasbags groaned with the sudden tension as the deck slewed drunkenly below them.

The captain grabbed hold of her chair with one hand and held onto her daughter with the other, "You alright?" she shouted, over the blare of the bridge alarms.

"Aye Ma'am," replied the young girl, attempting a salute.

"Good Girl, strap yourself in, it's going to get bumpier before it gets calmer; Mr. Hadleigh!"

"Aye Ma'am?"

"Keep us headed in the direction of the Bolivar, but initiate a crazy Ivan, let's give them a few broadsides and clear ourselves a gap."

"Aye, all hands! Prepare for violent manoeuvres, we will be

initiating a crazy Ivan in five seconds." the ship slewed hard right, as Mary pointed towards the enemy she fired, scooping great swathes of Spiders out of the cloud, then the Hammer came full broadside to them and the turrets fired another cannonade. The left-right movement continued for two miles until the Helmsman cried, "Captain, I'm getting a signal from the Bolivar!"

"Onscreen!"

Through the interference on the viewscreen, the unmistakable silhouette of the Baron appeared, he had his favourite monomer edged cutlass in one hand and a repeating ion pistol in the other, he was in mid-flow, "... Damn your eyes, man if I thought for a second you were running from your post I'd show you your own liver before making you eat it..." the picture faded and then snapped back into sudden clarity, "Get off my bloody ship!"

He had the head of a Spider impaled on the end of his sword and was rapidly beating it against the bulkhead.

"Massimo?"

"I'll kill ye, I'll kill every one of ye, you'll wish you'd never been riveted..."

"Massimo!"

"I'll hunt down where ye wuz made, an' I'll kill everyone there, then I'll find where the constructs that made ye wuz made, and I'll kill them, then I'll..."

"MASSIMO! – I think it's dead!"

"Aye, whut?" the bear of a man that was Baron Massimo Lohlephel blinked the red mist from his eyes and looked at his screen, "Ah, hullo my Sweet Flower, Mist of my Midsummer Morning! Ah... I'm... a bit busy at the moment, I'll pull off your face you clanking contraption... No, not you dear, I'll get back to you in a wee while..." he turned away from the camera and yelled, "get that bloody million legged abomination off my bridge Mr. Varloth!" And with that, the connection went dead.

"Alexander, can you contact the Slut?"

Dorleith giggled, 'The Slut' was her mother's pet name for Angelina, the A.I. on board her father's ship.

"Aye Ma'am, connection established."

"Get a status report on the Bolivar's systems."

"They have multiple hull breaches, Spider boarding craft cover the entire fore-section of the ship, and there are more mechanical life-signs on board than the internal sensors can reliably count."

"Damn! Are we close enough to fire on the Spiders without hitting the Bolivar?"

"Not with any degree of certainty Ma'am, no," replied Hadleigh with an air of regret.

"Take us in, weapons free, fire at will!"

The Hammer lurched forward, Mary and the other cannons killing Spiders in all directions as they went.

"Captain?" called Hadleigh, questioningly.

"Aye?"

"We're slowing!"

"What do you mean?"

"We're slowing down, I've lost control of the throttles. We're... we're in full reverse?"

"Alexander, what in the seven hells is going on?"

"The Simon Bolivar has invoked remote access; they are controlling us for the moment."

"What? Can we over-ride the signal?"

"No Ma'am, Angelina has locked me out of my own control systems; I will be having stern words with her when we get back to the Roost... Ah!"

"What now?"

"I am detecting a massive Heptium leak in the Simon Bolivar's starboard engine, there are signs of an impending cascade event."

"Get them onscreen... Now!"

The main viewer sprung into life, Baron Lohlephel was sat, calmly, in his command chair. The bridge was swathed in smoke and the sound of gunfire could be heard in the distance.

"Hullo my Jewel, I'm sorry about pushing you away."

"What're you doing Goat?"

"I'm saving your life..."

"I don't…"

"Angelina informs me that our engines are just about to go critical, and the life-pods are so thick with Spiders that we can't launch them, so I'm going to take as many of these mechanical monsters with me as I can."

"No! I… I fought my way here; I've come to save you… we can…"

He smiled and shook his head, "You know this is the only way, is Dorleith there?"

She nodded stoically and beckoned her daughter across, "Daddy wants to talk to you."

"Hello Daddy!"

"Hello Beautiful Girl, hope you're alright." There was the beginning of a tear in the corner of his eye as he continued, *"I'm sorry, but I've got to go now, I know you'll keep on fighting though. You won't let the Spiders win will you? Try to stop 'em any way you can."*

"I will Daddy, I promise!"

"I know Baby. I love you both so much." He put his hand on the viewscreen, *"I….."*

A freezing cloud of Heptium gas rapidly expanded from the rupturing engine, which instantly ignited in a ball of fire two miles across. The main windows of the Hammer's bridge exploded into dagger sized shards which spread across the room, narrowly missing the dumbfounded crew.

"DADDY!"

"I beg your pardon?" J'syah Preen's calm voice brought the captain back to the present, she slowly looked around and realised that she was back in her cabin on the Edward Teach.

"Nothing. I… I just remembered…"

"Yes, indeed, nasty business, your mother has been given the details, if you wish to help."

"Help?"

"Your father needs rescuing."

"Rescuing?"

"Yes, rescuing. You have been following my conversation

haven't you? About the Spire? The Confused Consciousness?"

"Well, no, I..."

Preen sighed and shook his head. "I see, well I suggest you talk to your mother. As I said, I've just given her the details and she suggested that I inform you. Now, I need to leave, I'm afraid that I have other important errands to attend to."

"Can we drop you anywhere?"

"No, that won't be necessary, thank you," he replaced his hat, stepped back into the shadows, and was gone.

"I..." she pondered for a second before she turned and entered the bridge, "Set a course for the Roost, best speed, and get the ship tidied, we're going to visit the Baroness."

Chapter 19 : Assault

Duke Pytor lounged in the command chair of the Fist of Compliance, watching the small flashing marker move slowly north-west across the map of Eastern Europe being displayed on the main screen. There was something about the pirate's route that made him uneasy, "Compliance? Can we tell where our precious little rabbit is running to yet?"

"Excellency, if the target continues on its current course," a bright red line was overlaid on the map, "there are only a small number of populated areas of any real size. They include the trade centre at Belgrade, the commercial fur farms at Ankara and the engineering works at Munich, before they pass over Albion and into the Atlantic. The next landfall after that would be Greenland Excellency."

"I can see that we need to program you with a little flexibility of thought Compliance. I do not think for one second that our quarry is heading anywhere where there is a large Company presence." he regarded the projected course closely, "I would say that they're heading for a coastal area, these nouveau freebooters all still have a romantic attachment to the sea. Every single one of their bases that we've burned to the ground so far has been on an island or in a sea-cave or halfway up a..." the Duke's voice tailed off, "Compliance, where exactly does their course cross the coast of Albion?"

There was a pause between the terminal's indicators brightening and the Compliance starting to talk, conveying an air of confusion, then the display zoomed out to encompass the North Atlantic, "Their course intersects the coast at our pre-programmed destination co-ordinates Excellency, the capital of one of the larger independent Baronies, specifically the Barony of..."

"Rustholme?" suggested the Duke, finishing the A.I's report for it, "I knew that making an offering to the God of serendipitous circumstances was going to be a quarter of a credit well spent. It seems that we may be able to kill two birds with one..." The Duke's feline grin once more spread across his face, "well, I'm sure we can find a weapon much more interesting than a stone. Connect me to our defence research station at Orleans." There was a moment's delay as the connection was established and the stern face of Commander Brusilov replaced the Company logo on Pytor's display.

"Excellency?" Brusilov's bald head dipped low in a measured bow, displaying the web of pale scars that spread from crown to neck, "How may I serve you?"

"Commander, I need to instill the fear of the Gods into an enemy of the Company who have their own stronghold. I have my dreadnaught of course," he indicated the bridge around him with a wave of his hand, "but I wondered if you could suggest a portable weapon that would make a fitting statement? Something that says that I could remove them from existence with a flick of my wrist. Do you have such an item in your experimental arsenal?"

The Russian's mutilated face creased in thought, and then opened with a smile, "I believe that I have just the thing Excellency. Two of our heavy gunships have been outfitted with a new Torkan weapon, the details were on my last status report," the Duke shrugged and Brusilov continued, "I have been trying to think what best to test them on. They are of course, yours to command."

"Splendid, I will reach Paris in two hours, they will be waiting for me when I get there. I look forward to a demonstration."

"As you say Excellency, I will personally brief the pilots now."

"Do so."

Brusilov's screen went dead before he had chance to acknowledge his orders. He breathed out and wiped his expansive forehead with his ragged handkerchief as his neck and shoulder muscles began to relax. He had been working on the new gunboats for the last month or so almost as a hobby, and had hoped that he would have more time to iron out any kinks during the final phase of testing before he presented them to the board. If it wasn't for the fact that he had had to account for the expenditure on the last corporate status report, which obviously he had assumed that the Duke had read, he wouldn't have suggested their use in the first place.

"Samuel, make the two new gunships flight ready and inform the combat pilots that they are to report to the briefing room immediately."

The miniature A.I. terminal on his desk sprang into life, "Yes Commander, will the Torkan advisors be required on this mission? The aircraft are still listed as experimental in the manifest."

"No, just the pilots, if the worst comes to the worst, I can always requisition a few more of them. Only the Gods know where you would get another couple of live Torkans, or how much they'd cost me," the terminal pulsed brightly as it relayed his orders to both the ground and aircrew. He sat for a while, weighing up the pros and cons of providing the Duke with weaponry that had not yet been fully tested, and thinking where he might end up if they did not perform at peak efficiency. Unable to put it off any longer, he rose from his chair and made his way to the small classroom where the pilots were waiting for him. They rose as he entered the room and he gestured for them to sit, "At ease. As you may be aware, you have been chosen by Duke Pytor to provide a great service for the Company. Should the mission be successful, you will be ranked amongst the chosen few, raised to heights where eagles fear to fly and there's the definite possibility of medals for us all."

The pilots looked sceptically at each other; they had grown used to the commander's hyperbole. If they were ever to receive even half the amount of medals that they had been promised over the years, they wouldn't be able to walk with the weight, never mind actually fly.

"Once you have completed your checks, you are to make for

Paris airspace, where you will, within two hours, enter formation with Duke Pytor's personal dreadnaught, the Fist of Compliance. From there, you will travel to the stronghold of a known enemy of the Company and participate in a show of strength. You will be asked to demonstrate the new weaponry's use as a deterrent."

One of the pilots raised her hand, he nodded in her direction, "Will we be firing on live targets sir? I've never seen the effects of the weapon on a live target."

"In all honesty I have no idea Lieutenant McVeigh," an uncomfortable expression flicked across his face as he considered that this would be a very real possibility, "you will fire on whatever target the Duke identifies. You're there to support the dreadnaught and make a statement; I can't see a war starting over a little posturing though. The odd sabre will get rattled I'm sure, the odd nose put out of joint perhaps. Nothing more," he looked at the pilots, who didn't seem particularly convinced, "anyway, get to your gunships and launch when ready. Keep me informed when you can, but for the duration of this mission, you report to the Duke, not me."

Both pilots stood, gave a smart salute and started to head towards the hangar.

"Wait!" Brusilov shouted, "don't forget to enable your gun cameras; I'd like to look at whatever footage you manage to capture, for training purposes you understand."

A'Shara McVeigh squeezed herself into the tight cockpit, and went through the launch checklist, "Samuel, gunship controls to local,"

"Affirmative Lieutenant McVeigh, voiceprint recognised, you have local control."

The display screens brightened as the security lockouts were released and she deftly completed the checks that had almost become a ritual. She turned to the vacant rear seat, forgetting for a moment that her usual Torkan co-pilot was not joining her today, and sighed dejectedly. She would miss his constant chatter, even if most of it was purely cautionary advice, "Miss, please be aware of the fusion motor core temperature," or, "Miss, we are exceeding the optimum landing speed by a factor of three," try as she might, she could never get him to call her McVeigh, let alone A'Shara. The Torkans were just too polite.

Her communicator crackled into life, it was S'Thul, the pilot of the other gunship, "Finished polishing your instruments? Can we get some air underneath us or would you like a few more minutes to finish your embroidery?"

"Cool your jets S'Thul, you inbred throwback. Samuel, this is Tangler Flight requesting permission to launch."

"Tangler Flight, you have clearance to launch when ready, good hunting."

Both of the crab-like, black, gunships lifted into the air, shot out of the open hangar and spiralled into the air, twisting around each other as if they were competing for the same piece of sky, until they had broken through the cloud layer into the clear, but slowly darkening, dusk.

"OK, set course to fifteen degrees magnetic. We have," She checked her chronometer and tutted to herself, "a little under an hour to travel the fifty or so miles to the rendezvous, so there's no need to burn out the engines or let anything important go flying off."

"I seem to remember that the last mechanical failure was due to you over-stressing a control vane whilst performing a negative-G loop. You commented at the time that it was unusual, but very convenient that Torkans can't vomit."

She laughed, "Yes S'Thul, I think you might be right. I also think it's time we practiced some low altitude manoeuvres, see you on the deck." The two aircraft rolled upside down and disappeared back down through the clouds. They chased each other haphazardly through the river valley that ran north towards Paris until the jagged outline of the Tower itself came into view.

"Showing nothing on scanners, well, nothing big enough to deserve calling itself a dreadnaught at least. Switching to long-range. Oh…"

"Oh?" the lieutenant increased the range of her own scanner, and although the resolution was reduced, she could still see two large contacts, flying line-astern and closing at high speed.

"I thought we were meeting the CEO's personal dreadnaught?"

"Maybe he has two, in case one bursts," reasoned McVeigh.

"Yes boss, that'll be it exactly, I can see why you're in charge."

"Gunship flight, this is the dreadnaught Fist of Compliance, are you receiving me?"

"Affirmative Fist of Compliance, this is Tangler Flight, Lieutenant A'Shara McVeigh, awaiting your orders," there was a brief exchange between the two groups until slowly the huge airships appeared in the distance, "well, I guess it wasn't a sensor echo then," she whispered to herself.

The two giant ships continued to get closer at an almost alarming rate, and within minutes had stopped, one either side of the Eiffel Tower, Each of them longer than the tower was tall. A new voice issued from her communicator, "Lieutenant, this is Duke Pytor, the Compliance has Clouded the coordinates of our target to you, confirm receipt."

She looked at her navigational display, "Acknowledged, Excellency, target is four hundred miles north, a set of coastal fortifications."

"Correct, when we arrive you will perform a weapons test on the structure itself and then continue that test on any vehicles that try to escape. Do you understand?"

"Excellency, I..."

"Your weaponry is operational and you are a combat pilot?"

"Yes."

"Then you will follow my orders to the letter for as long as you wish to remain so, is that clear enough for you?"

"Excellency."

"Tangler Flight, Fist of Correction, this is the Fist of Compliance, time to target forty minutes. Move out."

The gunships turned north and fell into formation behind the dreadnaughts. Their next stop was the shores of Albion and the ancient walls of the Roost.

ABOUT THE AUTHOR

Rob Grimes has been writing for a very long time; some would say too long. But this is his first full-length novel and it's also the first volume of 'The Windspider Chronicles', he hopes that you've enjoyed it enough to look forward to buying volume 2 (Child of Space) But don't hold your breath, he's been 'writing' this one for five years.

This entire story sprang from an abortive shopping trip that his daughter once took, where she tried to buy some shoes, but failed spectacularly. (So now you know). It features many hidden references for those of you who are 'in the know'.

He lives, with his family, in Derby in the East Midlands of the UK and is looking for any excuse, no matter how tenuous, to give up his day job in the heady world of Trains & IT and write full time. You can help make this happen by buying copies of this book for your friends, family and people you hardly know on Facebook and Twitter.

People on the Internet love stuff like this, trust me.

If you feel inclined, please feel free to follow my random thoughts on Twitter at @Chimping_Dandy (yes, really) or drop me an email to rob.p.grimes@hotmail.co.uk – I can't guarantee that I'll answer, but I'll certainly do my best, after all – I wouldn't be anything without you guys.

P.S. The main font used in this book is Calibri, and if that doesn't make you smile, you've not been paying attention.

29222898R00185

Printed in Great Britain
by Amazon